The
LOST
HIGHWAY

Shortlisted for the
Thomas Head Raddall Atlantic Fiction Prize

"Timely and timeless. The language and lyricism . . . capture the immediacy of vernacular speech from Northern New Brunswick, while echoing almost biblical poets."

—*The Chronicle Herald* (Halifax)

"[*The Lost Highway*] could be his best work to date. . . . Richards creates and then dissects his characters with a flawlessly sure hand, and lays a web of tension over a community that can barely remember its better days." —*Ottawa Citizen*

"A thrilling and exhilarating work of suspense . . . *The Lost Highway* dares to explore new themes of religious and secular uncertainty, while maintaining the author's distinct voice and vision. . . . [T]he book comes to life slowly and skilfully, its quirky characters masterfully sculpted . . . . Once the reader gets into the narrative groove, however, the book becomes infectious and impossible to put down. . . . *The Lost Highway* is the masterwork of an artist at the very pinnacle of his talent . . . . David Adams Richards has firmly established himself as among Canada's foremost literary craftsmen and finest storytellers."

—*The Globe and Mail*

The

LOST
HIGHWAY

A NOVEL

DAVID
ADAMS
RICHARDS

ANCHOR CANADA

LIBRARY AND ARCHIVES CANADA CATALOGUING IN PUBLICATION

Richards, David Adams, 1950–
The lost highway : a novel / David Adams Richards.

ISBN 978-0-385-66497-4

I. Title.

PS8585.I17L68 2008   C813'.54   C2008-901159-7

Cover image: Benjamin Rondel / Corbis
Cover and text design: CS Richardson
Printed and bound in Canada

Published in Canada by
Anchor Canada, a division of
Random House of Canada Limited

Visit Random House of Canada Limited's website: www.randomhouse.ca

TRANS   10   9   8   7   6   5   4   3   2   1

FOR PEGGY
AND FOR PAT

=

BURTON TUCKER MOVED TO THE HAYSTACK AND SAT DOWN in the brine of hay, and looked down across the barn and into the open, in the space beyond his house where in the sky was a cloud the shape and color of black gunpowder. The day was still murky and warm, and a feeling of oppressive, ragged heat surrounded him.

"What is hidden will be revealed," Tucker said. This is what old Muriel Chapman said to him once when he was visiting her. She had smiled at him, when he said he had no idea what was going to happen if things did not get better—for now everyone was talking about a big war. And he heard this war would be closer than ever, perhaps as close as Fredericton. They would come in the night, and at night be like thieves. He had been to Fredericton once as a bat boy with a baseball team.

"What is hidden will be revealed," she had said, simply. This of course implied nothing or everything depending on how one viewed it, but made her seem very wise to Burton at any rate. And he had heard of both night and nightly thieves from the Bible, which he kept together with his trophies and his pictures in his office drawer.

Mrs. Chapman had, as people said, lived an exemplary life. She did charity work for many people and it was known that she had baked for the community Christmas dinner for thirty-nine years. The problem in her life was her great-nephew Alex Chapman. She gave him everything, went to the principal's office in high school, and took up for him. Tried to do this for him, tried to do that.

He had had problems many times in his life, and things did not turn out. He had come home a few years ago, and worked for his great-uncle Jim off and on, disillusioned and ill tempered, for the great "turn of events" that he had hoped and longed for had not happened to him. Some day, as he often said, or said often enough, these great events would come and he would be recognized.

"Then the fools will be sorry," he had said.

"Yes they will," Burton said.

"The fools will be sorry, Burton."

"I'm sure of it," Burton acknowledged.

When Alex was young and small, his great-uncle put him to work after school in the junkyard, or back at the pit burning garbage. The boy would go to school, with three feet of snow on the ground, smelling of soot from a fire. Though they had money, the uncle was parsimonious, and sometimes he would clutch a dollar in his hand for an hour before he finally gave it to the boy.

Alex left work, went into study for the priesthood, and then left to wander the world. He went to university and worked with the anti-poverty league. He got very angry, and said things like: Why don't people give it away!

Then, abused and worn out, he came back and tried to fit in. For the last five years he had taught a course on ethics at the community college. He taught it from September to December and was paid $3500. That seemed to get him through the winter if his uncle helped him. Without his uncle's help there was no telling what would happen.

People—and there are gossips in the world—said that for a man who wanted to live like an ascetic, Alex hoped a little too much for some kind of inheritance. But others said he deserved something from his relationship with his uncle, who treated him too harsh for too long. Others, too, said his uncle would never leave him with nothing, that in the end the uncle had always been there for him.

Tucker had thought of Mrs. Chapman all day. The war as yet had not come. But perhaps it would soon. The highway drifted on below his garage—drifted away forever, to the east; a garage so out of the way the company had taken his pumps from him, and he had to make up his lost revenue by giving deals and working later every week. In the lonely, darkening stretch of country road the light of Poppy Bourque's sawdust truck could be seen rising and falling though the black, heavy trees. He remembered lights like these on a summer night long ago, when his friends and he came home from baseball games. But his friends eventually outgrew him, and he stayed as he was, with, it seemed, no real prospects or future. He called on them to come over, but after a time they had little to say to him, and got married, and his room filled with mementos from his youth, when they were happy together, did not seem to contain them.

He would go and sit with his cousin Amy, for an hour or two, and they would talk about all her plans that seemed nice and innocent. She played the guitar and had a box of CDs and was the kindest of all to him.

Burton wondered what would happen to the children like little Amy if there was a war. Well, who could say? No one wanted to bomb children. Almost every general said, "We are against the killing of women and children," and Burton would say, "Thank God," but then they proceeded to bomb them with great aplomb.

Burton was told by some people that he had to stop being so friendly to children—especially Amy, who they said now had her own boobs—and that many children didn't want him stopping them up on the highway to speak to them as they waited for the bus in the freezing January mornings. That it was a new age, and certainly he had a right to say hello, but there were a lot of mothers and fathers who were suspicious of people like Burton Tucker.

Then the police came one day, and took him aside—a young man and woman with blue uniforms and guns on their belts—and told him he shouldn't pick little girls up and swing them around so their underwear showed. The young female officer looked at him with a triumphant smile—as if all her life she had wanted to say something just like this. He started to cry as he always did, and told these officers he was an attendant at the open-air rink and at the community center dinners, and to prove this he showed them his hat, much like theirs, that said BURTON on the front.

Later, Markus Paul, the First Nations constable he liked, came in and told him not to worry and that things would turn out in the end, and wasn't the garage a place where everyone gathered, and didn't people look up to him, well there you go.

=

LAST WEEK BURTON HAD BEEN IN HIS GARAGE, AND THE DOOR was opened and James Chapman came in. He walked now with a game leg and a cane, and his face, which could show almost immediate anger whenever he wanted, was gray. And he didn't like dogs. He asked abruptly for the oil to be changed on his truck, and Tucker did so while Chapman waited in the heat of the office. This was Chapman's roadway, a roadway he more or less thought he owned for the last fifty-five years. But the politics and the times had shifted, and he realized he was forgotten. His business was forgotten, his friends were dead. This had made him take to playing pool every weeknight at Brennen's, and having one too many drinks.

He told Burton he would write his great-nephew out of the will. But this was at least the twentieth time he had told Burton this.

"I asked him to bring my truck in and he said that he was too busy, so I've had it and he is gone from my life—he will not be allowed in my house, on my property, or have anything to do with my estate."

He had changed the locks on his doors, and for once he was going to use these locks.

Alex had been a disappointment, Mrs. Chapman had told Burton. She said nothing more than this.

"Oh, Alex has been a terrible disappointment," she said. "He hates us, you see—that is the only way to think of it—deep, deep down his life has made him hate us. And the fact is that when you hate one person, you hate all mankind. Do you see—the instance that you hate one person, then you hate the world."

Old Chapman's business had failed, and he accused men of stealing, and fired them. He fired the one man who might have helped him keep his company: Sammy Patch. His wife, Muriel, had died, and now he was alone. It was all reckless, and all done within a year, and now his lifetime of work was a memory.

So he brought his truck in to have the oil changed, because his nephew would not.

"He's a ungrateful lad," the old man said, sitting in the office that smelled of gas and wire. "He was a creature left out of the world. Well, who brought him here? I did. Who gave him a name? I did. Who gave him money? Me. Who paid for his education? You are looking at him. Who hired him on again? Sitting here now! But we will see, won't we, Tuck, my boy—we will see what he gets up to—ha!—where will he go now—he's forty years old. Doesn't have no woman, has no kid, has no work, has no nothing. Talks big—anyone can talk big; reads books—anyone can do that; says the world is in bad shape—don't need books to know that—"

Burton said yes as he changed the oil (which was one of three things he knew how to do) that made his hands as black as squid ink, and thought of how Old Chapman had once ruled everything about him in an uncaring way that dull-thinking men have. He was an old man now, he talked with and smelled of the physical respiratory restraint of the old, and one might have the common enough decency to feel some sympathy for him at the end. That so many didn't was part of his legacy as well. They talked about him before he got to Brennen's tavern, and spoke about him after he left.

"He's a no-good bigot bastard," Leo Bourque called Old Chapman one day.

"Yes he is," Poppy Bourque agreed with his delightful, child-like smile—a smile far more childlike than Burton Tucker's, "and sometimes we can be said to be ourselves—and the Indians can be said to be too—and if there was a Dutch family here they could be too. Bigoted, my word. And the Lithuanians, have you ever in your life—and the Spanish and Portuguese, especially their fishermen—and of course one should not forget the Africans."

So how could Leo answer, except to spit and curse?

—

Alex and Jim Chapman had been warring off and on for twenty years, ever since the boy had left the priesthood under what were called suspicious circumstances, which only enlivened some against him, and so it had finally come to this.

Alex thought he would at least have the house.

That's what he had said to Burton one day last year: "I will never be rich—well, I wouldn't want to be—who would want to be rich—no, not me—but I will at least have the house."

"He won't have the house," the old man had told Burton last week. "I will burn it before he ever sets foot in it again. I will tear it apart one board at a time before he sets a toe in it—or a toenail, if you ask me. I don't want him close enough to smell the chimney smoke. If he gets close enough to smell the chimney smoke, I will phone the police—"

So Alex lived in a small cabin that used to be the old man's icehouse, off the main shore. And the old man said he was going to kick him out of that. "Any day now—yes, any day—"

After changing the oil and wiping his hand on a piece of paper towel, Tucker did what he always did. He took Old Chapman's money and gave him a complimentary lotto ticket, as advertised on the office door.

The draw had been on Wednesday night, last night, just as it was every week.

Today, after Tucker walked to the garage and cleaned the backroom and took a mouse from the mousetrap near the door, he saw the numbers in the paper. He was going to phone Mr. Chapman, and ask him to see if he had these numbers: 11, 17, 22, 26, 37, 41—for those were the winning lotto numbers.

Last week Chapman had taken the ticket along with the receipt, and Burton had copied the numbers in his small notebook that hung on a string from the glass counter. Still, he had copied them very hurriedly and might have gotten one or two of them wrong. But by chance if he hadn't, those were the numbers. And they were worth a lot of money. It was now August 10. He'd given out only one other ticket for this draw, to Poppy Bourque.

But his numbers didn't come close. So it had to be Mr. Chapman's ticket.

But before he could phone the old man came in again, and asked for a carton of Players cigarettes and some oil for his chain saw.

"I will have to cut my own wood," he said. He told Burton he wanted to have a cord or two done before he went fishing.

Burton only nodded and smiled. Burton was waiting for Chapman to say he was set, and had won the great prize, but the old man betrayed nothing about the ticket.

The dwindling summer air came through the door. It had been hot all summer—any squalls were soon gone. Just a dry, dead feeling in the air, and the plastic flags that ran up the poles as advertisement lay limp in the sun. Again the old man asked about Alex. Have you seen him, what is he up to, how does he manage to get by—you'd think gosh almighty this and that! Is he going to teach his course this year—what does he teach, have you heard him? Ethics? What is that! Is it about molecules or people—?

Once, when Burton was frightened because he had heard there was going to be a war, and actually started crying though he didn't want to, Mrs. Chapman had smiled and said: "Dear Burton—don't you know we have always been at war?"

"Where?" Burton had asked.

Mrs. Chapman had pointed to her heart.

Perhaps she had been thinking of the war between old Chapman and young.

=

BURTON CLOSED THE GARAGE AFTER EIGHT THAT EVENING. It was still light, and dark dying bugs flitted under the bulb above the door, with its smell of warm dry and cracked paint, which reinforced the idea of a summer night, and Burton made his way by foot across to the old wharf, with its clustered dry and deadened seaweed, and then along the dusty ambivalent rocks on the shore, where ticks of heat from the nearby woods were still heard, like soft mutinies in the very fabric of nature. Far across the river he saw the lights of the giant Ferris wheel from the exhibition. He tried to think of what he was on his way to do. Having the mind of a child—or one might say, not quite a child—presented its difficulties in a difficult world. From the teasing he got as a child, to the beatings he had taken as a big teenaged boy—when he asked a girl to go on a date and her brother heard about it—all of this he had forgotten. Yet all of this had left on him the scars of an indelible truth that indicted the world he belonged to.

He was not competent in keeping the garage, and his small cousin Amy came over one or two nights a week to make sure of his paperwork. Many were telling him to sell out, and that his chocolate bars were stale.

He made his way to Old Chapman's house, to tell him about the good fortune that had befallen them both. It had befallen Burton because he would receive 1 percent of the windfall—and when he calculated it, it came to a pretty penny, although he wasn't competent enough to know what that was. In fact, Burton thought only in terms of $1000, so if anyone told him the winning ticket would be worth to him well over $100,000, and to Mr. Chapman much, much, much more, he would only be confused. Now, as he walked, he wasn't entirely sure if he had the numbers right. Since Old Chapman had never said anything about it, Burton might very well have gotten them wrong.

So then, since everyone had always told him he was slow, or stupid, he believed this himself. If they had told him that because of what he was able to do he was wise, instead of telling him that because of what he could not do he was stupid, he might have had a happier life. But people did not care about that.

Still, it would be a terrible trick to play on someone, especially an older gentleman, if you told him he had won a large jackpot, and he did not have the right numbers. Say, if he traveled all the way to Moncton to get his prize and ended up with a teacup. Now, plagued by worry, Burton was trying to remember the numbers.

But soon 11 turned into 22 and 17 turned into 33. He should head back to the garage and bring the papers and the notepad where he wrote the lotto number down. He turned to plod his way back.

Then something happened as he passed the old Catholic church with its grotto of the Virgin, who needed a paint job herself. "A sprucing up" about her halo. Here he heard something, and turning saw Young Chapman walking toward him—not really to meet him, but simply to pass him, on his way home. Young Chapman, with his hair sticking up above his sweatband, was dressed in summer sandals, something that Burton had never in his life worn. He was tall with a bent back and, as is sometimes the case with tall men, he had often become hysterical at a moment's notice.

Alex once told Burton (this was late last year) that he could have made a million and a half trillion dollars but he didn't want to be like all the other "smucks." Burton only nodded. He said he could have written ten bestsellers if he wanted to "cash in" or "sell out." Burton nodded. Also, that he had loved one woman, but he would not tell anyone who that was. It was a night when Alex had let his guard down and become maudlin. He had drunk six beer, which for him was an awful amount.

"I won't tell you who she is, but I loved her with all my heart and soul. But I never touched her—never, never!"

Nonetheless, Burton knew who this woman was. Alex loved Burton's Aunt Minnie—would always and forever love her and her alone. Her husband, Sam Patch, had worked for Alex and his uncle, but was let go last year and was now working out west, with his wife and child, Amy Patch, still here. Sometimes (and people were not fools) Alex would walk up the back road, just to stare at the house, standing in the shadows in the rain.

Burton now told Alex of the good news he had. He felt that this news supplanted any animosity the young man might have for the older Chapman. Burton said in the great gusts of words he always had when he began to speak: "I don't think anyone will have to do anything for James now on—which is what I am trying to say, boys oh boy."

Alex looked puzzled. And then alarmed. "Why, did something happen—did he die?"

"Not so likely," Burton said.

"What did he come into, some windfall?" he asked now.

"Yes," Burton said, lighting a cigarette so its smoke drifted on the air. He had never learned to puff on a cigarette. In some ways he simply spit into it, and then held it. Took it to his mouth and spit into it again, and watched the person he was speaking to for some sign of approval.

"What kind of windfall?" Young Chapman asked, looking back out toward the bay, at darkness coming over the waves. Yesterday he had phoned his uncle to ask for his copy of *Moby Dick* back.

"*Moby Dick*—you won't even get a copy of Moby dickless. And who would ever want to have a copy of *Moby Dick*—what a bad name for a book—I could have made up a better name than that in my sleep—and who would write such a godawful book named like that—"

Most people ignored Young Chapman. They would see him coming and they would raise their arms in the air as if to fend him off, turn and go away. One night he began to talk to a man who hardly recognized him, and it was discovered that Alex was continuing a conversation he had had with this man six years before— and continuing it at the very same part of the logic.

"I am simply saying that, for instance—Stalin—Joe—would he have kept money away from his own nephew?"

"You're an idiot," the man said. "He killed his nephew."

But Alex plodded on, certain that he had a right to say what he had to say. And this year his course on ethics was once again going to be offered. He was going to talk in this course about the wise man being the good man, bereft of petty desire. And in the last moment he was going to mention his uncle keeping the house from him.

"Lotto," Burton sniffed now.

"Lotto," Alex whispered, perplexed, as if it didn't register. He had never thought of anyone actually winning a lotto. He pressed his lips together as if he were a child. It might have been the pool hall lotto worth $60 every Tuesday night. But there was a feeling deep in his body that it was very much more.

He kept his face to the bay for another moment, and shoved his hands into his jeans pockets. The sand was now cooling. He did not completely trust Burton Tucker to know this.

Burton, too, was thinking this. For as long as he was alive it seemed that nothing important had been given to Burton except, in a strange way, life itself. But there was also, especially about a lottery—yes, especially about a lottery—an enticement to believe in fate, some design from the heavens themselves. Yes, the witch's hurly-burly still captivated even professors of economics. So many people played lotto on the auspiciousness of birthdays and wedding anniversaries, or some dim remembered date that they had tucked away in their mind, all thinking that these particular moments were sweet wormholes into the deity of luck.

Alex knew Minnie Patch played the lotto every week. He thought of this now.

"Lotto," Burton said again, with the infuriating self-righteousness slow people sometimes have, and nodded goodbye, as if his mission to Alex's great-uncle bore all the certainty of purpose of a saintly pilgrimage.

Alex looked up toward the steeple off to his left, to the fading grotto of the Virgin.

"Come," he said, suddenly holding Tucker's arm, "where you off to?"

"To tell Mr. Chapman."

Alex's whole rationalization, for life itself, was Darwinism modified by randomness.

This, too, is what he taught in his course. In fact, his life was known by this kind of secular obstinacy, and he had defined himself by it in a way which had set him apart from others. Oh, there were many on the river who didn't believe in anything anymore, just like he, but his crusade against everything his uncle was had taken it to a different level.

In fact, he believed that what had happened to him over the last twenty-three years proved conclusively, once and for all time, the absence of any divinity. He was both fair and honest, and yet never got ahead. He had remembered his mother dying with such pain, when two days before her death it was his birthday and she had struggled that day to get up and celebrate with him. Each time he thought of this, his legs would begin to tremble and water would start in his eyes. He was correct when he said to his students, in his course: "You can be a good man, a kind man, an officer of the human race, without having luck on your side. I have suffered enough, and have harmed no one."

The worst of it was, it was all true.

Some nights at the garage over the past summer he would tell Burton, with great poignancy, that his mother's death had caused a death in him. And that for a long while religion had replaced her, for he felt he had nothing else. Until he said he finally understood something grander: that there was nothing in shadows but whimsy, that religion was a corporation, and that the cardinals were shareholders in the deceit. So he told Burton that a fly was not ordered to light upon the table, and there was no consequential determination when it put its little hairy feet down. From that fly one could move up or down the entire genetic scale, far past his great-uncle's "brutal" construction firm, to realize that a whole universe could explode and no god ordered it or cared. It was empty and devoid of meaning until we made it so. He said it was ridiculous for a priest, in this day and age, of all days and ages, to think he could take holy water and bless something. Especially a house. Burton remembered Alex said that the poorer the Catholics were the more they were blessed, but they never seemed to get any richer. They even stunk. He said: "If God cared, there would have been no Holocaust."

"Sure, God don't care," Burton would say, more to keep a friend than to reveal an opinion. And the man would nod, as if he had a friend. "Sure—God never cared—and if I saw God, I'd tell him so."

And then Burton would trail off and try to go somewhere, and say he liked to get home early to watch *The Dukes of Hazzard* and he hoped Alex didn't mind. For Burton was simple-minded and went to church because others did.

Alex's master's thesis was on Stalin's five-year plans and the historical significance of the battle of Stalingrad, and how the Second World War was really one against Stalin and his progressive ideology.

"If I was Stalin," he would often tell Burton, "no uncle would bother me."

"No, of course not—if you was Stalin—haven't met him myself—nor do I expect to, but if I do—well, boys oh boys—" Then silence would overcome him. There would be a long embarrassed moment.

"I'm only saying," Alex would declare.

"I know," Burton would say. "You is only saying."

"God loves you too—just like he loves me," Poppy said to Alex one night.

Alex disliked this particular association, for he felt and he always had felt superior to Poppy Bourque, who always wore a big T-shirt with a lobster saluting you and saying, BON AMI!

"Where are you going?" Alex asked Burton now.

"Tell him," Burton said.

"Tell who—?"

"Tell Old Jimmy Chapman."

"Tell him what?"

"Tell him he won the lotto—and is rich as can be."

"You mean he doesn't know?" Suddenly Alex's face expanded slightly, as if brightening on this darkening night, the one frail and undeniably elusive glimmer of hope.

"No—unless he's keeping it all to himself."

They were on the shore slope, in the dark and the spent day, where they could smell idle oil on the waves and hear the last calls of gulls sweeping over the water, near the little island called Chapman's Island. Alex's house was on the left, up a wooden staircase from the beach, into the dark stand of wood. It was a small place, hidden by half-dead spruce trees. The dooryard was dirt, and the trees in back had been scorched by a forest fire twenty-three years before, and Alex as a boy had gone out and helped beat back the flames with a broom.

"How do you know he has won?" Alex asked, curious. "If he doesn't—shouldn't he know—shouldn't he have come to tell you?"

"I wrote down his number after I give him the ticket for the oil change. He mustn't have looked at it yet."

It struck Young Chapman as absolutely absurd, this moment, for just as the stars were now coming alive in the sky above the evening smoke, above the wonderful river and the twinkling lights, so was his imagination being kindled by all of this. For wasn't it he who had convinced poor Burton to give out free lotto tickets? (They weren't free; he just charged it on the oil change.)

But more to the point, wasn't it Alex who had been asked by James Chapman to take the truck in for an oil change on that day? And what had he said?

"Take it in yourself, I'm no longer under your thumb—"

"Fine—then my thumb won't be lifted to help you—" Old Chapman had retorted.

And both had tried to slam the receivers into each other's ear.

What a moment to pick to say no. How could he have decided at that moment to? What was he thinking? Well, there might be an answer. The answer, of course, explained by his former religion, was that he never decided—that he had chosen freely, but had not decided. He thought of this explanation given in his first year of Catholic study: God either wills or allows, and so Satan sweeping toward the heavenly host did not know that every beat of the great expanse of his wings, toward his own destruction, had been understood a million, million, and plus a million years, and yet it was still Satan's choice. The old priest who explained this seemed very pleased, as if he himself was getting back, if not at Satan, at some form of pestilence that had plagued him in his youth. And then all of them traipsed behind him as they went down to the wharf to bless the herring boats. That night two boats were lost in a storm. Leo Bourque's captain, Eugene Gallant, died.

"I'll write you out of the will," the old man had said in exasperation last week.

"You have nothing left anyway," Alex had gloated. Well, he shouldn't have said that. That wasn't very nice.

"We'll see," Chapman answered, "all the things I have and will have and you will have nothing—you'll freeze your little rat-shaped arse off!"

"Ya—we'll see old Jimmy boy." Alex said, "Go blow yer nose."

When he went back to the house three days ago to pick up some of his books, he was ordered not to come within five hundred feet of the house.

"You are not allowed to see my chimney smoke—that's what the officer said."

Alex would stand five hundred feet away, and the old man would yell at him:

"If that is 499, I'm phoning."

"Its exactly five hundred—I counted them—exactly five hundred."

"Well, my feet are bigger than yours and it's my feet that count."

"The only time your feet counted was when you were booting me in the arse."

"Ya, well you might need another one."

"I am five hundred feet."

"I will go get my measure."

"Measure me all you want."

They would yell back and forth at one another like mountain hikers yodeling away. It was all fine. And the more people knew that they yelled and squabbled, the better it was. This childish insanity had been perfectly fine, this brutal infantile tit-for-tat, until this horrible moment.

Alex now picked up a stone, threw it to the water sullenly. Then he looked at Burton, and grimaced slightly and put his hand on his arm.

"Listen, Burton, my buddy. How much?"

"A lot—if you think I don't know," Burton said, sniffing and spitting and grimacing.

"Come on up to my house," Alex said.

Burton shrugged as if it didn't matter one way or the other, and the two of them trudged off toward the wooden stairs that led up to the soft, dark woods above.

═

WHEN HE GOT TO THE TOP, BURTON TUCKER LOOKED BACK toward the shore and saw the last bit of twilight against the languid waters and thought fleetingly of old Mrs. Chapman, who he used to carry down the stairs of her own place to rest a while on the beach. She would always wear the big ludicrous sun hat and smoke her Players cigarettes as she painted some seagull on the waves and talked about her nephew, in between bouts of smoker's cough and her talk of gin rummy, in hopeful terms—even when the company was going under and in the heat of midday you could hear from across the field Alex being shouted at by his uncle in the small office on the construction sight.

"Fine communist you are—even a communist knows how to use a peevie."

"I did not say I was a communist—that's what you say."

"Ya, you're just like every other communist I ever met."

"Ya, well how many did you meet?"

"You're the first."

"You call me a communist and I will sue you blind."

"Like I said, fine communist you are."

The old lady would shake her head and smoke and cough.

Burton thought of what Muriel used to say to him because he was kind to both her and her husband.

"Burton, someday, maybe a year or so after I have died, you will look down from the cliff and you will remember that I sat here this day, and when you look down across the shoreline and see a sunset that I painted with my brush, I will be thinking of you and already you will know that I have brought you a great gift for doing all these kind things for me now—and that we are all God's children caught within his painting."

And of course it was easy to believe, because he now could never not think of Mrs. Chapman when he looked toward the shore.

But he also knew she had died a year ago today. And now her two remaining loved ones, her husband and her great-nephew, were at each other's throats like weasels. And he wondered, as well as he could, if there wasn't some awful art in that.

After Sammy Patch left, the Chapman construction business sat moribund like a wounded bull moose in a bog. Men just did not come back in to work. They knew that like a dying animal, the business was done.

Old Chapman in panic tried to get a buyer. Some men tried to buy him out. The offer was good, even legitimate—but Jim couldn't see himself selling out to people who had once worked for him. The deal went sour. And the men drifted away.

Now the old man for spite had put Alex off the property. There were books—two more shelves that he wanted to take out of the house—and his thesis. If only he had taken the truck in to have the oil changed things may have worked. The one favor the old man had asked of him.

"Take the truck in."

"Go fuck yourself."

Alex thought over his life—in a fleeting second, yet a multitude of events were presented to him. And this was clear: If Old Chapman got back on his feet, Alex would pay the price for that terrible falling out, and for everything else. He would be crucified if Jim got rich again. The whole point of their back and forth tit-for-tat is that neither had anything. If one of them suddenly had something, what then might happen to the other?

Of course, fleetingly he thought this: Cicero, his favorite philosopher, would tell him to let it go—that his life was more worthy than anything anyone might say or do to him. Yet Cicero didn't convince him at this moment. For he knew that those who mocked him now would mock him worse if Jim got the money. He tried to think of a way around this. But he couldn't. The only thing he knew was that Jimmy, with his big shaggy head of hair, his cold and indifferent meanness of spirit, would humiliate him if he ever got that money, because he had humiliated him so much when he was a boy.

He'll find a stairs to kick me down, Alex thought.

He asked Burton about this ticket and if he had sold it, or had just given it away.

"I didn't sell it," Burton said. "I give it as part of the deal on oil change—just like you advised."

"I never advised that," he said, "you made some mistake—I never did." Everything about this night was suddenly trancelike. His shelf of books, the wondrous world of history and philosophy, stared him in the face. Those bold secular humanists whom he believed in. Could they help him now? Why couldn't belief in those books give him peace now? For what he argued at least as well as most was his indifference to the desires of man.

"Yes," he would say drinking at the tavern, after his sixth or seventh beer, "I am completely indifferent to the desires of man—" Of course he knew he wasn't. But he liked to say it. It impressed a few indifferent people.

"Well—" he answered now, "what I mean to say is if you didn't sell it, then you won't get the percentage—I don't think."

"Oh," Burton said. And he did look wounded, slightly, by this remark. Burton was easily wounded, and would for days disappear because of an uncalled-for remark. But still and all, he was wounded because of the hidden glee in Alex's remark—the kind that says: I will not be happy if you get a sniff more than I do.

"So would your percentage be a big score or what?" Alex asked, putting his hand through his matted hair and down the back of his neck.

"I don't know," Burton said. "But I should tell him anyways— if I get the percentage or not."

"You mightn't have the numbers right," Young Chapman said fitfully. "That would be terrible if you didn't."

He was now in a panic, and offered to make Burton supper. Burton said he had had supper. So Alex offered an after-supper lunch. Burton said he was not so hungry at the moment.

The idea that simple people had that this lotto was a sign from the divine when it was just a clever maneuver by a callous government to rake in millions he suddenly told Burton, exasperatedly. Burton simply nodded.

"I know that," Burton said. "Government is like everyone else."

"And do you remember when he beat me when I was eleven?" he asked. "He was the one who started calling me the big cheese. Remember—Big Cheese this and Big Cheese that?"

"Of course," Burton nodded, though he didn't remember, and would have been two or three.

"He beat me all the time—beat my head off, beat the snot out of me, half crippled me, cuffed me on the side of the head, twisted my ears," Alex said, rubbing his dirty hands together and looking about. "Sometimes on occasion my ribs still pain," he said. "Day in and day out I worked for nothing, and tried to please him—and I was always being kept in or yelled at. Just because I didn't bring the wood in from under that tub and dry it—do you remember that tub?"

"Oh yes," Burton said, though he did not remember, "that was quite the tub."

"About this ticket—we have to be sure—you wouldn't want to startle anyone into believing something they have no right to believe. That's what the church does—do you want to be like the church?" he asked.

"Not on your life," Burton said. "Who would want to be like a church?"

After this remark, Alex said nothing more. He was of course terribly ashamed of himself at this moment. But he was furious with Burton, as intelligent people are at times when they believe a person's lack of intelligence is an affront and a danger to themselves.

Burton stared at the floor in a strange reflective manner, as if ashamed of himself too, and as always he was trying to do right.

Alex's unemployment insurance would be gone in a week. But he had his course on ethics. Or at least he hoped he did. They were supposed to let him know. Now he asked whether Burton knew how much this lotto ticket was worth. His hands were shaking slightly as he asked the question, for a part of him didn't want to know.

"Oh yes, I know," Burton said, not looking at him. "I know very well what it is worth."

"Well—what?" Young Chapman asked impatiently.

"Thirteen million," Burton said, shrugging. "If there is such a thing as million."

=

ALEX THOUGHT, THIRTEEN MILLION. THAT WAS TOO MUCH for someone who was his enemy. An enemy having thirteen million could do untold damage. He would be the laughingstock of the river all over again as he was, as he was, as he was. The old man having thirteen million was worse then Beaverbrook having it. Yes, Beaverbrook and he wouldn't have gotten along either.

But there was also another consideration—that of Minnie Patch. Long had he wanted her. But if Sam came back, with his money—his little bit of money—but money much more than he had before?

She would leave Patch for thirteen million, she would have to. Though he was a defender of the rights of women, and no one on the river could say that he wasn't—in fact, he thought of himself as the only defender of the triangular rights of women: the right to choose, equal pay for equal work, and affordable daycare; he had made his life's duty to maintain this ideology—any woman would succumb for thirteen million.

But the pricklier and more feared problem was his uncle. He was suddenly terrified of what his uncle would say about him if he got his grubby hands on all that cash. He'd be worse than the popes, Alex thought. "Burnt at the stake no doubt."

So what he thought was this: If he could somehow get this money, he would do more good with it than his uncle, who had lost himself in anger over the company. Minnie might just come to him, and leave Sam Patch where he was, out west working. They would send Sam Patch some money, with a letter saying that they both still liked him.

The idea always in his mind, like those of unrequited lovers, was that Minnie really still loved him. He could not escape that hope. And it would be worth thirteen million to find out.

But then again, if James Chapman ever got this money, Alex's life may as well be over—that is how sure he was of the old man's enmity at this moment.

I may as well be buried up to my neck in pig slop, he thought. And then he thought again of jail. For if Jim Chapman got the money, Leo Bourque would tell about something Alex Chapman had done to the company a year ago. A very small little thing, but nonetheless it had destroyed the company completely.

How could I know I'd ruin the company, he had thought many times. Though he knew because he taught ethics that he had known, and that he didn't even have to teach ethics to have known.

That could mean jail. He would be like an angel falling from heaven—that's how low he would have sunk. He remembered the picture in his bedroom when he was a boy, of Satan and his herd falling through the sky. He always stared at the impassive non-expressive clouds about them as they fell, hurling through, as his great-aunt once said, "their own baleful conscience."

What a mess, he thought, panicking slightly. He stared at his wide and almost terrified eyes looking back at him from his mirror across the room. All those books, what good had they ever done—he may as well have eaten them, rather than have read them. And all those silly self-centered, pick-arsed authors that he wanted to be. What had they ever done? Did one of them win thirteen million?

Over the last few months, since the business went under, he had been waiting for the other shoe to drop. For in a way he was the one who had caused the business to fail, and left Old Jim and his employees broke.

So now the shoe had dropped.

If there was a lost highway where souls traveled, this was it. It was a lost highway because those going downriver met the French communities that didn't belong to them. Those French who came upriver met the English communities where they would never be welcome. The signs in both languages led nowhere at all, and right in among them were the Micmac, with their own language and as many problems.

Such was this lost highway that sat along the edge of the bay and called itself a land. James Chapman himself had done much to aggravate this isolation by tearing French signs down in the 1970s, and so too had a mayor from the French side by painting over the English signs with the Acadian flag.

But things had changed three years ago. The highway bids along this section of the province were now under French control, and people in power remembered Mr. Chapman, the Englishman who had tried to destroy them with his bids. Alex had blamed his uncle for his bigotry rather than the French who put Jim under; Alex had long ago decided his uncle and not the French was bigoted. He had believed for a time that his real father was in fact French.

Now, about this other stuff—the millions—he would have to act, he knew this. He would have to do something he never did before—break into the house and steal that ticket. Or if he was being watched, as he was, find someone else to. He would have to, if he wanted to survive. Or he could let James Chapman have his winning, and it would mean the end of his life. That is, he would never be able to live down Jim Chapman's hubris, nor would he be able to crawl back.

So it was now, at this moment, that Young Chapman became resolved never to tell Old Chapman what he may have won, even unto death. He would do everything to get this ticket for himself. He would be resolved to do so, and not lessen his resolve until he had succeeded. This is what he must do in order to secure his independence. There was one moment when he thought he should not do this, and this was the time to let the idea go.

But he couldn't.

There was a profound silence in the little room. And in this silence it was as if some kind of voice were pleading with him to let it all be.

It was, of course, the conversation he had had last week with likable, illiterate Poppy Bourque.

"Yes," Poppy had said, "I remember your mother, and I liked her very much, and what she would say to you is if we live as we must everything will turn out." Poor Poppy Bourque thought Alex would agree with this, and was startled by his absolutely disgusted look.

The voice of Poppy was in his mind for just a second, and then lost again.

Alex paused and quite to his surprise felt weak, breaking out in sweat. Finally he said this to Burton: "I'm his nephew, I'll tell him about the money and check his ticket. I'll tell him he should give you your 1 percent—"

"But I thought—well, thinking you didn't like him."

"Well I'm not doing this for him or me but for you, Burton."

"Oh," Burton said.

"I have a responsibility to you is how I look at it."

Burton paused, screwed up his eyebrows, and felt that this was good thinking, for already he had gotten the numbers entirely mixed up. To say someone who hadn't had won the lotto would be bad. In fact, he realized that the old man might think he was tormenting him. So he took his leave from Young Chapman and made his way back down the desolate beach, looking at the last of the seagulls and the terns skimming, and in the darkening grove above the nighthawks weaving in and out. He was perplexed and angry at not being able to remember, and why would God, if there was a God, do this to him. For this had always been the way. People had always teased him because of it—told him he owed them money when he did not because of it. Children would come in and say: "You have to give the $5 you owe me—momma says." And he would prolong his stare, and mumble, but he would give the $5. It was, as some said, a fail-safe way to make some spare change. Burton knew this, often after the fact. And he had always got up to a new day, and tried it all again. The only one he had protecting him from this was Amy.

When he got home what seemed exciting seemed after reflection to be nothing at all. Most of the things in his life he had been talked out of. From his pocket knife when young to his Mario Lemieux autograph he once had in his garage window.

"We will wait and see," he said. "It could be a big heap of change in my pocket. It could be."

There was one thing that bothered him. And it was what Mrs. Chapman had said, about a gift a year after her death. In the way of the world, stranger things had happened, and Burton himself was a strange thing—a person who wasn't even supposed to exist, because his own mother, a scared young girl of sixteen, had left him out in the snow to die, down on the Gum Road, behind the chicken coop. He had been left out on February 5, 1971, and when they found him on February 6, people said he was frozen solid and the hens had begun to peck at him. They took him to the hospital and thawed him out, and as they did he began to breathe and cry. So here he was, flesh and blood. When he met his mother years and years later, he had no idea what to do or say, so he broke out stepdancing in front of her, a smile on his face.

=

Five minutes after Burton left, Young Chapman had torn the place apart and found the local paper with the numbers printed on the second page, on the left-hand column at the very bottom: 11 17 22 26 37 41. He was in a daze now, as he put his dirty finger against one number and then the next. Were these the numbers Old Jim had at this moment in his pocket? All his life Jim had money-grubbed, and Alex had laughed at him last week: "Look where yer money-grubbing got ya."

Again, that wasn't the wisest thing to say.

Now he was doing things, which he seemed to witness outside of his body. He had heard that people sometimes acted this way. But this was perhaps the first time it had happened to him. Or maybe that long ago time when he had seen Minnie Patch's skirt blow above her waist.

He hated the lotto. Like many cross men studied by university and polemical in nature, he thought it was foolhardy nonsense and very much beneath him. Yes, he had teased Minnie about it often, saying she was a fool, saying she was raising her daughter to be a fool.

"Barefoot and pregnant," he had said, "that's how you ended up."

In fact, in the last year he could not see Minnie without saying something unpleasant, for hadn't she turned out exactly like he himself had predicted?

Now he began to shake as he sat at the table. Because he wanted the same thing as everyone else. He wanted the money. With the money, he would win Minnie back. He would be as wise as Cicero told him to be. But he had to have the money.

That thing which dreams are made of. He thought of when he was a runner and how with his training and his absorption of pasta and lettuce, and grains of various kinds, he had almost managed to run a marathon. Yes, that ethically minded, self-absorbed, self-indulgent, self-righteous sport. Yes, he had made much of his running aloofness—his passion for endurance and ecological restraint. But he had not run in years.

He took some water and tried to think. His medicine was on the windowsill—medicine for the ailment he had with his heart

that had come to him with age. This had happened since the fall of
the business. It had happened since he had seen Minnie again. He
had thought he had conquered his desire for her. It was obvious he
had not. "Just a valve," the doctor had told him. He tried to picture this valve and could not sleep some nights thinking of it, flop-
ping back and forth in his heart like a wagging tail. When it hurt
him, he would say: "It is nothing," or "Stop hurting me if you are
nothing," and keep plodding on.

When it pained he would sit up nights and read—and what an
authority he had become on the dazzling stupidity of man. So
then he must steal this ticket. For what did it matter to others if
he did or did not? Who would say in ten years that he had, and if
they did, who would care? He had read enough of the world to
know that!

Did Beaverbrook steal? Yes. Did Roosevelt and the Kennedys?
A whole lot.

His well-publicized disbelief in God made it certain that no
one was answerable to God. And if he believed this fully then he
had to act. In fact, he was morally obligated to. This was what it
finally came down to now. It was his moral duty to take the money
and help the unfortunate. All his predisposition told him so.

He left his house and went out into the warm, pulpy air. Far
across the river he could see the giant Ferris wheel, looking like
fate in the wind, going round and round, like one of those wheels
of Dante crushing, tumbling, and catapulting the grand illusion-
ary Middle Ages into the din of the past. If he listened, he could
hear the howls of children across the waters, as if they were falling
into some new estimation of the cabala.

He walked through the woods and out to the highway. He was
agitated that this had happened to him even though, in a way,
nothing had happened to him.

Yet now Young Chapman was consumed by the idea that it
had. He had not taken the truck in, and his uncle had received
the ticket.

He was on his way to Minnie (Tucker) Patch, the woman he loved and Amy Patch's mother. Because of the company's decline, her husband Sam was away working, and about to bring home a large amount of money. They were not rich—but when he came home they would be able to afford things.

Young Chapman used to trudge up Minnie's roadway in the winter, when they were both teenagers, and stand by the gate, looking in at those old yellow curtains hanging across blank, dirty windows in the small, cold house. He would stand in the cold almost all day long. It was as if that sad little house—filled with old and vagrant furniture, and cases of empty wine bottles stacked in the small, cold porch, with snow swishing and swashing over the back shed roof—was a place of mystery and worship. He worshipped Minnie—he actually did.

Thou shalt have no false gods before me, he remembered thinking, and yet he would stand in the cold unable to go home. "Just one glimpse at her peaked little Irish face and I'll bolt home," he would say.

When he got home, his uncle would often reprimand him for something he had left undone, or tell him he had to go to seven o'clock mass before he ate, stretching up to put the food away.

"Oh, let him eat," Muriel would say.

"Not until after mass. He has communion before he gobbles food—"

So he would trudge out angry and fretful, his belly gnawing at his bones, and then come to life when he realized Minnie was at mass as well. He longed for the host, just to establish something in his guts. His uncle had the habit of kicking him when they knelt, if he didn't answer the priest well. He was teased by some children that his father was French, and that is why his uncle despised him. So he began, then, to look for the name of his father in the phone book, and imagine himself a LeBlanc, or a Terrieux.

And each chance he had, he would walk up Minnie's lane. This is where he was free, and where she who freed him was. This is where the snow smelled more pure, the sounds of the highway were muffled by the great pine trees. The cold hung over his land and he was in deep despair, for it was love, and he could not give her up.

"Stay away from her," Old Jim told him once, bluntly. "You don't need no young dark-haired cunt from the back road—have some common decency."

But he disobeyed. He had to. It was his first rebellion.

He left notes in her mailbox, professing what he called then his "like" for her. And he was sick at heart, and this feeling was some-how satisfying in itself. Her mother always said she wasn't home. He knew that her older sister, June Tucker, had a child at sixteen and hid the fact from the family, put the baby boy behind the chicken coop, and fled to Toronto. The child, Burton, lived.

Because of this, Minnie's father said she wasn't allowed to speak to boys until she was twenty-six. Alex was dejected, but later that winter Minnie had the little boy, Burton, bring him a note. It was written in a light green ink, on paper from her history scribbler, and said she would like to see him, and maybe go to the sock hop if she could get permission. That she would try to get permission from her father. This, Alex knew, and so did she, was impossible. But still, in her youthful heart, in her love of life, as boys and girls so often have, did she hope for this.

Alex wrote back saying they would meet.

Minnie was a convent girl, with a spotless white blouse and a skirt, and on that dark night in frigid weather he thought of her soul, like that white blouse she wore. He thought of this when he saw her one day walking through the old creamery lot, with its junked pipes and tattered blocks.

She had black hair, and small crooked teeth, that he loved. She, too, at this time was in the Lenten crosshairs and fasted. The convent was in deep despair because it was closing, the nuns being sent elsewhere and the town being thrust forward into the secular age. But still fifteen students remained at the convent, and she was one.

Then came the night when she told him her father had found out, and would not allow her to see him anymore. The sock hop was out of the question. It was reported that the old man had taken her socks.

"Did he?" Alex asked infuriated.

She hauled up her pants over her ankles to show her sockless boots.

Alex said that when he saw her father, he would give him a piece of his mind. They walked along the Gum Road, in the freshly fallen snow, and he felt at home for the first time since his own mother's death. He did what his uncle said without complaint, because he was thinking of her.

Then he found out when her birthday was.

"I will meet you Thursday at the forks of Arron Falls," he said, "after four o'clock. I will have a gift for you. After school."

"I don't know if I can," she said. She was wearing a scarf and her eyes shone in the dooryard light, as a bit of snow fell out of the twilight and landed on the old sled path and fell more gloomy in the trees. All of this might seem or look depressing to one who did not know or revel in its great beauty as he did. The fields filled with snow, and acres and acres of lots stretching down the long highway into the void, with prip-props holding pulp wood extending into the night. There was nothing sweeter in the world, and if he traveled one million miles he would come back to its sparse and terrible beauty some day.

"No—you have to," he said. "I promise you I will be there."

"Then I promise you I will be," she replied, squeezing his hand, and turning and running toward her house, her woolen coat flying behind her, snow flying about her bare ankles.

He listened that night to what his uncle said about the state of their affairs, and what did he, an orphan like him, think he was going to get if he traipsed off with the daughter of a boozer.

"Her face'll get old and tired and you'll be looking for a woman who has some class," the old man said in fitful duty to some regulation. He jabbed at the bowl of his pipe with a pick, and looked quickly at his nephew. He had married a woman with some class, he said, and he expected as much from Alex.

Alex did his chores in the warehouse (rolling a barrel from one end to the other, which he had just rolled to the other end the day before) and said nothing. Collected the rats from the traps in the back of the barn and threw them out. Some nights, his uncle might wake him. He would get up, under the flare of a lantern, to go out along the back hall and cross into the barn, where a moose was hanging from a tripod, or a deer stiffened in death hung upon a hook, and Alex would help his uncle take the hide off these animals with a three and a half–inch knife. It was a long, disgusting process to Alex, for his uncle did not need the meat or the money. Alex was always conscious of how these animals died.

The meat was cut up and sold to people along the highway. His uncle tallied the earnings every year from this illegal enterprise, and bought things he needed for the barn or house. Most of the money he stored away. Alex could not stand the look of a rifle, and on those darkish days he became opposed to everything associated with them.

Now and again, when his uncle lashed out at him, Alex would look up at the catwalk above that ran from the big warehouse to the small, and say, "I am going to walk that someday—prove that I can—then I will be able to leave this place forever."

When he finally was paid that winter he bought an album for Minnie, The Beatles' collected hits. He moved sacks of grain that his uncle sold to nine farms, and had to take feed from bags the rats had gotten to and redistribute it before the buyers found out. He could see those farms in his mind's eye up and down the lost highway, and how his uncle tried to squeeze the last cent from all of them, on occasion traveling along the road with one of the priests. Sometimes Alex would go along, lugging the sack into the barn.

So then, for this work, Alex had this Beatles album as token of his love.

Thursday after coming home from school he started up the road, in the evening air that smelled of smoke and soft glazed ice on the trees, with the album under his arm. He had his coat unzippered and the wind blew against his small but strong body, the smell of wood ash lingering along Fanny Groat's ditch. Sometimes Fanny would call to him and invite him inside. There in the small room she would ask him about his aunt, with a particular light in her eyes, and Alex would think, I am glad she cares so much for Aunt Muriel.

Fanny Groat with her large fake pearl necklace and her fake fur stole.

He passed this dilapidated house now, and moved up the road. As he came to the corner of the tote road, where old Jameson used to carry his winter supplies up to the camps, a dark form appeared on the landscape and walked toward him along a row of poplar trees in the dusk. It was Minnie Tucker's father, Harold, who was drunk—as he was every second day, and as he promised not to be every fourth day. He had beaten Minnie to keep her inside.

"I've had one fuckin' trollop, I won't have no more," he sniffed with self-righteous conformity.

She was, he said, not to be mixed up with boys, but she had eluded him on this day, her seventeenth birthday, and had gotten out.

Alex, now tried to go around Harold on the road, but he made the mistake of keeping his head down and trembling. The old man, filled with mischievous meanness—a coward when sober and a bother when drunk—grabbed the record from the boy's gloved hand and looked at it, then waved it back and forth.

"Eh—let's see now, what have you got here—sompun' for someone—"

"A record," Alex said.

"A record, is it?"

The man held the record up and looked at it, and with the certainty of the ignorant, said, "Them lads are com-mu-nists—don't believe in God, is what I hear."

He smashed it over his knee, as if performing a service even Alex would approve of. Then, overcome by what he had done, he looked alarmed, his body reeking of wine. Alex tried to get the record back and go around him, but the man, seeing his prey was nervous and delighting in the fact that he had scared a young boy, kept pushing him back up the tote road in the dark. Each time Alex tried to push him back, enraged by this deliberate narrow-mindedness, or stepped to go around him, the man would raise his arms in front of him, fending the boy off, and smile, a slave to his own idea of power.

Tears came to Alex's eyes. "I'll tell my uncle," he said.

Harold only laughed at this. "Jimmy Chapman don't sceer me. If you think I don't know about him screwing the box off that slut Fanny Groat—while his own wife a cripple—and he makes sure she and you goes off to church. Praying like the cunt he is, then he goes up and diddles Fanny, or gets me to help him lift moose out of the bog. Then pays me and Fanny to keep it all quiet. Don't think we all don't know."

Alex in a second knew this to be true. He knew why he always felt an outcast in the house. He knew why Fanny asked him about his aunt, with scheming eyes. He knew why he skinned animals in the night. He knew why his uncle did not want him traveling up to see Minnie. Suddenly he was overwhelmed by the idea of who his uncle was. That large yet small man.

He could not go down to meet Minnie and turned to go home. Her father, who had so changed his day, had actually changed the direction of his daughter's life. Harold followed the boy back up the road, shouting triumphantly, "Fanny Groat!" and swinging his arms in frantic jubilation, with the evening sun on the back of his canvas winter jacket.

If this had not happened, Alex was to think later, what destiny would Minnie and he have had?

Alex went home and sat alone in the darkening parlor, with the cold mirrors and the pictures of geese on the wing, of his great uncle's large old house, with the broken album in his hand. It had taken his savings to buy it. He shook for a day and a half, in anger but also in shame for his fear. When he finally spoke to his uncle about Harold breaking his album, Old Jimmy looked at it and said, "No need for records like this anyhow," his cheeks emitting the scent of aftershave. And then he said this strange remark: "Some people can stand up to people and some can't."

The revelation about this remark came later that afternoon. His uncle was at the big cabinet on the second floor, had just locked it with the key he kept in his vest, and he turned to Alex. He was tall, but his back was bending—and his height, which pleased him, did more to reveal his smallness of mind than anything. The moment they stared at each other, Alex knew that Jimmy Chapman had hired Harold Tucker with wine money to do what he had done, because he knew Alex would run away. This is how well he knew his nephew. However, the old man didn't know that Harold Tucker, filled with wine and ashamed of betraying his own daughter, would tell about him and Fanny.

"I will never let this happen to me again," Alex said. "Never!"

That Sunday they went to church, and Old Jim genuflected and said his prayers and blew his nose.

OVER TIME, ALEX DISCOVERED THAT MINNIE HAD GONE TO Arron Falls to wait, on that long ago frigid February afternoon, with the smell of snow and ash on the wind and without a sock on her foot, and had not met him. But she had met someone else. This, too, seemed preordained.

She had met Sammy Patch at that very spot on that very moment Alex was supposed to meet her. Sam Patch, a boy with grade 7 education who had left school to help his mother and who worked for Alex's uncle, paid next to nothing. Even as a boy he could pick up large timber and throw them about. Many times he and Old Jim were out on a scow at the far side of Chapman's Island lifting nets. But his uncle did have a real affection for the boy, and Alex was jealous of this.

"If you could be half the man Sammy Patch is, I'd give me right fuckin' arm," he said one night at dusk, the summer before.

"I am better than Sam Patch," Alex had replied, and to prove this he tried to pick up one of the large pallets near the barn, and couldn't. When he looked up from this impossible task, the loud old man simply shrugged and walked away.

One day in late February, Sam Patch asked Alex if Minnie was his girl.

"Hell," Alex said, "I hardly know her." He had no idea why he said his, except he had been hurt that she would have spoken to someone else so easily.

Up until that time, Alex had liked and felt sorry for Sam, even beyond the envy he had. Now, their positions were not only competitive but completely reversed.

Two weeks after the incident, Harold was found frozen to death in a snowbank after being drunk for days, Minnie was at a dance with Sam Patch, and Alex was a memory.

A year passed when he pined over her, and every night after school he would watch her leave the bus but proudly refused to speak when he saw her, even though she looked at him and waved. On the bus, he was always bullied by Leo Bourque, who accused his uncle of being bigoted toward the French. Leo was Poppy's nephew, though a different breed. He was one of the last of the French boys forced to go to the English school. He was sent by his father.

Though Alex tried to be polite and understanding, he was confused and frightened. Over the year, he had withdrawn from the world. He kept pens in a pocket protector in his shirt—ballpoint, and fountain, and three of different colors. He carried a briefcase, with his books and notes he liked to make on the shore birds he saw. Yet every night he went back to that dim old house, to work for his uncle.

He had no friends.

Over a certain time Bourque became inflexible in his demands. Finally, he demanded money. This came one afternoon about a year after the incident with Minnie's father.

"You will not get on the bus again if I don't have some money—you have lots, everyone knows—"

The worst of this was, no one knew he was being tormented. Also, Alex had told Leo that he had a lot of money. He had said this when they first got to know each other to impress the boy. Now Bourque was simply asking for some, and he would look hurt if Alex couldn't bring him some.

Alex had to ask his uncle for advances on an allowance he himself almost never got.

"No!" the old man shouted at him. "What's this money business about!"

When he couldn't give this money to Leo, his pens would be taken from him. He would arrive at school with a pen missing from his white holder. Then, Bourque said he would not need any more money if Alex got him a job for the summer. It was the first time Bourque was nice to him. It was as if both of them could be released from their grip upon one another if only this would happen.

"Get me the job, Alex, and I will be the best friend you ever had," Leo said. He had grown up with nothing and this job meant everything to him.

At the table that very night Alex asked his uncle, while Bourque waited near the ferns up along the highway. There was a dark smell of March; winter still lingered and the snowbanks were raw and shrunken.

"Please hire him, Uncle Jim—I promise I will work twice as hard as he does if you do!"

"If you work twice as hard as he does, I'll never need him," Old Jim laughed. Even Muriel laughed at this quip. Jim could not hire him. They had no need to. And Jim never did anything that wasn't needed.

So Alex had to tell Leo that they were full.

"But I thought you had some pull," Bourque said. "I believed you had pull."

"I do," Alex said, "I do—but—well, not that much."

"Not that much—what in hell do you mean, not that much?" And he slapped Alex, and Alex went reeling.

"I'll pay you back," Alex said instantly.

"You'll never be man enough to pay me back."

After this, it got harder to ride the bus. Bourque would sometimes be kindly. If he took some money, he would say that he didn't like to torture people. It wasn't his way. But that Alex's uncle had cheated the highway and things had to be done.

"You think I like this?" Leo would say shaking his head sadly. When he waved his hand there was a good amount of power with that wave, as if he were dismissing you with tolerance.

But then one day Leo was not on the bus. It rattled down the road without him. Then the next day as well—and then a week and a month. First, he had gone to a foster home; then they said he had gone up north with his uncle Poppy, and would never be back. Alex was free, or he thought he was.

In a strange turn of fate, the only one Leo sent a postcard to was Alex.

Leo had had a copy of the local paper sent to him, and in that issue there was an article on Alex, who'd won a contest in naming birds. And so Bourque changed his tack toward him:

> Dear Alex. Hope is all well, and use are on the bus.
> Well here it is good, I am not so angry at my dad
> you see they trated me rogh and I didn't tell
> noone but things was toug with my dad. Now Mis
> Samples sent me here with Poppy it is not to bad
> here. Saw you to in the paper there yesterday,
> would like to know birds to, and have to find a
> book on it, so someday get my name in the paper to.
> Your friend Leo Bourque.

It was the way he signed his name with a flair, as if he were trying to show a sophistication, that made Alex's heart go out to him, and see him with new eyes.

Cold days and dark and winter and such a note as that was forgotten, and in a bright January gust was taken away.

=

AT THIS TIME SAMMY WAS WORKING FOR ALEX'S UNCLE FOR $79 a week. It seemed that every cent caused blood, and that the boy didn't mind spending this blood. Alex's heart went out to the boy, but he was also wretched with jealousy. Especially when he saw Sammy pick up an organ his aunt wanted moved and carry it by himself upstairs.

"Don't worry," he had said to Alex, who had come to help.

Sometimes, meeting Minnie walking to the corner store with her mother, he would simply put his head down and walk by, or sometimes he would go in the opposite direction because of the humiliation he felt. She tried her best to dress neatly and care for herself, more he thought than the other children on the road. It hurt him to see her in this poverty and with this grace of character. Here was a child with an untold fountain of humanity and kindness. But, as he discovered, she was a young woman already. And she had distanced herself, and part of him resented this.

One night he saw Minnie come to the yard to wait for Sam. Suddenly, so suddenly she had no time to stop it, her dress blew up over her thighs to her white panties, the dark V visible underneath. She pushed the skirt down and smiled when Sam laughed, looked at Alex a second and looked away. He was overcome with pity and envy, desire and famine. It clung to him like a gray, wet cloak.

He planned to save money, to have things in his own life, to be happy. But weeks passed, and no one phoned or called. He then tried to take his life. It happened one day after rereading Bourque's postcard. He was so sad for that boy, and himself.

It was Muriel who stopped the superficial wound to his wrist. But sooner or later everyone knew. So he stayed at home. Weekends would go by and no one would see him in the yard. Then he began to take walks along the roadway. Some days he would walk as far as town, on others all the way to Burnt Church. His thoughts were wild, and he seemed forlorn, but something in his makeup was yearning to be free.

It was during this time that he decided to discover who his father was. He went up and down the road inquiring about his mother, who she might have liked and disliked, and was led to a name by those who remembered her as a young girl in the late 1950s, who sang in the glee club and played volleyball. The boy he heard his mother liked was named Eugene Gallant from Barryville, a man half Micmac and half French. So that was why his uncle disliked the French and Indians. This, then, was one way to get back at his great uncle or at least to proclaim freedom from him: by embracing his own people. This, in fact, was the hook on which his psychological health seemed to rest for a long while.

Some nights he would take off walking, in the snow or rain, and walk all the way down to the house, which stood back from the road, off the battered highway in a shroud of small barren spruce.

One late evening in inclement weather, Eugene met him at the gate, smiled and engaged him in conversation, and was moved to tears to find out who he was.

"Are you really Rosa's son—you are," he said hugging him. "Oh my God, how are you?"

Eugene Gallant was in his mid-forties then. He was the first kind adult to the boy, sometimes offering a stick of gum, sometimes telling him to come along on a partridge hunt. For Alex, this had to be his father. But Alex could not go on a partridge hunt because he was frightened of guns, and could not hide this fact.

"But that does not matter, for I am not frightened of guns," he said. That is, Eugene did not mind this, and did not hold it against him.

As Alex hiked back and forth, to and fro, he felt he belonged for the very first time.

No one said Eugene wasn't his father. Gallant also admitted just how much he had cared for Alex's mother—so much so, he said, that he went to Saint John, to find her grave and lay flowers. To Alex it was love, and Eugene was Alex's father. It was also fine to assume he had Indian blood, and he used to like to think how his people had to take care of the settlers when they first got here.

Yes, he would think, my uncle's ancestors were taken care of by people like me. He would smile.

There was only one problem with wanting this man to be his father. He had forgotten that the man his mother had loved had abandoned him. He was very young and remembered it in small moments, but nonetheless? This man, this Eugene Gallant, wouldn't have done so. Still, he clung to the hope, as wild as it might be, that some mistake had occurred and this Eugene Gallant, half Micmac and half French, was indeed his dad. His uncle worried about him now out on the road, and often waited up for him to get home.

"I worry about ya there, boy, fer I don't know what it is yer doing! Have ya found some young lady?"

Finally, one afternoon he mentioned to his uncle that he knew who his father was, and was not ashamed in the least to admit it. His uncle looked at him, perplexed, and asked him with deep gravity to tell him all he knew.

"Well, his name is Eugene Gallant. He is Micmac and French, and he's a damn straight guy, and he wants me to go fishing with him out in the bay. And he is kind and nice as anything, so you don't have to be ashamed, I can go live with him. I will learn how to fish and live my life just like he does."

Alex said this very quickly, and very hopefully. He shook somewhat when he spoke. For he was hoping he would have a life that was his own. And the old man nodded and said nothing. For days he said nothing. For days he said neither nay nor yea about this revelation. And Alex carried on.

And then, on Alex's birthday, Jim simply came into the room with documents he had collected and handed them to the boy, stiffly as if he were a postman, without a word, except there may have been some unintended mirth in him. Without saying a word, though, he turned and left the room. And Alex's life was opened up to him.

His mother had been a child when she got pregnant. His father was named Roach. He was from a family on the road. His grandfather Leopold was buried at the small Protestant graveyard near Hackerook. Leopold had been killed by a Chapman grader on a turn along the highway one late evening in February 1954. He was protesting the plowing job Chapman had been given (up until this time the road had been closed all winter).

"The man had come out to stop us, and we weren't able to stop. His family never forgave me for this, but his family were squatters on my land, on my property, and I could have put them off but didn't—more fool I. I left them their little farmhouse."

Though his family had long resented the Chapmans, and young Roach was fed on this resentment as much as any, he was taken in by Muriel, a war bride, and shown books and taught painting.

"He used her kind nature to gain audience with your mother," the old man wrote. "It was your mother he wanted."

Here, on those bleak winter days, Roach came as a respite from his little fallen farmyard. But he resented what they had and what his family lacked, and secretly blamed Chapman for it, and for the death of his own father.

Many times the old man would come in and see the young Roach boy there, pitiful and alone, his feet freezing from walking through a winter gale, and give him some money. Their niece Rosa, about fourteen years old, was living with them at the time.

"But I thought nothing of this then," Chapman said, "more fool I."

As time went on, it seemed only Muriel was alive to Roach's ambition, and encouraged him; he wanted to have a grand life, to escape the bitter hardship. He would spend late afternoons and evenings reading what she gave him, but dissatisfied with her and resentful of Chapman he would always mention what his father could have had if he had been treated better and not been killed at thirty-eight.

One day Roach left to work a mine in Quebec for the summer.

"Better off without him," Chapman told Muriel, who had been foolish enough to look upon him as a son. But Roach found nothing in those mines, and nothing in the subterranean jazz bars of Montreal where he and others tried to talk like the beatniks of New York. He was gone, and forgotten, and might have never returned, except the bar he worked at went out of business in 1959.

"You are here because Roach failed at bartending," Old Chapman cruelly wrote.

So in the dazzling heat of mid-July 1959 he returned, tall, thin, with bony arms and a serious gaze, a beard modeled after those who he could never be. He walked back up the Chapman lane, asking Chapman for a job.

"So we put him lifting scrap metal with old Harold Tucker," Chapman wrote. "He stayed with us, in the room that is now yours. Muriel looked upon him as the son she never had."

But it was as a conjugal to Rosa, not the woebegone son of a kind, naive British war bride, whom he secretly belittled, that he was interested in, and Rosa he made pregnant. At the end of November she fled with him, her room emptied only of one suitcase, her childhood toys left behind.

"Charlie thought he would get my money—because of you— you were his ACT OF REVENGE upon the Chapmans he accused without proof of killing his father, your grandfather. He NEVER would get my money—and so he left her and you, to try his hand in Montreal again. He died in 1971. There is a photo of him during the October Crisis. He is screaming at the soldiers on the street. He was a Quebec nationalist at that time, and gloating over the idea that Canada would be no more. This, I think, was his last great lashing out at us."

This was all that was revealed about where Alex came from and who he was. A picture of a man at the back of a crowd of five thousand, some arms raised against a black October sky.

There was also a long, detailed, and painful document on his father negotiating for money from Jim and Muriel if he allow "the boy to stay with you." This was written in his father's own shaking hand; at that time he could not have been much more than thirty-six or so. The arrived-at price for this boy, this Alex Roach to become and remain Alex Chapman was $4541.11. There was a check written out, not to his father but to a woman called Samantha Debelshoult. His last known address was Laval.

So Alex had not been Micmac after all, and now nothing remained of who he might have been. He knew nothing about this sad, angry man or his family. So was doubly orphaned. He trembled all that night as he sat at the table. Muriel came in and hugged him, and he flinched away from her, his lanky, thin body frigid. She had known and had not said anything.

He trembled all the next day as he sat in class. Half of his teachers would have remembered his father and mother, and never had said a thing. Even Eugene Gallant, who had been so kind to him, would have known, and had said nothing to correct this love for a French-Micmac father who wasn't.

He knew his mother must have been used as a pawn in this act against Jim Chapman—and he too—and over the years details would come to the fore and be remembered by him about that long ago time.

For two months he did not speak to anyone. Then he went once to his real grandfather's house—near the South Talon Road off Arron Brook, in back of Minnie Patch's. There a doleful paddock and singed fence. It was autumn and the sky was furious, and one lame horse walked, and snow started, and he was alone. (The house would be left abandoned and then burn five years later in the Lean-to Creek fire—the fire that Alex himself had to beat back with a broom from his own small place.)

Afterwards, when his uncle looked at him, Alex trembled, and his uncle said nothing, except: "Don't worry, boy—don't worry. It ain't so bad to be a Roach or anything else. And he was a sad man at the end to jump from the Jacques Cartier Bridge."

This was something Alex did not know. He sat stunned, and couldn't respond.

Then one day the documents were removed from his room, and he never saw them again.

"Don't worry about your heritage, boy—you make your own," the old man said.

He sat in desolation another few days, and then recovered. And in a way this is what he decided: He would tell people he was whoever he wanted, if he wanted to, and continue on the way he was.

=

HE DID NOT KNOW WHAT TO DO ABOUT MINNIE TUCKER. He was still in love with her, deeply, when a missionary visited his aunt—because she was bound by a wheelchair, and Jim Chapman asked him to go down and cheer the girl up and give her communion. The idea that this priest was a special priest gave Jim a grand feeling of elation, and a look of piety when the priest spoke out in the dooryard to him. Piety of the kind always associated with privately violent men.

So the priest came in, through the doorway of the house that had seen so much bitterness and despair, with the host in a small locket, and said mass for Muriel, opened the locket, and produced the host. Alex was not going to go down and see him, remaining as he was in his room, but his uncle came up and insisted he go downstairs. He walked into the living room with his head down and his face turned away, trying to hide the blemishes of his acne.

"Ah, here you are," Father Hut said. "Sit down here and I will tell my story—and see if you don't find something about it interesting."

The priest, a small man with a dazzling face who used his whole arms to talk, began to tell the three of them about his great work among the natives of South America. He spoke for an hour, and then two, and then three. Alex, who tried to be disinterested, became more and more enthralled.

It was then, people along the highway said, that Alex turned toward holy orders. It was also in revenge against Minnie that he did so.

Holy orders was a sanctifying life—a life of great inner struggle—and a warrior's life, of sainthood. He knew this the first night when he went back to his room to pray. Who would talk about this life as being effeminate and who would not know that this was a life of spectacular grandeur—far surpassing the vow of marriage. This is what the priest had told him. He spoke of bravery in the face of death.

"I have faced death," he said truthfully, "and I will again. Many have contempt for life—they will do anything, it seems, and you think, ah, how brave they are—but the really brave have a contempt for death, and strive to enable life no matter how much death is around."

What truth in that line. Alex went and wrote it down.

Father Hut was as exuberant a person as Alex had ever seen. Grace seemed to glow about him—the blackness of his slacks and jacket did nothing to dampen the aura. And so Alex, thinking of his misadventures so far, turned away from temporal life.

But he found he was not like this priest—not exuberant and happy. He was rigidly fastidious. Perhaps like his Protestant grandfather, he was unmoved by spectacle. He became silent and pious. Still, for the very first time, the meanness of the world no longer mattered to him. Everything was less than a gnat's bite once he decided to live for God.

He went to church every morning at seven, and longed for the quiet of the pew and the stained glass. He had to be pure, for he took communion. He realized for the first time how much the world existed on lies. His uncle had for years insisted that Alex was not telling the truth when he was, and often students at school made fun of him for saying things which were true. And for the first time he realized this was his great sin, among those people. He had told the truth, about what made him happy, about what he longed for, for himself as well as others; how he had loved the grasses in the fields and the dour-looking shore birds. Many times he would pass Sam Patch coming to work as he was leaving for church, in the still silent hour of early morning, with the snow lying across the long yard like a cloth sheet.

It seemed that Alex becoming a priest was something the old man was proud of. He talked proudly about the boy, and even said: "He came up a hard road—rougher than most of us—rougher even than young Sam Patch; abandoned by his father and the death of his mom. I should have been much more considerate of him than I was. I should have let his mom get married to that boy long ago, but I didn't and can't change it now!"

The idea that he, Old Jim, had instilled piety and studious prayer in the boy made Jim gush when he spoke to the nuns.

One morning Sam was backing up a truck and almost hit Young Chapman as he left the yard. In fact, if Alex had not stopped to pick up a colored piece of glass, as reddish orange as the rising sun, he would have been struck and killed. As strange as it was, stopping to pick this up had saved his life.

"I'm sorry," Sam yelled, jumping down from the cab. "I didn't see you—I'm sorry."

The old man yelled from the office door: "Watch what in hell you're doing—that's me flesh and blood!"

Sam didn't want to lose his job, because he was preparing to get married. This is what Alex had heard. Sam and Minnie were taking a three-month course at the church. The one hitch in everything was this. Each time he saw Sam, the same dazzling jealousy returned. And in truth he thought only of her.

"I'll let him go if he came close to you—he's been careless with the big shifters," his uncle said that night at supper. "If I let him go he'll never have a cent—and he'll never afford to marry the Tucker girl."

But the boy knew this would be appalling. He also knew it was in his power to help destroy the relationship, at this moment. He swallowed hard.

"Don't be ridiculous," he told Jim. "It was an accident—and, in fact, I know it is not yet my time."

(That is, he tried to sound wise, but he also believed it at that moment.)

That night, going to bed, masturbating, thinking of her dress lifting, he was overcome with shame. He could not go to communion the next day, and when he went to confession, having to confess what he had done, in the privacy of his room he was certain the priest knew who he was.

"I'll not forget," Sam whispered the next weekend. "You taking up for me. And either will Minnie."

"Never mind it," Alex said angrily.

For the first time, Alex saw how the world stood—Sammy Patch with Minnie and him alone. Sam Patch with nothing but this dirt job that he, Alex, could take from him if he wanted to. But he felt the only way he would win approval is by going forward with his vocation, even if there were moments when he felt it was a sham. But who did he want to win approval from?

Minnie Tucker.

Then there came a test. One was his uncle asking him emphatically if he would or would not be available to work in the fall. Alex knew that this meant his uncle was asking if he was prepared to someday take over the business. That though they had not often got along, his uncle still considered him to be the one who would some day succeed him. In fact, because of his uncle's dislike for his father, he was always trying to make something up to Alex in the end.

"I don't think so—thank you for all you have done for me," Alex answered with insincerity, which he had already learned to evoke through piety.

The old man, however, caught unawares by this sudden compliment, had tears come to his eyes. He went over and patted Alex roughly on the shoulder (the only affection he ever showed) and walked away unsteadily.

But Minnie's test was worse. For he knew what she was asking him, and he didn't know she would. It was the unexpectedness of it that caused so much pain.

She met him one morning at church, and in the drizzle of a March storm walked up the church lane with him after mass. She spoke of non-essential things for a long time, and tried to rehabilitate her father to him just a little. He was, after all, a good soul. A man who had his moments of lively grace and humanity.

"I am sure he was," Alex said too stiffly. Again, the stiffness was a posture—a collaboration between saintly betterment and moral high-handedness. He knew this, and so did Minnie. This was the start of something that Alex had not had before, his pretentiousness toward goodness—this, in fact, is what one did not need religious study for. In fact, the world so opposed to religious study had this terrible pretentiousness as well.

Then she asked, as they stopped along the wet road and she suddenly took his hand: "Is it true you are going to be a priest?"

This was the moment, under the low clouds and drizzles of snow, amid the long sloping snowdrifts that ran down to the water, that said: There will be no other moment like this again. Tell her you love her and you will steal her back from Sammy Patch—for she is asking you what to do with her life. She is asking you to let her love you. This is the question she is asking—what is she to do, with her life. For she is prepared to live her life with you. It is not easy for her to ask this. And she would have to break up with him, but she is prepared to do so now.

But the idea of an ecclesiastical abandon surfaced in him—and the idea that he did not need these temporal things overcame him. For it was what he wanted her to believe, even if he was uncertain.

He thought, What will I say, how can I say I want her with someone else? He even thought of the moment he came when masturbating. Still, in pretentious casualness, and suddenly misinformed about his own agony, he said: "Of course—I have decided to go into the seminary of the Holy Cross next summer."

"You are—you will," she whispered, tightening her grip on his hand.

Her face was completely open in its vulnerable gaze, saying, If I let go your hand I will let go forever. But he could not overcome the idea that he was wounding her with this, and that she had wounded him. This meanness of spirit he suddenly remembered in his father, and yet could not correct it in himself. It was not so terribly harsh, but it was terrible it was present.

"And you have a good life." He smiled, but his lips trembled slightly. He would never understand why he spoke these words. But he was proof of Aristotle's disagreement with Socrates about men who have knowledge saying inconsistent things.

It was as if something beyond him compelled him to say this, as if the words had been in his mouth for a hundred million years. Both of them were still children really, standing in the early morning air along the lost and broken highway. What was so distressing is when he remembered her soft skin when her skirt blew up, and the triangle of dark hair. It was a mystery, and there was nothing temporal in it but a wondrous spirit of life that beckoned to him. But there was this: if he let his guard down, would she want him the same way? That was the question he was too frightened to have answered. He was frightened to give himself over to her question, and let her then control what she said in return. In hindsight this was one of the most significant moments of his life, on a windswept lonely lane.

He was pleased she had looked hurt, for a second.

She let go of his hand, kindly, and left him there. She turned and walked along the far side of the lane, and disappeared toward her house, rushing in the morning air, her head down. He could not stand to watch her go. So he tried to call to her but no words came.

And so he looked at his small Timex watch that his aunt had bought him for his seventeenth birthday and hurried home as well.

He did not swear, smoke, or drink, and would look piously

upon the world. But now his uncle's former activities bothered him, and he took a moment to reprimand his uncle one evening. In fact, he had many of them written down.

"Do you know how many times you whipped me?" he said. "I was chased outside in my underwear in February and slept in the barn. I was kept from friends. I never had a party in my life. I don't mind that—but there were other things. You tell me all the time how bad my mother was. And things I say which I know are true— and this is the most important thing: I know they are true—and I say them, and you tell me they aren't true. You say I made things up, when I never—and it torments me. Then you just laugh. And then, why did you have to tell me about my father—this Roach who hurt my mother—he is nothing to me."

The night was growing dark, and outside he heard the first robin of the spring twitter once in the trees. And so he spoke as if to the robin.

"Yes," Jim said, almost peevishly, "I know. But I want you to know something. I paid for your dad's funeral—I tried to put him to rest, and I didn't have to!"

Alex thought this was a great catharsis, but later on Jim would not speak to him, and looked away many times after. He was hurt, as men are when faced with something they always felt was incomprehensible.

And Alex's flaw was this: whenever he thought of Minnie he did something to harm himself, to end the body's desire, so he would not masturbate again. Somewhat like Saint Rosa of Lima. He cut himself, and distributed these cuts, hidden.

And it worked for a while. But still, in his deepest heart he knew this could not be sanctified, this was not what Christ wanted. So he tried harder to put all prurient thoughts out of his mind. But how could these thoughts, which were natural and over-came him at all hours, be unnatural?

He decided he would impress them all, and disprove his own desire, by becoming a saint. His aunt said he might be a little naive in thinking this, but was nonetheless thrilled by the idea.

"Saint—well, don't try it all at once."

"But that's what a saint does—tries it all at once," Alex said. "Well, not Saint Augustine perhaps, but Saint Francis and Saint Joan of Arc, and so many others!"

A saint had armor against the arrows of the world by not recognizing them as arrows. The great saints could walk through them because they did not acknowledge them. But on occasion, one thought would creep back into his mind. He would think of the day the wind blew her skirt high above her panties in the yard, enough to make him weak, and Sammy had laughed as if he had already seen it. And he remembered that she never left the house to walk down the Gum Road unless her blouse was pure and white—even on those days when her father had taken her socks—and one day, in the afternoon light through the trees, he saw that beneath her blouse she had no bra on, because the few she owned were on the line, her nipples taut as raisins in the sun.

Still, what had started in bravado and pride—the idea to show her up, by becoming a priest—continued in feverish hope. After a while this desire, and obligation, became his entire life. It had to— and why, because of people who were watching him, waiting for the flaw that would take him down. So he could not go down, he must keep the faith in all weather, until people saw it was not a pretense. That is, if it was pretense he must disprove it even to himself. And so he gritted his teeth and bore it.

The day before he entered the seminary of Holy Cross to study theology and Saint Augustine, his great uncle had a party for him, and invited every one of the young people. It was subdued because of the calling he had, because there was no beer for them, and because most of them did not know him well. But Minnie, whom he waited for, longed to see, did not come. Besides, though the venue was outside it was raining.

He sat on a lawn chair by himself a little away from every-one, and waited for Minnie. He looked like a boy who can only appear in rural Canada: clumsy, coming to manhood half-sophisticated, understanding the rudiments of society yet lacking in much, and trying to hide it all with sayings and ideas gleaned from the fringes of the broader world, all of this making him look gangly, self-conscious, and overly suspicious. That is, he was like a boy from everywhere, but in some aspects like one seen only here.

His uncle, with his tall boyish walk and his mat of white hair, stood above all, and impressed the young, as he could always do, with tales of the woods and war. He was filled with the kind of contrived outrageousness people have when they have little chance of being challenged. And he exuded the bravery that older naive men do in front of kids. And he sang old lumbering songs and told jokes to liven the party up, and drank homemade wine from his stash in the barn, and gave some to two of the more rugged boys who he wanted to approve of him. They drank and smiled at the jokes he told, and ignored Alex for the most part. He thought of their lives and wondered what would become of them. The old man also flirted with one of the young girls who had come, who responded to him out of politeness he misunderstood, and this made Alex embarrassed.

He took out his photos and showed his medals and spoke of his doings, and Alex himself sat alone. His aunt came to him and said, "I've had many dreams lately about Minnie—"

"Oh, I haven't," he said, lying, to bolster his virtue, though he had masturbated that week thinking of her.

Muriel knew he liked to sculpt and asked him if he wouldn't like to go to the School of Fine Arts in Halifax, she was sure she could make his uncle see the virtue of it. That he would someday be a fine sculptor. But he thought of the clay pieces he had done of those birds he once sketched, now lying in torment about the junkyard behind him, and said with perhaps as much naïveté as his uncle, "Well, we are all clay."

WHEN HE HAD BEEN IN THE SEMINARY A YEAR AND A HALF, and wore a silver cross on his chest, and had passed through his first series of exams, went to mass every day, and said prayers from seven until nine at night, was silent in certain parts of the seminary, he believed that he was better for it, and that he himself one day, as his older brothers in Christ had, would lay prostate on the altar in the hope of attaining the pleasure of Christ while snow fell on the dark ground. He wanted to be a young priest on the Bartibog and say his first mass where he had once served on the altar. He thought of pleasant afternoons in snow-laden February walking to small country houses to see the children—just as priests had done in the long ago. So many people his age wanted the same thing and sought so many ways to find it. But not he. He had already found it. He would return to it—to the idea of caring for the children's souls by loving them as human beings. He would do this for the memory of his mother. He tried not to think of his father, that failed musician who had died some time ago.

Great men had come from the Bartibog and great healers as well, and in truth great priests, who were known and written about. Priests who gave their lives for others, and served in the wars—walking into battle unarmed, like Father Morrissey and Father Hickey and Father Murdock. He knew this, and loved the idea of that kind of pure understanding, especially when the world understood so little now. And it did understand so little. He could tell Minnie understood so little, about true love and happiness, that he was as always awash in sympathy for her. And it was only this spiritual sympathy that allowed him to love and not want her, he believed.

He wanted the comfort of snowfall in the late autumn and picking out the decorations for Christmas celebrations at his little church. This is what he thought about. And so, in those moments, she did not matter.

But one thing plagued him. He was angered by something he

had been angered by before—just one thing, and it was this: his own false obsequiousness, the kind he had seen when his uncle met the nuns. He talked to MacIlvoy, a young man, a fine hockey player, who was studying for the church too, who simply said: "Give all these matters up—for there are other matters in the world far more important."

This was from a man who was drafted by the Montreal Canadiens and didn't accept because of his calling.

Then he received another postcard from Leo Bourque.

> Dear Alex—I have read a book on Balzac. I remem-
> ber you once saying that about Balzac he was very
> good as a righter as any England person, and I am
> sure you will be able to tell me other books I would
> like to get now. I am going with Doreen LeBlanc
> and she is very popular and I am sure to make a fool
> of myself, but if you got some news to me about
> other books I could read—your friend Leo Bourque.

He thought of answering it, but the address was obscured by a stain. And he didn't want to remember how he had been tormented by Leo. But there was something else: it was the basic instinct of pleasure he had at knowing Leo was trying to emulate him after once having tormented him and thinking, That'll never happen again.

He laughed at the fact that Bourque was short and lifted weights. It all seemed so ordinary to him.

"It's good he saw the error of his ways." He smiled, folding the letter up. He imagined as time went on how Leo would come to him, ask forgiveness, or do him unsolicited favors. And he felt special when he thought of how he would refuse all of this, all of the favors Leo would want to do for him.

He plunged into Saint Augustine and Thomas Merton, into the liturgy of the church, into masses and saints and fasts and feast days and calendars. To him, Saint Augustine was brilliant but obscure. So Alex thought Merton a man to emulate and a very great man. Yet what bothered him about *The Seven Storey Mountain* was Merton's mocking of physical love. If Merton, who Alex considered a great man, was wrong (as Alex believed he was) in this salient point, then might not other things be wrong?

He therefore now and then began to think of Minnie, and to wonder what she was doing at any given time during the long day—and if she ever thought of him. Twice, three times, he thought of phoning her—but did not, even though he walked to the phone booth on the highway. And then one day, out of the blue, he was struck by something. Rage. It just overcame him when he was in the field helping with the haying.

He was very jealous of her when he thought of what she might be doing. And he could not remain pure in his thoughts or deeds, as he lied continually to himself, saying he was. And just as he thought this, he knew others there were lying as well, just by their look, and he knew this grave falsehood followed them. That night he helped put the horse into the stall, and fed it oats, and walked toward the chapel to pray. He believed prayer to be the only thing that could combat what he was feeling. But that night something peculiar happened. All those young men were rushing up the road, some of them hobbling between a walk and a run, just as the sun was going down. They passed through some shafts of light falling through the trees and onto the dusty road as they ran to see the new Corvette that Mr. Cid Fouy had bought. Though they were supposed to be in chapel they had all rushed to see it, for someone told them Cid was giving people rides, and there were only two Corvettes on the whole river.

He could see them as they hobbled up the road, catching up to one another, shouting whispers. He was stunned by this covetousness, and stunned too by the naïveté of those young men, some born in poverty along the coast, who would rush out to see a car.

He went back to his room to be by himself, angered that they did not follow him. He realized it was very easy for them to agree with him when they had nothing else to do, but at any other time they were worse than the kids on the school bus.

Then, after a time, when he could not get Minnie out of his mind, Alex began to think that he would go to serve in some remote place in the north, among the Inuit, and not be seen here again. He was both kind and supportive of the native kids here, and he realized this might be for the best. Then in some manner—saving a village from the plague, a child from some plight—his name would drift over the hillocks of warm snow, south toward her. This daydream occurred in a necessary way, because of the feeble yet inextinguishable lamp lighted in some recess of his brain for Minnie Tucker. He heard too that she and Sam Patch had given up the idea of getting married, and that they saw each other only every couple of weeks.

But this strangely did not make him consider leaving his study. However, it made him feel pleased.

Yes, she would be a cause for concern as long as he lived—so best not to live on the Arron side of the great Bartibog. Hopefully if away, never a concern to be concerned about—however, he was still human. (He said this as if to anoint himself with the common ground without believing that it really applied to him.)

But there were two incidents back to back that came after he had been in seminary a year and a half.

The first was this: He had to go down to the reserve with a box of communion envelopes. There, the strangest thing happened to him. It was not reported about, no one found out, and in the annals of history it was perhaps never recorded. Coming out of the small church in the late afternoon, with drizzle in the air, he came face to face with a black bear suffering mange. Worse, her cub came toward him. The mother, famished from winter, gangly and cross, rushed toward him also. As he backed up he screamed, and tried to run. But just then a native boy about ten years of age, at the church preparing for his confirmation, jumped between the bear and him, and grabbing rocks from the dirt began throwing them. Two hit the mother in the head, stopping her up. She grunted and snorted but the youngster kept throwing. He kept throwing and throwing and would not give up. Each time the bear pressed forward the little boy, his hands bleeding, found more rocks in the frozen earth to dig up and throw. All this time Alex stood frozen to the wall of the church.

Finally, the bear turned sideways, collected her cub with a swat, and headed back into the woods.

"There you go, Fadder," the boy said cheerfully and breathing heavily, his black hair flat against his head. "That old bear's gone back home, there you go—no need to worry anymore."

The boy moved off and Alex stood in the wet with his cross, his legs still trembling. This moment would stick with him for years. The child would have given his life for him, and yet—what could he have done?

He went into the reserve and found the boy's house, saw where he lived and especially how he lived. But though he was going to help this child, and promised himself he would, he never got around to it. After a while he deliberately avoided the small lane where the boy lived. Yet without that little boy, Alex might never have lived to later teach his course on ethics.

The second incident might have been worse. A few weeks later, when he was sent out by Monsignor Plante to the store, he met a crowd of young men and women piled into one car going off to a party. There had been a thaw, the car was covered in streaks of dirt and salt, and now it was snowing mildly, with the gray sky almost meeting the ground, so he blinked incessantly as he made his way toward the village. As always when the weather turns warm, the young here dress like those in movies from the California south, wearing things unfit for our weather in order to belong to somewhere they never were and perhaps would never be.

The car revved its engine as Alex approached. It backfired, and then the driver revved it again, put it in gear, and squealed forward, so that mud came up against Alex's face.

He had already walked three miles and he was sweating and tired, and now mud spotted his cheeks and chin. He had always feared these boys in their cars, for they were the kind who had little or no use for him. And this might be a reason he had gone to the seminary—so he would not have to face them until he wore a collar. That would make it easier, and safer. He knew this secretly. And he knew why. Still, if he could not overcome this aversion to their swearing and nonsense, how could he later on preach to them?

So he approached the car with this in mind. He was going to knock on the window and reprimand them—in a calm and kindly way—about the mud on his cheek.

As he came toward the car, he could hear a boy saying, "Do it—do it," and people giggling and whispering. The window rolled down just as he came up to it.

He put his face into the window as a girl lifted her thin undershirt, and her breasts were an inch from his face. He could see snow falling down on those breasts, and his lips were near enough to kiss them. Everyone else roared and laughed.

Alex turned and ran. He did not stop until he got back to the seminary.

He thought of their mocking, and tried harder to pray. Then he saw himself praying in the mirror above his dresser, and throwing his boot, the mirror wobbled and fell, shattering. Two third-year boys ran in to look at him—and when he looked up at them, they backed away, for his face was now enraged. The day was gray, the mirror broken.

They sent the young MacIlvoy boy in and he calmed Alex. For Young MacIlvoy might just be considered the one boy there who was not bothered by people's sins. He was strong as a bear yet he never let on or cared that he was. He had been drafted by Montreal, and yet didn't even play hockey here. He didn't stay on the far left side of the old building where the hockey players were—the joke being that so many right wingers lived over on the left wing—the only ones not catching on to this double entendre were those hockey players themselves. But MacIlvoy stayed away from them, and had decided by reason of some miracle to lessen his life and disappear.

MacIlvoy sat beside him for an hour, and Alex thought only of the boy's intrusion and kept wishing he would go away. Or was it MacIlvoy's intuition, about him? When he finally looked at MacIlvoy's face, he realized the fellow was praying—and this bothered him even more.

"Do you have doubts?" Alex asked finally.

"About what?"

"About this—about us doing this?"

"A while ago I didn't even believe—I called Christ and the Blessed Virgin down to the ground, I mocked them all the time— and so it came to me all of a sudden. I haven't had time to doubt it yet." He smiled. "I am sure I will someday—I am sure in some place in a far-off time I will hate my calling and say I have lived my life for nothing. But I will tell you this—that there is nothing in the world a man or woman can do where they won't think this sooner or later about something—"

"You are saying there is no better life that this?"

"I am saying that no matter what life you choose, it will look at some point as if some other life is better."

Still, Alex knew that all his Lenten meals, his wonderful dialogue with God, and the sky, gave him nothing like that one brief moment when the woman lifted her shirt. And he wanted more moments like that. And each time he closed his eyes, in the warm classrooms, speaking of small ideas, the brief moment when Minnie's dress blew upward made him weak. He knew now, this is what Canadian poets were writing about, and he would bring these poetry books to his room, and try to read in them the essence of how he felt. But no matter how explicit these poems were, and probably because they were explicit, they did not corner the vast celebration of desire and human kindness that he felt for every woman he saw.

He read Saint Mark, and this calmed him, so often he would grit his teeth and keep going. Thinking of his mother, his old aunt—and even his uncle turning to smile at him and patting his shoulder. What would they say if he told them he had doubts? He went often to visit the ancient nuns who at one time had cared for the last lepers in Canada. And he was filled with gratitude while there, sitting in a small kitchen with sun coming through the small window, in a place so remote and barren that the furniture seemed alien. The nuns would smile at him, bring cookies and tea to his chair. But after he left, doubts would resurface. They would resurface because of the manufactured sympathy of priests he saw about him. He knew some of these priests were unholy and were kept here, out of sight, so they would not embarrass the diocese.

Still, he had been warned much about these doubts, and there was little you could do about them but pray. But of course it was not his relatives he thought about leaving him—walking away along a lane in spring a few years before. It was Minnie—it was her alone. And each day she was getting further away from him—becoming a speck so far away that the dazzling heavens made her disappear.

It was just at this time that a strange request came from Leo Bourque. He was getting married and hoped Alex would be his best man. The request came indirectly, from old Poppy Bourque, who came to see him and brought him blueberry cake. Alex said he would be best man, if that is what Leo wanted. And Poppy went away. But when the day came—when it came, Alex was at rehearsal for his Play of the Redemption and forgot all about it. The day wore on, and then the next day came before he thought about it. He found out that the wedding went on without him, that they waited an hour for him and Poppy acted as best man.

"Well, I am glad," Alex said. But he had told people that Doreen LeBlanc was making a mistake in marrying someone like him.

"He will abuse her," he said, with a sniff.

He once again disliked himself for saying what he still believed should be said, that women should not fall for people like Leo or Sam.

=

ONE DAY A MONTH OR SO LATER, IN EARLY MAY, WHEN HE got back from class, there was a letter waiting for him from Minnie Tucker. At first he was stunned. Then he suddenly felt vindicated and believed she wanted him back. And then once again this inconsistency of human nature: If she wanted him back, did he really need to go? For if she wanted him back, did it not mean that he had conquered her better than going back to her would? He was troubled by this determining, and decided not to open the letter. So it sat on the dresser in its white envelope on the far side of the room for over a week. One side of it had been twisted, and he could see a small tear in the top. For days he left it where it was, even though he felt pulled toward it every time he looked at it. Then, finally, he went to examine that tear. Sitting in the chair at his desk he hastily opened it.

It was Minnie at her simplest and most kindly. Telling him that, he was to be the first to know, she was expecting. And she wanted him to consider being the godfather.

"It would please my heart greatly," she wrote.

She did not want him to hear this news from anyone else. For certainly others would make much of the fact that she was not yet married. Sam was away with Alex's uncle, and she had not told him as yet. She wanted Alex to think kindly of her.

"I will marry him," she wrote, "but not until things are settled, and we have some money." Then she continued: "I do not know why I never married him yet. I think I was waiting for you to realize that you still wanted me. But that is over now, and I was childish to try to take you from your duty and your first love. I am sorry for this, and want to reconcile with you."

She didn't know if she could finish her secretarial course at the college. But she knew that Sam was a decent and good man.

Alex put the letter down, and he was shaking, and his body was cold.

"It is not up to me," he said. "She should have told me sooner!"

But as he sat there shaking, he thought, Why has God done this? He realized that not only did he still love her but he was torn apart by jealousy.

He thought for days what to do. I am sure she doesn't want to marry Sam Patch, he thought. And: Sam Patch is not for her.

And then this line, which he remembered: "I want to reconcile with you."

He thought long and hard about what this could mean.

To him it could only mean one thing, and one thing only: she wanted him, not Sam.

And why did he open the letter—so he could be tormented? He hated himself for thinking that she had in some way waited for him. And the more he thought of this, the more it plagued him, and the more he tried to reconstruct the letter and what it actually said.

And slowly he felt this: he must have opened the letter to act upon the letter. And she was hoping he would, and wanting him to reconcile with her. But how would he act? He thought, What does she want me to do? There was only one thing. And it was this: the idea of her having a child that wasn't his child was crucifying him and her. He suddenly believed that this is why she wrote, and why the word "reconcile" was used. That night he did not go down to supper, told everyone he was sick and locked himself away. He could hear an old priest in the other room, coughing and pleading with one of the younger priests that he was in pain. And the younger priest saying: "Yes, Father, I know—we are doing what we can—be brave—" And he heard the rosary being said.

Christ, is this what he wanted for himself?

That night he thought of what he was going to do for the rest of his life if he became a priest. He would take the vow of poverty—and he thought oppressively of how poor his side of the family had been. (That is why little Rosa had gone to live with his great-aunt and -uncle.) How this had always been brought up to him by his uncle. If he had been rich once like Saint Francis, this self-castigation might not be so bad, this seeking the cross might at times seem more natural—but he himself had never been rich. He disliked it here, too: the French students were superior and just as ignorant. Worse, everyone loved hockey, which he himself hated, and he had to stand in a cold arena and pretend to cheer for his brothers. Sometimes the convent girls would come over to watch and he would stare at their uniforms and think of Minnie. Think only of her.

The secret was, he had promised his mother he would do good. She had begged him to be a lawyer. And why shouldn't he? He had been dirt poor, and an orphan. She had been put out of his uncle's house after she became pregnant, and in a way everything he did was done in memory of this. But really it was done in anger. His father had not loved him, and when his French friends in Quebec rejected him he had jumped to his death.

Alex pondered this for another day—and thought, much like Sartre's character, of a "thing" growing inside Minnie with every passing moment, and she had written to him hoping he would help her. Each time he reread the letter it became more certain to him that Minnie wanted him to take action. This is what was crucifying him. Finally, he went out to the main highway and used the pay phone there. He asked his aunt how long Sam and his uncle would be away. Another five days, she thought. They were settling accounts and hiring a man who was going to haul wood for them, off Christmas Mountain.

Alex demanded that his great-aunt give him money. Baffled, she told him she hadn't the amount he wanted, for Old Chapman controlled it. But if Alex came home at Easter, she would have a present for him. She said this as if he were a little boy and acting impatient. Then she laughed and said: "Sometimes you remind me so much of your father, taking my books from my library and not giving them back!"

This infuriated him: "You old bat, you have never given me a thing," he said, hanging up. He turned and walked back down the cold dreary road, cursing at himself. He thought of all the deer and moose he had helped his uncle quarter—the salmon he had cleaned—the bear that was caught in a trap. Yet his uncle believed himself a good man.

So Alex would help Minnie do this one thing, as a form of reconciliation, and be no worse. And he knew what he was thinking. In fact, he knew he had to think it. That millions of educated men thought the same buoyed him now. Many millions today believed that being compliant was taking a moral stand, and refusing to take a stand on anything alleviated them the burden of self, which is what he believed Catholics were seeking in the first place. He was also relieved to understand that the Catholic church was a mess, and had been for some time. So this one thing was not so bad.

In the silence of the Holy Cross, all he could see was her—no vision of Christ, but only her. Though there was still ice in the ditches after the hard winter, the sky was warming and the birds had found homes in the eves. Those birds he had once wanted to sculpt. It was best to be outside. Here, the priest-ridden hallways, where he was supposed to learn, smelled of watered-down soup. Some of the old men looked to him like pedophiles, living out their days in sanctuary far away from their awful crimes.

The next morning, after mid-morning class when students were standing inside the foyer between those high-ceilinged classrooms, the Monsignor with his ample belly tucked round by a tied black shirt handed him money in a communion envelope, to deposit. He handed it to him saying: "Take this along to the credit union."

Young Chapman thought nothing of it as he went toward the small credit union up the highway. But halfway there he looked inside the envelope and realized it came to the exact amount he wanted: $700. That surely had to be a sign. It was money the whole residence had been saving for the missionary work the French priest with the lively face was doing in Guatemala. They had earned this money by the hockey games they played, their team called the Flying Brothers.

He got to the credit union, one of those little square brick buildings, with two or three skinny shrubs, that tried to look modern in the middle of nowhere, a kind of secular thinking business, with its few potted plants in the corner. It was also, this credit union, socialist enough to have the left wing of the church believe in it. And the church was becoming more left wing among the teachers and scholars if not among the practitioners. Many new leftist priests did not want to comment on productivity or the idea of when conception began, for they were driven by the current understandings.

But in the small credit union, in all of this he saw dreary, agonizing sterility. He refused to go in, but stood there long enough that people noticed him.

Then in a daze, still trying to look natural, he turned and headed back along the highway—and just where the French signs became English once again, both of them having been at one time or another torn out of the ground, he made his way toward the dark seminary with its vacant-looking windows, its ancient stones that were once the ballast of ships coming from Ireland or France.

That night, as the late evening sun was reclining, they had to go and bless the herring fleet, and he saw Leo Bourque on Eugene Gallant's boat, the *Samantha Rose*. (This was his mother's name. It inflamed in Alex the idea that he could still say he was First Nations if he chose.) Bourque and Eugene were fishing together. Wind blew as priests standing in their masculine robes batted the censor up and down, as men stood civilly in the crosshairs of a world now changing. Holy water fell against his face, and onto the hands of Leo Bourque, who was waving to him.

Later, Alex went to his small cubby room and put the stolen money under his mattress. He didn't even look inside the envelope. He would use this money to help Minnie, just as he believed her letter wanted him to, and then replace it before anyone found out. He would ask his uncle to replace it—he would have to—and say it was for Guatemala, which it was, and that he would work it off in the summer. That is, laying in bed, he underwent a fundamental change—one that came of a sudden and expurgated his former ideas of sacred duty. In fact, in sync with the times, the one true crown jewel of these liberal times started to become paramount, and this feeling would more or less rule his life from here on. It was the feeling all youth have, and feel blessed by: the feeling of cynicism.

"Who am I to think I could help the world far away, when I might help Minnie here," was the first volley in a war of will against himself that would continue unabated for years. Still, he had to try hard and long to convince himself that he wasn't doing this for himself but for her. This reconciliation that she wanted, and dreamed of, and he agreed to, for her. If he could stop the pregnancy, he could stop her humiliation. For it was the same humiliation his mother had suffered in 1959 with him, and she should have had the same option! (However, he did not consider that he was himself alive and so able to think this, and that the option he was pretending to want would have prevented his thinking it was a noble one.)

If she would do this, then Minnie wouldn't have to marry Sam Patch. If she did this, he would tell her he was leaving the priesthood, and she would come back to him. He was consumed by its rationale. That is, he should have held her on the church lane, but now was not too late! The rationale was also rational—this act would be a sacrifice for both him and her, and he would have to leave the priesthood by doing something against the church's ordinance. Therefore, they would both sacrifice something implicit and then be together forever. Just, he thought, as the radical Jesuit Barrigan brothers had done. For the Jesuits were forward-thinking, and so too was he. He decided he would become a lay preacher, and a benefactor to others here and now.

That wet night he snuck from his room, through the window, left the lower highway and walked many miles in the all-weather coat he had worn when he first arrived almost two years before. It was new then. Now, it showed him to be once again an orphan.

When he passed the phone booth he had a terrible feeling someone was going to call, and he began to run. Yet he was the only one on the highway. For miles, he and the sky shared nothing else but each other. The breezes, however, were warm.

He came to the house in the dark and waited until he was sure she was alone before he entered.

Minnie was startled to see him, and he felt she was a little ashamed to see him as well. This was not the case. She was happy, thinking in some way he would be pleased with her. That is, she was still innocent, though carrying within her something that others believed made her guilty. But, to her distress, Alex did not come to tell her he would be godfather to her child. There and then, he tried to convince her to go away, to the doctor he had heard about in Toronto, and abort what she carried. He said it within the first ten minutes he arrived, so the tea she had made him hadn't yet steeped.

"This is not as serious as you think—the baby hasn't even started—we must realize it is nothing—not even a little acorn," he told her. "As soon as you do this, I will leave the seminary and we can marry—we were meant to be together—that is, you will give up something, and I will too."

She looked at him, her face so alarmed it alarmed him. When she poured the tea, the spout shook the cup, and tea spilled.

But he continued on (for he had to). He had the schedule and money for the train ticket and "everything else." He took it out and pushed it across the table toward her, in an official, irritable manner.

"My mother was in the same boat as you and her life was terrible. Sam could even run off just like my father did. Who's to say he wouldn't? Then where will you be? I promised myself that if I could help it no one would suffer like my mother did. I promised myself that when I was a little boy. Your boyfriend will be away until next week," he continued. "He will get back and you will not be pregnant—it will be like it never happened. Then you can tell him that you have thought it over and do not want to marry. Then, after a time, I will start to see you. Not right away, but after a few months."

Now and again he would see her eyes drift sideways to catch a glimpse of him. She still wore her immaculately white blouse, her hair brooch gleaming under the kitchen light.

Then he said: "You know I love you."

When she looked at him, tears were in her eyes. He realized she was not thinking like he was, and became adamant to convince her. He began to talk against the church. He was filled at this moment with another great blessing the young have. How ironic it all was, and he delighted in the irony of broken church doctrine, by bishops and cardinals. That was irony for you.

"I will leave the church—I will leave it now!"

But finally he talked himself out, and she spoke: "But you did not come to the shore at Arron's, and when I asked you if you were going to be a priest, you hurt me to my soul with your answer. Well, I am not doing this because of the church, I am not doing this because of Sam, I'm doing this because of the child—it is not an acorn, it is a child. I wrote to you about a child, because I did not want you to think badly of me when you heard. It is a child."

He had convinced himself she had written him for exactly the opposite reason. "No," he said, confused. "I mean, we can stop it from becoming a child."

But she said: "When can we stop it from becoming a child? I could have stopped it from becoming a child, if I had not allowed Sam. But it did happen. So how did this child come about? Do you think that children are unplanned for? Who do you think plans for children like Burton? Or children like you—do you think you were unplanned for? What happened when your own father found out, that Mr. Roach? And would you give up one moment of your life, as hard as it is, for someone else's decision concerning your life? It was not my sister June who planned Burton's life. She only planned to run away.

"Long ago I waited for you—until my feet were blue—and at the last moment, when I was leaving to go home, Sammy comes with a sled filled with wood he had cut for your uncle—for your uncle always gives him the harshest work. You see, and I will tell you—Sam had to do work you will never have to do, because he had no one in his family but him to bring home money. So old Jim Chapman knows this, and uses him. So he comes up the back way, near Jameson landing—why was that? He could have turned and crossed the road much nearer the bridge, but on that one and only day he didn't. I was so cold, and he put his hands all over to warm me up, and who was I to tell him not to, I was freezing. So he acted like a boyfriend even then. Put me on the sled and brought me back to the Gum Road. Why weren't you there—my father spoke that night about a boy he had scared, and I thought it must have been you. You began to ignore me. You wouldn't speak to me at all. I have come to realize that the child is to be born because Sam, and not you, met me where you planned to that day—so it is not a jest but a gift of God."

"I suppose you still believe in the virgin birth," he said, shocking himself when he said it. But it was something that had bothered him since he had read Thomas Merton—this fiendish denial of physical love as a part of Catholic devotion. So he waited for her to answer with a lighthearted smile on his face. And her answer was surprising.

"Yes, and so do you—and let me tell you why and how—for the very opposite reason that you suppose. For if you think I have no child inside me, where do you think this child will come from—do you think that it doesn't grow or exist but is only human when it reveals itself fully formed from beneath my skin, when its head finally appears between my legs? Is that the only way you and the new world can deal with it as human? Then that is most miraculous—from thin air we come, from vapors we are formed—what angel would not come to us in the night and create our virgin births!"

He couldn't believe she had said this, with so much conviction and force. At that moment he was stunned by her passion and sudden brilliance. He was stunned that God, whoever it was or whatever form it took, would want her to have a child by Sammy Patch, who cut wood on the woodlot near the river, and not by him. It was a mistake all intellectuals make sooner or later: that God would naturally love them, and consider them more worthy than others. Few university degrees have ever expelled that sanctimony.

Still, he believed more than ever that he was doing all of this for the sake of his own mother.

Then, suddenly, another idea spawned. It was as a knife in his heart. Since God had decided this terrible trial for him, and her, he decided at that moment there must be no God. He hated Minnie at that moment, and hated the whole world because of it.

He stood, took the money, and left without another word.

As he walked back toward the seminary, a sliver of fine ice all along the highway that looked as if angels had made beds in the asphalt, and its trenches filled with weeds broken free from under the snow, he thought of what a great trick this God business was. Never again! Never, never again! He was enraged that this had happened to him. So often it happens that what God is perceived to have done creates denial of God. As he passed the phone booth, once again he hurried, and then and there, by some great chance, it started to ring.

He returned to the seminary and went to put the money back. When he opened the lock on the office door, with a calendar of Saint Jude hanging across the window, a hand touched his shoulder.

"Where is our money, Alex?" the Monsignor asked kindly. The manager of the credit union had phoned to tell them of his strange behavior the day before.

However, that same night in the rough weather, the herring fleet lost seven men out in the bay. So this story was the most important. They were looking for Leo Bourque, and the priest stayed with his family. Mr. Gallant, who Alex once thought of as his father, and who Leo went fishing with after he got married, had been lost. And Alex thought two things: the blessing of the fleet did nothing, and good men died in spite of what they prayed. That was irony for you.

Leo was found by the coast guard clinging to a board, and to life. He said that Mr. Gallant had given his life for him.

It took another two weeks for Alex to leave the seminary. He was asked to stay, to reconsider his vocation, but he couldn't. He was now ashamed in front of everyone.

Alex went home. His uncle—who had abandoned his trips into the woods to kill out of season, and Fanny Groat as well—now turned to him, and his face was livid with sad, overbearing anger. He stood in the back shed and blew his nose, and wiping it roughly shouted: "Hypocrite!"

When winter came, and just at the time he had no money, Alex was put out of the house during what can only be described as a heated exchange at supper. When winter came, he slept at the old icehouse. There he brooded, and turned colder against the world. For some months people did not see him. He tried to live off the land, and almost starved. This was also to his shame, for once having thought he was Micmac, now to realize who he was. Not that many, Micmac or no, would have done any better where he was.

Then one night, after being splashed on the road with slush from the wheel of one of his uncle's trucks, he in a kind of blinding and enraged epiphany decided to get back at his uncle and at Minnie Tucker. In the cold backroom of the icehouse he burned his religious books, at first hesitantly, peevishly, and then with renewed vigor. Going outside to throw them on a pyre, he stared off in the direction of his uncle's house, and cursed.

"I guarantee I will put you through hell," he whispered.

The next day he began to say and do things that he felt were necessary for a freethinking man. Anything that before was taboo was now no longer so. It did not come little by little. It came all at once, just like he wanted his sainthood to. All at once he wanted to destroy everyone who had hurt him, including Minnie. He remembered a woman Sam had when he was drunk one summer night, and so wrote Minnie about this.

"Yes, Minnie, it is not only you he's had."

He waited for Minnie to leave her man and come to him, and say she was sorry. She did not.

Alex lived like a hermit at Glidden's cove. He no longer spoke about the depth of the world; but believing he was free, he now spoke of how shallow it was. Belief in anything was given away to the cynicism so prevalent in this day. Not one man or woman given the chance would remain faithful. Everyone had been lied to, and so a new truth would have to emerge.

One day Alex watched Sam climb upon the catwalk in the snow and ice. He stared at him, in a kind of agony, because he knew the boy was exhausted, yet he knew the catwalk moved tenuously in the wind—and Alex was thinking: If he falls I am free.

In deep late December, the child, Amy, was born. He did not become godfather, and he refused to see the child even after he was invited to the christening. What did it matter to him, except to show his displeasure.

Old Muriel kept him fed and clothed, and endured the ranting of the old man, who blamed the great-nephew's failings on her. But the old man, even in his anger, could not in truth abandon the boy, and let Muriel have money for him, though he pretended he did not. A dollar, a five, or a ten would be on the table some bleak cold mornings when he left for work or mass.

One day Muriel, delivering this money, asked Alex why he and his uncle could not try to get along. "He is growing old now, and he is ill."

He turned and in a thoughtless moment said: "I'll tell you why if you are so eager to know! Did you ever hear about Fanny Groat and Uncle Jim—they have been together many times—when you are off being a slave of the church—that's what God thinks of you—God is acting on their behalf, a pimp, so they can have sex while you pray."

He saw in a brief moment of clarity the enormity of her suffering, and what his words had managed to do. There was something in her eyes that was wounded, not only because of what he said but because of who said it. He left the room shaking, but then came back in.

"Well you shouldn't cry about it," he said. "It's not that bad, is it? I mean, even if you left him—so what? Find another man—and see how he likes it."

But he could not believe he had said something so callow. Yet this only enraged him more, leading him to say more callow things. He became resourceful at saying things that would draw attention to himself, by saying things outrageous. Then he would try to take back what he said, and find he was unable to.

Then he did something which keeping it secret would preclude him from the adulation he wanted. On a cold March night, coming across a windswept field he went into the back of the feed shed, to keep warm. He had gone out to see if he had a string of rabbits, and was hungry and humiliated by his lack of expertise in the world of hunting and fishing. It was during this feeling of undeniable humiliation that he spied his great-uncle's black manifesto. The tyrant's "four-poster," people called it, because they said he verily carried his four-poster about in order to fuck you. It listed what people along the lost highway owed the tyrant for animal feed and hay and construction work. To touch it was anathema to good standing with the tyrant, but what did that matter now. Alex took it and in the cold, glassy, windswept field, lighted it afire. Because of the wind, it blew up in his hand and left a permanent scar. He saw it yawl and tumble in the wind, across the glassy ice toward Arron Brook, and disappear forever amid the windy trees.

The old man looked for his book for a week, and went to Alex's shed and asked Alex if he had it. He was perplexed and sad, and could not come to grips with the numbers in his head, and the many people who owed him. He tore and ranted and tore again, and ranted over it like a man lost at sea.

"This is almost $26,000 owed me this year—!"

"The last time I saw it, it was in your feedlot, where Sam Patch put it," Alex told him. That was almost not a lie, but it did instill the first vague uneasiness about Sam with the old man, whose tobacco-stained hands trembled as he went out the yard, seeking what he could not find.

Satisfied with this civil disobedience, he recounted it to two or three along the highway, who were most appreciative that the four-poster was gone.

"You never did it, Sam Patch did," they said. "You never done a fuckin' thing for us and never will. Why, your old uncle does ten times as much a service to us as yous do, and that is your trouble."

So what he counted on never came, his highway's acceptance of him and his reintroduction to them as a benefactor. What he did not count on came, that some (though, of course, not all) hearing of the old dictator losing his book, and knowing, tyrant though he was, how he'd helped them in lean times, took to estimating their debt and paying it off swifter.

Then, in the summer, came the first mention of Alex in the press. It did not start in earnest or even out of some lost desire, or the pungent scent of betrayal of one race over another and long ago negation of common decency, as the press indicated it had. It started only as a party on the shelled and drifted sand on the east side of his uncle's island. It started out as a joke, some Micmac men to go over for a party, and in fact only lasted for a week or so. But Alex rowed over on a small scow, asked by his uncle to see what those "chaps are doing" and ended up joining them, telling them he knew much about their suffering and had come to address it, and that ownership of land was theft.

It was not an exaggeration to say that once he was present, some papers in the region became interested in the plight of the First Peoples, so in the end it might have been a good moment and thing to do. For Alex, however, it became his sudden realization that agitation drew the press like blowflies to a moose gone down.

Alex had his picture taken with the natives on the shore, near their flat-bottomed skiff with a row of twenty-five salmon taken from the north cape of the island. He had another taken with seventeen-year-old Peggy Paul, who had come over in traditional dress to join the men. This was the picture that found its way into the papers.

Although vague and distant now in memory, this takeover and sit-in caused more of a rift between uncle and boy, who could just make out each other's heavy voices across the waves, the sound ebbing like the moment of the tide as the red sun danced and played on the black evening waves.

"Goddamnit, boy, you come back here!" the tyrant said, yelling though his throat was sore from yelling. "You get over here now, the press will pigeon you for a fool, if not today then tomorrow!"

"I will bring you a petition signed by everyone!" Alex shouted, though he had no petition, but he had a scribbler from the local paper writing everything down. He stared across to his uncle that late afternoon, and saw the old man fumble about on the shore, up to his knees in seaweed moving and undulating in the gray northern waves.

His uncle tried to stop them single-handedly two nights later and was driven back by stones. Alex could say he did not throw any. Yet like some defiant and forlorn Jewish settlement facing a roman division of AD 66, facing Vespasian in the sun.

Another day and Sam Patch was then sent over in a dory and spoke to the men, politic with an offer to pave the lower road on the reserve.

"It should have been paved a long time ago," Sam was instructed to tell them. "And we will get it done!"

"They don't want it," Alex spoke on their behalf.

Sam returned to a gloomy man sitting out on a pitch of dry earth, on a stool bent back, waiting for his man to approach, his eyes narrow upon him, as if he were just another enemy, or as if bringing back bad news he became the messenger one must blame. The tyrant's green tie was loosened and limp against his blue shirt, having come from a meeting in town, his neck chaffed and his nose and cheeks the color of browned-out maple bark.

"Will they take the paving deal?"

"I think they might if we can get Alex away from them."

Old Chapman said nothing as he spit his snuff.

"I'll give it one more week—and they'll tire of where they are," Jim told him.

In fact, he was absolutely prophetic. A week and a half later, the men from the reserve tired of Alex and in a squabble left the improvised encampment of birch and rocks, which to this day was still visible from the shore. They took as treasure Alex's scow, and he was left alone to swim back if he could. He could not swim.

Still, Alex said he would stay on the island, and tried to construct a shelter. He thought of his name in the paper, his martyrdom secure. Yet he lasted only another three days. Finally, stranded there during two days of withering rains, he called over to Sam Patch to come and bring him home. All one morning, half the neighbors could hear him call.

The paving was done, just as Jim had said. It was also said that Jim had secretly paid some of the families to get their men to come off.

Still, over the years people pointed to this as the second act of the Chapman downfall.

"The First Nations have suffered, that's for sure," Kevin Dulse's girl said, and she of course was right.

ALEX MOVED AWAY. HE TOOK UP RESIDENCE AT THE university.

He became a protégé of one of the professors, Dr. Doug Cavanaugh. The man, not to be outdone by nostalgia or precedent, dressed in tweed and smoked a pipe, and you could see its smoke almost blue in the winter sky, and he balanced his courses on semantics with his love affair with a former colleague's wife, Fiona. For a while Alex was in their circle and believed in their circle more than any other. He loved their kind and bookish house like he loved paradise. There was no religious calendar to evoke shame, no base Christ on the wall, no bible in the corner—except an ancient one picked up at an auction. They spoke of politics and the inherent power shift that must come.

Over time, sitting in the dark living room with the drapes drawn to the outside and the noises ebbing to nothing on the streets, they spoke of revolution and change as the coffee was passed around. Sometimes Alex did not leave that little house, sheltered by university buildings, until dawn, feeling the cold early dawn air on his skin for the first time since he had served mass. He would feel elation as he walked.

This was the great world, the world he was entitled to. He believed in their fair-mindedness and nurturing love of humanity until one day he approached them across the common, to ask them awkwardly enough about a specific child.

Doug and Fiona themselves had no children, and he believed he would perform a service. However, they said flatly that they wouldn't adopt when he approached them about Minnie's child, or about any of the children he was now concerned about.

He was surprised that day how, to prove various points, they likened other children not only as a burden but as a political problem that could be elevated and adjusted if certain men and women were forbidden to have them. The idea that they could decide who should and should not be allowed to have children was transforming to him.

They had their cat, and it seemed to be worth its weight in gold. The suggestion that he must love this cat as much as they, show tolerance toward their obsessive coddling of it, was always at the fore. And so he did, realizing how his uncle would be disgusted by them.

Still, Alex decided what they said was right for them, and what was right for them was also right for him. For who was he to judge them? (Except, of course, he had judged others closer to him.)

Many more evenings passed in their company, many more times he left at dawn.

And because he had been an orphan, he believed that he could now speak against orphans and be justified, if not for himself then for those two people he so admired. And so he did.

There were a few students in their inner circle, but he was the most favored, the one who could go into the house without knocking at any time.

But once, after supper in late April, he showed up in a rainfall, and heard them bitterly savage with each other. He backed away and went home. There was talk of some impropriety at the university that she did not know about.

The world moved on, and later that spring the couple moved away and Alex grew older. He wrote to them for a while, telling them of his plans, cynical and ironic, but after a while they no longer answered his letters. But he was becoming part of the new order that they had helped create, and that he himself believed he did. And after a few years, his tall, lanky body could be seen day in and day out amid the waning brick buildings of long ago, crossing the commons with frost in the soil.

Walking home one clear cold night in February, staring up at the great clock as it struck seven, he realized he had found his calling, and his home, and was secure. A great meaning now filled his life, and he was ecstatic.

By the end of seven years at university he was, he believed, his own man, and had given up any semblance of the man he had been formerly. He refused to talk about his past, that cold dark area of his life, which left people thinking he had been deeply betrayed. People whispered that he was brilliant and more so because there was nothing he believed in, but everything was questioned.

After he completed his master's he began to teach a course on modern ethics. This attracted the young to him, and by the time he was given his first appointment he had protégés and devotees among the young women who came to his class. The young women mightn't always agree with him, but they knew, in this age, he felt safer if he agreed with them.

Then he realized something. And because he was bright he realized it somewhat quicker than most. In this new age, people were actually expressing something they might not realize. It was this: at least among the people he admired, forgiveness was no longer an essential part of man's hope. What so many people had, as borne out by these privileged and radicalized young men and women, was one of two possible states. These two possible states were simply approval or disapproval. That is all that was required.

This new unspoken proclamation went on in all departments and in all circumstances. That is, approval or disapproval had replaced justice and humanity, while posturing as the exact same laws. He himself would not debate the discrepancy, for he felt it was a moot point. What was fascinating about it was that to the clever, like himself, it could be manipulated as seeming to be one and the same, and to the naive, like himself, what was determined in university was supposedly more impartial than anywhere else.

Yet many sophomores at university, along with the university professors, mistakenly denoted one for the other, and approved or disapproved at whim. Like any social worker who came into a family might do, or a professor correcting an essay. This is what Alex started to do as well, at first tenuously but by the time he was twenty-six it was a part of his nature, almost a definitive one.

At times, especially during the first snow falling on bare streets, he would remember another time and be sad. But that time, no matter what he wished for, could not come again.

He disapproved greatly and he sought one thing only: the approval of others. Though approval and disapproval were never spoken about as a replacement for anything, the eyes of certain people immediately told you that they had replaced forgiveness. And the more aggressive and certain his students were, the more they relied on disapproval.

So, after a certain time, by his logic and the logic of many of his radicalized friends, there was no wrong action, only action approved or disapproved. For any action he sought approval. And in this approval, he pandered to what was in vogue and disapproved of what was not.

His articles in the paper were many, and he became locally notorious. He still wrote about Chapman Island in his weekly column, and was certain to mention the anniversary of the Chapman Island takeover every year, and have the picture of he and Peggy Paul published.

He began over time to embellish his role in it, and the adverse toll taken on the First Nations by others, especially his uncle. Of course he was true in speaking of the terrible things the First Nations people had to endure by our hand. But he made the most of it by implicating those he disliked, and inflating the assistance he was giving, even by writing a column.

And during all of this time he was writing Minnie and telling her of his new life, and his new views, and in a certain way ridiculing her for hers. That is, he disapproved of her now, and wanted her to approve of him.

IF HE ADMITTED IT, HE HAD BEEN FRIGHTENED OF HIS former mentor and the mentor's high-strung wife, herself a former nun—for they believed that everything they believed was correct, and that the slightest deviation from it was incorrect, and he had tried to maintain their approval by saying exactly what would please them, even though at times he went against his better nature and the natural instinct he had to protect the memory of his mother.

That is, his former mentors saw his mother as being a simplistic product of her time who believed she needed a child to fulfill her. It was the first time he had ever witnessed the negation of the sanctity of life for a woman whose memory he treasured. This stung him deeply but he had said nothing. Therefore, when they said they were living for themselves and their careers and could not envision taking over the responsibility of someone else's child, someone else's mistake, he could not see it as being affected if they themselves did not. After they moved away and their apparent dissatisfaction with each other and with their lives became apparent, he told others that they shouldn't make too, too much of it.

Strangely enough, on occasion Leo Bourque would send him a note, saying: "I read you in the papers, you give it to the rednecks good," or "I heard you on the radio—someday I'd like to say a few things on the radio too. I will see you sometime for sure!"

It was wonderful that he was considered accomplished. So, too, was the comfortable fact that he himself would never have to leave university to be looked upon as a man.

THEN IN HIS NINTH YEAR AT UNIVERSITY HE WAS ASSURED of a tenured position. He knew this, and felt safe in assuming it. The debates within the halls of university were important and non-threatening to a person such as himself. And he believed that his own life was set.

Yet in all of this there was one salient point he did not admit to. He was, like most men who have never really stood on their own, frightened of being disapproved of, while pretending radical theory that was really the standard theory of a coddled academia. As long as they were the theories of many who never worked a day with their hands, he was in tune and safe, and being secure he could say he was radical.

But that year, one incident happened to change his life forever, and looking back on it he had no need to have ever been involved.

A woman came one late September day to the university, blocked in fog upon the old hill, with lamplights on wooden poles gleaming on the wet streets and blank-looking windows of those lace-curtain Irish so many of us are from. Walking the walkway was a woman who seemed to be the personification of this new idea that had taken him away from the stubble of his uncle's farm and construction company. This idea of how the world must change, in all ways, from the very surface of the lakes to the mountain of spruce across dark and forlorn barrens, so that the very singing of the birds no longer brought forth the sun but the great egalitarian and proletarian design that whirred like a fan in his skull would be realized.

She was the one, or came to be the one he was waiting for. She walked in with a funny hat and a sharp look, a rather official and predatory look, and was granted entrance as a mature student.

At first, it was true, he or no one paid much attention to her. She looked dowdy and common. In fact, he later remembered meeting her at two or three townhouses the students had, in those blocks of ambivalent and sour buildings, with cement walkways cracked and littered, and thinking nothing at all about her. But then it became apparent to people at the university, and to him especially, that she fit the criteria of those who believed in a certain kind of independence for women. (That is, as an independent woman some believed you could only be one kind—and Alex had forcefully come to this point of view.)

At first she was shy, as she sipped wine at those townhouses, digesting all she heard with the wine she drank, but as she became more aware of her younger and less experienced peers, she realized there was nothing at all to fear from them. At times her eyes would give a certain flare, as if recognizing not the greatness of a person, a professor or student, but their common smallness.

Men were frightened of her tongue, of her crudeness, and tried to pacify her, not by forgiving what she had done but by approving what she had done, and would do. Soon it was evident that past faults, whatever they were, were considered her attributes.

The dark fall came on. The trees emptied of leaves and bitter cold hung in a yellowish sky. She was seen each day at 8:30 in the morning, walking to class with her bundle of books, leotards and knee warmers, and a woolen coat. Soon Alex discovered two things: he feared her, and he wanted more than anyone else to impress her, and have her like and approve of him more than she approved of others.

Alex discovered when dealing with her that she could look wise or sad at any moment when she spoke of her life. And her life is what caught the attention of everyone she spoke to. Most of what she spoke about was her life on the Gum Road, and how she was a victim of abuse. And her stare, if anything else, told you so.

She had been beaten at an early age, forced to do housework, and what seemed worst of all, to this egalitarian group lead by Alex Chapman, forced to go to Catholic mass.

She rebelled against all this, she said, and began going with a man down the highway, who made her drunk and ambivalent to her own welfare, in those places of comfort long destroyed.

Then a moment came one winter night that year when she revealed to people that she had left her bastard child in the snow and ran away, covered still in the hot and tumultuous blood of birth, her legs shaking like a newborn moose, she scrambled to the river and fled, first in a canoe across the frozen water and then in a boxcar.

She broached this subject in a class on ethics, where Alex was the underdoctorate assistant professor, and watched the faces of the students go blank and twitch under the light, indecisively wondering how to respond.

"Yes, and I got myself away and took off to Toronto, got there with the blood still hard upon me crotch. I must have smelled some sweet!"

One callow boy laughed, then there was simply dead silence. Someone crumpled a paper. Another student stood and went to the washroom.

No one else wanted to speak.

"Everyone will think I am wrong," she said.

But no one spoke.

No one blamed her. Not really. That is, most had forgiveness for her, forgiveness forever, for being a child in the snow. Yet forgiveness here at this moment was an outmoded concept to Alex, who suddenly and frankly concluded that they approved of her, as he did. They approved of this act and could therefore sanction it. This great naïveté overcame him.

"She proves everything," Alex said later that night to Professor Scone, who almost instantly agreed.

For Alex, her past suffering became her greatest asset, and suddenly it became his. For some reason he wanted to take this asset and control it. And this is what he set out to do, even if he denied to himself he was doing it. For there was only one professor he wanted to impress and emulate now, and that was Professor David Scone.

"I will help her—I will write a column about her," he told his new mentor that day.

It was as if, though not believing in God, God had sent her to him, to make the most of. So he set about doing that.

Therefore, Alex invented her over the next few months, and the more he did, the more her action was mythologized and sanctified, so professors would speak of her to him, and on some occasions relate the story he had taken and reinvented.

"I am staggered by her bravery," one professor, his white beard offset by shining youthful eyes, said simply because he wanted the attention of having said it. And both Professor Scone and Young Chapman agreed.

Her dyed hair stuck out under the afternoon lights, her cheeks suffered rouge, her face, strong and opinionated, was soon enough a vague complaint against them all. And Alex became captivated by her. He wanted to show that he understood her suffering more than anyone else. In fact, he claimed her. He kept her captive for himself in his own mind.

And there was something else. In fact, it was the main thing. Alex, knowing who she was—June Tucker—believed he could hold her worth up against the worth of her younger sister, to show her younger sister up, and he did so by writing Minnie. The letter was simply a note of information, until the last paragraph: "You should look to your sister," he wrote. "She might just put that Madonna of yours to shame, for she suffered as much—having to carry a child nine long months!" It was in a way a long overdue insult to Minnie's child, who Minnie had carried. "So she left and you did not, and got away and you did not, and is now at university and you are not!"

He felt badly sending this letter, in the midst of a snowstorm, on a bleak cold day.

"Be careful," Minnie wrote back. Short and to the point. He ignored it. And for a little while, things worked to his favor.

But then, after a time, Minnie's warning became more and more credible.

One day, he hurried to class, his arms filled to overflowing with books, his corduroy jacket flapping behind him. She was sitting at the back near the door and he got the feeling that she suddenly understood he was saying things about her for his own benefit, and what was more, that she could use this against him. This was just a split second in that day, but he realized that his position with her had changed. Later that day she did not sit with him, but with Professor Scone. And seeing this as he entered the cafeteria, he felt a sudden betrayal.

Afterwards, June slowly and then more convincingly disapproved of and disliked him. At first he ignored this. He ignored that she was not his but the property of David Scone and a few others. But after a while, he tried to win her approval any way he could. In some ways he had created her, and wanted to take credit for it. In other ways what he had created was now more powerful than he was. For instance, she never once had to knock on Professor Scone's door, as he did. And since he had championed her as being truthful, he could not now easily say she was being untruthful about him.

He had to carry on, because the situation he had produced was his own. So he helped her in the department with research. He even at points agreed with her sudden disrespectful remarks about him. He knew that some of these remarks came from Professor Scone himself. He felt that both she and Scone were ridiculing him. He now, too late, saw many things in her he disliked: a vulgar pride that her sister would be ashamed of, a rapacious ego that she managed to betray without qualms, although he could not say so. Because her sister had warned him and he did not believe it. He saw too late how she had used him, but could not say so either.

Especially to Scone, who was now her protector, who had now as department head invaded Alex's territory. That is, Alex tried to deny what he felt, and champion what he secretly disapproved of in order for her to sanction him. He realized that Scone resented his rise, and had created a pincer movement to stop it, or at least to make more of a case for himself. He could not believe anyone could do anything so obvious. He was enraged at June Tucker for playing her part as well. Why had he not seen it coming?

So by mid-winter—by the second week back from Christmas break—some people had a different opinion of him because of all this. He secretly resented and hated her, but pretended to himself and others that he did not. He knew this and tried the best he could to ignore it. He began to hope she would go away and not influence those he relied upon against him. But she did not go.

So he tried harder. But he was never able to try hard enough.

Then in early spring it was revealed that the U.S. assistant secretary of state was to be given an honorary doctorate. Alex had not thought of this as an important thing at all until June Tucker herself, with great style as she butted out her cigarette, said this was an awful capitulation of all Canada's hard-fought values. She had just read this in the paper that morning, and only repeated it because it sounded wise.

She was sitting by Alex when she said it, and accidentally blew smoke in his face when she butted out her cigarette. It could have been forgotten.

He blushed, stood, and left the room. "Wait and you'll see," he said to her, believing this was a direct challenge to himself.

Alex, to win back the approval of those whose approval so mattered to him, started a campaign to try to have this granting of an honorary doctorate reversed and rescinded on the ground of modern Canadian moral principle. He hoped Scone would be forced to join him. But Scone said nothing at all.

It was at first an argument interdepartmental and contained, which no one paid much attention to. Each day as the students left the buildings, and the dry lights shone on the old hallways and crooked doors of lost offices, he pedaled about his applications and petitions. He asked June Tucker to help him, but she refused, so he recruited two young women with pierced tongues whose names he did not know. They went about each day with this petition.

Scone suddenly stopped all communication with him. This was the most unusual counteroffensive he had ever seen. Then Scone and June Tucker and others simply did not recognize him as he passed them in the hall. It was very painful, to wonder whether he should stop and nod or engage them in conversation. He did not. June looked hurt, as if he had done something very unpleasant.

He was stopped one April day on the steps by the vice-president of the university, a square-headed crewcut man with a heavy chest and a limp who took him aside quietly and indicated he was on the bubble for tenure.

Alex, seeing his position challenged, said he would resign from the department if the conferral happened.

"Well, that is unfortunate," the vice-president said, fidgeting in the dry cold spring wind and the smell of ice breaking in the river.

"Yes, it is," he countered.

This statement unfortunately was repeated to his students the next day and found its way to the paper, and he was interviewed on the CBC, which in the way of journalists egged him on. The president finally weighed in, saying he would be sorry to see Chapman leave—no one was a better professor, but he would not change university policy because of someone else's posture. The assistant secretary of state was a fine human being and would be honored, and any disruption would only make this conference more necessary.

"Posture, is it?" Alex said.

All the while, June Tucker was on his mind. All the while, he was furious at Professor Scone's pilfering of her. All the while, he wanted to prove that he was deserving of her approval.

For whatever reason, he could not stop now.

At first, many students backed him, and talked very bravely about it all. He clung to the two young women he had recruited, in hopes of revitalizing his stature.

But in the end none wanted to stay away from their own graduation. He found out, in fact, once he started this, how many actually disliked him. Some people saw him to be exaggerating and self-important.

The assistant secretary of state received his diploma on May 11, and spoke of tolerance in the conducting of our lives, the benefit of foreign service. Sincere or not, he was given a standing ovation.

Alex had stayed away, and was alone. Frightened of having overplayed his hand, and suddenly realizing what was at stake, he wanted to hang on to his job. But he felt forced to carry out what he said he would. So, on the verge of tenure, when all things were his, he resigned on May 12—and no one noticed. A month later, at the end of June, he tried to get reinstated, but his job had been given to a colleague of his. He tried to start a petition on his own behalf and began to show up in the department speaking of a lawsuit; finally, he was put off campus.

Alex tried other universities to no avail. Finally, he came home, at the urging of his aunt, and once again lived in the same small icehouse on Old Chapman's property.

For five months he did nothing at all.

Then he decided to become a sculptor. This, after all, was his first love. Could he not do it? He used his uncle's grand old junkyard as his inspiration. An inspiration into the beauty and degradation of human existence. All those pieces set up like proletariats struggling under the winter sun.

Blowtorches and steel and iron, and his sculpted pieces cried out, lying twisted in the snow, naked men and women convulsed and staggered like Frankenstein's burnt creatures asking for love.

One day the priest, Father MacIlvoy, saw him, and engaged him in conversation. Alex was still bitter about what had happened to him at the seminary and at the university, and felt both were conspiratorial. MacIlvoy took his arm and leading him aside said: "Do you remember if the phone rang in the booth along the highway that night?"

Alex said nothing, stunned into silence.

"It was me—trying to warn you about old Plante finding out money was missing. I thought you could get it back—I wanted to help you—but I must have been too late. Something must have happened in your soul to want what you wanted."

"Don't be ridiculous, nothing happened to my soul. You're cutting wood near my property," Alex said, "and I won't feed my hemlock to a church."

Yet the next day his aunt asked him if he could sculpt a grotto of the Virgin for the church—that Father MacIlvoy had seen some of his work and had asked. He was in fact simply too poor not to say yes. It was commissioned for $1700 (his own price) and he did it in four weeks day and night—the flares of the torch seen in the dark wood, against the shale and pitiless dead machines of our age. He was once again happy. Not only this but the idea that he had come back home as a prodigal, also a little enticing to him, alleviated by this idea of the romantic artist. The idea that there had been an enormous falling out between him and his uncle, between him and the priest, helped him in this one regard—to hold on to his self-esteem. People watched him as he worked, and realized he was a man of some talent. And sometimes at night, finishing work, he would look like all artists somehow look: the loneliest man in the world.

Yet over the last two weeks of his job, the face of the Virgin eluded him. For he hadn't believed in her since he was twenty. She was a myth out of the offensive mouths of centuries and centuries of opulent, vulgar men.

He walked and walked in the snow—he did not pray, for there was no one to pray to. He had, as James Joyce's Stephen Dedalus said, forged out of the smithy of his soul some other implantation, and these were in the statues and corroded figures of men and women in twisted and longing agony at his feet. However, he did worry that the whole piece would be lost without the right tempo in her face. Some noticeable characteristic, once elusive and yet forever permanent. And he did not know how to achieve it. Looking in books of pictures did no good. Her divinity had been captured in the pictures of old, but they did nothing for him. Her face always startlingly beautiful and yet humble. Each night under the moon, he walked down to the end of the giant yard and saw his Virgin, arms reaching out toward him in love, yet without a face, the wind blowing cold off the bay. But Alex could not give up. He worked on, as if something that wasn't in his own hands was prodding him forward.

Two evenings later, filled with a sense of failure, he went to the store to buy cigarettes. There he saw a young girl buying some milk and bread, and as she turned to him, she smiled. He followed her outside, and she looked back and smiled once more.

That's it, he thought.

Of course, there was no real Virgin—not at Fatima or Guadalupe (he had often written about this hypocrisy, and believed in making great jests toward it)—but still, this was the face that people might like for the Virgin. And this is what he was after. So that night he went back with a chisel and blowtorch. There the face, human and sorrowful and wondrous, was formed suddenly and completely out of the alloy of a junkyard under the frozen moon—and it was much like the face of that child.

⸻

TWO DAYS LATER ALEX, AFTER YEARS OF BEING ALONE, SAW Minnie as he was walking down the highway to tell the priest that the statue was finished. It happened during a snowstorm with big flakes falling down between the shadowy evening trees. She was trying to push her car, which had gotten stuck near a culvert by the church lane. Her face looked drawn and pale, her eyes tired.

Alex looked old now, and sad, his face and coarse beard. It was true that at first she did not recognize him at all. Still, his old feelings for her came back, all the deep love, the anguish, the hurt pride, her day at the churchyard. His hands were blackened and twisted from holding the blowtorches, his throat was marked by small burns. When he smiled, his teeth were gray.

Suddenly someone came out from the passenger door, saying: "I'll help you push—you get behind the wheel, Mommy."

It was the girl—Amy—the one he had left the seminary for, the one he had tried to be rid of. She was now about twelve or thirteen. He recognized her. She was the very girl he had used as a model for the face of Mary, Mother of God.

He was so startled he looked away, as if stung—without them seeing, but it left him shaken. He helped push and stood beside this child for the first time, her hands next to his, her various small fingernails painted green and blue and orange and pink.

Afterwards he turned and walked back through the woods path, the snow falling on his bared wet head.

He took the statue in a truck the next day, and he was very worried that the priest would not like it—call it unfinished or too modern—that the congregation, many of whom were older, would balk at it as well. That is, he was like so many artists, terrified of being rejected by the people he believed were not important. In fact, a few didn't like it at all—but most, the priest included, thought it was wonderful. The priest gave him an invitation back to mass. He did not go. Though he thought for a moment that he might, he could not and keep his self-respect.

The grotto was placed at the front edge of our little church.

=

HE ASKED HIS UNCLE FOR A JOB LATER THAT YEAR. HE HAD no real authority, and many of the men took no orders from him. Still, he tried his best to help his uncle. Yet he hated what he perceived to be the happiness of Minnie and Sam. But it was his own unhappiness jutting out.

And as the weeks passed, he longed for a time of retribution.

Every moment he had suffered, every suggestion of inadequacy, every syllable pitched against him from some flagrant mouth was remembered. He brooded, pitied himself, and longed for just one chance to do something. He taught one small course on ethics at the community college. He cherished that! But his heart was no longer in life. Once, when no one knew it, he drove to Arron Falls, stood on the bridge railing, and almost jumped onto the rocks, but could not bring himself to do so. He was lucky enough to climb down just before a truck went by. He went home confused and shattered.

Then last year it came, suddenly—a way to rid himself of Sam Patch, a way perhaps to get the business for himself once and for all, and to impress Minnie Patch once more. This in fact might be his last chance—a way, if he was brave, like those revolutionaries—to create something for himself. And then once he was rich, he would do things far better than his uncle, he would become a beneficiary to the whole highway, to the Micmac people he loved and to the poor families he had always longed to help. He thought of that Micmac boy who had saved him years ago, and said: "Yes—he will be the first I give a job to!"

He would live up to the expectations of those who once approved of him, and those whose approval he sought.

He put his blowtorch down, and listened.

Old Jim Chapman was in trouble. He had no contract to plow the shopping malls anymore and wanted the government contract to do the plowing down toward Neguac. He had been informed that he would have a chance to bid on tender. This in itself, bidding on a tender like a common business, was a slap in the face to a man of Jim Chapman's stature. Everyone was silent about it, but everyone knew. From the moment he had lost that black book— that four-poster, as people called it—certain things had happened, occasioned by his suspicion of Sam Patch, and reinforced when bad luck and new companies began to override him.

This might be the last chance to keep the firm afloat, and he must rely upon his foreman now.

So the plowing job was meticulously researched by Sam.

Sam knew the men could do it—and Jim was willing to bid what Sam Patch told him to. Patch worked on the numbers for well over a month, decided he and the men, to save the company, would take only three-quarters pay, and said they should bid $120,000 for the winter. Old Chapman was in a position he had never been in before—that is, he was no longer assured of anything, and must bid like a company in business for a month. That is why he needed Sam to arrive at a dollar figure for this contract.

"No one will be able to go lower," Sam said. "It's a long, tough job—and will be hard on the plows. Think of eighteen definite plow days, working eighteen hours a day. If we get this done, we will have other opportunities—we can do down to the French side, and Fouy can do it back toward us."

This was Cid Fouy, the man with the Corvette so long ago, that made all those childish seminarians rush up the lane expectantly into the twilight for a drive.

What Alex saw (yet he offered no helping hand himself) was that this man Sam working for twenty years had never had a credible salary or any good benefits—no dental plan, and little paid vacation—and yet he worked for the tyrant because it was the only thing he knew. And this tyrant depended on him, and loved him more than he loved Alex. This tyrant was the one obstacle preventing Alex from doing something for the people he cared for. What Alex knew, though he couldn't imagine it was for the same reasons, is that the paid employees at the university had no dental plan and very little pension plan themselves, and he had neglected to concern himself with it as he was seeking the comfort of being a professor.

Alex did have legitimate concerns here, however. He needed to know the business would be solvent in five to ten years. If not, his hope of being left a legacy and helping who he wanted to was moot. And he wanted to be left the legacy, if for anything, for his mother's memory. He wanted to live his middle age in comfort and write a book on all of the things he had suffered, or a historical book on the First Nations. The tyrant would no doubt ruin his plans.

Except for teaching his little course on ethics, his life had been set in stone.

So Alex went to Patch and spoke about these concerns in the little office on a quiet night. He could smell new paint in the backroom, and some flies buzzed here and there, and a gold string hung from the lone light bulb. Sam, a year or so older than Alex, was about three inches shorter and thirty pounds heavier. He was hard of hearing, and had huge shoulders that sloped forward, like his forehead did. His hair was curly black and he kept it short. He had the charm of personal comfort, knew who he was, and therefore was never offended by those who did not have comfort with themselves but only showed a kind of perplexity.

"If there are real storms this year, Uncle Jim will be in trouble—he will lose money—maybe everything he has worked for," Alex said, looking away as he spoke.

"I know, but you must then pray," Sam said, simplistically just like his wife, "for he needs this contract." He scratched his nose and smiled.

Sam had learned this piety from his wife, who he tried to emulate because he admired her, although he sensed that she did not love him but someone from her past. (For everyone's talk and gossip and assertions, he did not know she had loved Alex Chapman. He always believed it was some other boy perhaps.)

Although Alex had made his own estimation of $155,000 (which was still low) his uncle did not take him seriously, and said he had long relied upon Sammy Patch, and that almost any advice Alex gave had no meaning at this moment.

"I don't think you have the wisdom to offer a bid—you haven't been here, yous was never on a loader—you wasn't on the road, not even as my flagger when we had to redo the bridge, so what are you coming up so big feelinged now," he declared in front of all the men there. Alex, who had worked on his own figures for six days, couldn't look at them as he walked away, but could feel all of their eyes on his back.

Alex was coughing now, continually. His body was weak, and

his back stooped when he walked. He told his uncle that if it was a bad winter, they would lose money and perhaps the business.

He went back to his cabin and thought of what to do. And then made his soup of beets and corn.

Alex believed the tender was far too low, if there was any amount of snow—that was the catch. One must have faith that this winter wouldn't be too severe when they bid on the job. That is, the less they plowed the more money they made in the end. If they came out on top they were considered shrewd. And that was part of what Alex disliked about this process: they were relying on chance—or what was worse, fate—to be called shrewd and have a good year! This was the way the baffled highway worked.

The next day he complained about this to Sam, and Patch did something that to him was obscene. Sam Patch, to stop his worry, took him into the woods beyond Arron Brook Falls, to see where the bees had built their hives, and delighted in showing him that they were close to the ground, which was the true sign of temperate weather.

He then tried to put Alex's mind at rest: "If God is with us," Sam Patch said, "then we'll be okay—why don't you light a candle to the Virgin you carved?"

Thinking he was being made fun of, Alex roared at him, and turned away in the mud and rain, leaving Sam to wipe his nose with his sleeve and watch his old friend walk off.

So as he ate his corn and beet soup, Alex, in a very deliberate way, was prepared to save his company by giving up the bid. Taking the amount—secret from everyone except him, Sam Patch, and his uncle—to his uncle's main competition. If his uncle did not get the bid, he would have to take desperate action, and finally call on him, Alex, to save him, and Alex had a plan with which to save him, and would save him when he was called on. But first he must destroy the old man's faith in one person: Sam Patch. He did not look upon this as revenge but as business acumen.

Deciding such, Alex went downriver for the first time in years, along the cold broken highway of his youth. He was struggling through a great sadness when he saw the same potholes and ruts along the road he had seen as a child, and the same trees bent forward in the summer wind.

He made a call from the phone booth, and made an appointment with someone. The only man he knew, down here, who would meet him. He was now in a fight for his very existence, and so had to rely upon someone from his past.

That night at a place called the Old Seminary where he had once studied Saint Augustine and which was now a nightclub and a strip bar, in the haze of late summer he met a man very low on the totem pole at Geru Fouy Construction. Alex was forced to trust him, he decided after he had met with him.

The man was Leo Bourque.

Leo, who had survived many difficulties. Leo, the boy who had bullied Alex but then wanted to be his friend when Alex had his name in the paper about his bird drawings, and who had written him a postcard. Leo, who had asked him to be best man at his wedding, thinking he would impress everyone if Alex Chapman, who wrote columns, turned up to be his best man!

Leo was ecstatic to meet with him, and had prepared what he would say. But it came out a garbled profusion of big words. He also wanted to show his authority by ordering drinks and snapping his fingers. This appalled Alex, but he was in no position to say so.

Leo wore a summer shirt which showed his strong chest and heavy, muscled forearms, each with a tattoo.

"A hundred and twenty—that's pretty low for such a highway," Leo said. But he was interested in this bid, and Alex found himself thinking, in passing, that this was a man who would never be a threat or concern to him anymore—

"So you are giving this to me to take to Fouy?"

Alex nodded.

"Why?" Leo asked.

Alex bent forward and spoke softly. He told Leo he wanted to save his uncle from the disaster of bidding on a plowing job that might cost him everything. But this was not at all the case—or not all the case.

Bourque reached over and grabbed his arm, and said: "But you think Fouy should then go lower." For he believed that he had made a mistake about Alex, who had proven himself, and now he wanted to respect him.

"I am trying to have this work out for everyone. I am only saying if you want the bid, bid lower—even a thousand dollars, that will stop Chapman. You already have the French side, so your losses could be offset. I want to stop my uncle just this once. Next year I'll take over and we can work something out—maybe you can work for me."

"That would be something," Leo said, very pleased at this unexpected change of fortune.

Bourque tried to think of something to say which would reflect his intellectual reason, but then shrugged. He had thought a lot about the world and his place in it, and in the last two years he had been trying desperately to hold on to his marriage by proving he was as bright as Cid Fouy, who he knew his wife was somewhat interested in.

This, then, might be the one last chance he had to do it.

In truth Mr. Bourque was far more intelligent in these things and had known men like Patch and Alex's uncle all his life. He was, however, a simple man, he had had no advantage that Alex himself had. You could see in his face that he was perplexed by what Alex was doing. (And then, of course, not perplexed.)

"I will see—but I don't know—this is a big thing to do," Bourque said, suddenly looking cunning, like he had on that school bus. "I mean, sometimes you do something like this, and if it backfires you are in trouble."

"How could it backfire?"

"I don't know."

"Think of how good things will be for you if you do it," Alex said, positively. "You'll be something like a hero!"

"Sure I will. But if I do it, and it does backfire, will you help?"

"Of course," Alex said. "Why, of course."

They parted like old friends. And, in fact, they were.

＝

BUT ON THE WAY HOME, ALEX HIMSELF STARTED TO SHAKE. God, whoever it was, was playing with him. For the first time in his life he sensed this. And yet what nonsense. When he got home, he walked by his uncle's house and saw Old Chapman calmly reading the paper, calmly drinking his evening tea. Later, Young Chapman hid his face in the pillow. Why had he decided this? Out of some terrible spite!

For once let me have some spite, he thought.

He did not sleep all night. Like others, he gathered at the office two days later to discover if they had got the tender. Some of the men walked outside with their hands behind their backs, staring at half-dried clay-caked puddles. Others leaned against the trucks and loaders, their whole lives teaching them that it was better to be resigned.

Down at Geru Fouy, Bourque went through with it, worried if he did, and more worried if he didn't. Alex was the one boy he had written to when he was in the Far North, and he felt strangely that he had a camaraderie with him. Whether he did or did not would be borne out soon enough.

＝

THE BID, HIS UNCLE'S BID, AND SAMMY PATCH'S GUARANTEE, failed by $1000. Everyone turned to one another in shock and spoke about what to do. Old Chapman left the office and walked back toward the house without a sound.

The old man was too smart not to know that someone had given up the bid. For three nights he stood out in the yard, amid the swarm of gnats and blackflies, impervious to sight or sound, as he drank one bottle of wine after another. And at the height of his despair, Alex, terrified that he himself would be suspected, told his uncle that he believed it had to be Sam himself.

"Why would he do it?" Old Chapman said, lurching forward, his face coming up close to Alex's, his breath hot and smelling of alcohol. Alex once again face to face with this tyrant, as old and as tired as he was, became as he always did, a little boy.

"I don't know—but he was the one who guaranteed the bid, and was adamant that you bid just that amount. Why couldn't you have bid a thousand lower—that's what I was after!"

Of course, he had been after a bid thirty-five thousand higher.

At first the old man looked puzzled, and then furious.

The next evening he called Sam Patch, and over an hour— speaking, arguing, and haranguing—he told his foreman to go. He did it in front of men there, to show that though broken he still had authority. He said that after twenty years it might be time to find another manager. It was in fact like a general firing his commander at the end of a poor campaign.

Sam could not believe it. There was in him a feeling like the end of a marriage. He actually broke down and cried in the yard.

"I think we can get it all back," he was saying. Out on the highway Minnie stood watching. Amy stood behind her, looking out under her arm.

Alex could not bear to watch and turned his back and shook.

Three weeks later Sam left to work out west in the oil patch north of Edmonton. It was perhaps the best thing he ever did.

Alex went to his uncle and said, penitently, that he would do what he could to save the business.

"What can you do?" the old man asked in a kind of terrible resignation, mashing his hands together.

"You will thank your stars when you see how much money Fouy loses, and next year we will be back in business."

This, too, was the old man's one hope: that Fouy would lose everything on the grade this winter.

Alex set about that late fall, reorganizing the business on much leaner terms, laying off men left and right, men who had been faithful to his uncle for years—just the very thing he had believed he himself would never do. They stood in the office bewildered and feigning a kind of imperial wisdom as they were let go.

There was just one thing: there was almost no snow all that long winter. They could have easily made a profit of about $100,000. But without the main contract the business went down. Alex Chapman was in charge.

The old man looked at him almost heartbroken.

Alex tried to forget that look and go back to sculpting. But he couldn't. The talent he had seemed blocked. He found that he was only half as good as he once was. And that wasn't good enough for him. The idea that Sam was blamed and he didn't stand up for him, but in fact accused him, was a great cloud over his spirit. The last piece he had done, and was ever to do properly, was the stupid Virgin Mary.

What he had done to all those men, to his old uncle, seemed to close talent off from him.

It was twelve months ago that Muriel died in her sleep, ancient prayer beads laced in her fingers.

After this, a rumor started that Old Chapman was senile and quite dangerous to himself. People were afraid of a suicide. If Minnie had not gone to the house and fed him, people said he would not have eaten. And why would Minnie have done this? What inexorable law of self-denial or human understanding allowed her to? She simply did, for no one else did, and the business was over.

Alex hoped to get the man recognized as having diminished capacity, so he could take over what was left before it was gone. With this in mind he went to the lawyers three times in the last few months. But the three different lawyers would not take the case. For the name Jim Chapman still retained that!

⸗

BUT WHAT WAS WORSE WAS STILL TO COME. LEO BOURQUE was himself out of work. How did it happen?

In a strange way it happened exactly because he had done what Alex had asked.

One hot day, a few months ago, something terrible happened. He fell from the loader and busted his hip. His boss fired him. His wife then left him for the boss. Bourque discovered they had been waiting for some time to do this. Now that Fouy had the entire old highway in his grasp, they did not care what happened to Leo. When he got out of the hospital, she had moved out.

In the resulting family dispute his boss sided with his wife, managed to protect her from Leo's "horrible temper."

Fouy's takeover from Chapman enabled him to seduce the wife, who had worked in his office.

Bourque was left reeling, stunned, and shaken. He went to Alex, looking for help. His bank account was emptied and he had nowhere to go. In his own rambling fashion he blamed Alex for his wife's unfaithfulness, and wanted one thing: money. All the money Alex could get. At first Alex did not catch on. Then he realized it was blackmail. Bourque was taking pills because of the pain in his hip, and he was becoming addicted.

Alex, the ethicist, did not understand the urgency. Bourque, whose life was at stake, did.

"I gave you the bid," Alex said. "Why would you come here— I will get the police is what I will do."

But Bourque was no longer under the mistaken impression that Alex was someone very special, the boy he had tried to communicate with when he was up north. Now angry at having done Alex's dirty work, he was just as incensed at himself.

"Oh, go get the police—but before you do, you have to give me five hundred. Before the big bid, Cid was always worried—now he's a success and my wife's gone to him—and whose fault is that!"

There was in a strange way some truth to what he was saying. But he was more dumbfounded than malevolent, and he looked at the ground as he spoke. His left hand shook, as if he couldn't control it. This, too, had happened since he fell from the loader. He had taken night courses to try and learn English better, and now this was given up. That is, in mid-life, with as many delusions and false hopes as most people, his life was put on hold, or turned in another direction.

It was the mirror image of what Alex had wanted to happen to himself in regards to Sammy Patch. Sammy to go away, the business to succeed, and he to have Minnie. It had simply happened on the other side of the lost highway to chubby Cid Fouy.

In spite of everything, Alex asked Leo to wait for the five hundred, and prayed for him not to come back. But he did.

"You said you would have it—I have people I have to pay, bills and things."

Alex realized it was in some way his doing, and could not rid himself of the responsibility of Leo Bourque. Alex's stomach pained, and his chest hurt. He had no more money—not a bit.

"But you have to, I am already living in Poppy Bourque's shed!"

"Okay, we will see," Alex said. "Give me another week or so and I promise things will be better! I'll meet you at Brennen's and give you the money then!"

They had been on the school bus together as kids, and now this! But as always with Alex, he was sure there was some way to extricate himself from responsibility, and do what he had to do to make the best of it.

That was when he refused to take Jim's truck unless he was paid the five hundred he felt owing to him. He needed the money desperately and could tell no one why.

"You won't do this one thing for me?" Jim had said, sounding more hurt then he had in years.

"Not until you pay me."

"Pay you for what?"

"My severance from the company."

But there was no severance. There was no company.

So his uncle took the truck in.

—

AS MUCH AS HE HATED HER FOR HER BETRAYAL, ALEX STILL wanted his first love. So tonight he was going over to see Minnie and to fool her. Intellectually, he was in a terrible position. In a way he was planning to steal the lotto ticket from his uncle, the tyrant, to keep her respect. What would come of his self-respect if he was a derelict left with nothing, after years of preaching his wisdom to her? In fact, his vanity had always allowed a lack of personal integrity that became more pronounced now that he was in this bind. Alex knew Sam Patch would come home sometime at the end of the summer, perhaps with as much as $80,000 in his pocket, maybe more. Alex, who had always said Sam needed a better life, now hated the prospect that Sam might return and allow his wife and daughter to have one. A life that would in fact shine brighter than his own. This alone allowed a pathological reassessment of his role in the world. He became more driven to succeed at something.

But as Alex came to the small house, off the back highway, near Arron Falls Road, a place of quiet mystery, he suddenly thought, as if he was studying Thomas Merton again: Is this the way of my and Leo's chastisement? (For some reason, he did not know why, he included Leo.)

He waited for an answer in the dull silence, one that of course didn't come. In fact, he had waited for an answer for twenty years, ever since Harold Tucker had refused to allow him to pass.

There was a smell of heavy water in the clouds, and he looked up at the dark murky sky, as if there were strange beings above his head he might touch. They might be all about him now, just as many people believed, watching him, praying for him, asking him to be still and know that I am God.

A first tentative flash of lightning was seen.

Inside was like all small houses here along the dark back road. The kitchen was where people lived. The living room had an old sunken couch and a huge TV—but the old house was in a poor location and they could get only one channel. There was a bear head on the wall, from a Sam Patch hunt long ago. Could Sam have earned more, and better, if he had not been a protégé of old Jim Chapman for twenty years. Of course. Jim had taken advantage of his poverty and uncertainty at a time when he was a boy to keep him in poverty. Was this heartless? Chapman had grown up himself in the same way, even more brutal, and knew nothing better. So to Jim it was just business.

In the back room Amy, the child, slept at night, with a statue of the Virgin Mary by her bed.

Tonight Alex asked the little girl how she was, though he could not forget that he had once placed money in his back pocket to implement her destruction. So no matter how much he wanted to reassure Minnie of his care, his smile always showed insincerity. It was just that way. It had been fine when he was at university, where all his concerns, sincere or insincere, were the same concerns manufactured by others. But here, in this backwater—as he at one time liked to call it—it was different. Your concerns were understood to be manufactured or not. They had known him from a child. He was simply one of them, no matter how much he believed he knew.

He looked at the little girl now, and she smiled, her eyes like burning and beautiful beads. She was terribly shy, and had been all her young life. She was sitting at the table putting snaps on her jeans and one of her shirts.

"They will make me glow in the dark," she said, laughing. But she was really putting them on because she loved to play the guitar and liked to look like a music star.

——

ALEX WAS BRIEF. DID THEY BY ANY CHANCE BUY A LOTTO ticket? Yes, Minnie said, for they had started to buy them every week. His look was pale and agitated and hair stuck out over his head in curls, his nose was sharp and white and still had some freckles. In fact, if he had done nothing in his life but collect garbage along the road, he would have looked the same. He wore thick, heavy glasses that he was continually taking off and putting on.

When and where did they buy this ticket, he asked, adjusting his glasses once more. They bought it for the Wednesday draw, at the grocery store in town. He could hear himself sounding officious and earnest—he suddenly realized he disliked this kind of voice in almost everyone else. The little girl looked at him curiously, smiled slightly, and then put her head down again. Then she looked up under her eyebrows at him, for a second.

Did they still have it?

His Minnie Mouse looked puzzled, but said she must have and went into the den where the TV sat, to look among the papers. He watched her movement as if in a trance. Finally she came out with the ticket, held it in her hands, and started to tear it in two.

"For God sake, no!" he yelled, jumping up and grabbing it. He took the ticket and looked at it. The numbers were not even close: 5, 7, 14, 20, 31, 45. Still, it would have to do.

"Can I have it—please." His lips moved despite himself, and he tried to remain calm. Yet he was sweating. Was this in fact (and this thought came so suddenly he felt cold) just another way to destroy them? Did he want to destroy them completely and was this a way to do it? He looked at Minnie, her tired warm eyes confused, and smiled.

The little girl, Amy, took the ticket and examined it, looked at him curiously. She rubbed her nose and listened to the wind picking up. Then she went and got the numbers of the winning ticket from the paper and read them very seriously.

"I don't know why you would want it," she said. "I don't think it won."

"If I work this out, we might get some money—and it will be for all of us," he said now. He coughed into his hand and tried to look nonchalant.

"Oh," Amy said. That was all. She was in bare feet and wearing a long slip, not knowing that at almost fifteen she was a young woman, and looked like Minnie herself had at that age.

He adjusted his glasses once more and smiled at her. She looked at him impishly with her mouth twisted up into a half smile.

Now things must be done, before everything in his life fell away. It was either do this or die.

"Maybe a few hundred dollars, who knows," he said hoarsely. "If so, I will give you half, Amy, how is that?" He moved his hand through his hair, and tried to dispel the ever-present cynical smile of his worst angels.

"Fine," Minnie said. Amy simply nodded, and managed to look both serene and elfin at the same time, her ears sticking up through her dark tossed hair, her lips sticky from eating taffy.

"Yes," he continued, "but there is something I have to see about before the money comes. So fair is fair—don't worry—it is not so bad—just something I have to see about."

At that moment he was calculating how many millions he would actually give them. He thought that for over half his life he had dealt in papers and research, and now in grubby lotto tickets. He would give them something—but not Sam Patch. Not after all he had been through.

He was somewhat at a loss for words and wanted to say something nice. He smiled and said he put Amy's name in to take his night course on ethics. That he would teach her the great subjects, and they could transform her.

"I don't know if I want to," she said. She smiled up at her mother, as if asking for help.

"Oh, you'd love it—it would be good for you to use your brain," he said offhandedly. "It would challenge you—to hear what I have to say!" He smiled at this nonchalantly and then was silent.

"I put your name in, at any rate. Don't worry, you won't have to pay—you will just be allowed to go. Did you get the book on ethics by Aristotle I sent over?"

"I did," Amy said.

"And what do you think—I mean, of a man who lived three hundred years before Christ?"

"Very ethical—" Amy said, laughing.

It was then that Minnie told Amy to thank him, and she did. He nodded. She folded her thin hands together and sighed, and thought of the ticket was diminished.

He stayed for a cup of tea, and could not help but slurp it nervously. He was in fact out of tea at his house. He was ashamed to go to the welfare office because the main worker there had once been a student of his in university. So though he stalked the welfare office, he could not go in.

The wind blew, and tree limbs tapped against the window. As soon as the storm came Minnie stood and, taking holy water from the crisper in the fridge, began to sprinkle the room. She rushed over and touched Amy's forehead and Amy blessed herself nonchalantly, not so much out of commitment as out of practice. When she tried to touch Alex's forehead he brushed her hand away, miffed that after all these years she would not know him.

"Oh, I am sorry," she said.

She hauled the plugs out of the wall sockets for precaution, turned off the kettle, and sat down.

"I'll be back," he said, sticking a piece of raisin bread into his pocket. He stood, touched Amy's cheek, and smiled.

"Don't go out, it's lightning," Minnie cautioned.

So he stood at the door.

"Well," he answered boldly, "I know for a fact we have little chance to be hit by lightning."

"Except if God wants," Amy said, as if speaking to herself. He took no notice of what she said.

And with this, he took a step out the door.

———

He walked along in the night, which was still warm, and witnessed sections of the forest light up with a peculiar crackle, so that he could see his boots over mud, see fern cones in among the slopes along the hidden forest floor.

He had decided that he would switch tickets. But he had to have luck in this regard. That is, he was fortunate enough to know his uncle. Old Chapman had had lotto tickets before—and they lay for months in a cupboard without him even checking what they said. Alex was willing to bet Chapman had no idea he had in his shirt property worth $13 million.

And why shouldn't Young Chapman take it? He remembered asking for money one night to go to a dance at school, and Old Jim pinching the money out of his hand as rain dripped off the loose door of the barn, as if he was squeezing it out of his pores—so anguished he was to let go of it.

"I never went to no dance when I was young," he kept saying. "I worked from the time I was thirteen—me and Artie."

"Who is Artie?"

The old man let go of the money and said, "Never you mind who Artie is."

Later, much later, Alex found out that Artie was his grandfather, Rosa's dad, whom Jim had frozen out of the business because of that grader accident that ironically had taken his other grandfather. Artie had died broken-hearted about this death in 1957.

"Don't worry," Jim said after Alex discovered this. "He would be proud of you!"

But it was always like that. His own life was an enigma the world kept from him. So now he would pay his great-uncle back. To pay someone back it was best to negate who they were as a human being.

As Alex walked a huge bolt of lightning, energized in the pulpy warmth of night, flashed over his head, and showed the reddish mud at his feet, and even lighted up his shadow before him, so close he could feel heat. And he thought a strange thought: What if I was killed now, when I am so close to becoming so rich? It was a strange, strange sensation, so he picked up his walk to quicken his homecoming.

Taking off her clothes, Amy went over and said good night to her pollywogs, which were growing legs. She had four plastic cartons. In one was "the first stage," then came "the noticeable changes," then "almost croaking," and finally, "happy hoppers." At the happy hoppers stage she would band them and let them go into Glidden's pool, only to return the next summer to see if she could find any.

She had a pet skunk, and a beehive. The skunk was not descented, but would not spray her. It usually hung about under the porch, and there was a raccoon that slept in a maple at the side wagon road. The beehive was active, and she watched the drones day in and day out, sitting beside it without being stung.

On her wall, besides a picture of Tony Stewart the NASCAR driver and a picture of her father pitching horseshoes, was the picture of her in the local paper, for winning the mathematics prize. In the far corner was a picture of her and Rory. Rory and she were supposed to get married when they were seven, but had not managed to do so. So now Rory was her love and she had his ring. But as long as she had known him, and had waited, he had not kissed her. It seemed as if he did not quite know how. And this summer they had drifted apart, and she knew he sometimes only said hello because he felt he had to, and spent more time down at the cottage with Robin Anderson, whose mom and dad were rich. She felt a loss deep in her heart, not because she thought of marrying him but because in one way it was the loss of her youth. There was a time, on the first spring days, when changing to his short underwear he would strip off his pants, and she hers, and in his shorts and her panties they would run about in the yard, until twilight bade them stop. But one year they both realized they could not do it anymore, and it was a loss that was both understandable and melancholy. That the springtime would never again smell so sweet or be so inviting. And so was this loss.

In her own way she tried to hang on to him and disliked that Robin Anderson a whole lot.

She picked up her guitar and began to play. She played almost every night by herself. For she spent most every night and day alone. So with her feet going, and her legs and her bum moving, she strummed for thirty-five minutes "All Along the Watchtower," which she had been trying to learn now for three weeks.

Finally, after the fourth request to turn the music off, she put her guitar down, snapped off the amp, and lay on the bed with her hands tucked behind her head, her impish face suddenly looking serene and beautiful.

On the wall near the NASCAR driver was a picture Father MacIlvoy gave her three years ago. It was of a little girl crossing a bridge over troubled water, at night, and a guardian angel guiding her way. Father MacIlvoy gave this to her at her confirmation, because Amy was frightened of water and had never learned to swim.

Amy got into bed in her underwear and thought of what she would do if Alex actually gave them $700. She found herself dividing it up, between so many people she didn't have a cent left for herself.

She now stared at the ceiling, and listened to the night. The trouble was summer was fast coming to an end, and she had lost touch with Rory and everyone, and some didn't speak to her anymore, for Amy was busy with Fanny Groat and did not see them. She thought of this, and thought of the demands Fanny made on her time.

The night whispered around her, and rain fell on the tin roof. After a while, she rolled over, touched the statue of the Virgin for luck, and fell asleep.

Once Minnie turned out her light, and the house became silent, the skunk walked up on the back porch and chewed at an apple left out on the arm of the veranda chair. The raccoon sat at the far end of the porch, watching the skunk carefully, now and then shaking water from its thick gray fur and lifting its paw.

=

ALEX CHAPMAN WANTED TO SEE THE NUMBERS THAT
Burton had written down. He would do that in the morning by
bringing in the ticket he had taken from Minnie, and saying it was
his uncle's. They would check the numbers and find they were not
the ones—convince Burton he was mistaken. That would square
him with Burton, and give him time to find the real ticket and
claim it as his own.

He would get into the house, find the ticket, switch it, and—
he thought of what he would do with thirteen million. Once he did
that, and got his hands on the money, no one would be the wiser.
No one at all. Of course he would help everyone, and become the
benefactor he believed his uncle could and should have been.

Except, perhaps—Amy might know. She was a very wise little
girl. But he would put her in his ethics course, and she taking this
course would see how wise he was—especially as concerned young
women. (This was in fact his main hope, to be considered by
young women to be considerate of young women—especially, for
some reason, Amy.) So, seeing this, she would realize he wasn't like
her father and all the others. Yes, and so it would all work out!

He was overcome with giddiness, for in his mind the person he
wanted to impress besides Minnie was her daughter.

Seeing Amy tonight had brought back an uncomfortable memory, however. A few years ago, something had nagged at him. He
wondered if he could ever have children. He wondered why
Minnie would randomly meet Sammy at the shore, and then have
a child, when he was the one who had saved for the album. He tried
to forget this, but could not.

He went to Dr. Miller, and got a sperm test done. This sperm
test proved he was sterile. That in fact, he probably never would
be able to have a child. It was what in a sense he had known from
the first. He never told a soul about this, and sometimes late at
night he would take out the letter from Miller and read it, then

stare at the vast expanse of sky and all those stars, born and dying, and try to understand how the world worked. Was shy little Amy planned for in a way that superseded everything Alex himself intended? If this was the case, everything was known and understood, even the love that he and Minnie had for one another. If one wanted to believe such stupid things. But then sometimes he would think, what did he believe that was any better? That was, he thought, the one predominant question, and was either yea or nay.

Lately he had again attacked Minnie for being supplicant to the wishes of society, to religion, and to other impediments, and believed or wanted to that it was he, not she, who had fallen away from love. But he hadn't fallen away from love. Each time he saw her he still trembled. Little Amy noticed this but was too polite to say anything. And he sometimes felt badly saying sarcastic things with the little one there. He knew he shouldn't. But at times he couldn't help it. It seemed that the only friend Amy had this summer was her mother—he had noticed this. Therefore, it made it worse if he was sarcastic to the woman the little girl admired and relied upon.

"But sometimes," he decided, "you have to say what you know! How can she just sit around waiting for Sam—not a woman I respect would do that!"

Perhaps he was remembering his mother here.

—

THE SAME WIND THAT YESTERDAY BLEW HOT ON HIS FACE now was tinged with the very first trace of autumn, and Burton stood in the garage behind the glass counter and said nothing about the ticket that Alex had passed him. He was angry at everyone today—and said he might close up his garage or sell it. Kids teased him, stole his chocolate bars, and older people tried to fool him always with that mischief, easily laughed at, that lessened human integrity. All summer long they played in his skiff, out on the Bartibog, and he never minded that—but yesterday a boy had thrown an oarlock into the water and had set his boat adrift. It had taken him an hour to find it, far down the shore in a swell of incoming tide. Sometimes they took and hid it up Arron Brook, or far down the shore. And he was mad at this as well.

Alex had spent the morning polishing his shoes, so he still smelled of polish, and was wearing a crumpled white shirt that he had not worn in two years. For some reason he believed he would find the ticket today and make his way to Moncton to claim his winnings.

"This is my uncle's ticket," he said, and he tried to catch his breath, which he almost always did when he lied.

"What's this then?" Burton said with authority. He took the ticket and checked the numbers he had written. He looked at Young Chapman and sniffed. He then shook his head as if he distrusted a former idea, and rubbed his nose quickly.

The only sign that he was June Tucker's son was the perplexed look that sometimes overcame him. Other than this, there was no resemblance—for June Tucker had organized the world about her, and demanded the world, and Burton had not. Alex had written June Tucker three letters, never mentioning that he knew her son but asking her opinions on various subjects he was writing columns on. She never answered him, but once in a while she would be quoted by someone else, and it always made him jealous. He did not know why. She had studied sociology, so therefore to him her views must be important.

"I was far off," Burton said and put the ticket up to the light. After he did this he stared at Alex strangely. Again the suspicious look that made him resemble his mother overcame him. Then he scratched the numbers over, that he had written next to Jim Chapman's truck's serial numbers, and painfully copied Alex's numbers down, which to Alex seemed to be to his benefit. It was at this time that you got to see something of the problem. Burton had two fingers on one hand, and three on the other, and when he walked he hobbled, because one foot had been amputated halfway back on the day after his birth.

"The only other ticket I give out that day was Poppy—but he always checks his ticket here, and he didn't say nothing. I don't think he was the winner."

Any other ticket that had been sold had not been registered.

"That's all right—" Alex said, putting the ticket away. "We all make mistakes, Burton. But I'm glad we didn't tell him," he said. "He would never forgive you. So I told him I wanted to look at his ticket and here it is. He has never forgiven me for dozens of things. I still have the welts and sore ribs to prove it."

Burton nodded, scratched his face with his scarred right hand, and said nothing.

"Never mind, Burton," Alex said, remembering his own tears as a child, "everything will work out. Lots of people get tickets here—I often buy one." (He was happy he planted that seed.)

Alex stayed for a minute and then turned and walked out across the dusty front parking lot and the road, his suit pants billowing in the morning sunshine.

He had managed to see the numbers Burton had crossed out. Yes, those were the exact winning numbers and the sight of them was both exhilarating and scalding. For those were the numbers Burton had told him, and the ones his uncle must have. But where would the ticket be?

The trouble was Alex had lived on his own—but he was very worried about doing this all on his own. Still, who might he get to help him? Burton was out of the question—for obvious reasons. He wondered if he went to Minnie, might he entice her? "Entice" was the word, and just this once, too. Then his thoughts fell briefly to Amy. She perhaps was the one to try and entice.

She would never do it, he thought, but he did not say, "She is too principled." He said, "She is too straitlaced." And he had the uneasy feeling again, of realizing he was trying to fool a woman and young girl, who for months had had only each other, who all last winter had lived alone in the little house. Alex knew as well that Amy's friends had moved on to other friends. One day he was there she spent half an hour showing him her pollywogs just so she could talk.

This caused him to reflect on what he was doing, and to think once again of going to tell his uncle the truth and have a moment of reconciliation. This really seemed the best thing to do. And he started out toward his uncle's house, with his heart lighter for thinking of this.

When he got to the drive, however, he saw his uncle holding his fly rod up to examine it. His uncle didn't see him. He looked to Young Chapman to be old and sad standing at the front of his 120-acre lot, with old crushed drywall and cinder block about his feet, staring at this rod he had made himself some fifteen years back, and had taken over two hundred salmon with. Perhaps the only thing he was justifiably proud of. As much as he tried to get Alex to fish with him, Alex could never seem to manage the motion to cast.

It was very strange, but the sun seemed to come out furiously at this moment, and hit the eyes on the rod and make them gleam. Alex scratched his pointed nose and tried to think of what to do.

Apologize, he thought, get it over and everything will be all right.

He was set to do this, but something prevented him.

What would happen after that reconciliation? Too many things disallowed it. His uncle's cantankerousness. His constant displeasure at Alex's democratic stands. Old Jim's idea that God was just and therefore would have given him the ticket because of this supposed justice. All this would be held against Alex, so Alex would be forced to grovel, and he couldn't do it again!

Since all of this would come into play, he would not, could not, bring himself to tell his uncle anything. And he turned and walked back toward his house, as the wind blew against his face. He thought again of Amy and her mother, hoping he would get them a few dollars.

Tell him tell him tell him, the wind seemed to say.

=

ALEX WALKED ON TOWARD HIS HOUSE, AND AS HE DID HE thought of his former belief in Christ and his hardness of heart when it came to this belief now. His constant response, at once cynical and satirical against it, was that millions upon millions had died because of this belief.

In the seminary there were older men, teachers who believed in the winged serpents that were sent north by the devil, swept on the wild wind of the earth, to whisper sweet nothings into the innocent ears of children, all sleeping in innocent poses half-dressed, disheveled but sweet flowing hair, with lilacs and roses, and the blue, blue eyes of God. The devils, with red tongues, there to harm them; the guardian angels there to protect them.

A fairy tale, almost sexual, among men who held power and very much power over others—simpering, confused, and arro-gant men who until the end of the 1950s controlled whole house-holds in their palsied grips, decided who was good or not, what families could be singled out for castigation at any time. (In fact, this was why the Tuckers and their counterparts the Patches stayed so destitute.)

However, Alex's uncle understood these men, and feared them, and they counseled and feared him.

Alex, too, had believed in those angels and serpents, when he was a helpless child. But a child was so helpless he had to believe. Once he entered the seminary he was embarrassed by these men, with their fairy tales, their belief that there was nothing beyond our own earth and sun, and at that time he began to think of his uncle being exactly like them. Some of them believed man had not landed on the moon, that it was an atheistic conspiracy.

So came Alex's first rebellious act: "I will believe in God—but I will not believe in fairy tales," he said. It wasn't a tremendous rebellion, but still—he had been rebelling ever since. First he gave up Mother Goose, and then the Easter Bunny, and then Santa

Claus, and then those guardian angels that never helped him when he prayed, and then the saints like Saint Jude and Saint Francis who were supposedly able to do so much for so many, and then the Virgin who so many believed they saw in apparitions, and finally Christ and God himself. With that, everything was complete. It took some years. But now everything was complete.

He did not understand that even priests and nuns themselves, while remaining in the vestiges of holy orders, had given up these beliefs and did so with the compunction of our compliant age, and that for many of them nothing that secular man believed in would at all bother them.

Still the guardian angel his mother had told him about, the one who would watch over him if she died, had never appeared. One day he had led himself to believe he saw a beautiful angel by the curtain, just for his mother's sake, when she was very ill and told him she had prayed one visit him. This was in 1969 in a small little apartment in gloomy Saint John.

He had prayed to that angel that his mother not die. It didn't help. He prayed that he be helped. Later on in the dead of winter, he prayed that his uncle not beat him anymore. It didn't work either. He was not so silly as to believe in guardian anything anymore.

He turned down along the shore. As he watched children rushing past him he thought this. Where were the guardian angels for millions and millions of suffering children? Who, then, did God send? But then as he said this, something came over him—a small epiphany—and he realized he heard something inside himself: "We have sent you."

He shuddered, remembering that priest, Father Hut, with his exuberant face speaking to him, whose body turned up in a river in Guatemala riddled with bullets.

"We have sent you—it is not God but you who have turned your back on these children."

But he himself was too practical to give up his life to help a bunch of children he had no hand in making.

"I had no fun in making the bastards, why would I do anything for them?" This was, in his mind, ethical liberal thinking and because of this there was no greater scapegoat for the liberal mind than Mother Teresa. He once had thought of sending money away and adopting a child in a foreign land, but it came down to this: he was too wise, and no hypocrite—while his uncle, who was a hypocrite, sent money away every month to two children in Chile.

The only thing he remembered about the day he went to the foster home was standing at the corner of his street looking back at the house where he and his mom had lived in an apartment, a card she had gotten him for his birthday in his hand, tears running down his face. Now he was stunned by how Minnie and Amy lived this same way.

Yet that was the day when he had first learned that there was no archangel with a sword or guardian angel either. He saw how adults looked upon him with irritation and pity. And he had become disgusted with himself, and with the fact that he had peed his pants after his mother died. He was sent to a foster home with seven children. He remembered smiling obsequiously at them trying to share the things, toys and chocolate, a funeral director had given him out of pity. But he soon realized these other boys were hardened and cold to him. As cold as the ice outside. So he tried to fit in with them, act and be like them.

Alex took out a nicotine gum and put it in his mouth, for he longed for and wanted a cigarette.

But then as Alex walked a voice came to him; always he had associated this voice with his mother: "Well, how did Old Chapman find you? Remember everyone said it was a complete accident, a stroke of luck—that he spoke to a man in Bathurst who happened to know the woman who had taken you to Jacket River, that he had seen you in church—when you went to confession and asked the old priest for help. That they then realized you had been taken to this place 250 miles away. And when he saw you at that place Old James started to cry—they brought their great-nephew to be with them. We know Old James treated you rough—but you don't think he loved you? And you wouldn't drive the old man's truck over for an oil change? What was waiting for you if you did?"

He tried to stop this voice, for the same things were always repeated, and his breathing became labored, and he cursed. For the first time in weeks Alex grabbed at his chest for a second, and not wanting anyone to see him in distress (for there were moments when he was very brave) he let go of his chest and suffered the pain by grimacing. He kept on walking and this voice wouldn't go away. He was sweating, his face was pale, which made him look very much older. He climbed the steps to his house slowly, with his hand on the pole banister.

"Leave me alone—" he said.

Still it did not leave him, this insistent voice that he had always associated with that red-headed girl, his mom. He fumbled about, sat down on his couch, waiting for the pain to subside.

All of those others Alex had spoken to, as he sat in the university cafeteria in the middle of the day, all those exceptional people were gone and all his long discussions in the cafeteria with the young radicals meant nothing now. Most of them worked nine to five, and went home to their mortgages just as their parents had. And yet what was wrong with that, he thought now.

He had not wanted Amy to be born. In fact, he had insisted she not be, and was often enraged that Minnie had not heeded his advice. He hoped or had hoped for Minnie to regret the child, for the marriage to fail, and for the child to somehow ruin it. That is, he hoped for vindication at their expense. He had visited Minnie and Amy last winter, speaking about the ethics course Amy should enroll in, believing that now the marriage had failed with Sam gone west to work. But the marriage as yet had not failed, hanging as it might be on only threadbare love.

"My mother is independent," Amy had told him one night last spring, trying to sound stern, her little eyes lowered, when she overheard him saying something belittling. Perhaps Alex did not think it was belittling. "Yes—she is independent too," she whispered. Then she looked up with a carefree elfish grin, showing her small crooked teeth, so that her nose wrinkled.

He almost choked on the tea he was drinking.

"Oh—of who?" he asked, thinking it would be impossible for her to answer and smiling at Minnie, as if she too should take this as a joke.

But little Amy lifted her head and spoke proudly. "Of you," she said. "Why—she is independent of you."

And she smiled.

Of course in so many ways our little elf only wanted to be known as smart too, so he would approve of her, for she knew how important he was. Some days she asked in her prayers if she could be just a little bit important too!

At noon the next day, Alex decided to go and tell his friends he was mistaken about their ticket. He went back to Minnie's and sat there for an hour staring at the tea and cheesecake put in front of him.

"I am sorry about all that false hope," he said, and then added philosophically, "Hope in this world is so often dashed."

The heat had made Amy's forehead damp. The sound of birds outside in the near bushes, and a hummingbird coming to the sugar water Amy had placed on their windowsill. Everything round them was drowsy and green.

They didn't ask him about the money—the seven hundred he was supposed to give them.

"Just a big mistake—I thought four numbers were the same—" he said unapologetically. Then he shrugged. He too was sweating. It was very odd how much he felt like a criminal. They told him to never mind it, that Sam would have money when he got home. This rattled Alex as well.

"How much?" he asked, in a way that pretended he was happy for them.

"I don't know—because we are planning something, which I will let you know later, but quite a bit I think," Minnie said.

"What are you planning?" he asked, as if this secret was enjoyable.

But she simply shrugged and looked away. "I can't tell yet."

He never wanted to believe he could be poorer than Sam Patch. But by the end of the year he would be. He told Amy she would be in his ethics course, so she'd better sharpen up her debating skills. She looked at her mom, placed her hands on her lap and watched the hummingbird.

"Debates are not so much my line," she said.

The day was hot, and Fanny Groat was unwell, so Amy was going down to sit with her. Her temperature was 102 on a warm day. Amy had spent most of the summer with her, and that had alienated her from her friends. Yesterday, Fanny had told Minnie that she had dreamed that there would be blood on the statue of the Virgin before fall.

"Her life is almost over," Minnie said now.

"Yes, well, it comes to us all," Alex proselytized. (For some reason he had never forgiven Fanny Groat and disliked her.)

Alex took his leave and they saw him move across the dusty lane and into the distance.

Minnie told Amy that Alex was simply trying to be nice and to let it go, that she would learn much from him this fall.

"I know, and I do like him. And I do think he is smart—and I wouldn't go wrong in taking his course—but there is something about him" said Amy, in a way which did not accuse him, so much as baffle her. "Something—"

"Well, whatever—tomorrow you promised you would help Burton with his computer," Minnie said, to change the subject.

"And so I am," Amy said.

For Burton had bought a computer and needed her help in setting it up.

Amy was on her own this summer; as she told her pollywogs: "I was suppose to have fun. It's a complete fuddling disaster."

But her mother was so busy she did not see the little one's loneliness at this time. She didn't know that twice this summer Amy was not invited to parties. Amy had indicated to her mother that she wanted one, too. But Minnie did not seem to hear.

"Rory likes me, I'm sure," she would tell her pet skunk, "and all in all I think Robin too."

—

LEO BOURQUE LIVED HAND TO MOUTH. THIS IS WHAT THE highway became aware of. He was possessed of what so many were, a great ignorance about things outside of himself and his surroundings. He had tried to improve himself for his wife, had taken night classes and read articles written by Young Chapman, who he had tried to emulate, but it had not happened. He carried a pencil and two pens, but did not use them. And now his wife had gone away. And he longed to have her back.

Leo never had any of the chances Alex had. If Alex's life was tough, Bourque's was ten times worse. He'd been beaten by his father to within an inch of his life when he was twelve years old because he had been late for supper. He'd spent three months in the hospital. Later, he'd fished on the sea—on the very herring boats the priests had blessed—and saw Mr. Gallant drown in the storm of 1979 while making sure he, Leo, was safe. And now he lived in a shed behind his uncle's house. His uncle, Poppy Bourque, tried to find him work. It seemed that each thing Poppy did, Leo would find time to do something else, and wait patiently for his uncle to help him once more.

Poppy was now trying to get ready for the agricultural exhibition. He had grown fifty-five prize zucchinis, ten tubs of what he called Poppy's Patats—his wonderful white potatoes. The fair would stretch into September, ending at Labor Day, and he told

Leo he could earn $200 if he helped him set up and take down. Leo helped him so Poppy wouldn't have to do it alone. And though he grumbled and growled at Poppy, he did not want to take the money. He, however, had no choice now. This very human quality of his was hidden under so many shells it was at times hard to see.

The stand at the exhibition would be called Poppy's Place, just as it was for the past twenty years. But this year his young nieces would go with him on opening day. All of this Leo remained interested in to take his mind off his wife.

Leo had never heard what Aristotle had said about friendship, honor, or wisdom when he spoke to the young Alexander, never looked into the Book of Psalms when worried—and wouldn't care to anymore. The New Testament was a fairy tale now, as was the Old.

Funnily, he believed that not any of this would have happened if Alex had not come to him a year ago with the information about the bid. But the bid became his ticket, or so he thought. Since that time his wife had left and he had started owing money. Leo lived in a shed much like Alex did, except he was on the other side of the highway. Surrounded by smoky afternoons from the large empty fields, he could not believe his fate. If he had not given the bid, his wife would still be with him. That he had fallen and hurt himself at work, and that his boss laid him off for some kind of dereliction of duty, allowed his wife to leave him, the moment he needed her.

Leo only knew that it was in some way all Alex Chapman's fault. What enraged him about this was how he had looked up to the man, because he wrote articles about the dispossessed, about the First Nations. But in another way, very much because he was the grand-nephew of the great Jim Herbert Chapman, who had created out of his own muscle and blood the asphalt highway that stretched before him, shimmering in the summer and buckled and frozen in the winter months.

"The English get everything," he would say. And he believed this, even though not only was it less and less true, but the English were ridiculed as much as anyone else. Beyond that, Jim Chapman was only a quarter English and Young Alex a fifth. Alex was less English than Bourque himself.

Now Leo spent his time gambling at the tavern, on the money machines in the corner, certain that some day, in some way, he would make it rich. If and when he did, he would never lose anything again, he would get his wife back from Cid Fouy. Worse for Leo Bourque was this gnawing truth, that though with one hand he could knock Cid Fouy cold, he was frightened of the man, for the man had money and power Leo Bourque never could understand.

THE HEAT STILL LINGERED IN THE BACKROOM, WHEN ALEX woke the next morning. Another day of heat, the maple stand beyond his house shimmering under the blue sky. Would, he thought waking and sitting up, this be the day he found it? He wanted to know that—and he was going to flip a coin. Heads he would find the money, tails he would not. But he did not do this for two reasons. One, he was too practical and reasoned ever to believe in such nonsense. Secondly, he did not want to waste his luck by flipping a coin. The heat was oppressive—just as last winter the snow and cold were. The old stove had not been lit since mid-June, and Alex spied it thinking, Well then—once I have the ticket it will never have to be lit again, for I will build a house the likes they've not seen here.

But the truth of the matter was that Alex, who was the personification of a university system, believed he was against systems. Alex, who had more power because of how he thought, believed he was against the powerful. A man who disbelieved in evil and, though he made many mistakes, saw none of it in his own nature. Not once in his teaching ethics to students did any opinion form that was not the prized opinion of the secular. This then was his, Alex Chapman's, ethical purity, which was in a way not so far removed from the error of ethnical purity. This ticket hunt was just an extension of it, of what he had presumed to be ethical. The university had forsaken him. Well then, they would see what became of him. That is, in the realm of approval or disapproval, who would approve of him once he had this money?

He no longer had keys to the house, because his uncle had changed the locks, an old man proving his displeasure at the last of his life, but he didn't mind that. Poor old Jim once controlled the whole of the stinking highway from Route 8 to Route 11, and on to Route 224—no one would dare go against him. His door could have been left opened a million days and in that state, sublime and indifferent to the world, no one would have bothered his house. But now, his empire sinking, palsied, he locked the doors because his nephew had hurt him.

"I will not be held back by a lock—in fact I welcome them," Alex said.

Today his uncle went for a week to fish big salmon on the big Restigouche, which flowed like a grand giant between Quebec and New Brunswick, as he had done every year at the Feast of the Assumption. He had friends he met and continued to. They were all braggarts just like he was, Catholic boys too. This year would be no different. So Alex would wait until his uncle left the house today.

Then he would get inside, find the ticket, take it to Moncton. He would have to hire a lawyer, and remain absolutely anonymous. Then he would come back, and lay low for a while. Give his uncle $100,000 or so, say: "You see, this is what I saved for you."

But now the heat was bothering him, and he was dizzy, and he took his blood pressure pill. The trees above his shed and the great house beyond waved slightly in the gusts of hot wind, the shore-line was exquisite in its bluish waves. Across the way, the little island shimmered in green. All of this was majestic and, as he knew when young, worth more than any money. This is what he used to think when Old Jim refused him any.

"As long as I have a view like this, who can say I do not own the world?"

What had happened between them? Who could say? When did

that moment in Alex's childhood come when he thought he had been forsaken by the gruff old man? He didn't know. When was the smell of tea, and beans, and the sharp wind coming across the field at twilight not enough?

But now he thought of the coupons he had saved to buy his book on shore birds, and what had happened long ago, how his pens were thrown away, and how the whole school bus laughed when these things happened to him. That is, long forgotten pain, that had in some small ways been etched into his heart and on his face over the years, came back on a semi-regular basis.

But though Alex believed he had all and everything covered, something was going on that he had not thought of at all.

Burton, of the Tucker clan, of the poorest of the poor, who had by his own industry and the help of childhood friends from Chatham opened a garage four years ago, had now purchased the one thing he believed would make his life like other people's. That is, if he could not think, a computer could think for him. If he could not measure and scale and combobulate, a computer could do it. A computer could make him wise, all at once. Make him, he believed, like everyone else. He in his own mind had put that much faith in one.

And Amy had told Burton she would set up a computer he had bought the week before. Amy and Minnie had been with him that day, and both had tried to talk him out of buying it. Burton insisted, stamping his feet, and decided to make a scene if they didn't allow him to, for they did not know what he was thinking, that soon he would be as smart as they were.

After getting his way, Burton sat in the car's front seat, now and again tapping one of the big boxes with his deformed fingers, as they drove back down the dust-laden highway, with shore birds in the heavens circling far above.

He had no idea what to do with this computer, beyond tapping his fingers on the box. But Amy did, having helped set up the computers in the school. And the next morning, early enough that there was still dew on the grasses along the way, she walked down her lane, just as Alex, his eyes blinking from the sun, came out into Old Chapman's yard. She did not know if he saw her, but he didn't wave, and so she turned on the flat, pale highway and made her way to the garage.

She walked along, seeing the garage in the distance, it too looking desolate in the heat, with its white cement and curious broken cars. The garage was closed today, so it was the day to set the computer up.

In half an hour she had it up and going, so she began to copy Burton's crumpled receipts into it—day, month, year, payment, for each receipt he had piled in a shoebox. She had told him she would do this, and it would save him time, and he wouldn't lose any of his billing. That is, as she and her mother had always done, they made the best of what was offered them.

It wasn't a long process, the receipts going back only two months or so, which is when Burton started the business's fiscal year. (Not that he started it, but that the accountant from town, WP and Maine, came down to do his books at that time.) Amy thought little of the oil changes and oil sales, the filters and spark plugs and Goodyear tires—until she discovered that she was also compiling lotto numbers, tickets that had been given out as a bonus for these oil sales.

There were five of them since August 8.

So she copied them as well, thinking nothing much about this, until she came to the two first receipts—from that day in early August when there were two oil changes. One was Poppy Bourque. She almost overlooked the very first receipt, but found it too and began to copy it in.

The lotto number had been crossed and scratched out and another one written over it.

Name: Jim Chapman
Truck make/year: Ford 150/1996
Serial number: H987JH695
Lotto ticket number: 5, 7, 14, 20, 31, 45

She copied these numbers into the computer in a kind of stunned silence. How did her numbers get on the receipt? She glanced at the clock. It was twenty-seven minutes past ten. She felt sweat under her arms and along her back. She wondered if Mr. Chapman had gone yet or was still at home, or should she talk to him? She was in fact too shy to. Alex was an adult, after all, and a teacher too. So he would know what was best, wouldn't he? She took the old piece of paper, where Chapman's truck and lotto information was first written, and put it in her pocket. The problem was she could not tell what the crossed-out numbers were.

She must now rush to sit with Fanny Groat, and make her breakfast.

She rushed out the door, and up the silent highway. Her eyes were large, her lips pressed together. She was thinking of English literature. Strangely, she remembered a line from Browning: "Gazooks, here's a grey beginning."

ALEX HAD MADE HIS WAY TO HIS UNCLE'S, AND AMID SOME small birds sat on the narrow iron fence that separated his old ice-house from Jim Chapman's main yard. In his pocket he had stuffed a flyer that had been put in his mailbox. From Poppy Bourque: VISIT POPPY AT HIS POTATO STAND! It was always a delight to see his mailbox flag up, and so often a disappointment when he found nothing but these flyers.

Well, certainly he would find the ticket by the time that stand opened, Alex decided. Now and again he looked at his oversized pocket watch, scratched his nose. Then he took a walk toward the highway. From there he walked past Jim Chapman's gate and made his way along an old trail in back of the house, toward the water. He climbed the mechanical lighthouse, realizing suddenly that all of this activity was bothering him, and he was very dizzy. He sat down near the reflectors and using his binoculars began watching the house.

Jim Chapman's truck did not move; for three hours not a sound came from the desolate old place, the machines and cinder block of the back acres lay in silent turbulence. It was as if he was looking through a time machine into the past and seeing himself there as a child, a woebegone boy with nothing who sat about on a block and watched the men.

Now and again he looked at his pocket watch and imagined, as in the time machine, the clock whirring back through the years, the lighthouse he was on being the time machine itself. Yes, he was there as a child, amid those sheets of tin and broken, derelict machines.

Tin sheets that lay hot in the sun. Nothing moved. Just Amy walking back up the highway from someplace, and a fat bee or two quietly zigzagging, and now and again a ticking sound from somewhere amid the green bushes. He had studied bees, he thought, and he was content to think of bees for a while, and how they lived their lives. How the drones lived and died, and how once in anger a man had called him, Alex Chapman, an academic drone. Him of all people!

Yet if only he was!

Then, suddenly, he realized something. It came to him as he was thinking of going home to rest. The truck was actually telling him, by where it was parked, that the house was empty.

"Your uncle did not drive me—I am parked under the tree at the back because I will not be taken," the truck whispered through the casual wind of mid-morning, the still rich, abundant smell of summer.

It was like a shiver of hope ran through him. Jim had gone. The truck wasn't taken. He had left with someone else in the fishing party. The whole yard, the acres behind it, were left unattended. The truck, dumb in its physicality, now seemed wholly animated and alive.

"Song of joy," Alex whispered to himself, through half-burnt lips. "Song of joy—song of joy!"

He thought of his study of ethics and how he pinpointed various crimes committed by people like his uncle over the years. It would not be so bad, getting this ticket for himself.

He got down and moved along the old grasses, yellowed and burnt by the sun, his own hair lightened to orange by this sun, as the day was heating, and the sunlight left shafts of color on the great empty iron and steel bodies that lay crippled throughout the yards. His head moved barely visible among these gaunt and metallic stallions of other years.

In the great acres of Chapman's desolation was the smell of tar shingles and commodities of a bygone time, wasting away, that gave the scent of baking cardboard and dry shingles, and each acre he passed he seemed to relive some of his sad life. Here he was when he first came, the old rocking horse once in his room; here he was when he first saw; here he was when he first noticed—and all these memories were vague and seemingly sad. He moved through these acres like moving through time, remembering how his youthful hope was bled away in a thousand nights of reckless tyranny and forced labor. So now he was doing this for that child who was brought to this house as an orphan. In a way he was getting restitution for all orphans, and making good on a claim for them as well as he. He would pay Jim back not only for Chapman Island, which should belong to the Micmac, but for his mother as well, and the legacy she should have been left. What might he have lived like if Jim had given him a chance, he now decided.

He went to the house, however, like a scared child—the same child who had gone there in hope when he left the foster home, carrying a small cardboard suitcase. He went to the doors and tried them like he would some stranger's mansion, and found them locked. All the doors had new locks, as gaudy as brass on old woodwork, and his ancient key fit none. Even the shed was locked, for the first time he could remember.

But that is nothing now, he thought, I will have my revenge.

But still some small part of him felt desolated by being locked out, hurt that his uncle no longer trusted him. And some small part of him told himself he still loved his uncle and his uncle loved him. But now that was a very small part indeed.

What was more painful was knowing his uncle would never in a thousand years suspect him of ever breaking one of these locks! And did this not then make it a crime?

He went back to the lot, searched in the dry burn and scald of old paint in the wind and found a rusted crowbar in the soil. He began to think he had a reckless soul and he was very happy to have one.

"Yes, you don't fool with me—I will wait my time and then you will see."

He snapped the crowbar against his hand, and it hurt. He grimaced, once again like a child.

"And my name is not Chapman!" he shouted.

Of course in so many ways over the years the fight had been taken out of him. He had over the years almost accepted his role as an outsider and oddity on the highway, that desolate stretch where the heat now formed in the afternoon sun. Who else talked of Plato when fifteen? Who pushed him down when he had? Who anointed him with laughter when he tried to relate a story written by de Maupassant? Did he know that in order for some to exercise their manliness they set him up to be bullied and tormented, and then stepped in as his savior, hoping for a dollar? Of course he did. And he always had. And he hated himself for his knowledge without action. He was a weakling, and even now breaking into a house with a crowbar seemed to take too much from him.

He thought of this in despair. One day Old Chapman, seeing him bullied, had brought him to a cement single-story building, down on the property where he had a plant that housed bags of cement and lime.

"Come with me," he said, "and you can get stronger."

Old Chapman tried to make Alex lift these cement bags from the floor to the first staging, and told him Sam Patch would teach him. But nothing was more foreign to Alex than to force weights into the air, and his hands slipped. He was furious at the old man for making fun of him.

"I am not making fun," Jim said, confused and angered by this. "I just know it will make you stronger—give yourself six months—it is not a bad thing to do, I swear! You get at it now!"

Alex never could do it, and Sam took the task to himself while Alex sat in the corner day in and day out—watching up the yard for the old man to show. Then he would jump to his feet and pretend to have just lifted a bag.

So what, he thought, and he now thought of the millions in his grasp. So none of that mattered now!

Of course he would live much better than they would with this money. That is, he would give tons of it away. Minnie would come to see who he was. For as always Minnie was in his mind. She was the principal object and artistic quest, like Dante's Beatrice or Keats's Frannie; he too had a woman out of reach.

Yes, it was all possible now, as soon as he got the ticket!

But what he thought would be very easy to do, once his uncle went out, he discovered wasn't as easy as he supposed. If he got caught, he might end up in jail. The ticket would be lost. But what he also realized was this: the old man might still be home—upstairs asleep. What would happen? He would be caught at something that Burton or even little Amy might just figure out!

Well then he would make up an excuse, say he was coming for his books. Anyone would believe that! His uncle had said he would sell his books on Plato and Aristotle if he did not take them out of the house. Certainly he had a right to them.

"We will have to see," he said.

But then Sam Patch—how could he just blame him and have him fired? Because he thought he was better than Sam—and he realized this, and was slightly ashamed. But what he was most ashamed of is that things had worked out for Sam, after all of Alex's planning and subterfuge, and not for him, who believed always in being the master of his own fate.

So he bit down on his tongue and pried open the old shed door. The lock seemed to give way with a sudden immaculate spring, and the door fell open. It was quiet, musty, and the same internal smell of their lives that made it distinct prevalent in the air. He paused, heard nothing. He thought of his old aunt standing at the door, waving to him on the way home from school.

He had snapped the new lock open—the hinges were busted, and screws fell to the floor. He would have to replace all of this, he decided, and then he moved through the small archway into the house, thinking that his uncle was right, that he was an awful, ungrateful nephew.

"First time for everything," he muttered. He thought of himself now as a foster child coming back to deal with those who had raised him poorly. He realized how often in life this happened, and felt strangely enough as if his life had a meaning beyond his own consciousness because of this very act. When he turned a corner into the front hallway he saw himself in a mirror, and was surprised, and did not quite recognize himself.

The house, in its bareness, seemed to display the hidden facets of Young Chapman's life. He was reminded of himself playing in sections of the house no one went to now, when he walked through large old rooms and half-hidden sections. Sometimes he spent afternoons searching out places his mother might have stood, and standing there too.

Half the furniture was covered in white sheets. The grandfather clock had stopped. The calendar had not been changed since Muriel's death, and if truth be told he had not been in since then. Really, he had left his uncle to himself. After his aunt's death, his uncle tried to get him to come for supper and invited him to play cribbage. Old Chapman had left Muriel's apron—with its flowers, daisies with the smiling faces—hanging near the back stove, placed there by her on the last day of her life. Alex, who hated sentiment, was suddenly sorry for his uncle, without wanting to be.

Then he noticed something that froze him. His uncle's medication had been left behind, forgotten on the table. He had forgotten it and so would get dizzy spells if he did not have it. A panic set in.

Alex knew he should take him this bottle of medicine. But then, how could he?

For moments he stood petrified staring at this bottle of green and white pills.

"He must have another one with him," he said. But he knew this probably wasn't the case.

He did not know the house would bring this compassion for his foe to life.

He did not understand that crime was always better if done in groups of three or four—where no one played the ultimate role.

That is, sin was almost always a collaboration.

Still, he had to stay the course, keep going until the end. He was shaking violently and speaking to himself.

"If I get the ticket I will give so much of it away I will live in almost the same kind of poverty I do now. In fact, people will look upon me as an example of what a good man would do with money. People will know why I studied the way I did all these years. This is true, but first I have to find the ticket."

He thought of Minnie and the Beatles album that long ago day. She would come to him, once he had this ticket, and he would have what he had wanted from the moment he first saw her.

He searched that afternoon for almost four hours. The house was closed up, and when he came into the sunshine his eyes squinted as much as those of a condemned prisoner. He thought of what Father Hut had told him: "To give your life for others is both the greatest challenge and the greatest joy."

Nonsense, he now thought. At any rate, he knew all that.

And then he would think, Perhaps there is no ticket at all.

He went back to the kitchen and began to search through the drawers more and more forcefully, until the drawers themselves were messed up and he had to then try to straighten them out. But in his wild search some papers had fallen out onto the floor, and he didn't know which drawer they had fallen from. He hadn't even noticed, and it was as if a trick had been played upon him. He couldn't believe that he who wanted to be careful had left his boot prints on these papers. He picked them up hurriedly. He began to shake. It was of all things his great-aunt's recipe for the chocolate pie she made him when something bad had happened—when his pens had been taken, his coupons destroyed, or he'd had to walk home from a dance alone—and she had wanted to take his pain away.

"Give me the ticket!" he yelled.

ALEX THOUGHT OF HIS UNIVERSITY DAYS, AND HOW LITTLE he had done with all he had learned. He thought too of how many people had far less opportunity than he, and had made much more of their lives. He thought too of how he had tried to change and inflame Minnie, by writing her letters and telling her of how many women were independent. But no matter how angry his letters were to her—how much he accused her—he could not forget her for a second, and that she had married a man beneath him. He went to bed each night at university dreaming of Minnie coming to him.

"Sam will never take you off the river—I would have," he wrote her once. But at all these points in his dreaming, where they would fly away to some exotic spot, there was no little Amy sitting beside her. And in his mind Amy did not exist.

That is, he had been able to decide by all proper methods her demise, without ever seeing her. Until one day, after he had returned home, she simply appeared from behind the car, as fully alive as he had ever been, with her hands, feet, and eyes exquisitely her own—not just now her own, but her own eternally.

So now he had placed her, this brilliant, elfin, and awkward little girl, in his ethics course to instruct her on how to live.

He lay down that afternoon, and fell in and out of sleep. He began to remember other moments in his life, with his right arm over his eyes and his feet up on the couch arm.

He and his mother walking to the train station.

It was already after dark—and they had to go down a long street with almost no lights except the light of a store at the end, and there his mom stopped and bought him a bag of candy—he remembered her hands were raw in the cold. She had spent the afternoon dressing him up, making him presentable to a man he did not know very well at all. Then she instructed him on what to say, and how to say it. But when they got there, his father was leaving. That man called Roach who hated him for being born, who hated of all things Alex's nationality—for Roach disliked the Catholics, and didn't mind telling Rosa so.

But that night he even smiled at little Alex and touched his cheek in kindness. Alex didn't understand, and smiled back. But after that Mr. Roach didn't look at him. He didn't want to look at his son. He didn't know what to say to him. Alex lifted his bag of candy, and smiled. The man's lips trembled slightly, but he turned sideways. The smell of diesel signified a parting—and this man, Alex overheard, accused his mother of getting pregnant to make him stay.

It became evident that he thought she would have money from the Chapman business, and that she had been disowned because of this very man she tried now to hang on to. It took Alex years and years to understand this. This sorrow-laden evening in the snow. This sad, sad parting of people who should have loved.

Alex tried to understand by watching him, his movements. He remembered all of this now. There was a sudden Protestant reserve to Roach's hatred of them, their Catholicism, and his self-indulgence at what his family had put up with on their behalf. It had gone back, it seemed, to Alex's own grandfather, who had been in a dispute with Old Jim.

So now Roach reminded them. Yes, this was the right time to turn on them, when they were alone and defenseless.

His mother stood on the platform, and she did not cry while others were there in the sweet sorrow of parting. His mother was a young girl, really, in a cold foreign town. She had schedules for buses in her coat pocket to travel back through the drifts of snow to her apartment.

Thinking of this, Alex lying on the couch was so rigid he couldn't move.

Why did he think of these things now? Why did he think of Mr. Roach, his father? He tried not to believe he had become anything like his father. That Eugene Gallant was his father.

He had hated men like his father, Mr. Roach, all of his life. Those stiff, puritanical, edgy frauds of some past injury they never themselves partook in but could bring up in a second as their own. And thinking this, he realized he had done it too. On Chapman's Island with the Micmac, and many times in trying to control Minnie.

"No," he said, "I was never like that!"

Was this the reason he wanted Minnie not to have the child— to keep her from some disgrace he felt he had once caused his own mother? But would he have stopped his own existence to prevent such a disgrace?

In some ways Alex thought of all men as Mr. Roach, and all women as his mother.

=

THE NEXT MORNING ALEX WOKE IN A SWEAT, COUGHING. For a moment no thought came to him except a nice one, of being by the river as a child, watching fish in a pool. He thought of this and stretched. Another day, and the heat and soundlessness of the little shack. Then he sat bolt upright and remembered he hadn't fixed his uncle's shed door, he had left it open. Anyone could have gotten in. What if someone else found the ticket?

"Let me find the ticket today, and I will never ask you for another thing," he said, his heart pounding. He got out of bed, and walked to a chair where he sat.

"Get me the ticket!" he said, taking his blood pressure medicine.

But who was he saying this to?

Could man have hope in anything without believing in something beyond themselves? This was the whole idea of the lotto. Wasn't it?

It was perverted Christ worship. The sole idea of his ethics course was to debunk this.

Now he had come full circle.

He got up and pulled on his pants, went to the bathroom and washed—looked suddenly at his orange, ragged hair, and trembled to think how much he looked like his great-uncle.

He looked across the room into a mirror. His hair was matted, his beard gray and grizzled. He could pass for anyone along the lost highway now. Any of the dozens of men he had grown up with, who he at one time had thought he was so different than.

If he had money, nothing would ever bother him. He believed, in fact, he would get back at everyone. Except: no one had bothered him in years. No one had cared why or what he did, or what he said. After all his learning, the thousands of books he had read, he was waltzing with ghosts that no longer existed. Women who no longer knew him, who could pass him in the street and not recognize him, or ever say his name in longing. The breasts he once desired were now old. All gave and were given up, and still he evoked the idea that someone was waiting for him.

As he turned he saw the quote from Khrushchev on the wall above his books, a quote he had put there proudly when he came back to the river: "Get rid of the devil and priests will have nothing to do."

He wanted people to see that quote when they came into the house. Just after he made the grotto for the church, Father MacIlvoy came to his house one afternoon, to talk about old times and pay him for the statue.

Alex childishly said, "There is no devil in here—" and pointed to Khrushchev's words.

"I didn't expect there to be," MacIlvoy said humbly.

"I have nothing to confess," Alex said.

"Live long enough and you will," MacIlvoy answered merrily.

Money. Goddamn money.

He remembered his father, Mr. Roach, again, riddling her with guilt over money she was trying to get him.

"I will get it," she would say, closing her raw hands in determination, "just you wait and see." And she would nod with determination as rain fell over the greasy window of Lester's Coffee Shop. Roach would be annoyed, tell her to sit up straight, not to sniff.

"I'm sorry," she would answer, "I haven't been feeling so well."

"There are other girls in the office, Rosa," he would say. "There are other girls, they have outlooks—you don't have an outlook. They have plans—you don't have plans. They are interesting to be around."

"It must be nice for them," Rosa answered.

Later, when she tried to say that she did not have this money, it provoked a fight over him. Alex would listen to them, his face quiet and serene, hoping the arguing would stop. It never did.

He remembered how once, after an argument, Roach went out to his Christmas party and he and his mother stayed alone. Very late at night he came in singing, stumbling. He got angry when he saw Alex sleeping in the bed with his mom.

"Get him out of there!" he said. "Jesus Christ!"

He told Rosa there was a girl named Diane—and was she ever nice.

Alex would watch for the derelict, who always smiled at Alex when he saw him.

He decided this morning he would give Minnie money if she left Sam Patch. This was not as inexcusable as one might think. For Sam Patch, to his way of thinking, had deceived Minnie—and left her alone. Just like Mr. Roach had his mother. Simply speaking, why couldn't Sam have provided a better life for Minnie than he had, if he really loved her?

He gives her nothing, Alex thought in a practical way, and left her alone with that little child.

Of course Alex sent Sam away as much as anyone, and it was he who was worried Sam would come back to the lost highway with a lot of money as people from the oil patch were now doing.

How could he convince her, then, if he didn't find the ticket?

THERE WAS NO SIGHT OR SOUND FROM THE CHAPMAN house. A pale, thin cloud moved across the otherwise cloudless sky. On the radio, which sat on the counter inside Alex's own little house, he heard of the "two glorious weeks of summer left."

When he was very little he used to rush out and try to catch the first snowflake on his tongue. He would persuade his mother to come out and be with him, and watch as they melted away in Saint John's darker south end streets. It wasn't the Saint John of today with its fresh sidewalks and cafés and lights draped across pleasant walkways. It was the old postwar Saint John with its waterfront closed in by fog and battered timber, and streets twisting away in the fog. And how he loved it there. And now he thought of how young his mother had been when she died at twenty-nine, and how he was now much older than her, and how she lived with him alone, cut off from the inheritance because of this Roach man she had followed there, who was physically adverse to her, who disliked her in a visceral way once the money was not forthcoming.

When Old Jim found out she was pregnant, he said, "You marry no Protestant or you'll get not a sniff from me."

So she followed her man to Saint John, he already twenty-six years old. A manager of some warehouse of some small company. They waited for her uncle to change his mind. He, this man, thought she was rich. Why wouldn't he think this? Now he didn't even hide the fact that he blamed her for not being so. That is, he could not believe he had made such a disastrous mistake, a bad calculation from such a calculating man.

Roach had lived to the north of the highway, and he said he was always cut out of things by Chapman, who accused his family of being squatters.

He had learned to hate Chapman, and fear him.

And so he set his eyes on her! Her with her little bit of money and her music lessons!

He kept suggesting that she must be able to cash in some trust fund, would she not? At first she was surprised, then deeply empty, and would sit in Lester's Coffee Shop waiting for him after work, with Alex in the old iron stroller.

"I will get it," she said dreamily, "I promise I will."

"Because if you do, we live much better—that's all I am saying—I am saying nothing but that. I want a life for both of us."

"I know," she said dreamily, "yes."

Sometimes at nineteen she would pretend to be going to the post office for the money. But she would simply push Alex in his stroller about King's Square in the wind and rain, not knowing how to come home and tell Roach.

Alex went to first year elementary thinking, all three feet of him, of an inheritance that his mother would hand to him. By that time her man had gone.

Alex would walk up from St. Patrick's and St. Michael's, with his pants itching his legs, and his new bookbag, and each day it got a little colder. He remembered now the snap of the apple in his teeth, and the warm corner store where he bought his bag of chips. He remembered one year, at the first snow, she didn't want to go out because she couldn't find her pink scarf, and they searched everywhere for it, and he kept saying: "Come, Mom, or the snow will be gone."

There was a smell of tin and diesel in the air when they went out, along the black iron fence where cartons and paper cups were caught, and the snow came down in the alleyway, and his mother held him up to catch the first flake on his tongue.

What had happened, from those days until now? And why had it? And how had his life gone? And who was to blame? Or why did he think he had to blame anyone? Certainly he couldn't even blame Mr. Roach, caught in the same turmoil as everyone believing half-truths in order to blame other people.

Every year when the first snow fell, he thought more and more about his mother—and why she had done certain things. He remembered her one night drinking a whole bottle of wine, alone, and then laughing and singing and telling him all kinds of stories.

For a moment when thinking of her each day, he no longer wanted to rely upon approval or disapproval. He only wanted to love and to forgive.

≈

HE DID NOT KNOW DURING THAT LONG AGO CHILDHOOD time that she was having problems with another man at work (this was a year or so after his father, Roach, had left them), a business-man of a certain class who managed the store in his gray suit and flush face, who touched his female employees' breasts just slightly when he squeezed by them as they worked, or what was far worse, laughed at injury to others with a loud laugh, just as he did at any-one who held in his hand the gift of knowledge. He asked her out when he found out she was alone with a child. And that was it, wasn't it? Alex became a trump card for virile men who wanted to fuck her. His mother rebuffed this boss, with his paycheck and his loud suit, for she was waiting for her Mr. Roach to come back, because in her dreams she belonged to him, like those be-bop-a-lula songs he could sing into his microphone at the high school dances. So her boss then turned his attentions to Alex's mother's friend Pearl.

As far as Pearl believed, this boss was going to leave his wife and children and marry her. Alex's mother tried to dissuade this woman without telling her of the proposition she herself had had from that same plump boss, but to no avail. Alex saw this gentle-man once at the apartment. He had come in, with his short legs and mustache, abrasively speaking of someone who he had "got the better of." Seeing a painting that Miller Britain had given Alex's mother out of some deep kindness one day at Lester's Coffee Shop, the man had said, "He don't see the world like I do if you ask me," and guffawed.

His mother, with her little painting, the only one she had, was left little by this remark. She smiled plaintively, and it was the only kind of smile she had left.

"I like the painting," Alex said, standing up for his mother as he had done for no one else. He had met Mr. Britain, the day his mother was given that painting.

But his mother's boss hooted at the painters in Saint John, like Humphrey and Britain—and poets like Nowlan—those men who had, above all, visions of greatness and tramped the streets unknown. And of course, that was it—they were exposed to the elements of scandal and mocking, and this man who managed the south end Steadman's store knew if anything how to mock, titter, and be dismissive of greatness in his midst, for that was the way to herd together in this country—and Alex saw this later on in the seminary, among the "nose-picking boys" as he called them, and just as much, in the secularly conscious universities of the cluttered Maritimes, with women he once embraced as being independent, who said and did only what their friends said and did, and took that as freedom. It was all nonsense, he knew. So he must find the ticket.

"I could tell you lots about Miller Britain," the boss had sniffed. "Insane and everything else, if you ask me! Yells at the top of his lungs, if you ask me. Was up at the nuthouse there and wanted to jump off the reversing falls, and my cousin who's the custodian there says so for a fact! And don't even take care of his daughter!"

Perhaps it was then that Alex began to hate this kind of man, the BOSS, and then men, and took it upon himself to decide who was and was not that man. Who he could approve and disapprove of. But in his fury he could never decide well enough what kind of man he himself should be. He took ethics, studied hard, so he could see who was and who was not that kind of man. And now it came down to this: Sam Patch, good, kindly Sam Patch, was that kind of man. And he must save Minnie from him—for she at some point would still come to him.

His mother rebuffed this boss in hope her friend would see him for who he was, and he with proud moral effrontery began to talk about her behind her back to other employees in the store. She thought she came from a rich family but was just a Miramichi twat, and who were they but French-speaking and Irish rejects that were kicked out of Saint John—who should be cut off from the rest of the great province of New Brunswick. She had a man who left her too, just as she should be! She better be careful if she wanted to hang on to her job!

"That's why we is backwards like Maine, if you ask me!"

And she would arrive in the dreary damp of a Saint John morning, and hear against her the insignificant tattling of lonely, stupid women, one of whom was her friend Pearl, and guffawing, obedient men. Of course they were obedient, like schoolteachers and university professors; none of them in their lives had rebelled against anything or anyone that they weren't taught to.

Why did this insignificant life now matter so much to Alex, and why did he think of his mother? That she was at all those moments, in the harsh glare of this unsympathetic and pathetic life, dying. That each day she got up for work, waiting for the call from Roach who was going to take her away. She and their son, Alexander. And oh how happy they would be.

She was in fact the only one to ever call him Alexander. After she died, his name was hacked away, until in some ways he lost his name and who he was. And so after a while he could be First Nations if he wanted, and write the historical novel about "his people." Which is what he had been trying to do secretly for years.

"Alexander," his mother whispered, and clutched his hand. "Tomorrow—you go over to Lester's Coffee Shop—you sit at a table and order whatever you want." She tucked $10 into his jeans.

He lay down with her, and when he woke late the next morning her body was cold.

"Love and forgiveness," he whispered now.

What had happened to the Miller Britain painting, which might now be worth tens of thousands? He did not know; he never saw it again. He had tried to find it among the Britain paintings at the Beaverbrook Art Gallery one summer day, but could not. There in the still and broad-ceilinged rooms he walked about, with the gallery almost empty and the Salvador Dali painting taking up one wall, and everything to him at the moment seemed elusive and just out of reach. And what he realized was that it was his talent, his own talent that was now out of reach.

It, and his great-aunt's love of art, had propelled him to take up a blowtorch and hammer and chisel something out of his life. And once, once he knew, he could have been great. Perhaps not as great as Britain, but then again, perhaps, ah just perhaps greater. And so he made if nothing else the grotto for the local church—and suddenly he realized it was his great-aunt who had asked, and maybe paid, for his grotto to be made.

Tears in his eyes, a flood of half-forgotten memories resurfaced. On those days long ago he went to the rink with his mother, and she would tie his skates, and he would flounder on the ice. She wanted him to play hockey. But he did not understand the camaraderie of children playing. His mother could not get him to play, and now he understood something—that he had rebelled against Canada and its hockey all his life. He had scorned those who played it or liked it, had cheered for the Soviets against Canada to get back at those childhood boys, heroes to so many girls, to show independence. He hated and mocked Canadian hockey players. And along the way, he missed the entire country's essential grace and beauty, its magnificent poetic dance—for both men and women, a dance so captivating that not a ballerina in the world could ever match it.

Now, in his darkness, he was beginning to see he knew nothing of his country, much like those baseball-lauding academics whose friendships he'd once cultivated at the university so he could be called cerebral and obtuse.

He realized that he was, after all, much like his father, Roach.

What would happen now if the ticket wasn't found? He may as well die. So he would have to go back in the morning, he would have to search all over again, all day long.

His little mouth turned down, and he grimaced like a child.

"Send me a friend now, to help me—if you exist, you owe me that!"

Alexander never knew how much he demanded from the God he no longer believed in.

SOMETIME THE NEXT AFTERNOON, WITH THE HAZE OVER the highway, and the carcass of a porcupine in the center of the road, Leo Bourque left Brennen's tavern, one of those small red cedar buildings on an unpaved stony and water-holed lot, partially encompassed by a log fence, and went to the little garage on the highway. Along the black highway covered in a dusting of sawdust from the backs of trucks, one of them being his uncle's, cut away by the treads of cars, he felt it might be time to put up his thumb and leave this oblivion. For this oblivion was grounded into the trees and hard soil, and begged those who had failed to keep going. And he had failed, and what is more blamed that failure on others whom he trusted, like Alex Chapman.

Besides, he still owed $600 and had no idea how to get it. He thought Alex would help. Alex said he would meet him at Brennen's tomorrow, but he suspected it would be just to buy time again.

He was bitter and disappointed, and took pills to kill the pain of losing his wife and the pain still lingering in his hip. But these pills did not help. He was not a bad man so much as a man on the brink of despair. For instance, he had not taken cocaine until the pain in his hip became unbearable, and because of this he lost his wife. He had no pain until he gave the bid away and the boss gave him a new job, to operate a loader, and he fell from it. But he knew he was put on the loader because his boss wanted him out of his sight. And his boss wanted him out of his sight because of Leo's wife. His wife and his boss became friendly after Bourque brought in the bid that made his boss an extra $120,000 that year, and perhaps every year from now on. All of this happened without anyone predicting it would. And yet it happened simply and without the least trouble. And here he was. Worse, his wife had almost come back to him, but he in so much pain had taken too much cocaine and swung a fist at her. That destroyed any chance he might have had. Worse is how his boss held her, saying, "Let's go, we'll get your things in the morning—I knew this would happen."

But what was the worst was this: he knew in his heart that the boss would never love his wife like he, Leo, loved her. Yet Leo would never be able to convince her of this now.

He wondered much about his life, and it all seemed to have come to disgrace because of one thing: his meeting with Alex last year and his bringing the bid to his boss. Why had he taken the bid to his boss? Why didn't he bring it back to old Jim Chapman, and tell on Alex like he should have? Or have just let it go. Why had he been put on the large loader? Why had his wife left? How could she love a man with such a small mustache and such a large belly?

Alex.

That is, Bourque felt he had been deceived by the man he had tried to emulate for a number of years, and he could not forgive this in himself or anyone else.

=

LEO WENT INTO THE GARAGE, AND THE SMALL BELL TINKLED as if a country store. The little fan whirred in a corner, side to side. So one would feel the circulation of air like small tingles against your skin. He picked up a new lighter and lay it on the counter—he had come to buy matches, but the Bic lighter would do. It cost $2.79 and he placed $5 on the counter.

Burton was trying to operate a new computer sitting on the desk behind the counter—a wave of bright new possibility in a world so remote. Beyond starting it, it seemed Burton had no idea how to use it. He had forgotten his excitement at being talked into buying it from a man at Radio Shack as he had weaved back and forth on the mall floor one day last week.

Burton glared at it, as if it was alive and an enemy. Once in a while he would push a button and wait. His hands were deformed because he had been left out in the snow, and one foot was partially missing. Bourque had always thought of this—that is, that Burton had had all his fingers and toes, fresh and working, for about three hours, breathed with a brain as fine as most for a tiny little bit. And so he was always kind to him.

"Having a problem, is ya?" Leo asked. Outside the sunlight displayed the world in gold and greens against the old dusty windows, and slanted down on the hot pavement in the yard, and showed the garage to be emasculated, removed of pumps, and an old hose bleeding into nowhere. There was a smell of tar as cars passed along. Some junked cars lay hidden in the tall grasses behind the shop, their roofs blanched and peeled, and a curtain lay flat against the grimy back window, where flies buzzed and nubbed themselves into unconsciousness.

Burton was almost crying, because of the new computer that he thought would save his business. He cried very easily and if you asked him why he was crying he would say, "Why, don't you know—it's the world."

He had no idea a computer was like this. He thought computers made you money.

"The computer does everything for you—you don't even have to think," the salesman had related to him. And to Burton, who was always waiting for an instrument like this to appear, it seemed divine. But now, again, he was tricked.

Leo waited patiently, watching him. Then he said, "Double-click that there—and then give me my change!"

"Here?"

"Right there," Leo said.

Burton did, and quite suddenly all the work Amy had entered and saved came to the screen.

"There," Burton said, proud of himself.

Leo went behind the counter to make his own change, for he was tired of waiting—and in doing so he saw the entry, first Poppy and his lotto number, 3, 5, 8, 19, 29, 31; and then Chapman's name and the lotto ticket number: 5, 7, 14, 20, 31, 45.

"What is this?" Leo said, pointing with his smudged finger at the top left-hand side.

"Lotto," Burton said.

"You sell tickets."

"Yes, and give them to people who had their oil changed."

Leo looked them over, thinking nothing of it, his blunt face impassive.

Then Burton said, "Well, it was the wrong one—for Jim—Mr. Chapman—and it was the wrong number."

Leo didn't think any more about this, and was preparing to leave, lighting a cigarette in the grand dimness of late afternoon, when Burton said, as if he must expostulate because something was bothering him: "I thought they were the winning numbers—but I was wrong—"

"Well, that's a shame," Leo said. "You mean it didn't win anything—that number? My uncle didn't win anything either?" This was in the pedestrian quietude of late afternoon, a moment between two country-bred men standing over a machine that would open the world to them—as if in doing so, the world would be any better.

"No, yer uncle won nothing. Alex told me to forget about Jim's number," Burton said, "and erase it—and put these numbers down instead, so I done so."

"Who's Alex?" Leo asked, though he knew of course.

"Mr. Chapman's nephew. I met him on the beach and told him Mr. Chapman had won a lot of money—and he said he would go and tell him the good news."

"I bet," Bourque said, still not understanding the relevance of these comments.

"Then he come back and said it was the wrong numbers."

"Oh," Bourque said, catching his breath.

"But they were in the paper—"

"What was?"

"The numbers that I had written down before," Burton said. "They was in the paper as the winning numbers. Alex Chapman said to forget about it—and showed me the real ticket. So I erased them—and put these here."

"Alex showed you a ticket that didn't match."

"It didn't."

"And you thought Jim had the matching numbers?"

"For a while I did—I was sure he did for a while."

"Well that's too bad," Leo said to his childlike friend. "And what were the real numbers—I mean the winning numbers, what were they?"

"I forget by now," Burton said with immaculate arrogance.

Bourque opened the door to leave, but came back in.

"How much was a lotto like that worth—a few thousand maybe?"

"Oh—not so much—I heard thirteen million."

"Imagine to miss out on it," Leo smiled. "Old Jim hisself never said anything about it?"

"No."

"And Alex brought you his ticket?"

"Yes."

"And have you heard who won it? It must have come out who won it?"

"Of course not likely—" Burton said angrily. "And Mr. Chapman's gone fishing—he came in here to get leader before he left."

"I see," Leo said.

Bourque then left to go downriver to his small shed where there was a half quart of wine hidden under a plank. Wine on a hot day gave you a particular kind of drunk. He passed the old Chapman house, with his eye cast warily toward a window, door. Warily on this late hot day (the second day of Alex's search), he saw Alex Chapman leave by the side door and then move away into the back lots. Bourque watched him go, until one could only see his hair sticking up above the small reddish alders. Quite suddenly Leo was interested in the world again. Quite suddenly all his suffering seemed to be worth it once again. Of course he was furious with Alex Chapman, and why not? This man who he tried to emulate only thought he was superior to him, and had delivered a great blow against him, and then just walked away, impartial and imperial. Did he know that Bourque had taken night school in order to be more like Alex Chapman? And that even after all of that he was still called "right wing"?

No, but one must realize, that was long ago.

=

LEO BOURQUE WAS ALMOST LOST AT SEA AFTER THE BLESSING of the fleet. Much like Ishmael, he had hugged a board. The rest of the crew, kind Eugene Gallant included, was lost. A day and a half he was tossed in the Strait. At one moment he was sure he had seen the great fin of a huge shark rise out of the water and come toward him, then veer away when Leo slapped the water with his hands. He had bad dreams about this every night. He could not stand to go onto a wharf, and he'd never been on a boat again. If he smelled a herring it would make him sick. His wife had been able to relieve that pain, but now she was gone, and the steady numbing nightmare returned. Of course he had treated his wife badly, but he had not meant to. That is all he could say. Many nights he wished he could go to sleep and not wake again. He was actually the person Alex at one time had wanted to be, and Alex was much like the person Bourque had dreamed of being but could not become.

Yet over the last twenty-four hours Leo realized why he had lived. It was to obtain this ticket. What infuriated him was this. He had asked Alex for $500 to pay some bills, and was feeling guilty about it, whereas Alex—Alex, who he had tried to emulate—was after thirteen million, and had tricked poor old Burton Tucker, the least of all men!

Nothing made Bourque more conscious of his own gullibility than this. That is, he seemed to know immediately that the world did not care who became rich or who did not, who became success-ful or who did not.

Bourque looked for and found the numbers in the old paper at his uncle's, and stared at them. He couldn't take his mind off them: 11, 17, 22, 26, 37, 41.

As he drank, it came to him in a moment of blinding recog-nition. Think of how much more he could get from Alex if he played his cards right. Maybe they could share it! Did he want to share it or just take a million or so? And did he think really that Alex was in fact searching for this ticket? He pondered all of this, and decided that he would have to try, at least try to find out the truth. Then he decided that he would be culpable if he did not try, for the very reason he had learned of this was to benefit himself.

He walked back up the lonely highway and watched the old Chapman house all night—but was too frightened to go to the door himself. Finally, at about three in the morning, it colder than he wanted, he lay in the grass near the highway and slept.

At mid-morning, he saw Alex sneak up from the lighthouse, through the old lots, and into the house. Alex passed by so close he might have touched Leo. Bourque woke with his hand lying in the grass, and hauled it in quickly as Alex approached. But Alex did not see him as he passed, and went into the back shed and closed the door.

In three hours Alex came back out, and walked back toward his own shed, looking despondent.

So now Leo knew. The ticket was there, and the old man was away, and as long as the old man was away they had a chance.

Bourque had to decide how to treat Alex. It was as if he was talking to a strange being. Someone who read, and knew things Leo never could. And no matter what Alex thought, Bourque was intimidated by him. But Bourque realized he had one "in," so to speak. And that was the bid that Alex had given up and blamed on Sam Patch. This was the terrible secret that he knew. If he could hold this bid over his friend, things would work to his advantage, in a big score as well as a small one. Thinking this, he lay on his bunk in the dark smoking, agonizing over what to do, feeling that his faithless wife would someday envy him.

"If I find the ticket and get the money."

As chance would have it, everything seemed to work his way.

—

FOR BOURQUE, THIS TOO MUST HAVE BEEN AMAZING. THAT is, how easily things happened for his benefit. For once in his life he felt that things he had no control over were happening for him instead of against him.

Bourque had just sat down at the tavern the next evening when Alex Chapman came in. And why was Bourque always there? To escape, yet to play the money machines that he thought he controlled though he lost every night. He was also in such bad shape that people who were his friends now no longer bothered with him, and so he was in the advantageous position of being alone. He fidgeted as Alex came toward him. A deep emptiness flashed through him like a train, because he had no more pills.

But what was more important, at least psychologically, was why Alex Chapman was there. After three days Alex was exhausted from his search and felt he needed help. To quell the urge to ask Minnie for help, he entered to have a drink—time was running out, soon his uncle would be home, and he needed to know what to do! If his uncle came home and found such a thing as this ticket, he would either throw it out or claim it. Either way, this would be very bad. If he told his uncle, it would be worse.

Alex remembered when he came in that he had told Bourque he would meet him here this very night and give him the $500. Now, conscious of this, he decided to ask for another reprieve.

Leo Bourque, finished with the machine, was drinking his first beer at the moment when Alex Chapman entered. Alex sat down three tables away, opened his wallet and took out the dirty, crumpled five-dollar bill, and ordered three drafts. Then, remembering some change, he dug deep in his pocket, and what fell out was a loonie, which spun across the floor. As he ran after it, Leo put his foot on it.

"Tell me what year it was minted, and I'll give it to you," he said.

But he was smiling—and he lifted his muddied and weather-beaten boot. He sniffed, neither here nor there, at his old friend, and said, "Just jokin'."

Alex did not react, or even take time to thank Leo for stopping the runaway coin, but simply picked it up and turned away. He was both frightened and embarrassed. Leo watched him for a minute and then lighted a cigarette. Leo looked at Alex, holding a plastic cigarette box, familiar to anyone who rolls their own or buys native brand, out to his friend.

Alex took the cigarette, and Bourque moved to his table, and there they sat, speaking little as they drank.

"So, do you have the money?"

"What—oh, not yet," Alex said.

Bourque shrugged, but kept his eyes on him.

"You've had some harsh times," Bourque said after a long while. "Many times I thought to myself, Now that Alex Chapman is a nice fellow—but he has an uncle that is miserable. And you were teased a bunch when you were young by some lads who made sport of ya—I remember, on the bus—and it was just because you were a little orphan boy, that was the problem."

Alex nodded, feeling gracious that this man would recognize this fact. There was a particular sense of the lie that intimated Bourque was innocent of the "sport" Alex had been victim of, but if Alex registered this in any way, friendship would no longer be possible. And besides, he had seen this done dozens of times by women and men at the university when they, too, sought advantage. Even in ethics class. He had done it himself, when he spoke in tutorials, and at lectures. He had done it with June Tucker.

All of this was assessed in his mind in a millisecond, now.

"Well, your uncle Poppy was tough on you too," Alex said. He did not know if this was true—he did not know either the door he had just opened a crack. In fact, in this little bar, with the smell of beer and hashish in the air, he did not know how to act. He was that same boy who had sat out in the rain on the day of his party. Everything he had done, was done to escape that woebegone child and get back at his overbearing uncle. The fact was, almost everyone recognized this but himself.

Bourque recognized this most of all. He spoke about his wife and how she had left him, and how he needed to regain his self-respect. How he knew he would get that $500 from Alex any day, as Alex had promised.

"Yes—yes, yes," Alex said, commiserating with him. And he drank.

Alex knew this would not be the way he'd have spoken of this in university. In university, he would say what he had to, about a woman making a break for a happy life and leaving someone as miserable as Bourque. Even if it betrayed and harmed someone like Leo Bourque. But it was to his favor not to say this now.

When Bourque lighted some hash, Alex, who had never tried it in years, had some. It made his head dizzy. He said Alex need not worry about a thing, that he didn't blame him anymore if the blessing of the herring fleet "did not help." Even though he had lived and had spent three days in open water praying, and remembered the holy water splashed on his hands, he did not believe it was those hands that had saved him anymore. He also said he was not going to demand payment—"or anything like that there, anymore."

"Is that so?"

"No, never mind the five hundred—you keep it—I insist." Bourque smiled.

The relief was visible on Alex Chapman's face.

After a bit, Alex ventured to ask why Bourque had been in jail two months ago.

"Oh—you know as much about it as I do. I was always kept in the dark as to why—nor did I ever get a fair trial."

To Leo this was true. For there were so many unfair things done to him, what would it matter if not all things done were unfair?

"I suppose you think I am a big criminal," Leo said.

Alex shook his head and muttered that this was not true, that he always had liked Leo, and that he knew a much bigger criminal.

"A bigger criminal than me wouldn't be hard," Leo smiled. "But who?"

"My uncle," Alex said, in a way he hoped would shock.

"Yer uncle—?"

Suddenly Alex became that foster child once more: "He stole everything off me—and the roadway—you know that, Leo. You know how I tried to get you a job. I was always on your side. Everything was supposed to go to my mother—but he got it all—it's an internecine kind of thing—"

Why did he say this? Did he really believe it? Or could he assume to himself that he believed it for the moment? In fact, he was thinking of his uncle's will. What would happen if he was not in it, and didn't get the ticket?

"Well, why don't you go and take your property back?" Leo asked humbly. "I would if he took it from me!"

"Can't—it's impossible," Alex said.

"Ah, impossible—well nothing is impossible," Leo said. "There is always a way."

"I hope that is true—I hope nothing is impossible—I heard that when I was young, when I did my thesis, that nothing in the world was impossible—"

"Well there you go," Leo said. "You been to university so you should know them things."

Then Alex started to drink his third draft beer. They were silent, and the wind seemed to penetrate the walls of this forlorn little tavern. A minute passed and then ten, and Bourque was silent—staring at his friend, and now and again smoothing his mustache.

"Do you think we'll ever have any money?" Bourque said finally.

"Oh someday, maybe," Alex said.

"Remember when you brought me that bid—do you remember?"

Alex nodded.

"I thought we were set," Bourque added, "I thought I was set for the rest of my life."

"So did I—I thought it would all turn out for us!"

"Well, that bid destroyed my life," Bourque said, moving his hands together and looking out the window. It was true—all of this seemed to happen after that bid. "How do things like this happen?"

"I don't know."

"Are there plans in the world we don't know about, or are we masters of our fate?"

"We are masters of our fate, Leo—each and every one of us—and as long as we acted with this knowledge the world would be much better off. That is why I left the church, that is why there is no God."

Here Bourque nodded. But he said: "Well, if that is true then you knew what would happen to me—that my wife would fall for our boss after I gave the bid. That Cid would lie about the bid, and say it was his ingenuity. And that everything would go against me. That he was trying to seduce her and, with the bid, he managed to."

"I never knew any of that. I thought you would be happy—set for life."

"Yes—of course—well there you have it—I am set for life! You took matters into your own hands, and you must have hoped for a different end. And now, look what happened to me. Without that bid, I wouldn't have been put on the loader, I wouldn't have been let go at work, and lost my wife. But as you say, we are masters of our own fate!"

"But you decided to," Alex said.

"Did you want me to or not?"

Alex did not know whether to nod yes or no. He was silent.

Leo watched him for a moment. Then he said, "You know you were my hero once upon a time. When you talked about all the bad things that happened to the Indians and French."

Alex flushed.

There was another immensely long pause, and Bourque shrugged. Alex had thought the conversation was over when Bourque spoke again: "But if you could set me up for life—if you could—though I am not hoping for it—but if you could—would you? I mean because of the bid. I never told your uncle. Quite the contrary, I kept it to myself, just as the deal said I should do. Now let me think. What if I told him it was you? You would never be able to sit in this tavern again—because so many men were put out of work. You lied and got Sam fired, so even Minnie would never forgive you—nor would you be able to go into your uncle's house."

"I don't go into my uncle's house!" Alex snapped.

"Of course you do—you were there last night, and the day before—I watched you come up from the lighthouse."

"Oh, that—I'm just watching it because he's away."

"It's not any of my business," Bourque said, as if he were giving a reprimand. "But if you could help me get rich—you would?"

Alex shrugged uneasily. The truth was now emerging into something else. Into a trap hidden somewhere behind the smile. Alex began to stare uneasily at his friend and see a different man underneath—the man he had taken to be dull and stupid, because others had, wasn't at all so stupid. The man who had written to him because he had seen his name in the paper—mesmerized by some kind of fame—was much more than Alex assumed, and this startled him suddenly. Alex's own face turned calculating, as it sometimes did behind the desk in his office with an overbearing student. But now he felt a trap set, and maneuvered to get out of it.

"Sure," he said. "I would if I could."

"Are you positive you would if you could—I mean, I am not hoping for it—but if you could make me rich, you would?"

"Yes, of course—for you, yes," Alex said. "I brought you the bid, didn't I?" he countered hopefully.

Bourque looked away, and then looked back quickly and sharply, and with sudden pursed lips moved a stub of paper to the center of the table. "Forget the five hundred dollars," he said, "let's concentrate on this!"

Alex looked down, and said nothing. His face, however, said everything, and all at once. He was thinking of Minnie, and what would happen to him if the betrayal over the bid became known. How would Sam Patch react to him after years and years of being belittled by him?

But all of this was suddenly secondary and nothing seemed to make sense—just the numbers: 11, 17, 22, 26, 37, 41.

"Do you know where they are?" Bourque whispered.

"Know what?" Alex managed.

"Where these numbers are—do you know—what part of the house they are in?"

"I don't have a clue what you are talking about—" Alex said. He shook his head and looked away. His whole body began to tremble.

"But I know what I am talking about," Bourque whispered. "And if I explained now, yelled out that you were the one to give Fouy the bid, you wouldn't get out of this tavern. But should I do that—should I?"

Bourque then acted like he had reconsidered: "Look, all I want is a chance to get my wife back. You need someone to help you—are you going to take it to the lotto yourself—there will be no way they can take it from you? Well, how many people will suspect? How many might suspect already? What about others—what about the fact that you gave Burton a false ticket—who will figure that out and what will happen once they do?"

Alex immediately thought the gods were against him— though he didn't believe in gods of any sort. He remembered Saint Paul speaking to the Greeks about a god unknown. He now thought of Icarus flying far too close to the sun. He suddenly looked crushed, as certain smart men will when faced with unexpected circumstances. But he also remembered this. He knew he had used Leo by giving him the bid. So look what he had created?

"Don't be so alarmed," Bourque said in French. "I can help you find it—and I will take only a part—" Then, realizing the blank stare of the Englishman, he spoke in English: "Don't worry—we will get it together—or I will go now, and wait for a few days until your uncle comes home. If I tell him, I get a finder's fee—maybe, what, a million? If I am wrong about it, so what? I have been wrong before!"

His voice was somehow fierce, because he was thinking of money he couldn't possibly have dreamed of before. Never in his wildest dreams did he ever think of so much to be gained. He shook as he sat there. Just as Alex did. That was comical to anyone who might have noticed them on this warm night. Both of them shaking as they sat drinking a beer.

"Untold wealth," Bourque kept saying, shaking, "untold, untold wealth!"

Then he gave an ultimatum. He told Alex to agree to him having some of the money, or he would go to Old Chapman. "You have a minute to tell me," he said. He spit the words out, his body trembling. Alex couldn't speak. Leo looked at his watch, and suddenly he shoved out his chair. Alex sat mute, his eyes lowered.

Leo got up, finished his beer, and left the tavern, so abruptly that Alex was staggered. He didn't know what to do. So, feeling weak in the legs, he too got up and left.

Leo had almost disappeared down beyond the corner when Alex got out to the road under those terrible waving trees, waving like the trees of his youth.

"I'm telling you the truth—wait up," he said. "I don't know what you are talking about."

"Then why did you bother to follow me?" Bourque said, turning on him. "You do know, and so do I—I will mention it to your uncle in a second, when he comes back. Then, after the finder's fee, I will let people know what you did with the company. Either that or we will get the money together—I have no other choice!" Bourque turned and walked away clumsily.

"Okay—wait—we will be partners," Alex said too hastily.

Bourque kept walking to the corner, swinging his arms dramatically, and then stopped and waited.

As he walked, Alex remembered that for the last few days he had been going over a line of Syrus, the ancient philosopher, that had been attributed to Stalin, or Lenin—he did not know which: "For great good a crime is then virtuous." This is what he was trying to convince himself of as he broke into the house. It was in fact a plausible ethical stance—say, the murder of a tyrant to free people. So from that, couldn't other legitimate stances be taken?

"WE WILL BE PARTNERS, I SAID!"

Suddenly he realized that in order to save himself he had to not only come to grips with this, but convince Bourque not to go for the finder's fee. In fact, the finder's fee was probably easier to go for. So Alex caught up to his friend and tried to talk him out of this.

"There is no need of that," he said. He realized, too, that Bourque at one time had tried to sound and look like him, modeled himself after him. So then, couldn't he control him? He grabbed Bourque by the shirt. "Partners?" Alex said. "Come on—we will find it together?"

"I am not sure; I could just give the information to your uncle—there would be no questions and no trouble, I would demand a million, and that would be that." This in fact would be the most legitimate way to proceed, and both knew it.

But Leo smiled a slightly reconciliatory smile when he said this—thank God.

Alex waited.

"Come on—what a man wouldn't do for thirteen million." Leo smiled. "I mean, I might even kill for thirteen million." And he slapped Alex on the back—a slap that almost took his breath away.

They moved together in the night air, and soft music was heard far off from Amy Patch's room. After ten minutes they came to the main road, their shoes covered in dust and the night still sweet smelling of clover and hay. Once on the highway, Bourque went over everything. The first thing was to make sure the uncle had no knowledge about the ticket.

"Fine—as long as he doesn't know?"

"No—he doesn't know."

"But who will cash this ticket for us, if we get it—"

"I thought I would," Alex said.

Bourque thought a moment and then told him that would be impossible. Too many people would suspect. Alex, in fact, couldn't be seen to have anything to do with it.

"Why?"

"Because of Burton—you told him he was mistaken—he will know. By the way, where did you get the other ticket, was it yours?"

Alex went numb—his lips closed tight and he stared ahead. "No—it was Minnie's," he answered quietly.

"That's a mistake," Bourque said, "so you have to stay out of it."

Alex realized he was right. Leo said nothing for a moment. They looked at each other.

"Well, I am not going to give it to you," Alex said.

"No one asked you to," Bourque answered briskly as they walked, the activity of walking seeming to heighten their drama. "But someone who can get the money for us." He picked a blade of grass and put it in his mouth, chewing upon it as if he was deciding something.

And then Bourque, turning to Alex and grabbing his arm, said, "Of course! My uncle had his oil changed for his sawdust truck—so who would ever know. He could just claim it—Burton wouldn't know either. Once Poppy has it, who is going to question it—a kind old man like that!"

It seemed like an obvious choice. The old uncle. Alex thought for a moment, and he was conscious of some trick coming into play. So he answered, "But that means—I mean, it means you and your uncle will have the damn ticket."

"Don't be silly—you will get your share," Leo answered in a split second, staring at him inquisitively.

The word "share" bothered Alex a very great deal. He did not let on, but he was too bright not to know that this was a signal that meant something had changed in their positions, from the time of the bid. Even from the time they had left the tavern. It was a shifting of circumstance and position, within the tenuous dimensions of their association.

He thought it over as they walked toward his cabin. It was becoming difficult to breathe again, and he was worried about all kinds of things. He had always prided himself on being able to control this fellow. But now? Well, who controlled who?

When they got to his shed, his little garden illuminated in the moonlight, Alex felt his heart thumping wildly. He went into the kitchen and got some water. When he came back, Leo was curled up on the floor, sound asleep. Strangely, there was this: Alex's seven-inch hunting knife on the counter. It was there as if a signal or a warning—or perhaps to tempt Alex to murder. He thought of this. But then how could he? He had been called "a voice crying in the wilderness" by a local reporter who'd liked what he said. Some voice if he went around stabbing Frenchmen.

So he went to bed.

The next morning Alex woke with a start, knowing in his heart he had done and said much too much. He ran into the small living room, sweating and feeble, and found no one there.

He should have killed him.

"For great virtue a great crime might be necessary."

This is what he decided to put faith in now. Still and all, if he played his cards right, what could go wrong?

The only thing amiss was that Bourque had taken Alex's old hunting knife.

=

IT WAS AUGUST 15, THE FEAST OF THE ASSUMPTION. VERY few people in the world might know this. Far, far less would observe it. It was now a few days before the agricultural fair started, where Poppy Bourque sold his lettuce and potatoes, with a big sign that read: Poppy's Radish, Turnip, and Patats!

Amy had been told all her life about the Feast of the Assumption by her mother and father. She came from the store, where she bought a pop and a bag of chips, which she did on Friday nights, and then walked along the beach to see if there were any starfish. There was an east wind now. Across on a flat, near the steps down to the beach, stood the grotto and the Virgin, and Amy Patch walked there and lit one candle, and it, protected from the wind, burned. Her hair was dark and unruly about her ears, her skin smelled of salt and seaweed. She had a tiny mole on the same side of her face as Minnie.

Amy knelt before the Virgin, and looked at the face staring at her: childlike, intense, kind, human. The weather had made it more so in the last five years, and had given it more "truth." The Virgin's right hand was lifted out toward her, as in greeting, her left hand across her heart. The statue had never moved, yet the elements had made her more transfigured than before.

Amy blessed herself, kissed her hand, and touched the Virgin's heart. She was about to leave, and then she turned and came back.

"Do you know what I think," Amy whispered to the Virgin, far away from the steps and in the darkness. "I think old Mr. Chapman has a ticket worth a lot of money and doesn't even know—that's what I think—but if I told Mom that this is what Alex did, she wouldn't believe me. Besides, I don't want to tell on him. It is so strange a thing—I can see his whole brain working away trying to get this money, with no one else knowing! But if I am wrong—what a thing to say! So tell me what to do."

But of course no answer came. Who would believe in virgins anymore, or in God, or in Jesus, Moses, or any other mythology? All had been trampled underfoot by the somewhat smug and pedestrian certainty of modern man.

Man was not powerful? Ha, not a religion in the world man couldn't topple with a shrug! And Amy had seen this shrug among her friends, all dallying toward something else, precocious and certain of their invincibility.

But, as always, that was the way of youth!

=

OVER THE ROOF OF MINNIE'S HOUSE THE RAIN FELL, AND through the woods, where all the paths led to trout pools, the paths of boys and girls, the paths of fairies and hobbits so innocent that, like Amy, their sexuality or desire was never a question until someone commanded that it should be, and beat them down for it, and submitted them to the idea that their human desire was foul, when it was God given and as brilliant as the sun.

There would be no child left in the snow, if as God intended, love and forgiveness were understood. Amy, too, dreamed that night of a boy meeting her in the field where sweet black-eyed Susans waved, and as she lay down her clothes were taken away, until she wore nothing and the sun beat down upon her, and her legs were opened. Who then was this boy she didn't know who came into her dream to strip her naked?

She woke one time to the sound of the raccoon against the window, and fell back to sleep and the dream was gone.

=

THROUGH THE GREAT LONG UNCUT FIELD BEHIND McDurmot's tired old house, and down the church lane, a lone figure stood. Rain sweeping in from the bay fell over the top spire of the church, and he passed by the grotto to see the candle flicker and in the wet, dreary night to smell wax.

Now, after six months in the wilderness, Bourque decided this is how he would proceed. He was now much more resolute in what he had to do. Tragedy allowed his psyche to expand. He would act with decisive strokes and attain all that he sought. He would do it within the next week or two. He would do it for one reason: to get back at his wife who had betrayed him. He would also pay Alex back for having brought him the bid.

This, to him, was a betrayal of his whole life, and he could not let it rest. He had never hurt his wife, had loved her, and he was gullible enough to think that she loved him. So things would have to change, and he knew in his heart that this ticket was the only way to change them.

What would he ever do with Alex, that nephew, the foster child and orphan, who remained his biggest obstacle? Bourque did not know. But his estimation of what he might be able to do had changed from his admiration of that man, and he was fraught with pent-up expectation. The man, with or without his degree, was simply a boy, and Bourque knew he could control him. Now the money was so close, no X factor could make him fail. But what if it did fail? Then what? Well, he must do everything in his power not to have it fail. And he recognized that sooner or later Alex would be a problem. This came to him just as a slight shudder, and he tried to dismiss it; that is, dismiss considering what to do about it now.

He had watched Amy leave the church without much thought of how important she would be in his quest to finally achieve all of this. She was always on the outside, this Amy. And this was significant, too—because she spent much of her time with her cousin Burton. She had one friend, Rory. But everyone said he had gone off with someone else.

Yes, I will have to watch her, he thought. That is, Bourque was suspicious of her because her solitude had made her a companion of a mentally disabled man who had the computer. Amy had no idea of this, of course. Other girls went in twos and threes to the store on Friday night, Amy walked alone, and this had registered on Leo, who was smart enough to know that she might be a problem.

Leo stepped beyond the grotto, picked up a Styrofoam cup half filled with water and threw it in childish glee at the candle. It sputtered and went dead, but as he descended the lonely twisted steps, the candle Amy had lit came to life again and flickered against the dark.

≡

ALEX WAS NOT ASLEEP. HE HAD BUILT A FIRE, AND WAS staring into the dark where his fireplace, still lighted by some embers, burned low. He was shivering, and though not destitute, he felt he was. For he knew he had made a large mistake. How could he have been so foolish? Drink, of course. Even at university—a place where he placed certainty in his morality—he got drunk too easily.

He had trusted the wrong someone, and now that someone was deciding how everything would work. Alex was jealous of this. But he had no strength of character to stop it. This is what his study of ethics did. It challenged him to do better, but he always failed. And he thought this: Leo would search for and find the ticket. It would be over for him, then. He had to stop it—had to, but how?

Then the idea came that all might turn out and that Leo was his friend.

Alex thought of all the past ridicule he had suffered as a boy, after his mother died. And for what? For what reason was so much ridicule heaped upon him? The horrible death of his mother. The taunting of kids on the bus. The failure to win Minnie. The ultimate failure with his doctorate—and his consequential ouster at the university, a place where he had placed all his pride and certitude. All had floundered.

Last year, when he went back to visit an old professor, the man had forgotten his name. But as much as he was terrified of this past coming back to haunt him, as much as he hoped it would not, there was no answer.

Just silence and in the silence the words: You have done what you have done.

That was all. The sum total of all his plans and ambitions came to this sentence: You have done what you have done.

He shivered and tears came to his eyes. For suddenly he thought of the time his uncle bought him a bicycle, and couldn't teach Alex how to ride it because he had never ridden one himself.

"I'm sorry—I was put to work when I was nine," was all he said.

And then once when they were alone not so long ago, just when night was falling, the old man had looked over at him and said, "I'm sorry." Not for anything in particular, but for everything altogether.

There was something else he had seen on the third day when searching his uncle's house. In a drawer in his uncle's room, a dozen or more faded personal ads that had been put into the papers between 1960 and 1965: "Rosa Beth Chapman, traveling or living with son or daughter, or anyone knowing of her whereabouts, please contact James Oliver Chapman, 506-987-9017. Concern for her safety. Reward to be offered." Just as Aunt Muriel had once told him. After Rosa left his uncle had never given up looking for her. Alex had not believed it. At that time he didn't have to.

The personal ads had been stuffed away in an envelope, things that make the heart go weak. There was also something else—it was a bank notice of payment in the amount of $4541.11, the year Old Jim brought him home from the foster home. It was a payment—one time—for Mr. Roach to be out of their life—his son's life—money for nothing, part of the legacy Mr. Roach had connived for. What was worse was the realization that Mr. Roach had taken this money, and never came back. What was worse was the seemingly insignificant amount.

Still, beyond all the rectitude of Muriel, this showed more than anything the old man's troubled love.

≡

THE EMBERS FELL AND THE COALS BRIGHTENED, AND THERE was a knock on the door.

Bourque walked in, and Alex was stunned to discover how short he was. His black eyes were penetrating, however, and matched his toss of black hair and his thick mustache and thicker neck. He sat on the couch and put his right arm around Alex, like a man might with a woman. Alex had once mocked Leo behind his back. He would not dare now. But still and all, might he have to outsmart him?

Leo placed his right arm, which Alex could tell was as strong as an iron bar, over Alex's shoulder and said, "You won't have to worry anymore—and we will figure this all out together—but we have to do it very quickly and get Poppy onside. I think of you as my friend. I always have!"

Alex tried to calm himself, but he could feel his high blood pressure, which caused his legs to ache suddenly. He did not know what to say, and finally said, "It is all a dream—if it was there, I should have found it by now. And I think we should try to tell my uncle about it—he did do some awful kind things for me, you know!"

Leo slapped him on the back of the head. "Not your uncle, no! Trust me! I'll take care of it for you. Later you have your uncle to deal with—now is the time—is *our* time! I've never had my time, now is it!"

"Why can't we tell my uncle?"

"Because it is too late—for you have told me—and have already told Toes." (This was unfortunate Burton's nickname, because of his amputated foot.) "If you go to your uncle, everything will fall apart—he won't give me a cent! That is the position you are in now, so get used to it. Besides, once you have the money you can be more generous to your old uncle than he would be to you."

Alex was beginning to feel the deep betrayal of his uncle, and the substantial part he had played in his own Aunt Muriel's heartbreak.

Then, after a considerable pause, Leo said, "But I want at least a little bit more."

"More—what do you mean?" Alex asked. In all his travels, in all the time he had spent on the earth, he suddenly realized this was the moment bound to happen. He suddenly felt as if he had joined some other part of the highway—that part his uncle had always fought against—but he couldn't pinpoint exactly what part of the highway he was now being loyal to. Leo, too, after a lifetime of trying hard to please the better angels of his nature had now fallen into somewhere darker than ever before, because of this promised ticket.

Leo, knowing the power of being mysterious, simply said very quietly, "A little more, not much—three quarters."

There was a long pause.

Leo kept his hand on Alex's shoulder and said, "I am willing to take care of it all for you! Burton hasn't caught on, has he—and that's the thing, to keep Burton in the dark—"

"Yes," Alex said, "but I will give you half—no more."

Leo only shrugged.

Alex asked for his pills, in the cupboard, and tried as best he could to look serene, but his heart was pounding, and as always his left arm became weak.

Kill him or it will be a disaster, came a sudden thought. Bourque's back was turned, he was whistling. Still Alex could not.

"Pills," Bourque said, "poor little fella—you on pills—on the pills." And he brought the pills over to his friend. "Don't die on us yet," he said, smiling.

Alex shuddered, took two pills with some water, and sat at the table trying to catch his breath, while Leo stood over him, hand on his shoulder. He could smell the damp evening air.

"A bit of asthma," Alex said.

"It's all this weather and chemicals in the air," Leo said sympathetically. "It's the government—we should have a revolution. Something like in Cuba."

"That's exactly what I said for years," Alex commented. "That was the whole purpose of my doctorate. I wanted an ethical revolution—one that brought us all together."

"Yes, well that's what we will have—a big friendly revolution, starting tonight!" And Bourque tossed Alex's orange hair with his big friendly hand.

Alex found it hard to breathe again. Staring at this man, he knew if he did or did not do anything, helped or not helped, it no longer mattered, because the lie he invested in was already out, and this man had taken flight into dreams of wealth and power.

He stared in astonishment as Leo spoke about the ticket, about what he would do when he got it. That he would "put a few things to rest, let me tell you."

He spoke like a man who had been tormented all his life and was now willing to get back at everyone.

"Sooner or later I knew it would come my way," he said.

How could this be happening? Leo stood, short, blunt, with an impassive jovial face. The one who had written Alex as a schoolboy.

That friend from his past Alex had boldly demanded had come back.

ALEX HAD THOUGHT THAT WHO WOULD COME BACK WERE the friends he so desired to have near, those boys and girls all practiced in the art of easy common-room revolution, piqued and galled, protected, ineffectual and cowardly. The ones he could easily impress with progressive thought.

But someone else had returned. That erstwhile right winger into his left-wing world. He'd returned and was deciding in quick measure what direction Alex's life should now take. Alex realized the great respect this man had for him, and would continue to have for him—as long as he performed the way this man believed he should. But wasn't that like his friends in the common room as well?

Leo was curious about Alex now. "All that learning and after the same thing I am," he said. He smiled roughly wondering about this.

And Alex didn't like his look, or his wondering.

"I am going over to your uncle's and find the ticket."

"When, now—tonight?"

"No, tomorrow afternoon—of course tonight—why not tonight! Your uncle might be back tomorrow—"

"Well don't touch anything else!"

Bourque turned at the door, and a look of displeasure at this command crossed his face, and then he shrugged.

ALEX STARED AT THE DOOR LONG, LONG AFTER THE MAN had gone. He thought of sin, and himself as a child. How he worried about sin in the priesthood, and how he combated the idea of any sin in university among the professorial. To believe there was sin was to conjure up forgiveness—which he refused to do. Approval or disapproval was better. One might say the priests themselves instigated this with their demonic irrelevance in the modern world, and how everything to some of them was a sin.

He did not know that Amy now lived her life in constant worry about Fanny Groat who was dying, about Burton who was teased, and that the money he had promised her was to be given all away, to help get Fanny Groat a bed at the senior citizens' home.

He did not know that she believed him, and wanted to like him. Would he then approve or disapprove?

"I need the ticket—and I will do whatever it takes to get it," he decided again.

He followed Leo Bourque into the dark, across the wet field, and stopped dead, looking up at the windows of the house. There, from his vantage point, he could see a small flashlight zigzag crazily against the inside night, spraying the walls and certain curtains, illuminating for a second some artifact Alex had long held in private affection. For some reason this horrified him, and he could not move—as that flashlight moved, from one dark room to the next, and then up the long dark stairs.

Alex watched, then remembering the money his uncle had written to Mr. Roach, the messages he had placed in the papers looking for Alex's mother, he was unable to come to terms with his betrayal, and turned and went home.

Bourque stayed in Chapman's house another hour, searching every room. He tried to be calm but he left much on the dull hardwood floors. Agitated and sweating he moved to the last few rooms on the third floor. There he paused and lit a cigarette. For five minutes he conjured up visions of the ticket and tried to remain calm.

I will find it—and no one will get it before I do, he thought.

When he entered the last small room upstairs, Alex's, the moon was just coming out—the rain had stopped, and light glowed on the top of the truck and made it shimmer. He saw all of this in a daze because of his long hard day—but again the truck, parked behind the house and up against the willows at the edge of the property, struck him. He glanced up at the moon, and decided to leave. Then, quite suddenly, he was sure he knew where the ticket must be.

He turned and headed back toward Alex's. He was sorry that Alex was mixed up in this, and wondered if there was any way to keep him quiet if he found the ticket and did not want to share it. But this was a fleeting thought.

"For now it is better if we share—for it will be one less person

THE LOST HIGHWAY 173

to worry about—later—later we will see." He could not help but think this, even though he did not take it seriously. Of course he would give Alex his share, even though he still blamed the man for his difficulty. Again something plagued him, and he was uncertain as to exactly what. Then he shivered. Amy Patch.

Leo Bourque crossed over the great desolation and moved under the moon, in the direction of Chapman's little cabin.

He had deduced certain things. Some people would get their noses bent out of joint by this, and he was certain some people would want an investigation. Poppy Bourque, therefore, was the key. Everyone loved him, just as everyone distrusted Jim Chapman. Poppy must cash this out for them—and say nothing about it too!

≡

"WELL THEN WE FIND THE TICKET AND GO OUR SEPARATE ways—"

"Yes," Alex said, "that might be okay."

Bourque had come in without even knocking, and taken wine from the cupboard without even asking, and drank from the bottle without even hesitating. Thus began Alex's true reversal of fortune. Up until this moment, as certain as he said he didn't, he had always felt superior to this man. Now this man ran him, maneuvered him the way he wished.

For the time being, Alex thought now, and he suddenly became animated.

They began to discuss where the ticket might be. Leo was calm as he drank.

"Let's just say I have a firm idea of where it is," Bourque said. "I might be wrong—and if I am we are still flat broke—if I am not wrong, however!"

Bourque talked of his mother, and how she never had a penny and he was doing it for her. That all Poppy Bourque ever had was a pile of sawdust. Tears shimmering in his eyes, he talked about his father and his sister, and his look became fixated, his jaw set. But there was something that Alex could not readily put his finger on. Some self-deception unregistered yet present. For he had felt the same things himself.

"Fine," Alex said, shivering.

Alex had experienced this same feeling in university, this feeling that what was said was not true but elevated to the status of truth by people who hid their own natures from themselves, in a kind of weird juxtaposition between learning and falsehood that they embraced with great connivance, in pleasant clothes.

This, too, was how he felt about Bourque's analogy. There was a lie somewhere. He looked at Bourque and the vague and uneasy familiarity came back. In a fleeting moment, a voice said, "You are going deeper into the abyss and might never return."

Just at this same moment Bourque was speaking about all the people on the lost highway who he loved. In fact, he seemed to love everyone at that moment.

He spoke of his wife and said, "Yes, what could she do once I started taking pills—I was a mess. So she went out and got fucked by someone else, does that matter?" The way he said it showed he was trying to force himself to disregard it but could not.

Alex, though, was aware of this voice, this small authoritative warning from his mother: "Stop now."

When Bourque simply said, "Well let's go get this ticket—and no more fooling about."

"What do you want to do, search the house again—?"

"Not on your life," Bourque said, sniffing and smiling.

"Well, where?"

There was a pause and then Bourque smiled, as if he had just thought of something. "Will you give me an extra million or two if I get you this ticket right now?"

Alex did not know if he was serious. "What do you mean—if you have it you better tell me," Alex said, perhaps for the first time in his life asserting himself in front of a grown man. He was angry now, furious at this cat and mouse and also at this awful assumption Mr. Bourque had, that he could play this cat and mouse with his uncle's ticket, and that Alex wouldn't mind this horrible disregard of the Chapman family. Alex was also furious with himself for allowing this.

"Oh I will tell you," Bourque said, "and I will give it to you tonight—but I want an extra million out of your end to give to my uncle, for he is the key here. He must claim the ticket. We might have a problem if either of us did it—but we'll say it is his—he got his oil changed in his old sawdust truck at the same time. Well, how do tickets get mixed up when you have a retard like Burton. Once he has it, he has it, and no one will say nothing—"

Alex was silent. Then: "I don't want all my money taken away—in fact it was my idea—"

"But it is not your ticket—and I know where it is. It will still leave you with five million."

"Five!"

"I will get six—a finder's fee—since I know where it is—and my uncle gets two—he was going to get one anyway, but now he gets two—two is the amount. If we give him two it will shut him up—he is a wonderful man but he is a blabbermouth. Just a sawdust truck-driving fucker."

"Well what about my uncle—?"

"Your uncle is your problem—I want nothing to do with your uncle," Bourque said emphatically.

There was a long and desperate pause as Alex tried to calculate what he could not, with Bourque staring at him.

"What have you decided?"

"I have decided we will do it tomorrow—"

"Tomorrow might be too late."

"Tomorrow," Alex said, for some reason.

Doing it "tomorrow" instead of "tonight" would change their lives forever.

≡

WEDNESDAY AND SATURDAY NIGHTS AMY TOOK A COURSE
on Saint Mark at the church. So she would have to leave home
after supper and make her way down the road and along the
highway, with the sky clear and the distant stars steady and the
dull chunks of sawdust off old Poppy Bourque's truck, which
had small bits of shiny crystal in them, under her feet. He had,
that old man, loved Minnie's mother for years and she did not
love him back. He had waited for her but she had not. They said
he once bought her a diamond ring, and when she refused it he
threw it into the dirt on the Gum Road. To this day kids still
looked for that ring when they walked it. The only thing that
seemed to be left of this memory was his sawdust tracks on the
road.

As always people divide these journeys into sections, so did
Amy. The long section was from the point of Old Chapman's house
down the steep grade to the church lane. Here, if she was late, she
would leave the highway and walk through the junkyard, coming
out on Chapman's lane, then walking below Young Chapman's cottage and along the windswept beach, up the steps, and into the
church vestry, where chairs were set in a semicircle and a pot of tea
was brewing. It saved about ten minutes.

This, in fact, was her last night, the course finally coming to
an end.

Almost everyone at this study—from Irene McDurmot to
Betty and Lorne Everette—were senior citizens, some nearly
eighty, and Amy a fifteen-year-old girl sitting among them, wondering what she was doing here. She had come in here one night, to
sit in a pew. It was mainly just to get out of the rain for a time. But
people were sitting down in the vestry, and Father MacIlvoy beckoned loudly through the open door: "Well I'm glad some young
people still think this is great fun." And waved her in, before she
had a chance to close the big church door and escape.

When she entered, the door closed with a thud behind her, and the smell of oak and burning candles encompassed her, and she was trapped. So she signed up for a course on Saint Mark, who she decided, now that it was all coming to an end, was the practical saint among the four gospel writers. Yet whose message to her was not one of the law, but one of the spirit of the law. And the priest MacIlvoy seemed to embody this as well. Well, she had a crush on MacIlvoy because he was so kind, and that's why she couldn't say no to the course. He had been a tough boy, a good hockey player, and at one time a delinquent—or so was said. But something had happened to him, and overnight he had changed. He became a priest, even when the priesthood was being ridiculed and scorned, and seemed to say to one and all: "If it is scorned by so many then it must have some value."

He had come along the year after Father Porier had died, and made a few changes. One was to place the grotto of the Virgin at the front of the church—for it was said that it was to her he prayed after years of defiling her memory.

The way MacIlvoy spoke and what he thought important was not at all the law, even of the church, so much as the spirit of the law. The spirit of the law brokered all others, and made all law, in the end, insignificant. This is what so many parables, like the one about the good samaritan, stated, and the wind that came now and again reinforced it. That is, the nature of the law destroyed, and would always destroy, but the spirit of the law liberated you from all and everything. This what she had learned from the course. To the secular world the law mattered very much—for everything was based on approval or disapproval. But there was, MacIlvoy said, another greater law.

And when she realized what the priest said, what Mark was saying, she was staggered by beauty. That a man would write this, and then for two thousand years this would be used against others, and he, that man Mark, and all his brothers would be ridiculed and what they said cheapened. If this was the case, the world was doomed. She saw the grand dance of the world very much before her eyes this night.

Saint Mark's was of course a dangerous idea, a very bold one. Yet it was not thought about as bold or dangerous anymore, for those who promoted it seemed stymied and timid. Yet they had carried this message for two thousand years: That you could find freedom and ecstatic joy even when bound by a wheelchair.

This is what the spirit of the law not only allowed but requested people do. This is what MacIlvoy tried his best to instill in them. He was a very plain speaker, but one who was very comfortable with the things he said.

Tonight, listening to him, Amy's idea of life was an inextinguishable lamp of joy, and inside, beyond all the confusion of her mother and father, who did not love each other enough, and all the problems with money, and the problems besides of all and everything, hers was an inexplicable love of life told to her from some living word. Word that was as true as water in the earth springing forth to quench her soul at the lower end of Glidden's pool. As she listened to MacIlvoy read these words, she felt almost disembodied, and a part of the greater universe—but a universe not of form or substance but substantial and formless, vast as the creator.

Among old and young, when the recesses of the vestry were cast in dark and the walls were lighted far away with candles, the message of Mark, read by MacIlvoy, stirred in her this wonder of some great "other" meaning for herself and the rest of mankind, a meaning caught in erstwhile glimpse of a greater wonder than could ever be known. And she had not even known the course was going to take place until she had stumbled into the room to rest out of the spitting rain.

Now, she stared at Irene McDurmot's hands, and realized the difficulty of the journey—for Irene's journey was almost over, and yet still it was one that saw at moments the true and utter majesty of the world, even though now her head nodded, and she was asleep, and except for the wrinkles of her face like a child. One of the youngsters kicked Amy's foot and winked when Irene's head fell forward.

But Amy did not stir. Irene—to her, at this moment, and having known something of her life—was a great lady, and no kick would do for laughter. She was transfixed. The difficulty of the journey made it spellbinding, the glow along the old walls increased the message.

"Christ is with you," MacIlvoy said, and he touched her forehead and made the sign of the cross.

That alone, she thought at this moment, was greater than every bomb and torture man had ever devised.

"Whenever two of you meet in my name, I am present with you," MacIlvoy whispered.

Her heart beat as soft as the air. The place was serene and still, with worn daily mass missals lying on the far table. For a long while after the session ended she sat where she was, as others moved about her.

She left and walked alone along the beach, a radiant joy in her eyes.

So often the young are given this great gift of the heart in the autumn wind, seen only as spindly-legged children walking home in the cold, but when catching them at a right moment, you see their turbulent faces filled with awe.

As Amy walked up the pathway from the rock-strewn beach, toward the lane, and stepped beyond the first row of small fir trees, toward Chapman's lane, she heard two men arguing. It sounded strange and urgent, like a rustle of leaves—or "rats' feet over glass in our dry cellar." She slowed her walk and listened, curiously hoping for the telltale word, to make everything joyful once more.

"Look," one said, "it is over, leave it go—and you'll see how it all works out—and besides it weren't my fault it was yours! It was your fault too!"

The other, shaking his head, simply was saying, "Oh oh, oh, oh."

"I know, but still—nothing bad has happened at all—in fact, these things are unavoidable in cases like this."

At this moment she stopped in her tracks, then started to back up without even knowing why. But fear welled up in her. As she stumbled, both looked her way. She fell to the ground, but stood immediately and started to brush her slacks off.

"Hello there," Leo Bourque said.

She could just make out his eyes, as penetrating as a beam of light, glancing as he spoke. The other man turned, his own look somehow senile or deranged. He glanced back at her but for the first time did not nod.

"Hello Alex," she said.

She walked by them quickly. Jim Chapman's truck was sideways on the lane, as if its brakes had been jammed on, doors opened and engine running.

When she got to the corner she ran, for some strange reason plagued her heart. Along the highway she did not stop.

Alex saw and heard her as if in a dream. In fact, in the next few days he would not remember meeting her there, until Leo Bourque anxiously told him so. Told him they were looking for a truck. Told him she was the only one who knew.

—

TEN MINUTES BEFORE AMY HAD LEFT HER HOUSE TO WALK to the Saturday course on Saint Mark, old Jim Chapman's truck moved slowly downriver, with Alex driving. It was a strange moment for Alex. He thought fleetingly about it. For all his worldly energy had come to this; the boy who once bullied him was going with him to this rendezvous with the uncle they hoped would help them claim a ticket they had not yet found. Although Bourque, sure of himself, said he would show Alex the ticket that night. They were in the truck of the uncle whom Alex had disowned, after stealing the keys from the house. So the sum total of Alex's life had come to this, and he was the last person to think it would.

Alex Chapman believed that man was the creator of his own destiny. He dressed warmly because of it, made sure he took aspirin and vitamins and blood pressure pills. He had millions of intellectuals who agreed with him; the Canadian broadcast radio defined him and them every day as being the most rational and astute, and even the ones willing to save the world from itself. Politically correct thought abounded. Sanctity of the faith was almost always laughed at. He was devoted especially to the rights of women and the First Nations people. His many articles always said so. He was devoted especially to exposing social ills that others had created. He laughed at all religion as superstition. And if anyone called him on it he said, "I was a priest so I should know." He mocked G.K. Chesterton and C.S. Lewis and applauded Dan Brown.

There was not a moment of grandeur in the common man that could not be turned against the common man for the benefit of some new idea. He had learned at university as much falsehood as anywhere else—and how to give up others at the drop of a hat for personal gain—yet people made thousands and thousands a year clinging to this falsehood. Worse, as a student he had done whatever he could to shock adults—and in some ways he still did. There were always people singled out for blame. And for a few years Alex helped orchestrate this blame. Like his uncle, who he used as a scapegoat a hundred times. At one time other professors were frightened of him, for he might blame them, and so sided with him against those who were too weak or too honorable to side with anyone. The power given to him in small rooms of study was surprising, even to himself.

Knowing Minnie would have heard about his power he could not stop. He loved the idea of being outrageous. Of harming reputations. If he decided they needed to be harmed. That was up to him. In secret he had tried very hard to find the lie in Father MacIlvoy, which would entertain his friends. He did not, but as he said, that meant nothing. MacIlvoy was a priest and therefore culpable. He had been dazzled by his own rise to power within the student activists. He was mesmerized by the idea that he would get a tenure-track job, all the while feigning disinterest, knowing that they couldn't take it from him.

The same Alex who had attempted to disrupt the visit of the prime minister, over funding for the arts, was the Alex who wanted the poetry of a certain student banned for being too white and too male. He knew even as they tried to fire this student from the poetry journal, that the man was a fine and courageous writer. But the truth did not have to be present to pretend you were truthful. That was what masked truth at university. Alex became that man. The one who talked of Buddhism, but dismissed others with a calculating stare if they spoke of Christ. This was the same Alex who had sat in a circle and resigned his position; gave up his position on a point of honor, not knowing others would simply let him do so. That they wanted him gone just as he had distrusted them and wanted them gone. And that no other university in the cloistered Maritimes wanted him either. In fact, while traveling to those places seeking a job, he saw the safe, somewhat intellectually calculating faces he had left at his own, within the atmosphere of brick and brown and the studied aspect of the snow.

Always there were new ideas. It was an acquired taste promulgated at university, soured with cynicism and a feeling of superiority, a class consciousness based on the intellect, not much different in the final analysis than that of Leopold and Loeb. It was a vacuous condition of both men and women, certain of their entitlement. And it had brought him to exactly where he would have been if he had never finished grade 9. So he himself, over all this time, had no say in the matter. So he was not the master of his own fate he had set out to be. Thinking now of himself in his army jacket sitting in the mall, surrounded by his devotees and his protégés, he remembered his vast and rapacious ego, thinking the whole university would come down and his name be heralded. But he was turned on by his own group, betrayed by everyone including himself, and that's why he needed the ticket.

Bourque himself had imagined Alex as a great man who went to university and whose name was in the paper because he wrote articles about the underprivileged. From the time Leo had gone away as a boy he had taken an interest in this fellow he had been on the bus with. But he thought he would never see him again, nor could ever conceive a time when they would be friends. (Though he liked to tell his wife that he knew him. In fact, there was a point when he tried desperately to sound like him.)

Then Alex came back—with the bid. To Bourque, seemingly the impossible happened. And he went and bragged to his wife that Alex Chapman (a man as important as that) needed him. Yet what happened? Leo's life after that moment fell apart. Everything spiraled downhill for a variety of reasons, many of them having to do with the bid. And now this friendship seemed not as blessed as he thought it would be. And only the ticket seemed to him to be its saving grace.

The night was quiet and cooling, and small leaves were just beginning to be tinged with the faintest trace of gold—though Alex knew it would be another month before he would have to burn wood every evening, two months before the first uncertain snowfall, three months before the darkest days of winter. By that time, he decided, he would be in Greece and warm. No one would see him again—and he would bring to himself that quiet and peace he had longed for when he went to first communion with his mother. In those days, far away, in deep old Saint John, peace had seemed possible. What he tried not to think about was that he always remembered the church as being peaceful then, and his life of love and forgiveness, as naive as it was, better than his life of approval and disapproval.

He knew it wasn't, and tried not to be gulled again.

Why didn't she live, his mother, and was it possible that she had died of a broken heart—that in all the topsy-turvy of her life her uncle had been closer to the truth about that older man, that man named Roach, who left her without guilt or consequence?

That the old uncle, as mean as he was, wanted to protect her from a charlatan?

This is what Alex thought of now. And then suddenly of something else.

It was as if once again his mother was directing his thought. Asking him to reconsider.

For his thought was this: If Alex had started out to protect the memory of his mother, he had done a very poor job—for he had used her troubles as an excuse to try to destroy Minnie, who he loved. And he had used the carte blanche of easy and contrived and commercialized feminism to do so. In so much, then, Alex had failed, and he thought of this in a second and he became angry with himself.

You have done what you have done, came the voice, and this angered him more.

Therefore, the ticket was the life vest to the drowning man.

"You said you would show me the ticket," Alex said, trying not to show his impatience but unable to quell the tremor in his voice.

Bourque shrugged, now and then rolling down the window and spitting. All along the way he spoke about Poppy. Bourque would never be worried if Poppy had the ticket. Bourque loved Poppy. Bourque and Poppy were "like that." All of this he spoke with his certain charm that was disarming to a man like Alex.

"Poppy would never betray us, I know," Alex said finally, "even if it was twenty million." (For some reason the larger the amount, the more chance of betrayal—as if thirteen million wasn't enough to betray, but twenty was.)

"If it is where I say it is," Leo said abruptly, "then you will have to admit I am very bright—though I lived in the woods until I was nine and have never got out of school—some said I never sat in a chair until I was seven."

"Well of course I'd admit that—why wouldn't I admit that— I would be the first to admit that."

Bourque looked at Alex a moment, and shrugged as if slightly displeased by something. He was becoming displeased with Alex for the first time in years, he who had tried to emulate Alex at one time.

"Did you have to go to university to admit that I was bright?"

"No."

"Did you have to go to university to think the Indians were okay?"

"No."

"Did you know the band council was upset that you tried to take credit for Chapman Island?"

Alex of course did not know this at all, for the band council never said a thing to him, and there were those on the band council who wanted to use his name against his uncle. Bourque knew all of this—but for the first time he was allowing himself to agree with it.

"I have not had university or even high school. But so many people who have know very little, and that's a fact. Would you say I am smarter than you are?"

"Oh, I don't know—who cares."

"Oh—you care very much—you told my wife she was brighter than I and deserved much better—so I know how you think!"

"Not at all." Alex again trembled. "I never said that."

Of course he had said that. That one night when he heard she was marrying Bourque. Yes, that was exactly what he had said. And of course he didn't believe that a man like Bourque was anywhere near as bright as he was—but he never thought this comment would ever get back to Leo. Alex was the kind of fellow who never thought that Bourque being able to build a car from odds and ends, from used carburetors and cylinder heads, meant that he was bright.

But what would that matter, if they found the ticket?

Bourque said nothing for a while, then added: "You always thought you were much smarter than Sam Patch too." He said this so matter of fact it sounded sad, and filled with an uneasy rural pathos. "And Minnie and me, and my wife. But you will never screw Minnie, as much as you want to."

"I don't want to—never, ever did I say that!"

"Liar," Bourque said under his breath. But there was an added sting, a sadness again. "You wanted to for years and years, but a woman can tell when someone thinks they are better then them!" Then he added: "You didn't have to tell her. I always knew my wife was better than me!"

Then, after a suitable pause, Bourque added: "If the ticket is not where I think it is, we are back to square one—and I will not look for it anymore. I will walk away from it. For it has already given me a different opinion of you, and I am falling into hell. But if it is where I think, it changes everything. It changes our life—it makes me rich." And he rolled down the window again to spit.

"Makes *us* rich," Alex corrected. "So show me where it is—do you already have it in your pocket?"

They turned off on a log road fifty yards upriver from the old uncle's little house, with its sunken back shed and one light on in the hallway. This was the night, Bourque told him, that Poppy was to make his signs for the fair, so he would be up late.

Below this house was the phone booth. It was as if only this phone booth that the French and English both used was in constant communication with some outward spirits in the air. A communal phone booth that had both English and French graffiti, and one scrawled Micmac phrase: "Nitchi Gitch."

Only Bourque knew what it meant: "Suck my cock."

Alex shut off both the lights and the engine, and waited. The wind rocked the cab where they sat. There were perhaps fifty people in the world who would know this old logging road they had turned down, that at one time went down to the spring, which fed the old seminary with water.

"I have to go up there before he goes to bed," Bourque said. "I have to get him at the right time—just when he is finished painting his signs. He might be grumpy if I get him too soon."

"What do you want me to do?" Alex asked. He could see the light—far away in the night—and he wondered why this light provoked the strange feeling in him it did, a sudden profound lone-liness, not for Poppy Bourque but for himself. The shingles were all watered and weathered and brown.

"Do you actually know where the ticket is?"

There was another long silence. Alex was about to ask once more when his partner spoke.

"Ah," Bourque said, "where do you put a ticket you have no interest in—do you even bother to bring it into the house?"

"Why?" Alex asked, as if this was a trick of some kind, and at the end of this long road there was nothing but whimsy from Bourque.

But then Leo added: "I want you to open up the glove compartment, and tell me if you see the ticket."

It caught Alex by surprise, but then in a second he realized this too. Why had he even bothered to go into the house?

=

ALEX OPENED THE GLOVE COMPARTMENT—BY REACHING over Bourque—and there, sitting in Muriel's old knitting basket, was the ticket. It had been there almost a month. No one had thought of it, looked for it, or cared. The numbers were evident upon it when Alex picked it out. But before he even got a chance to look at them, before then, Bourque grabbed the ticket from him. He had to let go, or it would have torn.

"What a row this will cause!" Bourque said. "We should rip it to pieces! Well let me ask you one question—shouldn't we test our goodness and tear it into a hundred and one pieces?"

He said this as if in a trance. At first Alex had laughed but then became uncomfortable. He was uncomfortable because a new Alex was born, one who saw money making himself a powerful man.

Alex asked him to read the numbers back, to make sure they were the right ones, but Bourque simply said, "This will pay her back. I had no money—he had money—what will she do now? I could own him ten times over!"

"Don't think of that now," Alex said, frightened, "there is too much at stake."

"Don't tell me what is at stake—I know what is at stake—do not presume to tell me what is at stake." Bourque finished in French. Then he said, "I am going to lose it—what will I do—"

"Give it to me and I will keep it for us," Alex said.

Bourque looked at him and pushed him back with his hand so Alex banged his head. But then Leo guffawed, and said, "Didn't I say I was brighter than you—?"

"Yes you did," Alex said shaking, "you did—you are the brightest of all the bright men!"

Bourque then sat back in the seat and lit a cigarette, and puffed on it mercilessly, his eyes darting back and forth.

"What do you think?" he asked.

"Go get Poppy." Alex smiled. He was trying to be cautious.

"I don't think I should hand the ticket in myself—but if I did, what would the trouble be—decide now or forever hold your peace—if I handed it in myself and kept the profit, who would be the wiser? Isn't possession nine-tenths of the law?"

"I just think—people might know—"

"The only ones who know are you and I," Leo said suspiciously.

"But there is Burton—so if we get your uncle—it—it shuts Burton up."

"Yes yes, yes, yes, yes—I didn't think of that—yes! Where will I put the ticket?"

"Leave it in the truck with me."

"I have to take it to my uncle—I have to show him—show him what I got—"

"Just ask him, don't get in an argument or anything," Alex cautioned. "It's too important not to alienate him." All of a sudden that was the catch, as slight as it was, that they might do something to sow distrust in the old man. But this thought was fleeting and not taken seriously by either. You could see it in their smiles. Both of them were suddenly robust.

Bourque winked and opened the door. He got out of the truck, walked into the dark, then came back to the driver's side where Alex sat. His face looked terrified.

"I lost the ticket," he said. "It must have fallen—it's not in my pocket—"

"You put it in your zippered pocket," Alex whispered.

Bourque felt inside, and nodded. "Okay," he said. "Be quiet—you'll get your share—I always have to do everything—"

Before Alex could answer, Bourque turned and left, walking pigeon-toed into the dark. After a while Alex began to shiver, half with excitement and half with dread. He waited—then waited again—and longer. He began to fidget, and after a time he got out of the truck and, frightened to go to the house, went to the back of the truck and watched, now and again scratching his head. Then he suddenly broke into a step dance. But then he stopped, as if he were too refined.

About twenty minutes passed. Finally he saw Bourque come down over the hill, and Alex ran and got back into the cab.

He wanted to yell out and shout, but didn't.

There he sat. He kept watching for the door to open. It didn't. But as he turned, he saw Bourque staring in the side window at him, with a look of great suspicion. Alex jumped forward in fright, and then opened the window, but not all the way. He had an inclination to lock the door. Why, he didn't know.

Bourque pointed his finger. "He's coming with us—you let me do the talking—we are taking him for a drink—I haven't told him yet. Do you think everything will turn out okay? I mean, this is for my wife and daughter—nothing can go wrong, I have suffered too much for something to go wrong."

"I know." Alex nodded, and Bourque went to the passenger side and opened the door. Then, after about five minutes, Poppy came walking down the hill, a smile on his face, shaking his head, wearing his faded shirt with the large lobster, all of it covered with paint, and a bit of paint on his right ear.

"I've been painting my signs," he said, getting into the truck. But he declared he was very happy they were going up to Brennen's tavern to have a drink, and he settled back into the middle, look-ing first at one and then the other, his small nose scrubbed so it was shiny (to get the paint off). Poppy was a tiny man, so fit very easily between them. He kept looking from one to the other, smil-ing and watching them both.

It became apparent that he did not know yet about the ticket. Alex looked at Leo and he realized Leo was preparing to tell him, as he turned the truck on. Leo, in fact, was shaking. The lights shone on a large pile of sawdust old Poppy Bourque had placed there, in the center of the old side road. Poppy grinned sheepishly because he knew he wasn't allowed to do so—but he had to have the truck free of sawdust to load his vegetables.

=

IN A WAY THEY SEEMED TENSE, IN ANOTHER THEY WERE like two boys filled with bravado after having a drink. And this is how Bourque spoke, and this is how Alex reacted. But this bravado was perhaps just part of the reason their junket would fail tonight.

That is, Bourque did not know, and neither did Young Chapman, how immediately Poppy would say no to the scheme once he was told it was a scheme, and once he found out why he was the one to have to take the ticket to Moncton and claim it. At first they did not realize they would have to tell him it wasn't their ticket—but it became apparent that poor Poppy wanted to cele-brate, and he told them the winner should cash the ticket so they wouldn't get in any trouble. But this celebration was the last thing they wanted at the moment.

"No, you can't say a word," Bourque said. And that was Poppy's first inkling that all was not right. Once he decided it was a scheme, he was harder to convince that it wasn't, and that Leo, his nephew, once again was doing something he disapproved of.

"Why not—we're millionaires—why can't I say it? The owner

of the ticket has to appear in public, that's the law—you see, I know because I have been playing for twenty years! So you'll have to tell people sometime. I can't cash it, boys, because it's not my ticket—so take it down yourself."

He said this emphatically. Now that he had said this, they had to press on, for he already knew they had the ticket, and he suspected it wasn't theirs.

So Alex told him that it wasn't their ticket. It was someone else's. But that Poppy should not worry.

"It's mine but its someone else's too," he said.

"Whose?"

"Never mind." Bourque smiled, putting his arm as tight as a python around Poppy's neck.

They said they would do right by this other fellow with a million if Poppy just went along with it and cashed it for them.

Once Alex told him this, Poppy's face became a mass of stubborn wrinkles, and once he began to mull it over, the little man soured on the plan.

"You'll get two million," Bourque said, hugging him.

Poppy shook his head, his nose still shiny from its scrubbing, his ear with a little dab of paint. He wanted to know, what were they getting into and why were they doing this? And more importantly, who did the ticket belong to?

"You can't hide this," he said over and over again in French. "Sooner or later someone will know and we will have to go to jail or at least pay everything back and be a laughingstock. But even if we don't it's not the right thing to do."

For ten minutes they tried to convince him. Little by little he became argumentative and said they weren't being honest.

"Honesty has nothing to do with it—it's our ticket," Bourque said.

"If you found it on the road I would say yes, but if you took it from someone else—I would say no!"

"Well we found it on the road!" Alex said.

"No you didn't—or you would have already told me, and

anyway you would have cashed it yourself—you want me to cash it so people won't suspect."

"You are being very silly. Two million is staring you in the face!" Alex said.

Poppy shrugged and said he wanted to go home.

"Don't you say another word, Poppy," Leo kept saying, "or you won't get your million."

"But I don't want a million if it isn't mine," he replied.

"But it will be just like saying it is yours," Alex said, "so there is no problem."

Poppy looked at Alex quickly, with a sudden unfamiliar expression, for he hardly knew him, and who was this pipsqueak to give him orders? Then he turned and softly spoke in French to Bourque. Bourque could not convince him that this was for the best.

They had no idea he would say no, so emphatically. But once he did, something more tragic became apparent. It was this: They could not let him go home and keep the ticket for themselves. He would tell on them. So they had to convince him not to tell. And Alex pulled off on a side road.

"You can't tell anyone."

"I never said I would," Poppy answered.

But this was the problem: The more they spoke to him the more insane both of them seemed, Alex shouting in English and Bourque shouting in French, Alex slapping the steering wheel and Bourque banging his fist.

"You are making it all too complicated," Alex said. "It was supposed to be easy!"

Little Poppy sat with his arms folded, staring glumly straight ahead.

"Take me back home," he said. "I have to finish my signs—I don't want a beer."

And he said this glumly and emphatically, and sighed. Then he glanced at them quickly, sneezed, and folded his arms again.

Everyone was silent in the truck, hearing the tick-ticking after the engine shut off. No one spoke for five minutes.

But then, suddenly it dawned on them all at the same instant that they couldn't let him out of the truck until he said yes. Poor Poppy realized this at the same instant they did.

"Yes—okey-dokey—take me home and I will do it tomorrow!"

They were both silent and in deep fear, because by that time neither of them believed him. So Poppy said it again. He said it and also stated that he could walk home, because it wasn't that far. His legs started to tremble.

"Yes," he kept saying, "of course yes, of course yes."

But his legs were trembling so much they didn't believe him.

"You're just saying that now but you don't mean it," Alex said.

"Of course I mean it—I mean it a whole lot—just let me go home."

"Why do you want to know who the ticket belongs to—?"

"It will become known—that's all, boys—and why do I go to mass and take communion, to do something like this?" He told them the scheme would be discovered, and sooner or later they would regret it.

"Communion," Bourque said, slapping Poppy across the head.

Poppy became emotional, and began to plead. Tomorrow he would go to Moncton and cash it. Then he winked and shrugged.

"I have to see to my vegetables," he kept saying. "I don't want to have a drink." No, it was too late to go to Brennen's, he had to see about his vegetables. His dark, arthritic hands fidgeted on his lap as he sat there. "I want to see my nieces," he said. But his nephew kept pleading with him to understand that they couldn't let him go until he promised. So he promised and promised. He asked if they had a bible, and said he would swear on it.

"I don't have any bible!" Alex screamed.

The more Poppy promised, the more they believed he was lying. Then Leo began to beat him to make him promise. He promised and was beaten some more.

"I said I promise—how many times do I have to promise before I want to see my nieces! Stop hitting my ears!"

Alex listened to all of this, and became frightened when Poppy tried to climb over him to get out of the cab.

"Stop him—he is going to run away and tell!" Alex shouted as the little man tried to climb over him. Alex grabbed him by the shirt and held him.

"I want to see my nieces!" he cried, trying to open the door.

Then there was a sound as if air had escaped. Alex did not know that was the sound of a knife going into Old Poppy's lung. Poppy put his hands up and fell back, trying to breathe. He tried to breathe for thirty seconds, his face in agony, and then sat still, in almost the same position he had been in when he was sitting there talking.

"Uh-oh," Bourque said, "we're in trouble."

Alex was trembling. He remembered the lively little man shrugging his shoulders a moment before, his nose shiny, the paint on his ear.

Alex tried to speak but could not. Five minutes passed and neither spoke. Bourque kept nudging Poppy to wake up. But the body did not wake.

"We have to hide the body—no body, no crime—" Leo said finally.

But he himself was not so ruthless, just terrified. Because, he realized, they could not stop now. He had done some things in his life but never anything like this.

"I never believed I could do nothing like this," he said. "That's where the ticket got me!"

But after another long pause he added that all they had done had come to this moment, and in a way could be justified if they just kept going. But that keeping going was imperative to the nature of its justification.

"Well, well, well—we are in a pickle."

For some reason Alex remembered that one day while at the spring to get water, MacIlvoy told him to always remember that if there was a gathering of two or more, in the name of Jesus Christ, then Christ too would be present and ill would never happen. He thought of this when he looked at the faded palms from Palm Sunday made into a cross on his uncle's rear-view mirror. He snapped them away with his hand.

Leo looked at him now and took an instant dislike to who he saw.

"You bastard I should report you to the police for trying to pay me off—who do you think I am—can be bought off—who the fuck are you to decide if or not I can be bought off—that's what my boss thought—he didn't trust me after I brought him the bid."

"Shhh," Alex said.

"I tried to be like you. At one time I thought you were the big cheese. We have to get him somewhere—I don't want to, but God, what else are we going to do now?"

For a long time they said nothing to each other. Then Leo spoke softly.

He was rational. They had shortened the man's life by perhaps a year. But this was for thirteen million. You either went through with this now, or spent the rest of your life in jail. As a matter of fact, jail, he said, was even a better incentive to go through with it, for Bourque said he had been in jail and it had some mean characters.

"Mean—you don't know what mean is—you think your uncle was mean—wait, and you will see what mean is, and what mean can do!"

But after a deliberating silence both realized there was something else wrong. If Bourque took the ticket now, people would assume it was his uncle's—that was the catch now. The ticket would be assumed to be the reason for the death, and this is what reason assumed entirely. People would not understand it was even more complicated than that. So the body had to disappear. Forever.

"I was right," Bourque said, "I should have just cashed it myself. Nothing would have happened, you were the one to talk me out of it—I could have said I found it on the street, they would have to give me something—but no, you talked me out of it." And he stared unpleasantly at Alex. "You have done a lot to me in this life," he said, "and I won't forget it—I won't!"

"I can't do anything—we have to go to the police."

"Don't be absurd. You think your uncle thinks little of you now. Wait until he finds this out! You think Minnie is disappointed in you—wait!"

He then was silent. Now and again he would prop Poppy's head up, to see his eyes and wizened little face, and then drop it again. He was remarkably calm.

"I think he is really dead. Yes sirree. So we have to make sure the body isn't discovered—until—at least until after we get the money. If I have to do it all myself it will cost you another million." He said this not with any great belief that this would sway Alex, but because he felt he had to say it. Saving face was everything now, with this little Alex beside him.

Leo had to wrap his own right hand because it was cut, and he had to speak very moderately about why he did it. He also said Poppy was bothering him, and making him go to the Catholic church, which wasn't right.

"He kept saying it would change my life around—every Sunday he came by to pick me up for mass—every Sunday! He didn't know the pain I was in, to think a simple church could get rid of it. You know what that's like—no, I never liked Poppy."

Then after he settled down he said, "Think of the possibilities, and besides, I did it for you—"

Seeing that Alex was in a terrible state he tried to speak of other things. He spoke of how the moon was nice, as golden as a nugget, and asked Alex if he ever in his life snared rabbits, because he had when he was a boy. Besides, he said, Poppy wouldn't have stopped, he would have keep on until something bad happened. He would have told his nieces, and all of them were little snitches. They all of them walked about the house nosy for the sake of it. Best to get rid of the problem now. He sounded very rational. Perhaps as rational as anyone sounded in the common room in a dispute over world revolution. Those people, too, had lost their moral compass and floundered into middle age. The thing was, though there was uncertainty in his life, Bourque had never imagined himself killing anyone. Alex, who he had first bullied and then tried to emulate, had made him do this.

All this while the little body was propped between them, with the lobster on the T-shirt. Poppy's eyes, half opened, stared straight at Alex. His hands were folded on his lap, and his sneakers had been tied with big bows. It was as if he were about to sing Hank Williams.

When Alex saw his uncle's house he couldn't go in there, so he turned down the next lane, Chapman's lane, and jumped out of the truck and got sick, and Bourque ran and caught up to him. He made sure the body was hidden because the dash light was on. That was fortuitous. They were standing in the lane for three minutes or so before Amy, returning from her course on Saint Mark, came up the shore path in their direction.

"What are we going to do—what are we going to do?"

"I said we would find the ticket," Leo answered, "and we did. We just have to put the body somewhere where it will never be found. He was an old man, maybe he went for a walk and died— that's probably it, you see—so don't blame me. Think of the pressure I was under." Although Bourque had loved Poppy on the way down, now he had turned completely against him.

"I don't want the ticket—how in God's name could one want a ticket after this?" Alex asked.

"But that's totally absurd. Totally. And I will tell you why. Nothing makes any sense unless we use the ticket. Poppy's death is meaningless unless we go out and enjoy ourselves. I assure you this is why I did what I did—for the ticket—and I will do more for the ticket if I have to. If we give the ticket up, the world is absurd— and you can't go through with the least little thing—so answer me—do you want the ticket or not—"

Remembering nothing but the sweet smell of the pine air freshener in the cab and the heavy oppressive sound of Poppy's breath leaving his lungs, Alex turned and staggered away.

But Bourque called him back, and said simply, "In for a penny in for a pound—we have to take care of the body—have to or give me all your millions—remember you are back to six million now—I still get my finder's fee!"

MacIlvoy had told Alex something else that day at the spring. Alex had asked MacIlvoy what had happened to his dreams of playing hockey in Montreal. MacIlvoy had smiled and said, "Want to make God laugh? Tell him your plans."

Strange how soft the night was, and music coming from far across the river for the grand opening of the fair. And what else—yes, yes, yes, the most faint traces of Beethoven's song of joy.

≡

AMY HEARD THE SAME SONG OF JOY AS SHE WAS APPROACHING her house. She was trembling with anxiety.

She woke the next day and, for the first time in her life, felt a sense of dread. What had happened the night before?

Later that day, after she picked blueberries in the field, she heard that Poppy Bourque had disappeared. The first thing she thought of was how coincidental it was to have seen his nephew the night before. Then, standing with a pail of blueberries in her hand, waiting for her mother to come from across the field, a feeling of trepidation suddenly filled her.

Nonsense, she thought, it was nothing!

Alex Chapman was a well-known man all over the river who had done nothing if not treat her kindly.

Why, he was the one who wanted to give them $700. Maybe that's why he put their number on the receipt, to help them get it, who knows!

≡

ALEX DID NOT GO OUT UNTIL THE NEXT EVENING, AND HE crept up to the highway just before sunset. He had not washed in over a week, and he could smell his own sweat permeate the air. He had remembered the loonies in his pocket and was going to buy a small box of tea. With everything he saw, and every car that passed, he felt a kind of physical fault beyond endurance—an almost needlelike shame swept over him.

The little old man who had been painting his signs about his vegetables, the hands folded on the old man's lap, when he finally died, the picture of him Alex once saw, in front of a big heap of sawdust. Or the times he listened when Alex was upset and said: "Don't worry, trust in God and all will work out!"

What god did Poppy trust in, to go for a drink? And yet this is what he thought all day, what Poppy had told him: "Don't worry, trust in God and all will work out!"

It was now coming to the end of summer, and Alex heard from some of the men that Sam Patch was coming back to the river for vacation after a nine-month rotation.

"He'll have nice money," one of them said.

"Damn right," said a second.

"Ahhhh," Alex said bitterly, and he left into the dry dust settled across the parking lot.

Now they all went away to work, for there was nothing here. But Alex's problem had been that he in fact was trained for nothing and he could no more get a good job away than he could here. What could he do? Fix a roof? No. Run a motor? No. Clean an underground skip? But there was something more: he had always thought he was too good for those jobs, and now it was too late. The fact was Patch would bring back money—perhaps as much as $50,000. He would buy the car Minnie wanted, the furniture, and remodel the house.

What could Alex ever do to impress them now unless he stayed the course and cashed the ticket?

If Bourque wanted to impress his wife, who did Alex wish to impress?

He walked along the shoulder of the road with his head down, his little box of tea in his hand. After a time he could hear a truck slowly running along behind him. He turned, and stared. Leo Bourque was driving his old uncle Poppy's truck. When Alex turned, and not until he turned, Leo blew the horn, and Chapman jumped. Bourque pulled alongside and rolled down the window. Sitting beside Leo was his daughter and two little nieces. They were all dressed as big vegetables. They were supposed to go to the fair with Poppy, and stand by his booth as bean sprouts.

"Hello," Leo said. "We're looking for my uncle—you haven't seen him, have you?"

Alex stood on the side of the road, his mouth opened, in a kind of anticipatory agony, with mosquitoes coming up out of the ditch to land on his arms.

Leo said they thought Poppy might have come up here, as he sometimes did.

The little girl, Leo's daughter, Bridgette, smiled, some of her front teeth still missing; the other little girls smiled too, then they all spoke at the same time to Leo in French.

"Shhhh," Leo kept saying in a fatherly way, laughing at their antics. "They say your fly's down," he said.

Alex realized this was true, and that his shirttail was sticking out of it.

"I haven't seen him," Alex managed as he tucked his shirttail back in and zippered the zipper. The little girls started to laugh, grabbing at each other's hands.

"So," Leo said. "If you see him, tell him little Bridgette is waiting." And he winked. Bridgette was his daughter, who now stayed with his sister and her two cousins. She was, or had been, Poppy's favorite, and Bourque himself loved her and wanted only the best for her.

Alex had turned by then and gone into the woods, and at every shadow he pleaded forgiveness.

By the time he got home darkness had settled over the earth— and while he sat at the table wild thoughts came to him: of running up the road to Minnie and telling, or of going to confession. The idea—yes, the terrible idea—that if he confessed he would be free.

As he was thinking this, the telephone rang.

"Guess where I am? I am in Poppy's house—everything looks normal—you must know I am doing things normal. It is normal to look for my uncle, so I came up the road—you must learn to be calm—I can't let Bridgette know anything. I can't—if I have a chance I will do anything to keep her from knowing and get my wife back. So we can be a family again."

There was a long pause.

"Well?"

"Well, what?" Alex asked.

"Do you think I will get my family back with the money?"

"How should I know?"

"Well," Bourque said offhandedly, "let me tell you—if you think it's bad now, my sister is going to go to the police—"

That night she did just that!

≡

So many people believe that we do not want or celebrate murder. In fact, at all times we do. The police themselves need it, and so do lawyers need it, to make cases for or against, and prove themselves out. The papers, too, want and relish it, to make outrage and moral certitude against it. Rumor needs it to be salacious against it, or to have the very idea of salaciousness inform us. And who knew this but those in the twentieth century who used it for their own means and comfort? There was also, and Alex was just beginning to feel this, a certain moral compass attached to the very act. It was a horrible act—unless you discovered that by this act something civil and good might happen that could lessen the act itself or even make it appropriate. Alex knew this is what Leo was saying about shortening Poppy's life by only a year, but for a good reason. He also knew this is what murderers from all over the world said. "For great good a great crime might be necessary."

He also knew that the very ethics course he taught could dispense much intellectual energy discussing it.

By the second evening it was discovered that Poppy Bourque had disappeared into nowhere. The first thing on people's minds was that he had wandered off, that he was acting strangely, that in fact people should have kept an eye upon him for he might have been in the beginning stages of dementia or Alzheimer's, the way he dumped his sawdust. So in some ways it was looked upon as an ordinary event.

Still, it surfaced along the lost highway later that evening that something might be amiss. People spoke of a vendetta—perhaps a retaliation against Poppy for something. Because he had been a troublemaker when young. Still, who could ever have a vendetta now against Poppy Bourque, the little man with the vegetables? It was then that people became helpful to the family, saying they would try their best to find him. By ten that night it was all Leo himself spoke about.

The households on the highway, frightened by this event, were still ecstatic over their late-night conversations. It heightened everything at this time of year. You see, the nights were just starting to cool. So with the coolness came that faint dimension of eroticism. So those along the lost highway wanted scandal. The priest in Barryville wanted it, but did Father MacIlvoy? No, he did not. Again to the little group in his seminar he spoke of crime and how easy it was to justify something you yourself had done. He spoke not of the crime, if it was one, but of those who may have committed it. He said that at this moment they were convincing themselves it was for the best. They would go on trying to do this, he said, because it was the only way to negate what it was they had done. But, he said, they had lessened their own humanity by this venture.

Then he said that if anyone knew anything about this disappearance, perhaps they had better go to Markus Paul. He did not think that Amy was looking at him more intently than anyone else, until September 2. But by then it all had come and gone. The worry had settled on her compassionate, childlike face.

Yet in another way a greater imbalance was taking place. Everyone in some way was celebrating this crime and pretending not to. Father MacIlvoy said this was almost certain to happen. And he was right.

"People will love this, because so many have forsaken what they should love," he said.

Those who did not know the "victim" now said they did. Those who knew him said they knew him better. Acquaintances called him their best friend. Those who had outs with him—those people said they in fact were the ones who tried to protect him. Then the rumor started that his throat was cut, because they had found a knife. Leo Bourque went to see about this knife but was told it was simply a rumor. This rumor among others was the first indication that murder silenced no one and nothing, and that if Leo was suspicious and worried now, just you wait a day, and then two and then three, and that the person he would worry most about, of course, would be his partner in the crime.

But for now Leo simply acted as others did, saying the same things as them.

"It was the Indians down at the old hunting camp—it was that crew," certain people said.

People stared at each other's throats, wondering how easy they were to slice, and felt nauseous over this thought. All played in murder's bloody discourse and found it beneficial, for outrage or some other more venal reason. Even those who were hauled in for questioning puffed out their chests and wallowed in their infamy. For a while. The idea that Poppy had money, and his throat was cut for money, was something not taken seriously—except for the fact that some people could kill over ten dollars.

Of course this talk of murder was vastly premature. And people kept telling each other this. So a search was started, and each hour people were thinking this is the hour he will be found.

=

CONSTABLE MARKUS PAUL, HOWEVER, WAS NO FOOL, YOUNG
as he was, and he believed he had been given a murder to solve.
Rumors started as to who it might or might not be. The rumors
pointed to two men at Fouy Construction who'd had an argument
with the old fellow three days before over sawdust spilling off his
truck onto their car.

"That's the rub," some said.

They were interviewed and said they had nothing to do with it.

Constable Paul found no reason not to believe them, and let
them go. Constable Paul, as young as he was, had his eyes set upon
something: the turn of the wheel in the sawdust, of a truck on a
lane fifty yards from the house, where the old man in his laziness
had dumped some sawdust he was supposed to take upriver. That
was the problem, the old man had made a ton of enemies because
he dumped sawdust all over. He would dump sawdust on your lawn
and then try to steal away before you found out.

So, many people were interviewed.

"Who would kill old Poppy Bourque over dumping some sawdust?" people asked. It was annoying but, in retrospect, it was
endearing. But a truck had turned into this lane and onto a small
pile of sawdust, so the tracks remained—even though two police
cars had thoughtlessly turned there. Markus was trying to piece
the evidence together from this supposed truck. There was no
body to prove anything had ever taken place. But everyone knew it
wasn't the old man's truck there. Rumors soon got out of hand.
Young Markus Paul began to look around for this truck—it might
have been a Ford, it might have been wearing Goodyear tires. It
may have just been two lovers in the night—two kids drinking
their hopes away. Some people were saying it was a gang of criminals looking for drug money—one man said he knew there were
four people involved, that they had been seen on the road for days.
And then, supposedly, there was a woman with them dressed in

leotards, and they said wearing no bra whatsoever. Then there was the idea, and Sergeant Bauer was most interested in this, that at that old hunting camp on the barrens Micmac kids and young white men and women had parties and drugs.

Still, as they questioned people about the old man's impossible crime of dumping little piles of sawdust, the tracks got colder under the seemingly indifferent whitened sky. They searched inch by inch the long swamp behind the spring. Only Markus stubbornly, and many said stupidly, held to the fact that this truck was from the English side of the road, and was the truck they should be searching for.

"I think he went for a walk and got lost in the cedar swamp," Leo said, eating dinner at his sister's. For this is what most of the police themselves thought. All except for that troublemaker Markus Paul.

The little girls went looking for him, by themselves and then in groups, and others too, and then the search and rescue brought a helicopter and a Cessna plane. Dogs came with two RCMP officers. They searched from the cedar swamp to the old spring and back, inch by inch over the bug-fouled swamp. Every time they brought in some new equipment, or used a new tactic, they decided this would be the hour he was found. Bridgette was told to go out on the fringe of the barrens and call his name loudly, in case he was confused. She called his name so loudly she giggled, and then she began to cry.

Then Constable Paul brought one of the German shepherds Poppy's hat, and the dog went immediately along an old track to the pile of sawdust and then wagging its tail to the road. There, in the midst of traffic and heat, it turned in circles with the scent lost.

Constable Paul late on the second day said he believed it was foul play. But some others believed it was all a big stink over nothing. People said he went for a walk and got lost. Others said he had a woman in Quebec that he liked to go and shag.

But Markus Paul knew he had been painting his signs for the fair and seemed to have left the house suddenly.

No body, no proof, and at the small police station Markus Paul was a Micmac man on the highway between the French and English. By the third or fourth day they began to talk against Constable Paul on the road, saying he was trying to make a mountain out of a molehill and over what, a little hill of sawdust. That he was a renegade Micmac for sure, and should be looking to the hunting camp that his grandfather used to own, because that is where the real trouble was.

—

ALEX'S TERROR OVER THOSE HOT LONG DAYS WAS THAT JIM Chapman would come home and figure everything out. Alex stayed in the backroom with a jacket placed over his head and shook as if he was ill, waiting for something. He did not care about the ticket. Many times he ran to the toilet and was sick to his stomach.

But, as luck or fate or chance would have it, Jim Chapman did not return from his fishing trip. No one had paid much attention to this, because of the excitement over Old Poppy, but in fact it was common knowledge and others thought Young Chapman knew. Old Jim had taken a dizzy spell and fallen from the canoe, and gashed his head on a rock the very night Poppy Bourque disappeared. He had forgotten his medicine on the kitchen table. He was taken over the old camp road by Jeep to the hospital in Campbellton. A few days passed and Alex began to have all kinds of worry about what Jim's absence could mean. But then at about ten o'clock on the third day after he was to return, the phone rang. Alex finally picked it up. At first it was very confusing, and Alex thought the hospital was telephoning about Poppy Bourque, saying that he had regained consciousness.

The doctor said Jim needed a pacemaker, and his days of fishing were over.

"He is asking you to come and get him, though I would like him to stay here for another few days. He says he wants to go home."

Jim's fall had kept him unconscious, and when he woke he thought of his nephew. Alex, in trepidation (for some reason), asked to speak to his uncle. When the call went though, the old man spoke in a weak, almost terrified voice. In fact, he didn't seem to remember the argument they'd had over taking the truck for an oil change. He said it would be his last fishing trip. His friend's younger brother had been there and had made fun of him about going bankrupt and losing the bid to a Frenchman. He didn't like being made fun of, and he had gotten lost the first afternoon, trying to find Duggan's pool.

"I've fished up Duggan's pool all me life and couldn't find it."

"I am sorry they laughed at you," Alex said, his hand clutching the receiver.

"And I lost my compass—and now—" Here he was silent, knowing he was talking like a child and not wanting to.

Jim managed to say he had caught a large male salmon, about twenty-nine pounds, and had slipped in the bow of the canoe just after he had landed it. He said he did not want Mr. Lutes's brother to take his fish, and wondered if Alex could sort that out for him.

"He'll take it on me and say he caught it—so go up to the house and see if he has it in the fridge," Jim said.

The truck key was in its usual place, Jim said. "On the key board in the kitchen—if you have to get a key to the outside door, Minnie has the new one—"

Once again he said it would be his last fishing trip—that he got lost, and that he had lost his compass.

"I'm sorry," Alex said again.

That was that. The old man hung up without saying goodbye—but then he never said goodbye to anyone.

Alex sat in his hot room staring out over the trees toward Chapman's Island. For the first time Alex saw this relationship between he and his uncle as a kind of harsh and stupid love. An old man sitting in the office of the foster home with his hat in his hand, proudly saying, "I'll take care of the boy." As if the whole world was or should be interested in this decision. The party he threw for Alex was in fact calculated to show that he as an uncle was to be commended.

Tonight Alex realized things he had not taken the time to think of before. The roadway hated Jim, and Alex had learned to as well— and used the roadway's hatred to exact a victory by taking the bid and blaming it on Sam Patch. He did it with such smugness that suddenly he was overcome by shame. Sometimes, in his old age, Jim looked peevishly out at the world as if bearing in his old soul the hope of a final—not reconciliation, as Alex had once thought— no—more than this—a terrible peevish hope of vindication.

Alex sat in the dark, wondering how to extricate himself from all of this. It was a horrible moment, for he realized he had been cast into the role of a patsy by the universe. Just like everyone else. And that was no fun. He remembered reading about all those men forced into the role of patsy in their lifetimes. He never thought he would be one. But the instant he made the decision to go forward sparing no one in his chance to get the ticket, he had been tricked by his own malfeasance of spirit. He thought he knew how to play out a hand, but all along it was being played out in another way, on him instead of by him. Someone or something else was in charge. Now nothing he could do would change that decision not to tell his uncle about the ticket. That in fact the moment he had asked Burton to walk up those steps was Poppy Bourque's death warrant—no one aware of it. And if he was supposed to be aware and hold his fate in his own hands, which was the idea behind capturing the ticket in the first place, why was he not aware of that?

He decided to go the next day and bring his uncle home, and admit everything. That was the only way to clear it all up. Yes, but what was he clearing up? The death of a man who should have had no reason, ticket or no ticket, to fear anything about him. But now he realized with even more dread that none of this had had to happen.

For the first time in his life, Alex found himself pretending to be human, pretending to act in accordance with human ideals and humanity instead of simply being human. He found that this affected all manner of things: the way tea tasted, the way he walked, the way he could no longer look into a mirror face on. He had become a shadow even to himself, and all, and everything that he had mentioned in his youth now came back like bold writing to torment him.

As a man who did not believe in predetermination, or the laws of luck or chance, things he had no answer for were now happening. There was one more terribly strange sensation—and it hurt like hell. Thinking he must prove to Minnie something that essentially was unprovable, he had longed for her for years. And so he ended up stealing from her, and lying about her husband, to prove his love for her. And how much more would he do to prove love for someone he had never touched? He was a living refutation of Socrates, who blindly believed a wise man could not act against his own interest. (But of course Alex was not wise—or was he?) Now, once again, he was being pushed by events and the ticket, inconsistent in his thinking of how best to extricate himself from this. When just a few days ago he wouldn't have conceived of saying this, he said at this moment: "I will tell Old Jim tomorrow, and we will get out of this together, no matter."

He went to bed longing for clean sheets and an approving stare from someone—say, Amy Patch, or anyone at all.

He woke the next morning, but had a hard time walking to the truck. It seemed to stare at him as if it were living.

The long highway to Campbellton he drove—slowly and then much quicker, given to intemperate swings in his mood, he had no idea if he would make it. At times he pulled over and shook, he felt so terrible; at other times he was overcome with giddy speculation. He could not look at the seat beside him, so frightened he was.

When he arrived, the doctor took him aside and said he felt the old man would be more comfortable staying here, and that as a nephew and only living relative Alex must be aware that Jim had only weeks to live.

Alex, shaken by this news, asked Jim to stay where he was. But the old man said that was ridiculous. The hospital was short of beds—and he wasn't going to spend his last days in a johnny shirt in a hallway. The doctor said they were worried about a drop in blood pressure. What was particularly upsetting to Alex was seeing old men in johnny shirts staring at him from beds, hooked up to IVs—some walking the hallways with IV poles. All of these men looked exactly like little Poppy Bourque. Many of them spoke French, and prattled on, and Alex was confused and then amazed that Jim was answering them in French—that he had spoken French most of his life, something Alex never managed to do.

"Take me home," Old Chapman said to him, waving his trembling hand at nothing. Here was his fishing vest, his fishing rod, a road map, a cracked fly box, his waders covered in dried brown mud. The heavy-set nurse pointed to these with her left hand, as if indicating and even celebrating his demise. The old man's knuckles were blue and protruded from dark wrinkled skin, as if crying out at the end of his life for justice or mercy or both.

On the way home, Jim's voice was tired. He didn't like how Alex drove—too bumpy. And he wanted to know who had been sitting in the middle of the seat.

Alex didn't answer, and as they drove past certain places Jim became more and more giddy and animated. He then told Alex this: This building here, he constructed. That basement there—over there a warehouse—here is where he came to pick up a grader in 1960. When he got back home, Rosa had gone away.

"I never found her again—though I found her boy!"

Jim smiled and stared at Alex for a long time. It was unnerving. And then he said, "This is the road I built in 1955. This is my road. This road we drove when I got you at the foster home. When my search paid off! When I found you and brought you home—"

After a time he was silent. Then he said, "You know something now—you have everything that is mine."

"I don't need it," Alex said.

"Well I'm not asking you if you do—but it's yers—it always was—it was a promise I made to yer dead momma for treating her shabby." He said this weakly, as if to himself.

"It's all I have left."

It was the last thing he said. They were near Tabusintac hill. When Alex turned to look, old Jim Chapman was dead, his eyes glazed, and his hands folded on his lap—exactly like Poppy's had been. In death, Jim Chapman was seeming to tell Alex not to bother admitting what he now knew.

=

THE OLD MAN WAS WAKED IN THE SMALL CHAPEL AT ONE end of the church. It was what Jim had requested, and Alex was happy about this, first because so few came, and second because he could not have people in the old man's house. Nothing had been put straight in it since he and Leo had looked for the ticket, and he was worried someone would think a break-in had occurred.

The chapel was small. It was a closed coffin, with a picture of Jim sitting on it. In happier times it seemed. Fanny Groat was the first at the chapel, with Minnie and Amy. Fanny wore a fox shawl, and with her dyed black hair, her coarse-colored lipstick and her intensely self-absorbed face, she kept asking him questions about so many things that he finally went into the small side room and sat by himself, leaning ahead in his chair as if about to bolt. Burton stood alone with a kind of whimsy, his shadow cast by the light of one electric candle, and then some stragglers came in: some men from work, some women from the Catholic women's league, some old soldiers who seemed happy to see other old soldiers there.

Father MacIlvoy came up to Alex and said, "It comes to us all sooner or later."

A rather stupid saying, Alex decided.

The day was sweet and warm—one thought of a fine harvest—as they lowered the brown coffin into its resting place.

Two of the pallbearers were those rough boys Jim had given the wine to on the day he held the party for Alex. One was bald. The other had ballooned to 270 pounds.

Alex longed to see Minnie alone—but when she came toward him, he turned quickly away, as if he had been scalded, and when he turned back she had gone down the steps of the church. There, as he came down, Amy was walking up. For the first time they looked at each other with a kind of mutual terror that came from a certain hidden knowledge. Amy seemed to be trying to decide what this knowledge was.

She looked away, smiling slightly, and he, feeling he must, patted her shoulder, then rushed toward the long lane to go home.

=

IT WAS TWO HOURS AFTER THE FUNERAL OF JIM CHAPMAN before Leo came out of his old shed, chewing a radish. It had spitted rain a little, the drops falling on the deep dust in the driveway, making deep dark marks in the dust and then drying out, leaving a kind of spotted depth.

He had worked all day quietly in the yard, on the wood. He spoke to no one. He, however, did wave at some cars. At about four in the afternoon Markus Paul arrived in his squad car, after his other work was done, to tell Leo that he believed the search would have to be discontinued, at least discontinued with the assumption that Old Poppy was alive, and might now be continued and scaled back with the certainty that the man was dead. He then took a walk up and down the drive looking, for some reason, at the truck's tire marks.

"Dead—that's bad news," Leo said. They conversed in French—for Markus Paul was trilingual, knowing his own Micmac, French, and English.

"It will break the little girls' hearts," Leo said with certainty. "I will go out tonight and start the search again."

"Where would you go?" Markus asked, by way of asking.

"Perhaps, who knows, he took a walk on the highway and was hit by a truck—sometimes that happens and they don't report it."

"Well, that's true enough," Markus said. "He could be somewhere along a ditch, the poor old man. These are tire marks from Poppy's truck?"

Bourque nodded. "Why do you want to know?"

"Ah, nothing so much—just interested to know what truck was in that small woods lane." He asked this as an inquiry, and Bourque knew it.

Bourque shrugged.

"Which way," Markus asked, "would he have gone? I mean if he went out for a walk, late at night without his truck?"

"Up or down—one way or the other," Leo sniffed.

"Yes—but for the fact that he was an old man, he might have done so. But I believe—here is what I believe, between you and I, Leo, and keep this in confidence please—I believe he was in for the night, and someone came to his house. I believe they enticed him out for a drink—maybe they had something for him, or wanted him to do something for them. In fact, I have tried to put myself in his shoes. I am an old man in for the night, getting ready for the biggest day of the year. I haven't even finished loading my truck. Why would I expend energy going out? Perhaps I would go out if I knew someone—better yet since I was painting my signs and had no beer in the fridge, for the last bottle was empty with cigarette butts in it, then I might go for a beer—or if someone wanted to celebrate something with me. Someone who said he would come back later and help me get ready. So I am thinking someone French."

"How do you know that?"

"Well, I don't yet. But he spoke to Bridgette at quarter to nine, told her he was painting his signs and for her to get ready to be an ear of corn."

"Does that matter?"

Markus shook his head. "He could not have gone too far in the dark—he didn't take his flashlight. He didn't take his truck. He had no reason to go unless someone offered him a drink. Most of his life he spent alone—most of his visitors, all in the last five years, were Acadian—at least 90 percent of them were."

"Perhaps."

"There is no one nearby who had him over for a drink—I checked—and the first English house is six miles farther upriver. So."

"So."

"So that likely makes the visitor French—but where would they be going to—?"

Leo shrugged, and looked down as if inspecting something.

"Brennen's," Markus Paul said, his face suddenly emptying of gravity and becoming delighted. "What do you think—Brennen's?"

"Why?" Leo asked, his legs buckling just slightly.

"Simply because it is closest—fifteen miles closer than the bar downriver. So say they were on the way to Brennen's."

"Why couldn't they go to the French bar downriver?"

"Well I don't know—you got me there—but a couple of reasons: one, it was late, and they would want to get to the tavern before it closed, they would go to the closest one. He would go if he was told they wouldn't be all night—say, for an hour or so."

Leo shrugged again, turned his head away and immediately scratched his ear—a nervousness not lost on Markus.

"He mightn't have gone with anyone—or if he did he may be somewhere else right now—"

"True enough!"

"So why Brennen's if they were French?" Leo contended.

"Well, French go there," Markus said.

Leo shrugged.

"You go there at times?"

Leo shrugged.

"Or maybe there was someone with them—English guy?" Markus paused, and then nodding at his own answer continued. "You see, an English guy driving; a French guy goes to the door." (Here Markus pivoted on his legs a little to show his theory.)

"They started to take him somewhere. But they didn't make it. No one did—at least no one we can account for—so something happened on the way—"

"That's if any of it happened," Leo said.

"That's right—that's if any of it happened," Markus said, staring at Leo for a long moment. "I know it's far-fetched," he said quietly.

"Did you check the camp where Johnny Proud hangs out?" Leo asked.

"Oh yes—and I will again—it's all still open." He smiled.

"Well that's good," Leo said. "I just hope the old lad comes walking up me drive. I'd certainly give him a big hug!"

"So would I," Markus said.

Markus Paul believed it was murder over something—perhaps money. Probably committed late at night when Poppy was in a truck or fleeing from a truck. He believed Poppy had trusted those he was with. He believed it was two people. He also believed it was a French and an English man traveling together who knew the area. He believed it was an English man driving. All of this was easy for him. Police car tire marks didn't hide the fact that the passenger side of the truck had two people come to it: Poppy and someone else. This in fact was terribly easy for him, even though his colleagues' footprints hampered the evidence.

If it was an English-speaking and a French-speaking man—who were younger than the missing man—the French fellow would probably go to the door; the English man might be the one driving. That, to Markus, meant the truck came from upriver not downriver toward Shippigan or the French villages as Leo believed. He had already thought the truck was from the English side of the phone booth—simply because of where it was parked, on the English side. If it was from the French side, it would have been parked on a lane almost identical down from the house, not up. So all of this was suggested simply by the way the truck's front tires had been positioned on the little pile of sawdust on the old logging lane.

"Of course," Sergeant Bauer said, "that could have happened that morning or the evening before—and it may have been other people entirely."

And all that could be true, if one did not think like Markus Paul.

Markus believed something terrible had happened, and the men had hidden the body. In the last two days, some had wondered why Markus would get the case. People who knew him said wasn't his daddy worse than anyone, and what about his drop-her-pants sister and his renegade cousin Johnny Proud! This is what they were whispering already behind his back, and this is what he already knew. And they had begun to look at the reserve, which rested just in back of Poppy Bourque's, as the place where the real culprit came from.

Markus had searched Poppy's house for the last two days trying to discover something missing people might have wanted, but couldn't. Poppy had almost nothing at all.

After Markus Paul left, Leo sat out in his T-shirt that showed his body to be as strong as iron, and he stared down through the back woods that went for acres, as if he was thinking of something, or remembering something.

"Ah, yes," he said, "yes, well there you go."

How close to solving it Markus had come, just off the top of his head, just by noticing the beer was gone, and the painting was stopped, and the flashlight wasn't taken. How close someone could get to the truth over such incidental things, so Bourque knew they would have to hide the body soon. Far from trying to emulate Alex now, as he did when he was younger and wanted to be educated, he discovered Alex to be a weakling and a vast problem.

The big cheese, he thought, the big cheese!

But he suddenly realized there was a far greater problem, coming like a torpedo into view on the starboard side of his life.

He thought so suddenly of Amy it was physically painful, almost as if she were present beside him. That little girl who once gave him a cupcake she had made in her little girl's oven that Sam had gotten her for Christmas. The girl with the impish smile who could play a guitar as well as anyone he knew.

He remembered that he had stood at the door, and snow fell on the cupcake, and she said, "Oh, I will get you another one." And she ran back into the kitchen in her panties and T-shirt to get another, carefully bringing it to him. But snow fell on that cupcake too. Tears came to her eyes as she stared at the snow on her cupcakes, and she ran to get another.

"Oh my dear I like snow," Leo had said, laughing.

Now, he began to wonder. This was a dangerous moment. For what would happen if she went and told Markus she had seen Alex and him together? That would go a long way to prove the Indian's theory.

But then his thoughts would trail off. It would in a way prove nothing. Best to let it go. Then he thought: she was the only witness who saw them together that night. He was a relative of Poppy Bourque. He had told Sergeant Bauer and everyone who asked him that he was home. If she told people she saw him?

He would have to talk to Alex. To see what Alex would say, and just to see if the theory Alex preached about years ago at university held water. For Alex's was the classic intellectual idea that murder could hold juridical weight in the right circumstances. Alex himself had written an essay about this in the paper years before when he was trying to hold Chapman's Island for the native band.

"What if someone gets hurt?" a reporter with a little mustache and a crooked face had asked Alex, tantalizingly.

"Sometimes a person has to get hurt to understand things must change," Alex had said, born of the knowledge that he himself was almost certain not to be harmed.

Bourque had read it and thought it was very smart at the time, and it lingered in his mind later, when he took the bid to his boss. Now it was playing in his mind again.

But there was something else as well, and it has to be said now. To Bourque, the act of abortion was murder. It didn't obsess him or absorb him—he didn't bother marching against it, or ever think of blowing up clinics—and he knew in his heart that some intellectuals like Alex loved the thought that common, stupid men like Bourque thought this way. So he had kept it to himself much of his life. Still, he wouldn't or couldn't change his mind about the act. That is, he did not mind if people did the act, but he refused to call it anything else but what he considered it was. Do it if you want, but I refuse to legitimize it, he might say.

So this is what he felt Alex had wanted to make legal (for he wrote many times that it should be), and he knew, as did a lot of people his age, why Alex had left the priesthood, and how much he loved Minnie.

This is what "stupid" Bourque was thinking as he sat out on his sawhorse and scratched his arms, and watched as afternoon wore on.

Amy and the fair and the painted sign, and Poppy. All of this now swam in Bourque's mind.

"Loose ends," Leo said, "too many loose ends that I have to take care of all by myself."

He lit a cigarette, and loaded some wood, and crossed the field in the dark, where the east wind howled out like wounded monsters just at dusk.

Yes, he would have to talk to the big cheese soon. He would have to talk to the big cheese tonight.

—

LISTENING TO THE SAME WIND WAS ALEX CHAPMAN, WHO had not eaten in days. He had come back from the funeral, and was still in his suit. He sat in the corner of the largest of the three rooms. His whole world had been turned upside down from the moment he started to look for the ticket.

But most ironic was this: If he had just left things alone, he would have had the property and the ticket, and would now have

been safe and secure for life. In his anguish he had given the ticket
to his worst enemy.

At different points in the day he would remember his
mother's stringy hair, the drab yellow walls, the children crying
out in the apartment behind them, the little girl Pat who he
liked and who he believed he would remain with forever, the
great red dog that scared him (there was a red good dog and a
red bad dog, he remembered), the man who said he knew Miller
Britain. All of this made him cry out: "I have never done anything like that!"

And the answer: You have done what you have done.

He thought of what they should have done and might have
done differently, and came back to the same answer.

Go to the police, he heard.

How could he say anything to the police? What would happen
if he did say something?

Shame, jail, prison, death.

At his uncle's funeral he had listened to the mass in a kind of
anguish. So he had left the church early and far across the lot was
his grotto, its hood covered in falling leaves and a clear blistering
wind coming from off the bay. And just as he was looking in the
Virgin's direction, the sound of "Ave Maria," sung by Pavarotti,
that Jim had requested for his funeral mass, came to him in all its
wonder, as if reaching once again, and once more, and always,
always toward what life is supposed to be.

That old hypocrite, he thought, when he thought of Jim,
screwed every woman he could. Still and all, the song he requested
had no hypocrisy, and perhaps Jim had known this.

Fearing he would collapse, Alex turned as soon as the graveyard prayers were over, and hurried first to the little reception and
then back to his cabin. He hurried, walking alone up the dirt road,
so people watched him go, as if watching a madman.

Of course the house was his now, the debt was paid at death,
and the ticket was actually his as well. His uncle had left him

everything. In fact, he should ask Bourque to give it to him to cash. But no, the idea of Amy knowing something stifled that thought. They could not cash the ticket yet.

He went to his own shed and locked the door.

—
—

ALEX STAYED IN THE SMALL BACK BEDROOM, WITH THE plastic grocery bags over the small window and garbage bags with cans and bottles collected about the room, and hid.

He decided that it was time to go away, anywhere. And he packed his bags, and sat alone by the window. Then he thought that if he left, he left others to that man, Leo Bourque, and he could not do that. Bourque had to go away first. But that was not the only reason. Any sudden movement would turn all eyes upon him, he felt. He had to act natural.

—
—

BOURQUE, TOO, PRETENDED TO HIMSELF HE HAD NOT DONE this. In fact, he had discovered somewhat of an excuse. Poppy had been too friendly to those nieces of his? Well then—he found out, and had to protect them! You don't do that! Anyone could see! How dare he! Bean sprouts, my foot! So this is what he would say if he had to say it, that Poppy was trying things with the girls. But he didn't want to use that judicial plum unless he had to.

Then he turned his thoughts toward Alex, and what must now be done with the body of Poppy Bourque. Just as it is when doing a bad job putting in drywall that you were forced to continue, and make corrections as you went along to mask your mistakes, so too with this. But he was also thinking it wasn't too difficult to see that though Alex had done nothing, Bourque could say that Alex had done everything. That might be his real ticket out of this mess, and over the next few hours he began to slowly formulate Alex's culpability.

For he was too smart not to know that this is exactly what Alex must be doing with him.

One could surmise it was Alex who discovered the ticket, and went alone to Poppy Bourque—he driving his uncle's truck—he using the ticket from Minnie (his lover) to discredit his uncle's ticket to Burton. All of this was a calculation which showed malicious intent. Bourque believed he had enough on Alex now in fact to turn him in. The knife he had used was the hunting knife he took off Alex's table the first morning he woke there.

He went to the phone to call Markus Paul and then reassessed this. No, now was not the time to turn anyone in. Paul would realize in a second they were both involved. He simply must control Alex in order to protect himself, until he got the money.

In reality, Bourque wanted to change, be good like he was when a boy, but was in no position to change right now. He could change only after these things were accomplished. Then he could become a goodwill ambassador for his village. Shake hands, run for mayor. But until such time he had to stay near Alex, the big cheese.

That is, they had been locked in union from the first time Alex had stepped on the school bus. Bourque had started to torment him then as a joke. Then when he reversed his opinion he tried to emulate him, spout big words. Though he was sorry for both these actions, it was too late now to stop.

=

ALEX VOMITED SIX TIMES IN THE TWO HOURS SINCE HE GOT home.

As the day passed by, those who had not betrayed themselves in such a terrifying way went on with their lives. Alex had seen them at the funeral, and he had seen them in the small reception hall later on. He had seen Amy attending to old Irene McDurmot with such care and grace—something in all his life he himself had never been able to do.

"Don't let him get out of the truck!" he remembered yelling to Leo, as he threw up. That is what had caused everything to happen. His panic had caused Leo to panic as well. That split second had dissolved his life into wet ashes. Forever he would taste them. It might have been better not to panic.

It was after ten that night when Bourque arrived. All of a sudden, out of the dark cool night, he was at the door. There was the smell of a shore fire and the wind blew the tops of the old ragged spruce.

"So sorry about yer uncle," Bourque said, holding out his hand.

Alex simply watched Leo as he pulled up a seat.

"Why aren't you back over at your uncle's house—it's yours now," Bourque said.

He said the ticket was in a safe place and they would go down next week and get the money. That would be the best way to proceed. He said he had decided to give Alex his full share since he had been through so much, and justice called out for kindness.

"Now you have to come with me," Bourque said, soothingly. "You were the one who wanted me as a partner; now that I am, you have to help me as a partner would and should—for there is nothing you can do now to separate yourself from me. Once you decided, you decided—and now it is all up in the air. Just think," Bourque said with an almost philosophical seriousness, "if you had waited just a few more days the ticket would have come to you. If you had gone to Jim in the first place it all would have been yours, but," here he shrugged, "you did not—and now you are stuck. That is what is so particular about it, isn't it—that is what is so strange about it. Here people said you knew what you were doing—I used to hear people say that, very much—and it made me want to be like you. I tried to read like you and talk like you, and sometimes when people mentioned your name I would butt in to say I knew you on the bus, and then I tried to protect your reputation. What propelled you to make the biggest mistake?"

Here he continued, again philosophically, "So I have to protect you once more. If you don't do what I say no one will believe you didn't do what I say—for I will bring you down as far as I'm down."

"I don't care what people think of me now," Alex said, his head still lowered, fumbling still with his long thin fingers.

"Of course you do—that's who you are—"

Alex was silent. He felt he did not deserve people saying that to him.

"So come with me now," Bourque shrugged a powerful shrug, "and we will take care of it all together. Forget the old life you had, it is now no longer possible; the life you have now is the only one to concentrate on."

Caught off guard Alex looked up sheepishly, his eyes brimming with tears. "It was all a mistake, so why can't we just admit to it as a mistake and get on with our lives?"

"Quite impossible. We—Markus Paul and I—are looking for my uncle—so I don't know what direction that will lead us, but I am still hoping we find the old fellow safe and sound."

That sounded completely insane, except for one peculiar aspect: Bourque was now aligning himself with those on the outside who did not know anything about the sordidness that had happened.

"Just remember—I am far better at this than you are. Whatever you were better at is no longer able to protect you. What I am better at is what just might see you through."

He got up and left the cabin, and Alex, after a moment, followed.

They went out and down to the beach and walked along the cooling sand. Small waves limped to the shore saturated by seaweed and pebbles, and then drifted back, as if wanting no part of them. The clouds still moved above them, dreamy in August, and the moon shone down on a bit of the bay. They could smell driftwood smoke in the night from a party of boys and girls.

A buoy made an outline in this moonlight, and yet all of this once so mesmerizing to Alex was now a torture. How could living cause so much dread? So much fear in a handful of dust? Alex only wanted to die. In fact, one of the local criminals, after killing an old man, had said, as a way to gain his parole, "I wish I could trade places with him, I cry my little bitty eyes out." What this statement allowed was Alex to feel akin to a great and unwholesome shame.

He was unsure of where they were going, until crossing into the back lot of Chapman's he was suddenly aware. They had placed the body in the old junkyard behind the pilings near the collapsed cinder block—out of sight of the world. The place was a yard or two from where Alex had plodded up to break open the locks and look for the ticket. Only a few flies buzzed there during the funeral, and once when he saw one of the men walking toward the cinder block, he shouted, "No, not that way—go around if you need to get to the road!"

Bourque whispered that they would now take this body and place it somewhere it would never be found. Bourque was certain that this would free them—just a few more hiding places and they would be free. He turned and said to his friend, "Do you believe in Christ?"

"No," Alex said, stopping up right behind him. (He had to say this. Part of him knew it was asked just so he would say no, and in his present state he would be forced to say no, even if Christ himself had asked it. But always there was still an option to break through the cinder block and say, I do believe; even now.)

"Well then," Bourque answered as lightheartedly as he could, "what is there to worry about? This is just men meting out what they must." Leo smoothed his mustache, and smiled slightly.

Alex remembered here a line from Dostoevsky which he hated: "Without Christ in their lives mankind will fail." It was a strange time to think of this line but he could not help thinking of it. He could not get it out of his mind. His head pulsed as if the very moonlight was coming in and out of it.

"Big Cheese," Bourque said, slapping Alex on the back.

"Don't call me Big Cheese anymore," Alex said. It was what certain First Nations men had called him when he went to a band meeting and said he could solve their problems. Like so many professors he believed his one and only way to legitimacy was to posture intimacy with those who had lost everything.

Bourque went with certainty to the old boards behind the cinder blocks and began removing them. The first thing Alex saw in the moonlight was the black sneakers with the big bows. He had tried to put all of this out of his mind. He still in some part of his mind thought of this as a nightmare that he would wake up from. That he would be happy, that he would be safe.

Then when Bourque grabbed the man's shoulders and asked Alex to grab his feet, the sudden smell was so powerful Alex thought he might vomit.

"Now," Bourque said, "can't you tell—we have to bury it—that's the only decent thing to do. That is, now that we are in this position I want to do the decent thing!" He looked with questioning and real sympathy upon Alex.

"Where?" Alex said.

"Where—you haven't figured that out? In with your uncle—of course."

"What?"

"Who in the world would look into a new grave?"

"You can't be serious."

"Of course I am serious—!"

"I won't," Alex stammered.

But Bourque then simply moved away.

"Where are you going?"

"It's no longer my problem—it's on your uncle's land, in your uncle's truck—what in the world have I to do with it?"

He was walking toward the highway with almost carefree exuberance.

"Come back then," Alex said, "come back—but isn't it sacrilegious?"

Leo returned, hands in pockets and shuffling a bit, and shaking his head.

"You see, you are using old ideas—but Poppy needs a resting place too!"

For a moment Alex couldn't move, and then he did so, so quickly bending over to pick up the feet it startled Bourque.

They moved the body slowly out under cover of darkness and through the woods, Leopold Bourque carrying a spade shovel.

Far into the night, until after twelve, they waited for the priest's light to go out, the body stiffened before them, still with the big white bows expertly tied, the eyes still half opened, the matted gray hair covered now with maggots.

Then, struggling, they made it out to the freshly dug grave. In the distance was the grotto, with the candle Amy had lighted, still glowing. When Alex looked up he saw the Virgin's arms reaching out to him just the way he had imagined when he'd wrung it out of his consciousness, as Auguste Rodin must have.

But what was more burdensome was this: He knew of MacIlvoy's tough, tough life, and the so-called "miracle" that had happened to him when he was nineteen. He entered the Holy Cross the year before Alex, just after this so-called miracle.

He remembered Pavarotti's "Ave Maria," as he got on his knees and began to dig with his hands.

"Just a song—the world is sold for a song," Bourque commented when Alex mentioned it.

"Yes, yes, you are right!"

They were hidden by the big white pines that towered over all the other trees here, and they could hear the river sweep beneath them, just as Alex had when he first came here as a little boy. Using the name Chapman, until he realized it was unpopular—and then returning to his name, the name of his father, Roach. Then back to Chapman again, always a lost child searching for who he was. Still, he refused to look into the grave, as if by doing so he would be committing an injustice to the memory of the old man who had fed and clothed him all those years ago.

Almost a sacrilege, if he believed in such a thing.

They placed the body on top of the coffin, and Alex turned his head away.

Bourque informed him that Poppy's family had put up a reward of $500 for information. Well, he said seriously, they could afford no more—and the little girls themselves chipped in with their lemonade and cookie money. This only furthered Alex's feeling of being lost. But he decided that Bourque might be insane.

They went back to the cabin. Bourque then returned to normal conversation. He asked seriously if Alex would take possession of the house, and if he would try to start the construction company—plowing would still garner him some money, and he could build up the business again. He could get a good hay crop in, and use square bales instead of the big circular ones, for farmers liked them better. Besides, clover was in abundance over at Chapman's Island, and he could let Greg Henry's horses graze there.

There was still contracting to be done, but he must have the proper attitude. He must be more compassionate than the old uncle.

"Do it for the people," Bourque said.

But then Bourque stopped smiling. Lighting a cigarette, he spoke of predestination. He said he always had wondered about this idea—and did Alex? He was trying to be philosophical after a long day, like someone might after a hard day in the woods and gathered to camp at night.

"There is no predestination," Alex managed after a long enough pause.

"How can you be so sure? It is just strange that I am at all involved in this," he said, very seriously. "When if you had just been patient it all would have come your way. Say if you had just waited until today—this day—the ticket would have been yours, no one would have cared, and Poppy would still be dumping his sawdust."

His voice inflected a certain blame cast upon his friend. And he continued, not as an adult but now as an adolescent, a boy perhaps fourteen.

"I did not mean to kill him," he said. "He was going to phone your uncle—and I reacted—but you were the one who yelled. So it wouldn't have stopped until I had used the knife. But you see, if

I didn't, if I had used common sense, the ticket would still be yours—all would be solved. So what I am saying now is that your predestination did not have to do with the ticket—but had to do with certain people whose lives are now in danger because of it."

"What people?"

Bourque said nothing for a moment about what people. Bourque however realized that the initial plan had been the best—that is, the ticket should have nothing to do with him. He couldn't simply take the ticket and go to Moncton. It might be discovered that something had gone on between him and Poppy. He reflected upon this almost happily, in a way showing his authority.

"You see, we wanted them to think the ticket was Poppy's. Now they will suspect it was his, and we can't have that—we have to make them think you got it from your uncle. How strange. Everything is exactly the way it should be, except you have put yourself in a cage and have thrown away the key."

Alex listened, and stared strangely at this man who now seemed to control his breathing.

"There is of course another teeny-weeny, small, and insignificant loose end."

"What loose end?" Alex managed.

"Her."

"Who?"

"Amy. She had to come up the lane at that very time—she is the only one who can link us together with the truck. So, I am thinking something must be done!"

"Nothing—nothing more can be done," Alex said. "Not to her."

Bourque lifted his hand. "You don't think I killed someone—well, now you have to. I don't want Bridgette to find out," he said. "First of all, she will run and tell her mom!"

Alex didn't answer.

"It is easy to make it all go away—so there are only the two of us. Besides, drowning in the summer—a girl like her sneaking out at night to swim or see a boy—that's what we'll say happened—you see, it is what happened to Sam Patch's sister fifteen years ago—remember?—well, that's what happens—she'll have gone swimming—I will put a bathing suit on her—and bingo!"

"I won't do anything to her—she can't even swim, the little thing is frightened of water!"

Bourque shrugged. "Even better. If you want anything out of this, you decide—it was you made a mess of it with them!"

He stood. His presence towering over Alex but his voice was very reasonable, and who was he beginning to remind Alex of, with his mustache and his dark, blistering eyes? In some way Bourque had become what Alex had made him. His own portrait of Joseph Stalin, friend of the proletariat, that he once drew on the back of his scribbler when he was taking Russian history in 1982, and writing with faint wisdom against Ronald Reagan.

Bourque turned, his hands quickly waving at something in front of him. Then he turned and came back.

"I am simply saying that without God—or who you think is God—there is no truth, just a series of questions, and that means everything is true and nothing is true. So you have been implicated in a murder I could claim that I myself have had nothing to do with. I have as much of a chance as you to escape penitentiary."

Here he picked up the phone. Bourque seemed to be inflamed by his logic, and was perhaps dedicated to seeing out his threat.

"Put the phone down," Alex said, terrified. "Don't be so crazy—I thought you were logical—"

"I am—I am, at that! Who will ever miss a little girl from the Gum Road!"

Then Bourque took the ticket and gave it to him.

"You're the one who has to keep it," he said.

"What if I tear it up?" Alex asked, taking it, his long white fingers trembling with the pressure of holding it, and smiling with civility at his friend.

Bourque turned. He smiled slightly too. Then he said, "Go on—tear it—we are still in the same predicament! A dead body and a girl who knows we were together!"

Alex could not bring himself to tear the ticket. Yes, if they hadn't murdered he would have torn it—but now that they had murdered for it, how could he bring himself to waste so much money? It would be a waste of Poppy Bourque's life, and Poppy Bourque meant more to him than that!

≈

ALEX STARTED TO WALK THE HIGHWAY AT THREE IN THE morning. He didn't have a clue as to where he was going. But it seemed he was going to Minnie's house, along the old brook, staring at the rapids and the windfalls. What was he thinking of? He was thinking of suicide, of course. He could jump over the Arron Falls bridge, but he was unsure if that would do it. And if he didn't accomplish the job, he would be a cripple going off to jail. He was also thinking of warning Minnie—and telling her to go away. Take Amy away with her. This is what he really hoped to do. But there were other things, and other concerns.

Sam Patch was coming home with a lot of money from the tar sands. This, most of all, was his worry. And caused his great dejection. For after a lifetime of telling himself he wanted Sam to earn a respectable living, now he was jealous and fearful of falling beneath the radar in Minnie's eyes. Of being looked at with pity, as a broke and pitiful intellectual. He could stand anything but that.

He smelled tarpaper and vetch and cattails under the moonlight. Though he tried not to, he thought of all he had done to them. It flooded his mind, that he had not been continent. Amy, who he had wanted not to be born, under the guise of justice. Then he had taken Sam's job away, cut out from under him. Still with the idea that he was on their side. Then he had prepared to steal a ticket and used them to do so. He was even so bloody as to think he would not give them any, unless Minnie swore she would leave Sam Patch. That was at the height of his power, when they were thinking and dreaming of $700 to put Fanny in the home, and he was thinking of $13 million.

Now Amy knew, or she might know.

So what had happened? All that he said he wanted—their liberation and Sam's bounty—was about to come true, while all he secretly wanted—her suffering and Sam's castigation—was about to be overcome by his own destruction and humiliation.

But what had stopped him?

He thought of all of this while staring at this small, battered, innocent house. The house was so innocent because it asked for and expected nothing.

He turned about, and the moon shone down across the laneway, and he started to walk home. At one point he looked to his left and saw the old shed behind Fanny Groat's with the faded white paint still visible that Minnie had written to him one night when they were children.

"Don't you know how I feel, look, the writing is on the wall!"

He was staggered that it was still there.

But as soon as he got to the highway, lights came toward him, and he turned to see the squad car of Markus Paul. He put his head down, thrust his hands in his pockets, and kept walking. The car went by, and then turned at his uncle's lane and came back. It stopped and compelled him to stop as well.

"Hello, sir," Markus said, rolling his window down. "Out for a moonlit walk, are you—?"

"Sure," Alex answered. He tried not to shake. Still, there was a chill in the air, so shaking was okay, even appropriate.

"You're Mr. Chapman."

"Yes, that's me."

"Okay—pleased to meet you finally," Markus said, holding out his hand. "Everyone has heard so much about you over the years. I'm Markus Paul." He said this without indicating that he knew Alex had criticized him in two of his columns in the local paper over the last two years.

But nonetheless, both were silent for just a moment.

"Well then—it's late—have you been out long?" Paul asked.

"Oh, just for a walk."

"Yes—I'm afraid that's what happened to Poppy Bourque— have you seen him in your travels?"

"Who?"

"Old Mr. Bourque—the old gentleman with the sawdust truck. I am afraid he might still be wandering about not knowing where he is."

"No," Alex said. "I tell you I haven't seen him in a year or two."

"Really?"

"Yes—a year or two or three—that's when it was!"

There was a pause.

"Well I'm just driving and hoping—of course you heard he went missing?"

Alex nodded, patted the door, and turned away, saying, "If I do see him, I will call you."

"Yes, you do so." Markus waved.

Alex walked across the gravel as if on eggs, under the moon- light receding to daybreak as time went on.

=

CONSTABLE PAUL WAS ALREADY SO NEAR TO THE ANSWER. He was near to it as he watched Alex Chapman cross the road.

Two men.

English and French?

Who saw any English and French men together over the last week, either in the tavern at Neguac or in Brennen's?

Three men had seen Alex Chapman and Leo Bourque sitting together at Brennen's tavern arguing and shaking. What was strange is that they both were shaking and it was so warm. When was this? Two nights before Poppy's disappearance.

That is, forty-eight hours before the disappearance, they were sitting together. And that is, within forty-eight hours after the disappearance, Markus was almost certain he knew who had committed the crime—that it was most likely on the spur of the moment, but that it was a murder.

Now he had to find out why.

That is what made him drive the highway late at night. He was simply looking, and thinking. This is what made him stop and speak to Alex, his certainty that Alex had helped murder someone. When he watched him cross the road, he was positive.

Someone must have seen them together, sometime on that night. Someone must have seen them in or near the truck.

There was, however, one hitch: Other police officers believed it was someone else, and they knew who. An Indian who was down at Markus Paul's own camp. This is why they believed Markus wanted the investigation to go in another direction.

"If you accuse a French or English guy and it turns out to be someone renegade from your reserve," his superior, Sergeant Bauer, told him, "you are done—you may as well go peeling pulp."

Markus Paul did not have to be told anything so obvious.

═

THOUGH THEY SUDDENLY REALIZED THEY COULD NOT STAND the sight of each other, Bourque came to see Alex again two days later. In fact, Alex had phoned Bourque twice to see where he was but got no answer.

Leo said Markus Paul had been to see him too much.

"Twice in the last day, with his big chubby-cheeked smile on his fat chubby-cheeked face!"

He asked Alex again about the ticket, and again he realized the terrible predicament of not being able to cash it.

But then he came to the real purpose of his visit.

"If this harassment continues, I may have to go to the paper,"
he said, "and give my side of the story." He gave the kind of self-
important look he himself seemed impervious to, which men of
limited experience often do when discussing media.

"In what way?"

"Well I will just say, Many people like Markus Paul think I
killed my uncle, but I had no part in it. I have given to charity
every year since 1979! It is most likely an Indian, you know what
they're like—kill each other all the time!"

"You can't possibly do that—that's the same as admitting it—
no one just walks into the paper and does that. It's like signing a
confession," Alex said. "You'll be on the front page of every paper
in the province!"

"I will?"

"Yes."

"Is that so!"

"Yes."

"You don't say."

"I do say."

"But you wanted to give yourself in as well," Bourque said.

"No I didn't," Alex lied.

"Will we ever get to cash the ticket?" Bourque said specula-
tively, to offset Alex's hysteria and his realization that Alex was, at
least on this point, in the main, right.

"We will cash it next week, as soon as we are sure Amy can
keep her little trap shut," Alex said. "Say, if they go away—if we
can convince them to live somewhere else?"

"You wouldn't be able to stand it if Minnie left!"

"Well I am trying to think of reasonable alternatives!" Alex
yelled.

Bourque shrugged, and sniffed politically at this. "So what do
you think?"

"About what?"

"What should we do about her? Amy!"

"I don't know," Alex said.

Bourque looked at him a long moment. "Well, see what jail actually does to you and your high blood pressure pills!"

Now the beaches were metaphysically changing, so slightly one might not notice it unless one lived here. The sands were slightly harder, the seagulls' cries sharper, the sky was taking on a deeper blue—the edge of the island looked farther away.

"My boy—everyone knows you wanted her gone before," Leo said.

"That's not true," Alex said, his speaking muffled. "I did not want her gone—she was not who I wanted gone. I just did not want another woman to suffer."

"What do you mean by that?"

"I didn't want my Minnie to suffer—my God, she was just a kid—if I couldn't do that for her, what kind of friend would I be?"

Leo contemplated this. Then he continued: "Amy was to be a woman, and she would have suffered—for that little moment when they speared her like a fish." Bourque smiled.

When he said this, Alex again became weak and started to shake.

"Last week if you had asked me what I was up to, I would have told you I was on my way out west to work in the oil patch with Sam Patch, that Sam actually said he could get me hired," Leo said angrily. "What did I have to do this for? Oh Sam, I'll be out sometime but first I have to stick around for a day or two and kill Poppy, and then see to Amy. Then I'll be out. All as I did was go to the tavern, and then to Burton's—and then the numbers—why didn't I just go away? How do these things happen?"

Alex couldn't answer. He was in a daze for a long time, looking down at the floor.

And then struck by this memory, Alex told his friend.

One day the seminarians prayed over a child dying of leukemia. It was a standard practice for them to do this. They all traipsed up like little saints, mobile penitent things, and went into the room. Novices from the convent as well as young men from the Holy Cross, all pretending to be holier than one another, carrying the colors of their special disciplines into the room with them. It was a faded room with two small beds. Plastic sheets covered one of them. The room itself eschewed a kind of indolent mid-afternoon emptiness, a room overcome by bare walls on which small plaques were distributed at certain points.

The mother—heavy, with broad shoulders, and thick legs in torn stockings, smelling of wash—stood at the door looking in as they kneeled about the boy's bed. They were at the child's house up on the highway in his small bedroom. His whole life had been spent there in the opened aired emptiness of that particular room. As they prayed, the child opened his eyes and spoke for the first time in two weeks: "Mom, they are all here."

And the mother said, "Who is all here, sweetheart?"

And the boy said that all his relatives were there. "Uncle Pete and Dora and Uncle John Ross," he said. They were sitting beside the bed, smiling in comfort, ready to take him to heaven. "They are saying they will bring me to heaven today."

And he blessed himself, smiled, folded his hands on his lap, and died. He mentioned Uncle John Ross, who had died thirty-five years before in a hay bailing accident as a man of twenty and was someone the child wouldn't have known. He mentioned Dora, a girl of eight who had died twelve years before John Ross.

"A miracle," one of the novices said, blessing herself, her chubby cheeks red with emotion.

Alex remembered being very confused by all of this.

A bag of the boy's marbles were still sitting on the shelf. And when he had blessed himself, the boy's reflection was strangely caught up in the prism of these marbles. This is what Alex remembered seeing. They prayed the rosary and then they went out into the late sunshine and crossed the road.

The boys in the seminary debated this event for many a day, at first open to it all. But after a time cynicism crept in, even in those studying for the priesthood. And they decided it was a hallucinatory thing, that the boy had mistaken them for his relatives. This was the most obvious explanation. Alex walked in the fields and helped with the one old horse. Then Cid Fouy arrived in his new car, and they all chased it.

Later, some made fun of the novice who had blessed herself when she said it was a miracle. Some even began to make fun of the child, and the mother, and the house itself. There were certain areas of the seminary where silence and obedience were paramount, and it was in these places where they became most giddy.

"Yes," one kept saying, "hallelujah, God just came to New Jersey." (This was the name not of the state but of the small village along the broken highway.)

And once they began to make fun of it, they couldn't stop.

"Next we will see the Shroud of Turin," some said.

Alex was with the intellectuals at the seminary, who often mocked the faith they were embracing and kept it at arm's length. They would look at each other in church and burst out giggling, so four of them were brought before the Monsignor. But it gave them a fine intellectual feeling, because they were studying for the priesthood simply to call it a delusion. Alex, always a questioner, was quite happy to be so, and to make known that he could call a spade a spade. He became a kind of de facto leader of the group of boys who did this.

This moment came back to him now, as if it had happened just an hour ago. The room had been engulfed in sorrow when the child died, and yet the mother, shaken to her foundation, was ecstatic. She wanted to claim it a miracle, and went to the seminary to have the students back her account. But by that time they were skeptical of what they had heard, and wouldn't. Some, one or two, became angry with her. So she was silent in front of their mocking and went away. The child was buried simply, and the mother's belief was strengthened but theirs was not.

Alex told Bourque about this now and Bourque nodded, and said that was not a worry to him. Alex whispered that MacIlvoy, who hadn't been there, still believed in the miracle, and brought it up to him just last year.

"How can he believe when he wasn't present, and I who was present and heard it and saw it and should believe don't?"

But Bourque said that was because Alex knew how to figure things out the right way, and wasn't soft in the head like MacIlvoy.

"I think he got hit one too many times playing hockey!"

Then he flicked some dust off the table as if he was annoyed because Alex's newfound hope rested in something he had supposedly long given up.

"But I have to tell you who is buried on either side of my uncle," Alex insisted. "On one side is that kind, brave little boy (much braver than you or I, Bourque) and on the other is his uncle John Ross—how could this be! That is why I couldn't stay in the cemetery the day of my uncle's funeral, I was too confused."

"Well what do you propose?" Leo said with some measure of annoyance. "Let's pick a book off the shelf and read a line," Bourque said, "any line from a book, and we will do exactly what it says. What do you have, a bible—take a bible—no bible? What's this—*Stalin*—well, who was he, what did he have going on?"

"What did he have going on?" Alex mimicked, his face blushing.

Bourque was furious at this and threw the book toward him. Then he said, "Well the first thing you should do is clean the truck, and things like that—just in case. I would help but I can't."

"What do you mean?"

"I mean if the two of us were seen cleaning the truck it would seem obvious—there's the English and French guy cleaning the truck, I wonder what they are up to!"

Bourque smoothed his hair, lighted another smoke, and took his leave. Still, he was right. How long would it be before they asked about his uncle's truck?

Tomorrow.

Alex ran across the yard as if he was suddenly being chased by the seagulls above him, and moved the truck down toward the kiln, hidden to the road, and began scrubbing the seat later that day. Leo had assured him that Poppy had not bled on the seat, just on the throw blanket over it, which they had discarded along with the body.

But now, even though he was sure he couldn't see it, he knew it was there—spots of blood—yes, perhaps that is what Old Jim saw, before he died. He cleaned the seats and cut a small piece of carpet out of the floor that looked darker than the rest. He scrubbed the vinyl dashboard.

"There, that's better," he kept saying, his teeth chattering, his arms covered in soapsuds.

All the while the wind whistled in from the bay, the trees swayed, and summer was ending. The swaying of the trees now seemed to be so sad, as if when he looked he saw his mother standing under them turning to wave before she left for good. And why would she leave for good if she loved him? Amid all his certainty about the lifelessness of death, which was a big part of his new course on present-day morality, both Muriel and his mother were present with him all that afternoon. They stayed in the trees in the wind, by the branches down the lane, and seemed to be trying to help him in some way.

Then he thought that there was not a day during the fair for the past twenty years that he did not see Old Poppy's truck going by—you could hear it coming a mile or two away.

Strangely and desperately, he missed its sound.

He decided he would change the tires. He would go to Burton's the next afternoon and say he had decided to get the tires on sale. Burton always had a tire sale in the fall. That would be reasonable. No one would have anything to say about it. It was just the nephew coming over to get tires on his uncle's truck, growing a goatee and teaching at the university. Yes, that was it. He believed that Markus was a nice young man, but would not suspect him. He needed to distance himself from Leo. In fact he saw this as the ultimate test, to distance himself from Leo. He had the ticket again, and he could say once he got the tires changed that he had had nothing at all to do with Leo. As a matter of fact, whatever Leo said could be challenged.

Nothing he could do could bring Poppy back to life. He was not the one who had used the knife. In fact, Leo had bullied him into sharing the ticket!

But this is what he now knew. It was his ineffectualness that had caused him to get mixed up with Leo, to become what he had become. It was that same ineffectualness that prepared him for a world in which he didn't belong, and pampered him long and hard into believing he was indispensable to it. That's why he had played with fire over the ticket. He couldn't see his way clear not to be indispensable. How godawful. Worse, he realized, he could not get tires for the truck.

He went back home in a daze.

That night he started to go over the course he had to teach at community college. Yes, as he went over his notes and the texts he was going to tell his students to buy—Cicero, Aristotle, Plato— he realized it was a course where everything he had wanted to say about the crumbling moral structure of those fallen puppet popes could be said.

He had imagined all last spring (from the time her picture was in the paper for her provincial prize for mathematics and history) how he would channel Amy's great intelligence, and how her mother would come to appreciate him. He had even imagined that there might be a showdown of some kind with the school board over this child and how bright she was, and he would take her out of school completely. He imagined sooner or later Amy being influenced by him, and him alone, instead of her father, and leaving the school to be instructed by him. He imagined Minnie coming to thank him, Sam being chagrined, and Minnie saying, "I think I'll stay here the night." And Alex going to get bedding and making her comfortable, like a good friend. Finally, Minnie and Amy would move in with him, and he would have to have a confrontation with Sam. Sam, of course, would hang his head, and say, "I didn't understand!"

This was what he had thought about over the summer, on those walks. That is why he had taken that very walk on the night he met Burton. He was still thinking that Minnie would be his!

This is what he had dreamed of for years. And the worst of it now?

Why, of course, Amy's name was on the student list. With a little note about why she wanted to take the course (all prospective students had to write one) and describing her summer, and the fun she was having, and how she had tamed a skunk, and how she was helping take care of Fanny Groat.

﹅

THEN SOMETHING HAPPENED ON WHICH EVERYTHING ELSE hinged. It was not just the return of the heat, nor the sound of the bells for church. But something else. Yes, the heat was over, except it refused to go. It clung to the late summer foliage, and stated its case among the weeds in the yard. The small garden lay trampled, and yet the tick of insects was still evident among the paling flower beds. There was the pervasiveness of warmth even with the smell of cooling air, and in the evening certain walkers came into billows of warm gusts as they moved along the hidden pathways.

But as forlorn as Alex was, he did not know a cat and mouse game was about to start, which would make the previous days look sublime.

The seventh morning after Poppy Bourque went missing Alex woke to a loud knock on the door. It was the police officer Markus Paul. He stood like a form not quite understood in Alex's consciousness. Why would he be here—what would make him turn up? For a moment Alex did not know if he should open the door.

But he had to.

When Alex opened the door Markus smiled as if they were friends from long ago, and as if the meeting the other night between them had re-established this bond. That was it, the meeting the other night was indispensable, it seemed, to the meeting now. And it was as if this bond, like all bonds between friends, was somehow private and gracious. The smile said all of this in a second. And Markus came in.

"I think we might have an answer to the problem," he said.

"What problem?" Alex asked. It was not yet nine in the morning—and why would a man come to him so early and say I think we have an answer to the problem—as if he had something to do with it? This was indication enough of the peril he was in. Suddenly he was wide awake and quite frightened.

"Oh, we picked someone up last night—who they think might have done something to Poppy."

He looked at Alex a long moment, and Alex was almost ready to ask if it was Leo Bourque when by luck Markus said, "I am wondering, did you know your uncle's house was broken into—you haven't been over there lately?"

"No," Alex said. "When was it broken into?"

"I was sure you knew—but anyway, last night we caught him."

"Who?" Alex said.

"John Proud."

"Who?"

"John Proud. We knew someone was in there—but you see, here's the thing, he's—can I sit down?"

"Of course," Alex said.

They both sat at the small table in the ever-so-tiny kitchen so their knees were almost touching, and Alex felt uncomfortable with Markus's eyes resting upon him.

Then Markus continued speaking: "The thing is, he broke into Poppy Bourque's house—and a few others. My colleagues believe he was the one who is responsible for old Mr. Bourque disappearing. He was on a rampage over the last two and a half weeks—he was taking a lot of cooked meth—do you understand—you cook it up with household products, battery acid, hydrochloric acid, cold tablets, things of that nature. We are seeing it more on the river—it's bad stuff. It will kill a generation of Micmac if we don't put a stop to it. It is easy to become addicted. You might have heard of it—crank?"

"Oh," Alex said, stunned by this revelation. Stunned that he had no idea that Markus had been gallantly fighting this on a reserve ten miles away.

"When they saw him at Poppy's he tried to scramble out the back way into the woods with some things in his arms. To sell. So Johnny Proud's now the most notable suspect—and my people think he was in your uncle's house as well! By my people I don't mean First Nations—I mean cops." He smiled a little self-consciously here. Then he continued: "He has tried in his life to do good, but he hasn't had much of a chance—not that I'm saying that because he is First Nation—but you see others will think I am doing so, won't they—they say the case is solved QED. So they want me to let other things go, like the tire tracks and such."

It took a moment for Alex to digest this. They simply stared at one another for that moment, and Alex felt terrified.

"But you are skeptical?" Alex asked finally, his throat dry.

"Yes. I don't think he had anything to do with Poppy Bourque. I mean, I don't think he was the one who had anything to do with the disappearance. But it will be in the paper after a while."

"Well why did you say he did it? QED?" Alex asked.

"Oh, it's simply because others do—that's what others think—and they want me to approach it all as if the case is solved. My colleagues. You might have run into colleagues in your life—well, you are famous around here, I remember hearing about you as a boy, so you would know—who think the way they have been informed to think." He paused, looked into his pocket for something and continued while looking through a notebook with an eagle head on its front. "And in fact as long as they live will not be able to think any other way." Here he flipped some pages that seemed greasy and smudged. "They do not mean to rest and loiter in the world as hinderers, but they are hinderers. So I have these colleagues who believe the case is solved. But I am sure the case isn't solved."

"Why?"

"Well, I think—here—your uncle has a Ford—with standard half-ton box and tires—"

"Well, what do you want me to do? I mean—well, what I mean is why are you here at nine in the morning?"

It was a good question to ask and it caught Markus for a bit. He paused, looked at his watch.

"Oh, it is early, isn't it? Anyway, I want you to understand everything will be in confidence. You were the one who organized the First Nations takeover of Chapman's Island, so they could run their nets up along the bar. You were the one who went to the press, stood for your picture with First Nations men and women, so it would be put in *The Globe and Mail*." Here he smiled again a little bit. "So I thought I'd come to see you—for, well, ethical support—support from you, in a way—so I wouldn't have to charge Proud. I mean, if you spoke out it might allow a little time to continue looking in another direction. You are a voice for natives here, even if you are not one yourself!"

Alex had not forgotten that incident that had happened well over fifteen years ago. But now he said, "Oh—well—that was long ago—and—"

Markus put his notepad away.

"What do you think of Johnny Proud?"

"I don't know Johnny Proud."

"Ah—well, anyway, someday you might remember him."

"How could I remember him?"

"Someday you may. He's a real good candidate to do something like this—and we found a few things on him."

"I don't know what it is you are trying to say," Alex answered. He was suspicious now, and felt the back of his neck pain. His heart, too, became rapid, and he could feel the valve as it seemed to constrict his breath. "I can't stop the investigation!"

"Well, as you know, it is easy to blame an Indian, isn't it?"

Markus whispered. "I mean—I think someone told him these places were empty—and he needed money—then, well, after a while all the signs point to him. People simply forget the truck on the highway, forget how quickly Old Poppy left his house, forget that your uncle's house is so far away from the reserve Johnny would have had to hitchhike or walk—and in his state how could he? That is, I don't think the two break-ins are at all related. But you see he is First Nations, and so everyone thinks it's him, and he has had a bad life—his mother was murdered in front of him. But an Indian is an Indian." He said this almost as bait, and waited.

"I'm not sure if that's always so," Alex said, taking the opposite side of the issue for perhaps the first time and forgetting instantly his hero, the Vancouver sound poet who chanted Indian chants. "I believe there are a lot of people who no longer think that way—I certainly don't!"

Markus reflected upon this outburst, and was silent.

Then he nodded.

"Yes, that's the strange thing about ethics—it changes and yet it doesn't change at all. The world is a full canvas, isn't it—contradictions abound, no one knows exactly where anyone stands anymore—but I came on the quiet to see you. I mean, you'd give us a break, if you could!"

"What does that mean? 'On the quiet'?"

"Simply this: I think someone else is involved in Poppy's disappearance. Now I may be the only one to think this, and I may be in a bind. In fact, as the only First Nations member of the department I am sure I am in a bind—for me to come out and defend Johnny Proud, my first cousin—you see. You see, I know how ethics work—I know that a First Nations man got away with murder last year, because he was a First Nations man who killed another First Nations man. But now Johnny Proud comes along—a First Nations man who is suspected of having something to do with the disappearance of poor old Poppy Bourque. Someone will want to make up for last year, do you understand? So I am in a bind. My colleagues certainly do think he did it, and I am in the same department of law enforcement they are in—it is like a fraternity—so I have to bide my time. The pressure is to go along with them. Go along to get along. But you have always defended the underdog. So here I am, wondering if you think I am being too—well, unrealistic—and perhaps, well, you might write a column defending Proud—if you felt he was being set up."

He smiled at this, a little sheepishly, and said nothing.

Alex tried to respond philosophically. "But—I am just saying, if you caught him—"

Markus paused again, and kept his eyes on Alex. Then he shrugged.

"We caught him coming away from a house that was empty—and so some think he was in your uncle's house when it was empty—but does that mean he was there? I don't think so. What I want to know is, was anyone else in those houses before John Proud was? And could it have been the same two people in both of those houses before John Proud came onto the scene half out of his mind on methamphetamine?"

Here Markus looked straight at Alex, and waited almost without breathing for a reply.

"I didn't know anyone was in my uncle's house—when did you find that out?"

"Oh—some little while ago."

"Well how would I know? I can't write a positive thing about John Proud if I don't know—you know that!"

"Of course I do. You would have no way of knowing," Markus said not as a question but as an affirmation.

"Of course not," Alex laughed, "why would I? So I can't really do it—I mean, I would like to write about Proud as a fine man—but I don't know, do I? I mean, say if he isn't a fine man and I go around calling him a fine man when he isn't—well I shan't do that, shall I!"

There was a pause—just a slight one. Markus put his hand on the table and, trembling just slightly, picked up the salt shaker and tapped it twice, as if to calm himself. Then putting it down he looked at Alex again, and said, "You wouldn't allow anyone to ever get into trouble on your behalf?"

Alex's entire face seemed to freeze in still frame for twenty seconds or more.

"Why would I ever do that—I could never ever imagine doing so," he whispered.

Then Alex made what he considered a mistake. He became angry, and said he should be the last one suspected of trying to get anyone in trouble. He had stood against fire for the First Nations.

"I lost my position at the university defending the First Nations and walked away." He had a strange self-indulgent smile on his peaked little face when he said this, and his orange hair seemed to move slightly back and forth.

"You did?"

"I did!"

"You lost your position trying to defend First Nations people?"

"I did."

"Well, well."

"Yes!" Alex said, shaking his head sadly.

This, though not true, at the moment seemed as if it could be true. As if Alex's made-up life could be true. But this was strange to Markus, for he knew the one place on the river that often agitated on behalf of First Nations—sometimes rightly, sometimes wrongly—was the university. So he felt it very strange that a man like Young Chapman would lose his position for doing something 75 percent of university professors took as the norm.

Yet Alex said it, as if it was true. Markus nodded quickly as if he had just been put in his place about the First Nations people. There was a pause.

"Of course I didn't think you could blame anyone—but there is a problem," Markus said.

"What is it?"

"John Proud can't defend himself—he's been up for weeks on meth—he is now in hospital—so he is into the sleeps. He might sleep off and on for three weeks. He will never be able to say where he was or what he did. Of course you know John Proud—almost everyone on the river does—I am not defending him, but he's almost virtually harmless. But you see he will not be able to provide an alibi—he has two or three things he stole from Poppy Bourque's, one was a floor lamp—him trying to carry a floor lamp. He broke into other places down there. So they think he broke into your uncle's as well. X equals Y—Poppy gone—case closed. But he doesn't really have anything with him that I think came from your uncle's. Nothing at all."

"Well was my uncle's broken into?"

"Oh yes indeed—but by whom?"

Alex shrugged, and felt sweat on his forehead, which he quickly wiped away.

"Does it matter—it may have been someone else?" Alex asked.

"Yes—I think it was someone else; but I have a feeling this someone else has something to do with Poppy Bourque. But unfortunately for us, no one else seems to."

Alex shrugged.

"And the fact is this: All things being equal, people will believe that I will show my character and my ability by charging John with theft and implicating him in the murder of Poppy Bourque. But if I do, I forgo the investigation I am now engaged in, which is what those who think I am off on a wild goose chase want. I am in fact like a referee at a hockey game who must blow the whistle on his own hometown team even though it is late in the third period and they are already down a goal. They are waiting for me to prove I can do it, to prove myself loyal to the complexities of my job. If I do it, a possible promotion is in store, for the whole highway is abuzz this morning, saying it was John Proud. I am being asked to do the appropriate thing, to prove that I am not above the law. They are looking at me."

He smiled at this. But Alex had only heard one word.

"You said murder of Poppy?"

"What?"

"You said murder of Poppy?"

"I did—I said murder of Poppy Bourque—"

"Yes, you did."

"Well there you have it."

"Murder?"

"Absolutely," Markus Paul said without the least hesitation.

There was a long pause. Alex got up and took his medicine and sat down at the table once more. He took three pills, though he should only have taken two, and coughed a little when he drank some water.

"I see," Alex said. "Yes, I see."

"Do you?" Markus asked.

"Well yes—I think so!"

There was another pause. At this moment Alex became very much aware of how close Markus was to the telephone, and how he might pick it up if it rang—and what if it was Leo Bourque? He was also conscious of the fact that if Markus pressed the redial button, it would dial Bourque's number, who Alex had called in panic yesterday. In fact, both of them seemed to realize this at the same moment. Markus glanced casually at the phone. Then he looked back at Alex.

"But is the case closed?" Markus asked. "That's what you have to help me with." And here Markus took a chance. "Look, I am asking for your help because I am a First Nations man and have not dealt in the world like you have. One article claiming that I might be on the right track and that you want to get to the bottom of it because of your feelings against injustice—and it was your uncle's house!" He blinked and sighed.

Alex looked at him and nodded understandingly. Then he spoke: "I don't know—you see it—you are emotionally involved, and I think it could very well have been Johnny—and if he is in such terrible shape, he can't be held responsible—not morally or ethically, physically perhaps, but not otherwise—"

"That is what I think."

"You do?"

"Of course I do—did and will—especially when he admitted to it."

"He admitted to it?"

"Yes, and then he fell into his deep Rip Van Winkle snooze. He'll be kept under by medication for six or seven days or more. But you see, here is what I think—he would have admitted to the Kennedy assassination if we wanted him to, just to get out of the torment he was feeling at that moment. That is what is so painful to me at this moment—he blamed alcohol and drugs for the death of his mother and then over the last fifteen years goes on a rampage himself. Who in the world would not think he killed or at least misplaced Poppy—put him somewhere? I come to you because you are a teacher of ethics. You are teaching a course— you did your master's and doctoral thesis on ethics. I need some help here because I am in a bind."

"Well, I did my doctoral thesis—well—it isn't quite finished and it wasn't on ethics so much." Alex thought a moment, then gave a peculiar sniff and said, "If he did it he should be held responsible."

"If he did do it?"

"Yes."

"That, of course, is what I think. However, knowing your views on this, on the"—here he looked at his notebook once again—"'sometimes shared responsibility of society in the involvement of minority crime,' as you stated in a letter to the editor in 1980 during the Chapman's Island takeover, you seemed to want to protect some of the people more as victims. I just wanted to know—"

"Well, in the heat of the moment—" Alex began.

Had Markus simply read it and remembered, or was he researching him? Alex did not know that Markus had read many of Alex's articles three nights before, to prepare for this interview, even the articles Alex was preparing to use in his course on ethics. That he had interviewed many people about Alex already, that he had been up almost four days reading everything he could about him.

"So you think Proud might have?"

"Well, he could very well have," Alex said sheepishly, and he flushed deeply. "But then again I don't know if we can hold him responsible. Besides, my whole idea is that which you just said."

"Either do I," Markus said. "But I thought I was on the right track until last night when all this came out—I mean a very different track. I mean the truck track, and the idea that an English and a French guy are in this together!"

To Alex, a bomb had been placed in the room, and he was tied up, and it was now ticking.

But Markus simply continued: "Then it all came out and he is under guard at the hospital—and I am supposed to wrap things up. You should see the shape he is in. He has lost upwards of forty pounds and sixteen teeth—well, fourteen and two are loose—all because of methamphetamine. You can poke around in his mouth now that he is asleep and haul them out with your fingers!"

"That is awful."

"But right now I don't know—this is the difficulty I am in. I have my suspicions, based on signs about Poppy Bourque's, that it is not one but two people. Yet I am told not to pursue that, and if I do, I am a racist. This is what certain people are saying."

"That's silly," Alex managed, "and ethnically insensitive."

"Yes, there you have it! I knew you'd understand—" he said, still smiling.

"Yes of course—" Alex said, with a flash of emotion.

Markus smiled. He then asked Alex's permission to go into the uncle's house that afternoon, at about two.

"You can join me," he said.

Alex nodded but couldn't find the words.

=

ALEX MADE HIMSELF A CUP OF HERBAL TEA, AND LOOKED over the statement given about his uncle's death. His uncle wouldn't have ever lived beyond October, even if he hadn't fallen from the boat. He had cancer in his liver, which had spread to his lungs. He had left his nephew everything, but with kind instructions to provide for Amy Patch's scholarship. And if Alex reneged or declined the property in any way, it was to fall to Sam Patch. This had been talked about over the years between the old man and Muriel in order to do something for Sam and his family. It was in fact a largesse conditional upon the temperament of Alex himself. The old man felt he did not have to change it in order for Alex to be chagrined by what it said.

It was an old will, so maybe he had had no time to change his wishes. Or perhaps in the end he didn't really want to. Perhaps he was thinking of Rosa and the man who led her astray. So Alex had the entire property, including Chapman's Island and Bartibog wharf. That is, over 120 acres, warehouses, sheds, barn and paddock, and what was left of the equipment, some of which was in fair condition. Even without the ticket, he would have made some kind of life for himself. That is, though the old man had gone under, there was no requisite lien on the property, and Alex was now solvent. If this "thing" had not happened he could have been the gentleman farmer Mr. Roach had wanted to become, while still teaching his ethics course.

My God, what a beautiful life he might have had!

Perhaps one more little act would still allow it.

Not a thing had stopped him but himself. But if his "crime" was discovered, it would all go to Sam. This in its own way was calculated to scald him.

—

LATER THAT AFTERNOON ALEX WENT OVER TO THE HOUSE, and went inside and waited for Markus, who said he was going to be back to check inventory. In all of this there was a second sensation that he was feeling, a kind of cat and mouse, a flirtatious examination of Alex himself by Markus Paul that Alex tried not to notice. He sat on the chair in the dining room, a room he almost never went into unless called to do so, as long as he had lived here. It made him feel like an outsider in his own house. He felt the sweat on his back dry, and he shivered, as one does when they come inside out of the summer heat. He smelled the oak tables and dining room cabinets in this enclosed space. He thought he might try to put things back in order in the house—certain drawers had been pulled out, and many things were scattered. Then he decided that he couldn't do this. He would be accused of hampering the investigation. He had also a certain thrill come over him when he thought that he wouldn't be held accountable if this thing stuck against Mr. Proud. They would be completely liberated, which in a sense is how he thought. The crime wouldn't have been committed. He felt this euphoria, knowing it came from a native's wrongful accusation—the very thing he had fought all his life.

Yet he decided in a certain way it might be the best thing. For Proud could get the help he needed to overcome a methamphetamine addiction, while at the same time not be held completely accountable for his actions. It was also strangely timely that he had read an article in *The New Yorker* about methamphetamine moving into communities in the east, coming from the rural west. So that was not his fault. And John Proud might even get his teeth fixed. Perhaps it would work out. The only thing problematic was that Proud had already confessed. It struck him now that when Proud recovered they would press him to remember where the body was. Why this bothered Alex, he didn't know. But it was laid out upon a very grave feeling, disassociated from anything in particular, vague yet endlessly vast, surrounding him as dust surrounds a planet. He heard that there were theories and even seminars on vagueness, by various professors, and he wished he could listen to one. Say, if in the mud huts of all this vagueness, demons or terrors or angels were in the air, hovering about the microwave, making sure of things in some other dimension, a dimension that, if it did not control our lives, played out its part in a fascinating kind of exchange of which we ourselves were almost never aware.

His continual uneasy horror over what had really happened, and where the body actually was, and his underlying part in the mystery, was in fact surrounding him in a vague balloon, like chloroform. This now shaped everything about him and his relationship with the world. It certainly foretold of trouble. He tried to think moderately about the two books he was going to assign in his course on ethics, along with the old masters: *The Da Vinci Code* and *In Cold Blood*. Now, feeling outside his own sphere of recognizable armor, he decided he would not offer either book. They no longer pertained to what he really wanted to say. And what did he really want to say? Two weeks ago he could have rattled off his entire seminar.

"Once this is over," he whispered, "once this is all over."

Just then there was a knock on the half-opened door and the voice of Constable Paul.

"Yes," Alex said from the dining room. "I'm in here." Calmness came over him, and he was happy about this. He didn't want to be nervous and shaky in front of a police officer.

The one thing he did not know was that Constable Markus Paul was not at all convinced that Johnny Proud had done anything in this house. He was in fact convinced that Johnny, his cousin, had committed no serious crime. In fact, the very idea that Proud went into Poppy Bourque's house to search for something to sell showed he had no idea a disappearance had taken place, and that the police were watching the property twenty-four hours a day.

Markus now came to Old Chapman's house to prove that someone else was involved in the break-in here. That those who were actually responsible for the break-in at Chapman's were in the end responsible for Poppy Bourque's disappearance.

"Well this is a mess," he said.

"Yes, it was riffled through," Alex answered, trying his best to look annoyed. "This is what you hear about."

"What is that—what do you hear about?" Markus asked.

"Well, you know, the family is at a funeral and someone decides that's the best time to come in and go through your house."

"Oh, but this was done before the funeral—"

"It was?"

"Yes, I am sure of it—" Markus smiled again, his face brightening for a second as if to dispel the added cruelty of a break-in at the time of a funeral. Then, looking serious once more, he said he was going to look around, and asked if he could do so.

"Sure."

"I won't be long then," Markus said, and he climbed the stairs. Alex thought of following him but didn't. Then Markus came back down and walked by Alex. Alex got up and followed him into the kitchen.

"What is it?" Alex asked.

"What is what?"

"Have you found anything?"

"Nothing." He shook his head, and opened two or three drawers that Alex had opened.

"There is something strange here," he said. And it was a deepening mystery to him now. He looked very perplexed.

"What?"

"Items left exactly as they were—gun cabinet not broken into, radio and portable TV exactly where they were, microwave oven, all of it easy to sell or pawn—none of it taken—none of it moved—why?"

"I don't know."

"Either do I—but it is pretty strange."

"Yes—"

"Unless something else was going on."

"And what is that?"

"Unless the person was looking for something in particular—something small."

"Why small?"

"Cabinets are opened, nothing removed—but the three cabinet drawers are pulled out, vases turned over—a pencil holder upset—something small—a map of buried treasure on Chapman Isle." Markus smiled. "Something that could fit into a shoebox of bills, which was riffled through here—so a piece of paper, or a coin—"

Then Markus blushed, his face turning slightly redder, and said nothing.

"What?"

"Oh nothing—I was thinking perhaps a will, but I don't think that would fly. All I am saying is little Johnny Proud wouldn't have been searching through a shoebox of bills sitting on top a microwave oven. He would have taken the microwave oven. But someone who was looking for something in particular would have. Something not too random, as kids say today. But something special. Something in the family. John was in Poppy's, yes—but someone different was in here, looking for something different than John Proud was!"

Alex shrugged. And then his legs wobbled as if he had been shot, and he sat down.

That is because he suddenly, overwhelmingly, realized who John Proud was—strange that he remembered this, at this exact moment. John Proud was the boy who had thrown the rock at the bear to keep Alex from danger. That is exactly who they were talking about. Exactly!

"What's wrong?" Markus asked.

"Nothing," Alex said, though he couldn't stop his leg from trembling, so much that his knee bumped the table, and he kept his head down.

Markus only nodded, looked through some pages and notes that had been scattered, and picked up some old recipes.

As he did, he spoke, with his eyes cast down: "Look—I'd like to show you this."

"What?"

"Well, do you remember my sister Peg—during the Chapman's Island takeover?"

"I don't exactly—"

"Well," Markus said, almost happily, "she died of meth poisoning four months ago. So anyway." Here he handed an old picture to Alex that he had in the folder of his notebook. "See, you had your picture taken with her—on the front of the paper. See, she was proud, she died with that in her wallet. I was little but I remember the day that was taken. How proud she was of you standing right beside her."

"I was proud to do so."

"You were."

"Of course."

Markus paused, took the picture back, and nodded as if to himself.

"Yet, there is something. Over the years I thought, Who is giving up his property here—not one of the reporters from Toronto, none of those professors, only silly old Mr. Jim Chapman, who knew more about the First Nations than any one of them."

"I see," Alex said.

"That's why I felt so badly for your uncle. That's why I'd like to know who really broke in here—for your uncle's sake—because so often the truth is somewhere else!"

LATER IN THE AFTERNOON ALEX WENT HOME, AND TRIED to concentrate on his course on ethics, but could not manage to focus. All he could focus on was the horrible feeling that things in his past—his concern for women, his concern for First Nations—all which he prided himself on, were now being re-examined, and he of all people was found wanting.

Markus was using Alex's very claim of altruism to dismantle who he said he was. And Alex knew this, and could no longer pretend or prevent it!

Markus in fact was studying them both, and had been now for a week. He knew how Alex and Leo had come together on the school bus, and was piecing together how they had lived ever since, and how little by little their unsettled and unsettling lives came together once again to wreak havoc with one another.

Markus's little notebook with the emblematic eagle, which his colleagues derisively called the bible, had twenty new pages of notes. He kept that picture of his sister in it always. At first he had been proud of it, but as time went by his heart went against Alex's easy adopting of other people's misery to make a name for himself. And so now his gaze turned toward Alex and all he had done.

"They couldn't have gone there to kill him," Markus said to himself. "Poppy leaving so willingly seems to attest to amiability."

BOURQUE HAD BEEN REELING UNDER THE WEIGHT OF others' opinions of him, too. They told him he could do nothing most of his life. When he was young he had tried to prove them wrong. And at each juncture it seemed they were right. Yet he realized when he found the ticket that all opinions are subject to change—and that this change coming about by chance was even better. He could reclaim more than some measure of his former self. But for one thing. It was a self that would have had nothing to do with his former self. He would be very rich, and much different in one way, and not changed at all in another. That is what the lotto did. In fact, he thought many of the same thoughts Alex had, coming to them in the same way. And it also came down to the same two things: there were people who had injured him he could get back at, and his wife would return to him—his daughter Bridgette would live with them again. But he would have to make his wife suffer just a little. She had made him suffer unduly. He would think of how she got the job because of him—and then him being sent out on the loader so Cid could be alone with her. He would think of him telling his wife that he was the one who had made Cid rich, and how, after a life of being disappointed in him, she dismissed this claim. And thinking of all of this, he would shake and then hit something.

On the eighth day after the disappearance Bourque went for a walk along the herring-stinking beach, and looked out at the full water, light and milky blue, and he remembered his love of this land as a child. He sat on an old log, as he was wont to do, where from across the T—as they called the little inlet—he could watch his estranged wife in her boss's office. And what was vastly annoying to him, he saw her boss pat her behind as she walked around the desk. Confused by this, he jumped up and began to walk back up the beach, until he saw Markus Paul's police car driving along the narrow inlet road toward Fouy's Construction. It was as if someone had hit him very hard to make him realize something very important—so he turned and walked closer.

Paul disappeared into that clapboard office building for a moment, behind the door to the tired stairway and little pressboard door; so Bourque could follow him in his mind's eye. Then the front glassed door opened, so from where he was Bourque could see how Constable Paul brought his ex-wife to the police car, and began speaking to her.

Leo's emotion was akin to a patient learning that not only did they discover a bit of cancer, but in fact he only had a week to live.

What Leo noticed was his wife's body movement—her little gestures that he had witnessed ten thousand times—when she was confused or tried to please someone because she did not want an argument. And it was these gestures that made him forget what her obscenely self-confident boss had done—and made him love her all over again. He knew she was being questioned about him—Leo—and he knew he was being hunted. He knew why he feared when Markus Paul didn't come to see him, almost as much as he feared when he did.

It was about an hour and a half later, in his own shed, eating his supper alone, when Bourque's sister came to tell him that Constable Paul had been to the house, and had said they had picked up Johnny Proud for the disappearance.

"Oh I hope that's not true," Bourque said sadly. But he eyed his sister cautiously, thinking that Markus Paul might have sent her to trick him, and in one second remembering the thousand small betrayals that were committed by his sister's easy gaining of confidence from him over the years, even telling Doreen when he wouldn't be home so she could move her things. This betrayal was first and foremost in his mind now.

But after a time he thought he was very lucky to have Proud blamed. This made him euphoric for a bit, until he thought this: If Amy was ever to keep silent about the truck, which he had convinced himself she would, she couldn't if she believed they had arrested someone who had nothing to do with the crime. She would have to tell what she knew, as a moral obligation.

"But what are the possibilities of her thinking this," he wondered. "Tell me, what are the possibilities of her thinking she has to report us?"

And the answer came: VERY HIGH.

Sooner or later, even if it was a year from now, she would figure it out. At the very latest, on the day they cashed the ticket she would speak.

He poured himself a last glass of wine, and stared off into nothing at all.

John Proud being arrested actually upped the ante against them. They could not cash the ticket with Amy my love still alive.

He snuck out later, along the old back path. He did not trust the phone (every phone he could think of was now bugged, especially the one on the highway), and he walked along the dirt path silently until he came out on the road far above the turn.

He had to see Alex and convince him that Amy herself was their greatest liability, that certain specter called the angel of death. They could not fool themselves anymore. They must take action against Amy as quickly as possible.

He tried for the first time in a long time to think of his soul, and it registered in his mind as turning like a small leaf on the forest floor on a cold autumn day, shriveled and dark. One part of him was thinking that he had a soul—and thinking of his youth, of praying as he struggled not to drown long ago, perhaps a very great soul.

It would leave a scar, no doubt. But the soul would eventually heal. And in fact this is what Bourque said now: "This will scar us all."

He was not thinking of the body being scarred. Of course he was thinking of the soul. But the scar would heal over, and in some future day, in some way, things would be normal again.

—

BOURQUE HAD PIECES OF GRASS IN HIS HAIR, AND HE HAD frightened Alex to death by standing up in the garden when Young Chapman went to get his morning cucumber. Alex had run, thinking in a millisecond that Bourque had come to kill him.

It was 7:30 in the morning. And it was cold and gray and the trees blew like ghosts, and the whole bay was riled like a fever. The little cabin sat damp and friendless, the specter of autumn upon the ground.

For a while Bourque said nothing at all. He simply stood looking out at the bay.

Then he said, "The problem is John Proud—he is our scapegoat, but he is the one to hurt us too."

"Why is that?" Alex asked, rationally. "It might be that they can get him help—this is what I have been thinking about for the last little while. We might be doing him a favor. And if he is charged, and gets help, and it takes a few years—say, seven years—when he comes out we can give him a million dollars, and then and there it will all be for the best. I have thought much about this, and this might just work!"

"Audacious how you can help the Indian now by putting him into jail."

"I am not saying that."

"Truly audacious—" But then he added, "It is not how Amy will think of it."

"What do you mean?"

"I mean sooner or later the idea of a human tragedy named John Proud will make her see the truck as a pivotal bit of evidence to clear him, and she will want to do the right thing."

Alex, of course, was immensely pained by this. This idea of doing the right thing was in some ways his territory.

But what Bourque was saying was that if Amy—if Amy girl, as he sometimes called her; Amy my pigeon; Amy the pure of heart— was LESS of a girl, was LESS human, then she might not be compelled to tell the truth in this one instance and they might be able to pay her off, with a few hundred thousand and a convertible.

But he had seen her eyes when she had handed him the berries her mother had asked her to bring to him last week, and in those eyes were recognition and shock. So sooner or later her humanity would make her turn to the police and tell them they could not accuse John Proud. So what Bourque was telling Alex was what in his lively imagination Alex already was thinking: they must destroy her humanity, which Alex had failed to destroy before.

"If we can do something else—bring her here and offer her money—pay her money—I am open to it," Leo said. "But if not—and all I am saying is, if not—then what are the alternative solutions?"

Within this talk there was another conversation going on, one that was interwoven and demonstrably different than the conversation about the money. This other conversation concentrated on the fact that Bourque had been beaten half to death as a child trying to protect both his mother and his sister, that his life was utter hell, that he had found a young woman, Doreen LeBlanc, and loved her—that she had made him whole, but her leaving him was destroying him. And all of this detail made him livid.

But also, now and again, woven into these two subjects was a third—and this subject was Amy. And because of the first two subjects, it was perfectly obvious that something would have to be done with Amy very soon.

Still, no matter how desperate he felt, Alex tried to talk them out of it: "We would never get over it. We would be drowning ourselves!"

Bourque thought for a moment and answered quite rationally. "Okay—let us think this through. Let's say that our plight right now has given us these three options—jail or suicide or Amy. What if we do something to Amy—just something—and we are able to live with it. Then it negates the other two options, by which I mean no jail, no suicide. If we are not able to do this to Amy, jail and suicide are the options already available. And we can do them quickly!"

This seemed somewhat rational, notwithstanding the life of Amy herself, which Alex did not care to mention as a negative in the argument. If it came to light even now that John Proud had not committed this crime, there would be more hell to pay for them when it was discovered that they had. This suddenly seemed completely logical to Alex—even more so than the fact that Johnny Proud was completely innocent in the first place.

"If it is discovered in any way that he is innocent, we are doomed," Alex whispered. "Even at this moment! We are done for!"

Four times during this dialogue Bourque asked to see the ticket, now in Alex's possession, and four times Alex showed it to him, each time hoping for some kind of revelation inherent in the myth of riches that seemed so out of place now.

Here is what Leo said: They would open a youth center in Amy's name, and build a monument to her in front of this center, where children could go day and night from all over the river to be safe. "Its doors would never be locked!"

Then both nodded, because it seemed essential that this be done. That is, the murder seemed essential in order for them to build this center where they would be looked upon as humanitarians for doing so.

Yet this was exactly the point, in principle of all Alex's study. This isotopic debate that had spread itself over the surface of all his erudition for almost twenty years, that intellectualism held the key—and a somewhat golden key—to a door of discovery not dependent on faith. Now this had become quite suddenly the unexpected debate. He thought thus: If the religious moral in itself is bogus, then the idea that such a philosophy holds the certainty about good and evil is bogus too—as he often said, and usually said on behalf of women everywhere, who were the most victimized by the social idea of good and evil, and nothing in the world was more savage.

Therefore, if ecclesiastical study developed the faulty premise of good and evil, intellectualism could open the door to reduce it to nothing, to smash it to smithereens. This also was why he was teaching his fall semester course on ethics—all of these points were germane. And here was the point, the one point damning to Amy that had come to him suddenly. Something he could hold on to to help him, in his hour of need.

Amy, in a way, represented not womanhood (for didn't he admire that) but represented instead the repressed view of good and evil, held by the diabolical Catholic church, that had been as far as Alex was concerned almost entirely debunked by the turn of the twenty-first century.

So wasn't there a principle that could be expressed as being just as truthful, and where one could understand his premise as well as Amy's?

Well, wasn't there?

Well?

Yes there was, he decided.

It was in fact a cautious, intellectualized relative morality where the very strangeness of his position and its attending argument could be looked upon as a subject of required intellectual debate. And if it became the subject of intellectual debate in any classroom he was in, it could be raised upon learned stilts to almost ethical opera.

It was in fact where he now saw himself: in a common room with radical young nose pickers, debating this. And he would be able to find among those young postmodernists a few professors whose hatred of the church was such that they would at least warrant an examination of his point of view.

"Oh, well, yes, then in that case—yes, well, in that case it does work," he could hear them saying. ·

This sudden horrid cynicism is what kept him going at this moment. He did not understand how close his intellectualizing had brought him to Leo's own thinking. And that Leo, the smell of fear all over him, was in fact trying to stay alive just like he was, knowing that almost anyone they spoke to would condemn Proud—except Amy Patch.

"I don't like snitches," Bourque said. "A snitch is dead on this here river—'cause we don't play no games!"

Alex looked up from his reverie. Yes, the idea of the snitch was vaguely disliked everywhere—in ancient Rome and here—and this, both intellectually and emotionally, was satisfying.

He clutched the ticket like a drowning man. And Bourque himself was a man who had almost drowned.

⸻

As August wore on, Amy realized more and more that she was in the crosshairs of something simply because she had seen them that night. Alex couldn't look her way. And twice she saw Leo Bourque on the far side of the highway glaring at her and then turning his back. Five times she asked others if they had seen a truck on the highway, and looked pained when they said they hadn't. For she realized that things were up to her.

Worse, she tried to act as if everything were normal. When they sat in mass near the stained glass windows and heard MacIlvoy talk of honor and redemption, it all seemed wise and comforting as long as she did not have to go outside into the daylight.

Father Mac was the first one to mention that Markus Paul was indeed looking for information about a truck seen on the night of

August 16. At first she did not even think it pertained to *that* truck. But when she did, it struck her as if she was suddenly hit by a stone. So she began asking questions about this truck to the boys and girls at the wharf. But none had seen it.

"It's John Proud," someone told her.

She sat in her bedroom and read books for her course on ethics that she believed would help her.

Why did Alex not look at her anymore? She had long known Alex's flaw was one of false sympathy. And false sympathy, like tin notes in an orchestra, was always sooner or later understood exactly for what it was. It was similar to her father wearing a new shirt to go to an interview—it never seemed to fit over his dark hands and bull neck.

She went looking for her copy of the New Testament that she took with her to the seminar on Saint Mark, and couldn't find it. She searched the house, and then realized that she had not had it since that night, and it must have fallen from her pocket when she fell. She would think about it lying there, and wonder if she should go back to get it. But she couldn't go back to it, because she was frightened of that lane. Why was she?

The almost ecstatic reverie she had had over Saint Mark that wild night had also gone, just like that erotic dream early in the summer when her clothes were taken off. Now each day she helped Fanny Groat get from her bed to the toilet and back, would clean her bum and dress her, and sit and read to her in the afternoon. For the care of the elderly left to the young is still prevalent in places in the country.

Every day Fanny wanted her lipstick put on, and her fur stole. And Amy did so. Then Fanny, seated in a chair, her body having the aspect of a shell, waited for some interesting story, or gave orders to get her muffins, or to open a window or close it, or to light her cigarettes for her.

"It's too sticky—open the window—it's too sticky."

Then after five minutes: "It's cold, that east wind come up again—close that window, girl!"

Or: "Go get my slippers—you didn't bring them from the living room—I can't just sit here without slippers—what are ya, crazy!"

Or: "Tell me a story—"

Amy would tell her stories from history. But after relating the story of Joan of Arc—how the young maid of Orleans took on the English army, and was betrayed by Charles VII, the very king she had placed upon the throne, and was therefore burnt to death—Fanny sat before her, a sly smile on her face, and said, "You are lying—that never happened—that's the kind of stories a girl like you gets up to. It's better if you had a boyfriend to tickle your mustn't-touch-it—get screwed, then you'd not get up to all this mischief." And with an accusatory look said, "You are making it all up—!"

Amy knew that the truth could be held up as a lie, very easily. People did it all the time. That is why she didn't tell her mother about Alex and the ticket, because she did not want to be accused of lying. "Besides, if Alex has the ticket he would have cashed it!" she reprimanded herself. "He gave our ticket to Burton to try and help us—it just didn't work out—that's why he came back and told us!"

"What are you mumbling for—stop this mumbling and get me a muffin!"

Still, for some reason she wasn't quite sure of, Amy would try to get home before dark, but often she couldn't. Now, each night as darkness approached, there was a feeling of dread. She would look out at the water puddle halfway down the dirt drive. It was still and murky, and reflected the trees. One late afternoon, busy with Fanny, she turned to look at it, and she could see the water swaying and rippling, as if someone had just stepped through it. Her heart began to pound, and she felt a small unsettling terror pass through her. She looked in all directions, and went to all the windows but could see no one.

That was the day she learned Johnny Proud had been arrested. She sat by the front window and watched the lane until it got so dark she could not tell trees from shadows. And just as she took her eyes away, she was sure she saw something move from one side of the lane to the other once again—a shadow, she was sure, of a man. But of course she was aware that this was her imagination.

But he has been arrested, she thought about John Proud, so things must be getting back to normal!

She had Fanny pray with her, which she did often with the old woman, to give her comfort. "Our Father, who art in heaven, hallowed be thy Name," she whispered.

Then she stood up quietly, and went and locked the door. Suddenly, a deep belief that she must protect this old woman overcame her, from somewhere deep inside her. This old woman who had spilled coffee on her back when she was a child, and slapped her when her parents went away, so she would sit in the dooryard alone and cry.

She locked the door, and decided that there was darkness on the face of the deep, and that it was her job to protect this eighty-two-year-old.

Some nights when Mrs. Hanson couldn't get up, Amy would stay over with Fanny, sleep on the cot and stare into the darkness, listening to the tick-tock of the clock in the hall. Usually Minnie would come over as well. But once or twice Amy was left alone. It was at those times she did not sleep until she saw the morning sun.

—

MOST OF THAT SUMMER FANNY WANTED TO KNOW ABOUT Amy's love life. But Amy could tell her nothing, and Fanny was angered by this.

"I have a boyfriend called Rory, and I think he likes me—like on Friday night I go get my pop and bag of chips—sometimes he sits beside me on the steps, and talks about baseball—we knew each other since we were kids."

"Have you ever been kissed?"

"No!"

"Will you ever be kissed?"

"I don't know—maybe Rory will someday—I—"

"God, girl, yer useless, some young boy shoulda had a whiff of it by now, it's better if you went with some young buck," she said. And she laughed until the peppermint fell from her mouth.

Amy thought of this as she sat with Fanny. No, she would not be like this. For Fanny, people said, was once a brilliant girl.

So, for her mom and dad she must go on. Then she would become someone great, and even famous. That is, those who sometimes influence one to greatness are those who have lost their own.

Later that afternoon, she heard a board clatter again. She ran to the large front window, and saw a tree wave just beyond the lane.

She rationalized randomness in her mathematics as never being random, and every flare from the sun produced a wind across the lilacs where the hummingbirds trembled their wings. And she was certainly smart enough to understand it, more than many.

What was worse was this. Just as soon as she began to relax and think of everything as her imagination, just as soon as she would begin to think of things she would like to do, and how people would someday think she was a fine girl, and she would go on great long trips to exciting places, just when she relaxed, she would hear the snap of a branch outside—something would sway and then stop, and that small bit of terror inside her would begin again to grow.

She thought of the things she had discovered about Alex. She always tried her best not to have this influence her. That is, in so many ways she was far more considerate than Alex himself. She remembered the letters she had found in the back of a box in her mother's closet late last year. (She did not tell her mother she had read them.)

She remembered every line as she sat in the old hard-backed rocking chair looking out at the drive, with its ruts and puddles, keeping guard like a little picket.

She had been amazed to learn that Alex, fully alive himself, did not want her born. She felt nauseous when she read this, and a deep shame and anger over came her. He was adamant she would end up a terrible burden, and that Sam was "no father to be proud of or look up to!"

She thought of Sam coming home with his left hand bashed on a piece of machinery, blood on the old cloth he had wrapped it in. She was certainly proud, and loved him then!

Then another letter which to her seemed even more insidious: he did not want her baptized. His argument was a sound one. The child was innocent, and no he wouldn't be godfather to a baptized child, for what was more innocent than a child?

He had not wanted her born, but then he wanted to protect the idea of her innocence by keeping her from baptism.

Then she suddenly thought: What if it was Poppy Bourque's ticket? And they stole it—that's what it is about—

She tried to be polite to the elderly woman, who had her share of trouble, and who couldn't sit still without giving her some order so Amy was constantly run off her feet. At first Amy had tried to be pleasant about this, but there were so many orders she was now sullen and angry. When Mrs. Hanson came into the house, Fanny would say, "Oh thank God you're here, dear, this little child has no sense."

Mrs. Hanson would shrug and look over at her with preconceived disapproval.

But the next morning the orders would start again.

One afternoon when they were playing checkers, Fanny asked out of the blue: "Do you have yer hair between yer legs yet?"

At first she didn't answer.

"Come on, tell me! A beautiful girl like you! What, are ya too proud?"

Amy nodded. "Of course," she said.

"Why do girls need hair between their legs?" Fanny asked.

"I don't know," Amy said.

"To prove that women are stronger than men." Fanny said.

"How?"

"I tell you this—if you use it right, one little cunt hair of yours can pull a battleship." Fanny smiled.

This, Fanny said, was Fanny's advice and should be taken.

The heat, of course, had made the little house both rancid and decrepit, and by this time of year the weeds had grown up almost over the windows. It was a secluded place, off a lane and a side road on the lost highway, where people could come right up to the window and look in.

IF YOU GO ALONG THAT ROAD NOW YOU WILL SEE NOTHING there. It has been replaced by the hours that have passed since Amy walked home one afternoon and found her mother and father were buying a house out west, that Sam had been wanting to tell them all year that there was no need for him to return. On that day there were still two houses, a small shed here and there, a pouring stream that crossed from one side of Arron to the moss and stump-laden woods and ran into Bartibog. It was still there as yet. That was a few years ago now, when Amy walked home that noon hour with the sun falling on the blueberry field and the old gravel pit still visible beyond the beginning of Jameson's tote road, and the sun just above the trees.

That was when there was still life here, when Fanny still sat out in the sun on the withered steps, her head mirrored in the old paned window, with its paint-peeled frame, and one antenna sticking up behind the stovepipe near the second floor, and she complained that no one visited her, and when an osprey or two circled in the sky, and then in a swoop came down into Arron Brook talons to grab a fish, where an eagle, larger, would wait at the riverbank all day for the flash of a fin from a salmon. Or a bear or two walked silently through the tumbled-up fagots that had been cut along the power line years before that, or a panther still strode at dark, swiftly. It was gone now simply because there was no one left, and two hundred years of life on the Gum Road seemed to have gone away. Amy would be forced to leave her little place, her small bees and raccoon in the tree near Lean-to lane. What would happen to all those secret places she knew?

Amy was the last child born here, and she went home to discover that her mother was leaving for northern Alberta to meet her father, and they were going to finalize a deal on a house. That she would stay with Fanny and Mrs. Hanson at Fanny's for two days. That on the third day Amy would have to keep Fanny alone—but that Sam and her mother would be back by one o'clock in the morning, for it was a late flight coming out of the west, and Mrs. Hanson was driving down to pick them up.

They would be able to put Fanny in the home in Tabusintac, and Amy would be able to say goodbye before they all left for another life.

The old pathways she had traveled, no other child would; the place where she placed her pollywogs would be forgotten. The liveliness she had when she walked, so that it seemed the birds sang for her, would disappear as if someone were walking off camera and becoming invisible; and so everything she loved and desired here would never be the same. And in that, and perhaps because of that, a sadness would come to the birds and the leaves, and the eagle that waited in stillness waiting for a fin in the rip.

They were all going now—and it was as if after two hundred years this life was no longer worthy and some machine and men and piles of sludge out west were more frantic and needed, with cowboy hats and coats and the gloating idea of prosperity.

This is what Amy discovered wearing a kerchief around her neck, and watching the roadway with a sunburned face. When she walked home that day, the life she knew would change forever. What a sad place the Maritimes had become, for so many wonders to be longed for and forgotten, turned over to the dark earth, and like an old fence no longer recognizable as yours, a land gone away.

"It is for the best," Minnie said, "isn't it, dear?"

But what would happen to George the raccoon, and Lester the skunk—where would her pollywogs be next spring, and how many bees would fall into the bottom of the hive—where would everything go without her, those places she had been and believed she would always be? Those places deep in her heart that no one else knew. What other children would come to take care of them if she left and went away? What other child would be able to bring the buck deer, whose antlers were now in velvet, into the yard with an apple and a lick of salt. What would happen to that buck she had trained to know who she was, whenever she gave a soft doe call with her tongue? How many other young girls could do that? And who would care? Sometimes the buck came even now walking along the road toward her, its velvet antlers resembling a halo in the soft weather.

"We will have a good life yet," Minnie said. "Sam promised."

"I know," Amy said, with the first tinge of grown-up bitterness. "He has always sought your love! Always, no matter what!"

IN TWO DAYS ALEX KNEW THAT MINNIE AND SAM WERE leaving. Everyone knew. It came as an astonishment that the last twenty years of his life, in one way or the other spent scheming to get her back, were now irreversibly foiled.

How could he have had a life so stupid and meaningless? He was down to eating pabulum in the last two days, for his heartburn was so bad.

"I can't even munch a carrot," he said now.

"There is big, big money out on the oil patch," Bourque commented in appreciation of Sam and Minnie's decision. "He has to take advantage when he can! In fact, he'll be more appreciated out there than he ever was here! You never appreciated him. Old Jim never appreciated him. I always did myself. Did you ever see Minnie naked—I did, in a field one summer day."

"Don't talk about her like that!" Alex insisted.

Bourque shrugged. He was smiling and happy to have them out of his hair. "Gone daddy gone. Talk about luck—Proud in jail and Amy gone!"

He almost danced about the little kitchen. And Alex, too, felt relieved.

Yet after the initial euphoria of thinking that Amy would be out of sight, out of mind, and their problems would be over, came a sudden and startling twist. Both became aware at almost the same instant of what pressure Amy would be under to tell what she knew before she left the province. Or worse, as soon as she got away from them, so they couldn't stop her.

In fact, Leo was in the midst of celebrating when this realization struck him like a punch.

Suddenly both realized she would be out of reach.

The fact that Amy had not said anything yet only heightened their concern of what she would say as soon as she got a chance. So once this danger was recognized, by Alex and Leo, it became a significant prod to go through with the "act" against her.

"It is as if she hasn't realized what exactly she saw yet, and is trying to talk herself out of thinking she has seen anything," Bourque reasoned. "But sooner or later—well, we're dead, that's all there is to it!"

So in the early evening of the second day after they made certain she was going, with a cold east wind blowing the trees wildly and shadows playing dangerously across the walls, they had a meeting. The lights in Alex's cabin were turned off so no one would see them in there. They could just make out each other's features, if they got close, and once or twice they bumped into each other as they moved around.

"I know where Amy is now," Bourque said. "I've been over there four times. She sits there staring out the window—or reads a book. Do you know she reads really important books—not like the kind my wife reads, the trash romances, but the kind you read for your ethics course!" he said with some admiration.

Here Alex struggled not to sob.

"The problem is, she is with Fanny—and I don't want to have to kill her too, you understand, I am not a bad man. Amy stays at the house three nights a week. Then Mrs. Hanson comes and stays. But we have nothing against Mrs. Hanson. Or at least I don't. So Minnie leaves next week. The third day Amy is alone, this is what I learned from Burton. Mrs. Hanson is going down to pick them up. Minnie and Sam won't be home till later in the morning, maybe two or three. That is when we have to act. The problem is, even if Amy is alone with Fanny, as long as Minnie is near, or Mrs. Hanson, we are in a bind—but when they go—ACT," he said with great decisiveness.

"How do we act?"

"You know what I mean. Once she goes to Markus, once that happens, you may as well never have existed—every variance of your existence will matter not the least!"

This was said exactly, and even the word variance was used—meant as discrepancy more than clash—and Bourque used it because he felt himself able to, as he said as a child, "swing some words around!"

And now he walked with his hands behind his back, doing just this.

"The problem for Proud is that his camp is in the proximity of Old Poppy—and there had been disagreements with Poppy over Proud's friends and their habits, noise and Poppy's sawdust. This is what we have in our favor—you must understand that. It is the constant negative in Markus's theory—something he will not tell you when he tries to interrogate us. So we have this in our general favor, my friend."

Leo had always wanted to speak well, first in French, and when he went to school and was forced and beaten by his father to learn English, then in that language. It showed in fact how incredibly bright he truly was. He had often used these words in the wrong place to impress people he wanted to like him, and to try to be more like them. A few years before he would stand with his wife, spouting out great verbosity, until she was red in the face, and he would sputter the words again and again, entrenched in the idea that he must impress her friends to impress her. But now he didn't care what they meant—he was determined to use them as he saw fit, which made him in his new power of boasting slightly comic. But it did add a measure of danger to him. For a man who had the gumption to use them had to have the gumption to feel worthy enough to. He was unsure of the meaning of many of them, but they felt right.

The moon now was over Bourque's right shoulder—only half his face was visible. And quite suddenly he did remind Alex of one of his former heroes in the heroic struggle, Joseph Stalin. For the first time the terrible wish he had made—"send me someone from my past to help me find this ticket"—came to him as caustic divination.

He shuddered.

"It would be better if Amy had never been born," Bourque said now, philosophically. "Yes, much better if she had been snipped off when she was still in the acorn stage. We have the acorn stage of man, now, and that's when she should have been killed." He looked at Alex with a great deal of accusation. "But you didn't get the job done—and look what happened!"

"Don't say that," Alex said, for some reason shuddering.

"It would have saved a bucket of blood," Bourque said theoretically about what should have happened fifteen years before. Alex knew that in effect Amy's very life imposed upon him this further responsibility to protect himself, and that perhaps every footstep he had made since had in some way been instructed by her birth. And that his life had in fact been thrown into the maelstrom because of her.

Revenge might cure him of the last fifteen years of his life.

Both of them had now slipped into a moral coma where anything could be argued to be right, and if decided as right then nothing was wrong.

"Have you heard of Stalin?" Alex finally asked weakly, hoping that Bourque had not, even though he had mentioned the book a few days before.

"Who's he—does he know something?" Bourque said.

Here, even in his despair in this dark cold little room, Alex laughed.

"Does Stalin know something—ha, that's a good one."

Bourque was angered by this laughter. He didn't know what to say. But then he told Alex this: that he did not like to be laughed at, and Alex better not laugh at him again. This was his most humiliating fact! He had been nothing more than a janitor at Fouy Construction. When Bourque brought the bid over and Cid Fouy saw he was useful, he gave him a job—he took a course on loaders and began to work on one. All of this he did, thinking that Cid loved him. But Cid wanted him out of the yard on the loader to go at his wife's snatch. Then Cid told Bourque's wife that it was himself who had arranged to undercut the Chapman bid, by logic alone, and he was in a position of power where he and not Leo was believed.

Leo had fumed at this in front of his wife, but nothing he said was believed by her. He was a common laborer, and Cid was Cid.

This was the comic despair Leo was fighting. His wife left him because Cid convinced her Leo was delusional and lying. That's why he had to be rich, and that's why he had to have the ticket.

"And that's why I told Cid and Doreen last week I was going to buy a Porsche."

"You told them what?"

"Do not worry—they never believed me anyway," he smiled. "It's just that they made me so angry! So I told them I had more money than they could believe—so there!"

And this in a rambling way is what he told Alex about himself now: Some years ago Leo would go to dances and sputter his big words to Cid, and his wife would blush and say, "Please Leo." Yet he couldn't seem to stop, because he had wanted to follow Alex's lead and be important.

"Please Leo," his wife would say, as he tried to get his tongue around a set of words like "undulating like certain specter grasses that I saw as a boy." And the boss, with his huge tie and his tight pants stretched over his opulent rump, would smile, at first with utter surprise at how easily this wife, of all wives (for she was so innocent), would be delivered to him like an examining magistrate, and then more cynically, like a head on a plate, as his pecker imagined, and then finally amused at the bafflement before him, the apologia of a man's entire life, as if in trying to say "symmetrical tandem those queer-shaped undulating grasses of my bonny youth; and the elusive internal morass of coming to madness or adulthood I do not know," Leo was in effect spilling his rocky marriage upon the floor. For the words seemed to make no sense and— half in French, half in English—they were an utter bewilderment of phraseology under those cocksucking strobe lights. But in his own mind, in Leo's own mind, they were—these words, if he could possibly deliver them—the one balm to free himself of the restraints of the woods, where as they said of him, "He never sat upon a chair until seven."

Finally he was left sputtering and gesturing drunkenly by himself, ennobled only in his own mind, for that one moment a free man, and a clever one, and one that could if he wanted say: "Twizlewooded slope and fractured plates of clouds over the grand dark waters where I did wander, I tell you that much, I wandered through all the snapdragon grasses and the wind in the willow, until my cock itself came stiff."

And at the end of that night his wife was waltzing with the boss, his posterior raised to accommodate his small dancing feet, the dalliance obscene in its predictability, and Leo was at a table at the end of the hall in word and gesture drunk. The next afternoon he willed himself to jam gears and fell headfirst from the loader. Why? Because it was all meant to happen. He knew it now in his utter grief. He spoke to Alex with tears streaming down his cheeks.

But with the ticket he would buy the Porsche and prove them wrong. He would get back at anyone who laughed at him then.

He asked to see the ticket once more. He looked at it like a delicate flower. Like a willow filled with a soft delicate wind, as this gray dark night enclosed them.

"Yes—but we can't kill her, we just have to scare her," Alex said. "Why?"

Alex thought. "Because I'm her godfather," he said.

"Oh," Bourque said, astonished, and he spoke like an astonished child now. "Forever you would be worried about her—and if you cashed the ticket you would be more worried—and," he added with some soundness of mind, "if I suddenly impress my wife by becoming rich and then am charged with a murder it won't do any good at all. But if Amy is out of the way, no one will ever know—and think of the man Cid, and all he has done to harm women. I will put him out of business, slowly, little by little, and then, well, he will watch as she comes back to me. And as for you, Alex, with your seven million—yes, I can accommodate you by giving you seven—Minnie will soon tire of the tractor ruts and giant trucks and lost tundra out west and will long for you—her absence will make the heart grow fonder, even more so," Bourque whispered, "if the little girl is buried here and you build a recreation center in her name. AMY PATCH'S PLACE."

He continued now his postulization, with artificial humility, his eyes widened, and his legs planted against the table while he spoke, looking down all this time at the floor. This was said in a complete whisper in the semi-darkness: "Minnie will blame Sam for bringing her out there, she will even blame Sam for the death of the little girl—if it is done—and if Sam manages to come back, she will not stay with him. She will say: I went to buy a house in that graveyard out west, that mournful death knell for Maritime men, and the little girl my little baby drowned herself in a pool of water because she didn't want to leave the Miramichi for she was heartsick over Rory, a boy she was going to marry at seven, and why would anyone in their right mind ever connive to leave here.

Let me tell you, Amy was right and the only one who helped her was my dear friend Alex Chapman—you cocksucker, Sam, you have destroyed my life—you have destroyed it all! And Alex who we treated so deplorable, simply because he was a secular atheist, what did he do—what did he do, he went and built a recreation center for her, that's what he did, Samuel Patch."

Alex knew this to be true as well. All of this then he knew to be true, up until the moment he thought of Amy. Then he could not accomplish in his mind that which they were planning to do.

But his partner took another leap of logic and said this, while looking back down at the floor again and again whispering into the darkness before them, "I have long been interested in wife beating."

"What—what do you mean?" Alex said, breathing harshly against the quiet blackness.

"I simply mean this, fool. I have never hurt my wife, but she hurt me. And I know two women from downriver who killed their husbands, their defense being they feared for their lives—I am simply assuming the husbands did not have time to fear for theirs before they were shot. If they had taken the ultimate act, as bad as that was, they themselves would be living. This is what we must do in order to continue to live. Amy will terrorize us if we don't."

Alex's mother had died of a broken heart. He used to go out at night and search for his father so he would take his mother's heartbreak away.

"I will get the money," she kept telling him, "I will, just you wait and see!"

And Alex's life had started out with the deep conviction he could change this, change the very act of needing money or of ever hurting women. He could not stand to hear a woman cry.

Bourque told him that all that was beside the point now.

Alex tried to think of Socrates telling Plato one afternoon, after eating some soup, that he was going across the street for a moment to drown a child.

"Why?"

"So she won't snitch that I stole some ducks!"

And Plato saying, "Get her!"

Bourque in this darkness had taken a quantum leap to land on Stalin's plateau. That is, would it stop with Amy? Would they have to kill Fanny, and then Minnie, and then old Mrs. Hanson who owned the little store—or the nurse that came in twice a week?

Alex knew very well that poor little Koba the Dread had never any intention of stopping his killing until there was no one left but him.

He decided Bourque was a terrible right winger. So that, too, was in a way a mark against him. So now he looked at Bourque and tried to infuse the man with this kind of polar enmity.

But then he suddenly felt this: Leftism—the fashionable angst-ridden bullying kind he had known, that which paraded itself as just and morally superior and a balm to women, the kind he had used to subjugate Minnie—was now in limbo, or had been washed away, or at least it had entered a different stage, covered up in politics and perfume, where in its transition it had made the common justice seekers, who were now entitled and privileged, spoiled and infantile by their very views of the world. Were the right wingers better? Of course not. But the ideas Alex had of peace, along with other elaborate men and women of conscience, had by their varying forms of hypocrisy enabled war and bloodshed and the untold slaughter of millions.

"She is very, very sad about Rory—" Leo said. "That's what little Bridgette told me. She was his sweetheart and now he is— well, people drift apart—I know it's terrible, but they do! The only thing she has beyond that bridge in that little alcove is her pollywogs. And now they are taking that little spot away from her. It is tragic, really." Bourque actually had tears in his eyes.

"Terrible times," Alex whispered now.

It seemed all of this and more to Leo also, who asked Alex genuinely if he wanted to go and lie down, or have some tea.

"If worse comes to worse, and we have to, we can always blame Burton—everyone knows what he's like! A little girl-diddler if there ever was one!"

=

IT WAS STARTLING, BUT THAT NIGHT SITTING IN THE darkness Alex was compelled to tell Leo about the Maid of Orleans; that is, almost the same story that Amy told.

What he wanted to know was how "Bourquey," as Bourque was suddenly insisting he be called, would understand it, fathom it, and to what conclusions they might come regarding it, and did it have anything to do with them—that is, did 1430 have anything to do with them? Was it really more than five centuries ago, or could it have been just yesterday?

What did that little girl look like? In fact, could she have looked a bit like Amy Patch? In fact, at this moment Alex was sure she had. He asked this, as Bourquey was making him tea.

"I doubt it—" Bourque said.

"Can we be sure, Bourquey?" Alex's hair stuck up in huge curls from his forehead—because he hadn't managed to get it cut.

Leo shrugged and said, "It was probably a different case!"

Alex trembled. He spoke about her hearing the voice of God. He realized that atheists like himself (and he was the first, he said, to admit it) always had a problem with this little girl—oh, they wanted to admire her, for her courage, but they didn't in the end believe her. George Bernard Shaw was one. Perhaps it was her diet, who knew what they ate back then? Pig intestines, mostly.

"Really?"

"Pig guts was a big source of nourishment."

"I can see that," Bourque said. "They wouldn't be so bad in a stew!"

And of course the feminists found her problematic. He knew that. But, Alex said, as if he just had an epiphany, many feminists he knew found every woman outside their comfort zone of political gain problematic. Alex had always tried to agree with them, to agree with their sense of entitlement, cast in an arena of victimhood. How could he abandon them now for a little saint like Joan?

"You can't abandon them," Leo said, "for women had to bear the brunt!"

"Don't tell me, I know how women had to bear the brunt—I knew it before you!"

"Did not!"

"Well, at any rate so you see here it is—if Joan of Arc came along again, she would again be burned—so I am just following the new religion. They would have to burn her to a crisp."

"Well we aren't going to burn Amy—we are only going to drown her—!" Bourque answered victoriously.

It was strange for Alex to say all this. But did he want to change his opinions now? Could he protect Amy, who disagreed with everything he had ever said, if he himself was in danger to be put in jail for life? He would not last in jail. He would perhaps be raped. Most certainly killed. But to do it for Amy Patch? To go to jail in order to keep her alive? That was true courage. Of course he had been arrested for protesting the lack of a women's clinic. He had spent a night in jail, and was interviewed the next day. He had believed he was courting danger then!

But, he said, even the French didn't believe our little maid, and he asked Bourquey, as Bourque was insisting he be called, if they as atheists had a problem with Amy, just as atheists had a problem with little Joan.

"Not a bit of it, boy," Bourque sniffed.

"Well, she has taken a course on Saint Mark!"

"Lot of good it did her," Bourque said.

But Leo wanted to know what happened to Joan.

So Alex continued. The British controlled a good deal of France, and Charles VII was an absent king, a worldly king without a country.

"Is that so?"

This voice Joan heard. This voice of God coming to a peasant girl, and this voice told her to raise an army. Over persecution and ignorance, she did, and she battled the English and defeated them— it was a masterful, wondrous thing, Alex said. Yet she was captured.

"Cookie?" Bourque asked. He had brought a bag of homemade cookies from his sister.

Alex munched on the cookie as he spoke, a napkin on his knee. And then the dilemma for Charles, back in power on the throne: the little girl captured by the English; the English willing to leave him on the throne if he just gave them the little lady. Why? Because they did not want anything to do with a warrior who heard the living God. It would be better if she had heard the devil or nothing at all. In a way, the English gave Charles the option of keeping grand France in exchange for little Joan.

"Do you see how this was a predicament?"

"Absolument," Leo said, scratching his pocked face quickly—and quicker than usual.

"A worldly predicament?"

"Oui."

"And one without precedent, really, except maybe the inescapable quandary of—"

"Of who?"

"Why, of Pontius Pilate."

"Really."

"Yes."

"You don't say."

Bourque was now sitting at the table with him. They could see each other's eyes and faces and no more. Alex tried a bit more of the cookie.

Yes, the quandary was much the same. And they too, the judges of 1430, wanted to have Joan admit that she didn't hear the voice of God. She could not admit such a thing.

"I suppose she couldn't if she thought she did," Leo said, taking her side.

"No, they wanted her lessened, just as we want Amy lessened."

Bourque gave a start, and then nodded neither one way or the other. For Alex was making a comparison that was not entirely comforting. But Alex, if he had ever searched for the truth, must search for it here.

"And King Charlie was much like me—this big cheese didn't mind giving up his integrity—his soul, if he had any—by giving up the savior of his kingdom, by giving up this sweet child—like Amy keeping care of old Fanny Groat all summer long in the dark little place up the hill!"

"That stretches it," Bourque said. "That really stretches it!"

There was a long pause as he finished his cookie.

"And so what happened to the little girl?"

"She was burned at the stake—with an unfortunate aside."

"And what was this unfortunate aside—I mean, it seems unfortunate already."

"Ah—you see, for young girls especially, the executioner always had pity, and would strangle them just before the fire was lighted. But she was guarded by so many English troops he couldn't manage to do it, so she was burned alive."

"Ahh," Bourque said, spitting.

He told Alex to shut up. He talked about once getting a steam burn instead. Then he turned to go, back along the lost highway well after night had fallen.

—

MARKUS PAUL WAS BRILLIANT, AND TOUGH, AND WITHOUT debt in the world. Of course I am not talking about financial debt. He had enough of that. I am speaking of moral debt. He had nothing of that. And how did he know, how could he be sure of having no moral debt, when so many millions upon millions of people did? He knew that Johnny Proud did not kill Poppy Bourque, and he knew that everyone believed he had. Proud had lost thirty-four pounds and most of his teeth from meth. But even in his delusion he was not a murderer. But in defending Proud a defaming was set against Markus, to which he never believed he would be vulnerable. They said of him he was wanting to deflect guilt from his cousin to shadows who were never there. Some truck that may have been just a young boy getting jerked off by his girlfriend who wanted at this time in her life to remain a technical virgin. They laughed and told him one hot sour day that they would search for a spot of cum to prove it.

Markus saw how the whites simply assumed Proud's guilt, and were contented with being assured of it. And he saw how his own reserve believed it, and in fact like the whites around them, wanted it as well. For if it was John Proud, that little boy who had thrown the rocks at the bear to protect the seminary student—if it were him, well so many local and immediate problems would be solved on the reserve. He wouldn't be waking up drunk in other people's houses, or trying to break into cars. He would be out of the white man's hair and off the reserve as well.

In jail where he belonged. For he had finally gone and done it.

Bourque was right. Poppy had problems with the men at the camp, and had threatened to phone the police. So that was the tie-in that Bauer was using. Markus, though he knew of this, wanted to dispel it, for he believed it a red herring.

Still, if he had said it was that way, Markus would have solved the case and have gotten a promotion. QED. This is what everyone wanted; even the band chief, who stated he was angered they would immediately charge a First Nations man, secretly wanted Proud out of his hair.

All, then, were waiting for Markus to say the case was solved, and get a promotion and walk about like a big Indian. But he could not. And not being able to do this, caused those who he had admired, and who he believed had once admired him, to change toward him. To open doors for others, and close them when he approached, and to keep information about the case from him, so he was seriously hampered, even concerning the imprint of the tires. For everyone knew who did it, and who had confessed.

They wanted the Proud case solved.

Well, Markus stubbornly said, he could not solve that case. He might solve another one involving a truck late at night. He might be able to do that. But doing so would lead him down a darker, more harrowing, and less traveled road where even the more liberal of our society might blame him for so-called pettifogging. But he believed this was the road he must stay on. Until he was successful or until he was proven wrong.

It was quite simple, and he had already mentioned it to Alex. Nothing was taken from Old Chapman's house, and nothing was missing from Poppy Bourque's the night he disappeared. It was only after the fact that John Proud came back and tried to steal a floor lamp. But is that the reason he came back? Markus did not think so. That is, perhaps Leo Bourque, who knew him, and knew what shape he was in, sent him there as a decoy.

Yet others decided John Proud was breaking into old men's houses, and carrying them off and putting them somewhere where they could not be found. Markus wanted to talk to the professor of ethics about this, but as he did he became more and more aware of a man fudging his own moral standard. It was what people did, and Markus saw it all the time. But he was surprised how quickly Alex conceded guilt for Mr. Proud, when he had not conceded guilt on a man who a few years before had been guilty. That is, Alex had marched to a drum for the rights of the First Nations, and called anyone who would not see his point of view racist. Markus Paul himself did not march. He would be living proof of the rights of the First Nations. That is, he would be living proof of the dignity of a human being. That was unfortunate for him. Because it meant he could not fudge his moral standard, as did certain men who pretended to have a moral standard regarding his rights as a First Nations man. They had wanted him to become more visible, and he hadn't. They had wanted him not to charge the Penniac man, and he had. And as strange as it was, they wanted him to charge the Proud man, and he could not. So the idea was that this was favoritism for his cousin, and the worst case of native nepotism. If he was wrong it would be written about everyplace. He knew this and steadied himself.

Yet for those few who could see, it meant that Markus Paul was not in debt to the past or the future. It also meant that he might flounder on this small barren highway, and never get the promotion he, like all ambitious people, sought. He could have made more of his position if he had aligned himself with Alex Chapman. For Chapman, even though he might not himself know it, was considered on many levels to be above reproach. His battle for human rights alone was flamboyant enough to cause a stir over any issue he chose.

But Markus could not simply say what people wanted him to say. He was stubborn like that. And the last thing he would do is try to ingratiate himself with those who held this against him. So those in the department soon found him problematic, and often they did not tell him what they were doing. Nor at times did they let on he had received messages about the case he was trying to follow. Not because they were mean, but because they felt they were right and he was wrong.

So as the days passed Markus was more certain of the involvement of Chapman and Bourque, and everyone else was less certain.

It was so strange, almost unbelievable, and certainly, so far, unverifiable.

Yet why?

Why was a question that must be asked.

For a long time he sat in his small apartment, dazzled and depressed by this why. For to think of Alex Chapman as a murderer was certainly depressing. For he had followed Alex's career, and read his writings about the indignity suffered by the First Nations. At first he had admired him, but over the last few years he felt Alex to be a dishonest broker. Still, he wanted this Alex to be noble and, like Caesar's wife, above suspicion. But now, after compiling his facts, or assumptions, Alex, he concluded, was guilty of knowing something that happened, and not reporting what he knew. At its best, this scenario meant that Alex might have had information about Poppy (such as child molestation) that was so horrendous he took action. In fact, Alex's career to this point suggested that he might finally be tired of the courts and the menial sentencing of criminals. This would make him heroic, or might mitigate the stamp of guilt.

Yet to Markus, Poppy was the most innocent of old men. He

couldn't have done anything. The worst he had done, besides dumping his sawdust, was drinking too many beer and singing Hank Williams in his French twang.

Who could ever be so cold as to kill a man like this? Markus wondered. Oh, he knew who: those who had lost their childhood and blamed innocence and kindness for that loss.

Yet the more he was dazzled by it the less he slept. But he was certain, just as the priest was certain, that the two involved, whoever they were, if it was not John Proud, would be depressed and paranoid and sure to blame each other. Sooner or later they would have to confront what they had done, and begin to suspect one another. He thought (did he know how close he actually was?) that it might be over a will—something on a piece of paper.

So he kept thinking: what was it these people were after, what were they looking for? Did Poppy give it to them? The more he tried to answer this, the less and less successful he became. Until with a trick of the intellect he simply said, in Micmac, "What have they found?"

For a day or so, he let it register and said it again and again, but was puzzled by it. Maybe they had found the will and had to have it changed. And maybe Poppy found out!

That didn't make sense, but more sense then anything else. Then Markus decided it had to be something else—more communal and less private then a personal will. Something that would benefit Poppy as well. That is why they went to him. So he stared out the window, at the dry dark parking lot of his forlorn apartment building on the outskirts of his reserve, with paper wrappers being blown in the air. Everything seemed to be like a sad movie picture, in black and white, when he thought of Old Poppy and his vegetable stand. He wanted to let it go, that question: What had they found? But it wouldn't go away.

That was the day he went to visit Leo Bourque's ex-wife. He drove along the split highway that ran against the shore, against the sunlight shining over the corpses of a million seashells in the deepening afternoon, the water languid and milk-like, with the

smell of heavy equipment and creosote logs against the deepening
blues of the sky. With the pounding of the great hammer behind
them, shattering cars to nothing, he brought the petite woman
from the office and into the sunlight and asked questions, which
she tried to feint like a boxer. No, she did not know where Leo
went or what he did, or if he did or did not, and she was only certain that he had changed since she married him, like she supposed,
with her one whiff of learned and practiced and coddled superiority, that all men sooner or later did.

The innocent girl had become aloof.

"Ah yes," Markus said, nodding and smiling, his cheeks flush
and his eyes upon the office door where her opulent boss, in his ill-
fitting suit, stood as if watching guard, and as if he was there as
her moral protector—which was what men who had taken over a
woman's life on the pretext of setting them free of their husbands
so often did. This boss had tried to talk to Paul in the office about,
well, about himself—about how he'd had to get her away from Leo
Bourque. That is, as in situations like this, the other man wanted
the police to join him in moral disgust of the husband. And Paul
knew this, and had dealt with it as a police officer in all the ways
one could. He often disliked these men more than he did the abu-
sive husbands, or just as much. The boss then closed the door just
as the great hammer shattered and crushed down on the hood of a
car involved in an accident two weeks before.

Many looked upon Markus Paul as an Indian, too big-feeling
for his own good, harassing white men and women. This is what he
knew he would have to put up with for the rest of his life.

But this meeting was not unfruitful for him, as Markus
discovered.

Leo would drive about with his wife at night—and go by
houses of rich people, and say he would be as rich as this. This was
when he went to the parties for Fouy Construction and began to
talk with words she did not comprehend, dazzling them with his
need to prove to her that he was relevant to the world. It was then
that she was seen at a party and hired by Cid himself to work in

the office. Just as a temporary office worker at first. It was not long after this her boss would call her in at night to go over the tenders and contracts, and she would leave Bourque alone. She couldn't get home so she would dine with the boss at Taylor's restaurant.

Then, one day, Chapman went under. Cid got the bid on the entire road. And Bourque tried to tell her one night in their little kitchen, smiling like a Cheshire cat and waiting for her to open her arms to him, that it was he who had done it. She felt sorry for him, because Cid had told her it was himself. She smiled and patted his hand and told him he didn't have to lie. This infuriated him even more.

"It was me, it was me, it was me!" Leo kept saying, spit coming from his mouth. "Alex gave up the bid—to me!" But she did not believe him, with that infuriating, infallible certainty of mind.

"Alex Chapman wouldn't even talk to a man like you," she had said. Of course she regretted it. But it was said.

Markus looked at her broad white forehead, and her blunt little nose.

They had such a big contract because Chapman had gone under, and she was indispensable to her boss now. She went to Campbellton with him in his Cessna plane, to see about a road job, and spent the night.

"In separate rooms," Doreen said, as if Markus should be the one to understand this.

Leo, however, began to plead with her to leave the job, begged her to leave her job, because he could see the handwriting on the wall. She told him she would not. She wanted to learn to fly that Cessna plane. Cid said he would teach her.

Later that month, Leo fell from a heavy loader and busted his hip. He was out of work.

"He came to me last week and said he would get a lot of money."

"How?"

"I don't know—I am not sure—but Cid had nothing to do with it!" she said, protective of her man with the Cessna airplane. "But he said, 'I've won the jackpot.'"

Markus gave a start, and he flushed, his eyes widened, and he said nothing. Except he was thinking of ethics and a moral code of some kind, and the tragedy of Leo Bourque.

"Why would Alex give up a bid?" he asked himself.

She turned her head away, in the listless heat of tar and afternoon and a blood-red dying sky, as her boss looked out the door window, smiling at Markus Paul obsequiously—something he would never do to this dark-haired, small-breasted woman, who looked quite a bit like Minnie Patch, and Markus supposed something he would never have to do with Leo Bourque, with all his big words in the wrong place. Not that this boss would actually know what those words meant, or have ever read a text where those words would be placed, or have tried in some desperate winter storm near the back roads of Tracadie to struggle through Balzac. He did not have to impress anyone, having his new Cessna airplane, as Leo, alone and frantic, had tried to do.

"He said last week he was going to be rich," Doreen told him. "He told me he would have a surprise for everyone."

"He told me," Cid offered from the door, as the soft wind blew his tie back over his neck, "that he would buy a Porsche."

"He did."

"Yes," Cid said, hesitating and then laughing.

"How?"

"I do not know—but he often said things like that, from the first day I met him, but I never saw him with nothing trash like that!" Cid said.

"Like that, but not that," Markus answered, and looked toward the sun, blood-like against the wide sky.

"Pardon?"

Markus did not bother answering. He asked instead, "A jackpot. Do you know of any?"

"Pardon me? Pardon-moi?" Leo's wife asked.

"What jackpot, I wonder—?"

—

How long did it take to glean this information from this young and handsome woman and her altruistic boss? Ten minutes exactly. And did she have to say everything for Markus Paul to understand what had happened? She only had to say a tenth of it. And he knew. The young woman turned and went back inside, and the great large hammer fell again. The little mustached Cid, with his flat face and opulent rump, was waiting.

So now, this new development put more pieces together.

Alex had now floundered into middle age, and Alex's moral debt had to be paid. Would this jackpot pay it?

Markus Paul had watched this debt become apparent and increase exponentially over the last six or seven years. Could he go to Alex and confront him?

Markus Paul had no moral debt. He could stare you in the eye and tell the truth.

He wondered about this, as night fell, and the cry of gulls faded, and the shore birds slept, their wings turned inward like miniature pterodactyls on the waves.

Markus then went back to Poppy Bourque's house, up the crooked rock drive and in the back way. Just, as he decided, the murderer must have.

A small and untidy little spot of a house on an old road—where it seemed to hold the memories of a thousand family nights, now gone forever. A vase filled with papers and bills, where there had once been flowers. A picture of a horse-riding woman with a white cowboy hat. A picture of Madonna and child that seemed, though forty-five years old, still pristine.

An autographed picture of Rocket Richard.

But here is what Markus was thinking: why weren't the box of bills and vases with pencils turned over here, like they were at Chapman's, if both places were ransacked by John Proud? Of course that was the question.

Where would Poppy be, Markus thought, obviously very agitated at the idea of not being able to help the old man.

Earlier he had gone to the hospital. He took John Proud's shoes and looked at the bottom of them, then turned his stinking and fetid pants inside out, and opened his wallet again. Empty except for his name written in it. In his jacket pocket three Export cigarettes, a hash pipe, some tinfoil, and in his inside pocket, in Kleenex, a syringe.

Then he had woken Proud by shaking him slightly.

"What were you doing in the house—what were you looking for—what jackpot?"

But Proud could not help him—he didn't understand anything. He had not remembered much of where he was or why.

He had been on his way back to his hunting lodge when he was stopped.

"Why the lamp?"

"I don't know—I still have a sense of humor," John said.

Markus left his wasted body, the ribs protruding from his weakened chest, and went back to Poppy Bourque's. He stared out across the desolate back field toward Leo's small shed that looked forsaken in the wind. Far above, seagulls rested on the air; far above, a plane carrying uncaring people from London to Toronto, Markus a tiny speck on the ground.

"The only one who would feel free of being detected by Leo, was Leo. The only one who would feel comfortable at not being discovered by Alex, was Alex," Markus reasoned, thinking of the "break-ins" at the respective houses. He was looking for a jackpot. He even, or also, thought of digging in the dirt basement, where somebody had dug sometime before—but realized that the previous dig was only to find a sewer line, when the new sewer lines were being put in. And so he came upstairs and brushed off his shirt.

John Proud would be transferred down to the Richabucto jail in a week. Then the prosecutorial weight would be placed upon him, Markus Paul, to bring some kind of credible information for a charge. He entertained the idea that John Proud was with these other two, Bourque and Alex, but persuaded himself that this was not so. Proud had no friends, no one would trust him to go in with them on anything. In fact he was or could be considered the poster child of what happened to First Nations men because of generations of neglect and abuse.

Besides, as the kids liked to say, this was totally random. That is, it wasn't a crime until the actual crime was committed. At least this is what Markus Paul had decided, so it wasn't even a crime that came off the back of a botched robbery, Markus decided.

Markus Paul left the house and went back to his apartment. He had the hash pipe and the tinfoil with him, and the old syringe with some of John Proud's blood in it, and set them on the table, along with John Proud's wallet. The wallet looked immaculate, new, had been carried by John for a year. He never had a thing in it. He just wanted to have one. He set the wallet down, and then feeling guilty Markus Paul zippered the wallet back up, placed the hash pipe upon it, and set them both on the coffee table by themselves.

POPPY'S HOUSE HAD NO ONE IN IT FOR ABOUT AN HOUR AND a half. Then suddenly the door opened and Markus came in again. He began to look through the cupboards and baskets and cups, the drawers everywhere. He upset that vase, and looked through bills and receipts. Angry and resentful with himself that he had not discovered what should be discovered. But now his face was determined, his methods professional, and his search intricate.

Why?

Because he had gone home and cooked himself some spaghetti, was sitting before the TV waiting for the sports and saw an advertisement for the 649 lotto, and the information that a ticket worth thirteen million had been sold in northern New Brunswick and so far not claimed. He stood, and began looking here and there for a ticket he himself had bought three weeks before.

While doing so, he realized he was searching in very small places for a piece of paper.

Christ almighty, he thought, this is ridiculous.

He went to John Proud's wallet, and opened it carefully, looking through it. He zippered it up again. He went back and sat down, stared at his dinner, finished his tea, lit a cigarette, and thought of Alex, and Leo Bourque.

Over the last four days he had written down twelve things all of this might be about, scratching things off one minute and adding things the next, unsure of why he was doing so, like, as he thought, a gamester playing a Ouija board. He kept these silent thoughts away from Sergeant Bauer and others, for they had no use for his obsession with the truck.

Things like "car payment," "money owed," "hidden assets," "real estate," "fear of Poppy knowing something," "fear Poppy will tell something," "couldn't let him out of the truck," "couldn't let him go home," "couldn't let him go to the fair," "gambling money owed," "must have a weapon."

And every once in a while he kept coming back to "couldn't let him out of the truck."

And then this, after he initially came back from Poppy's: "Some small item at Mr. Chapman's house—they were looking for a piece of paper—a piece of paper—looking in drawers and small bill jars for what—it has to be a piece of paper—Poppy discovered they found this piece of paper. They didn't search Poppy's house for it!"

A piece of paper!

Over the last two days Markus Paul had thought of a piece of paper. And what would be on a piece of paper one was looking for. He had put down "numbers to a safe," and thought that had to be it. But what if Old Chapman had no safe? He would have to get into the house and look. But if that was the case, he was at a loss.

And then this, just now which even he laughed at: "lotto ticket worth $13 million."

But he knew from his work the old Sherlock Holmes adage, even if he himself never read Conan Doyle or watched Sherlock Holmes movies: If one excludes all other possibilities, the possibility that is left, no matter how unlikely, must be the one that is true.

=

BOURQUE WAS NOT AT ALL CALM, FOR MARKUS PAUL WAS AT his uncle's all day. He could see the squad car there, and wanted to go over and ask him what was going on. But he hesitated. He knew that if it was nothing to do with him, Markus would come over and speak. He waited, and Markus did not come over. Therefore, it had to be something to do with him. So he walked up the road, and thumbed a ride to Brennen's tavern. Then after a few beer, with his nerves settled, he went to see Alex. He was now very angry and knew things had to proceed quickly. He had to convince his Siamese twin or be doomed. The only way to convince him was to prove to him how esteemed he would be once this was done. This was the sleight of hand on which everything else hinged.

So he said, "We will have one opportunity and no more. We drown her in the current of Glidden's pool. The day she is alone— that day and no other!"

"People will find out," Alex said, as a challenge.

"No," Bourque explained. "They will say: 'That crazy little kid, she loved that boy so much that she couldn't stand going away.'"

This was the one and only hook on which it could all ride.

Yes, she had trouble with a boy and was depressed about leaving him and going out west. In fact, the idea of her leaving had not only made it imperative that they kill her but logical that she, depressed about going out west, would take her life.

Bourque knew very well what to say to his partner, and spoke now as if his life depended upon it: "That is what they will say, Alex—listen to me, they will say you visited her when Sam was away, and tried to comfort her. Got her into a course on ethics to cheer her little bauble head up. But you who knew she was depressed could not help her with this boy. The ethics course was done for that reason! SEE! Once that is realized nothing will stop us—we will be as free as birds! Look how it can be envisioned by people! To benefit you!"

Alex listened to this, and it seemed logical as long as Bourque spoke. It was Plato's noble lie that could catapult him into the future. Plato's noble lie stating that someone might be sacrificed and a lie be told, a public manipulated if great good could come of it. So if he held on to this, then it could be managed. That is, the very manipulating of the truth sounded far more tempting and very much more desirable than the truth. Alex wasn't immune to succumbing to it, as long as he listened to Bourque speak. In fact, he had manipulated the truth all of his life.

Bourque in a way had become the new Plato. Because Bourque by now knew exactly how to play on Alex's vanity and make it seem like reason. The desire to believe that his own altruism concerning this girl tried to prevent her from taking her life, even though the girl's mother had shunned him, was something the very noblest of humans could say was splendid. In fact, this alone urged him to carry out their plan.

There was even something else—it might be discovered that his family had set aside money for her scholarship, something in Chapman's will. Alex knew he could say very easily he had insisted upon this. And he would have, if he had thought of it, he decided.

"I knew she was bright—I tried to keep her alive!"

"Well," Markus Paul would say, "from the earliest time you have tried to show wisdom in the face of your enemies!"

"I am just an ordinary man!"

"How many of us would like to be as ordinary as you! Look what you have done—tried to give back whole islands and everything else!"

So Bourque continued in this soothing and in many respects brilliant vein: People would think that Amy had relied upon him and him alone, because she was so bright. That she could not rely upon her semi-illiterate father. In fact it might be better if she did die, so people could have Alex say, Yes, she was coming to visit me—brought me buckets of blueberries—I insisted she be allowed, because I knew I must try to help her. But there was this boy, and you know young girls and boys! Once she came from the church, from some course she was taking down there, and cried her little eyes out! Father Mac didn't understand!

"Oh, I'm not going to say that—I will only say she herself came to me."

And there was of course one more advantageous bit of fiction that could be catapulted into the truth: "Some very worthy people at the university know what you tried to have done—when she was about the size of a sweet pea—but they will see how you stood for life once she was born," Bourque said with sympathy and understanding. It was as if he himself were changing his stringent mind about this procedure.

And Alex was somewhat comforted. He mulled this over, and ate a carrot.

"My good God, you know—just like with John Proud he tried to protect them his whole life," Bourque whispered. "That's what they will say—you won't even have to grow a beard to be recognized as an intellectual!"

And Minnie; the idea that this might bring her to him some night was a fact not to be sneezed at.

"Not to be sneezed at," Bourque said, continuing his polemic, and rubbing Alex's shoulders as if he was a boxer getting ready to stand in the ring.

Alex thought of this for a moment.

"Paul is getting closer," Bourque said. "I don't think he has much figured out—and Sergeant Bauer and others are angry at him for leading the department on a wild goose chase and making a mockery of justice. So it might all quiet down once Proud is charged. Paul might face charges himself!"

"How do you know that?"

"I only know what everyone else on the damn highway knows. They are thinking of charging Markus Paul with impeding a police investigation—that's what some people say, and how angry the police are with him. Soon after this is all over, you will be the only man—the only one the river looks to."

—

Bourque told him to come with him, and they went down to the beach. It was cold again, and the waves looked mean and choppy toward the North Cape. Alex stared across the water to the island, and the old barricade he had helped the First Nations men build when they took over the island.

"Come with me now," Bourque said.

They walked along the shore all the way to Arron Brook and then back through the woods to Glidden's pool.

"What will happen to our souls?" he asked Bourque as they approached Glidden's pool in the evening, with the trees swaying above them. "I mean, on the very off chance that we have one?"

Bourque was startled, his hands moved slowly and he folded them and leaned against an old black spruce.

"Better off for it," Leo said, rubbing his nose.

"How in God's name will we be better off for it?"

"Makes it stronger," Bourque said.

"What do you mean?"

"I mean—" Bourque said angrily, "you are worse than my wife—what I mean is better off. What I mean in the intransigence of the morning air, in this small little square root of a place we now exist in—what I am saying, what I am saying is that, well, in a way we will be quite a bit better off—financially. And if we build that center and put Amy's statue up, we will end up helping far more children than we hurt—a thousand children helped, and one hurt—that is the only way to think of it. And if you don't think governments don't think of it this way, we must act then like a government just for this brief moment."

Bourque continued: "You will stand in by Vince's rock—you silly, stupid fucker—and I will stand about the turn near Glidden's pool. She won't come here alone, even when she puts her pollywoggles in she has someone come with her—so you will get her and bring her to me. But if she goes down on the road to seek help, I will be able to see her. We will get her, and we will quickly, without hesitation, put her in the water—we have to get a lot of water in her puny lungs. She won't feel so much—we will tell her we want to take her somewhere, her mom is sick or something!"

"But she is afraid of water," Alex said, smiling, as if this was a hitch in their whole plan.

"Can you swim?"

"No," Alex admitted, "I don't swim."

Bourque slapped him again. "There, for being stupid."

"Stop that, Jesus Christ!" Alex yelled.

"Don't you see, that doesn't matter—we are not going to ask her if she likes water—don't be ridiculous, you just don't do that. Besides," Bourque calculated, "the fact that she hates water shows the kind of state her poor little pea brain was in over this boy Rory. And this boy treated her bad, don't you worry—he needs a good slap, he treated her so bad, which means, when it all comes down to it, that killing herself was probably the only thing she could do!"

They were silent for a long time.

Then Bourque added with compassion, before they started to walk back, "So what do you think, how does that sound?"

MARKUS PAUL REMEMBERED IN THE NEW TESTAMENT HOW Jesus told his listeners they wanted a sign for everything, and he would not give them one for they lacked belief. They mocked belief and wanted a sign. Well, here it was. Everything pointed away from John Proud, but no one believed him. Sergeant Bauer, who was incensed that a man who had confessed was not yet in jail, was the worst. Yet the signs were everywhere and they did not see those signs.

The simplest things they did not understand. They did not understand ambition as much as greed. Greed they saw as being compatible to the estate of John Proud. Markus had come to see this as a crime of ambition. He did not know how or why, but he felt the two had killed Poppy for ambition. Perhaps, strangely enough, for a lotto ticket that Poppy himself did not have. And why? Because, as he said, of the rapacious ambition of those two. By "of those two" of course he meant Bourque and Chapman. They were both exceedingly ambitious. What was the ambition about? He knew Bourque had grown up in a house without a chair. That could make a man ambitious.

There was something else very obvious. Leo Bourque had been to Poppy Bourque's that night. Why? Simply a process of elimination. It had to be him, for no one else had visited old Mr. Bourque in the past twelve years except for the girls, their mother, and Leo Bourque himself. So unless Poppy left with a complete stranger then by easy process of elimination Markus had whittled it down to Leo. There was something else. Poppy Bourque's lights were out, but the porch light was left on. Poppy had turned the lights out, left the porch light on because he believed he would come back in the dark. So as far as Markus could fathom, Poppy was thinking of going out for an hour or so with someone he knew, at least coming back before daylight. That means he either got lost or was taken away. He did not take his flashlight, which, Markus was informed by Bridgette's aunt, he always did when he walked up the highway at night. This meant he was with someone and being driven somewhere. And it meant that most likely, with the porch light on, he went willingly. Also, all of this information he had acquired without the help of Leo, who was not forthcoming. But when Markus Paul said this to Sergeant Bauer, just as when he said things about the truck, few listened to him.

But Markus now had something else. He had confirmation of Leo Bourque's fingerprints on one item in Old Poppy's house. Bourque's fingerprints were on file because of him having gotten angry and threatening his wife. And one might say his fingerprints should be on everything in Poppy Bourque's house, because he was always there. But then again, it was what it was on that was the salient point, which no one seemed to think important. So Markus kept it to himself.

It was on the beer bottle that had cigarette butts in it. And that beer bottle very likely contained the last beer Poppy ever drank. It had been picked up by Bourque, who had dropped a cigarette into it. It was the only cigarette that was native brand. Poppy rolled his own from Players tobacco. Bourque had come into the house, and Poppy got ready to go out. Leo picked up the bottle and put his butt into it, just as Poppy was washing the paint off his hands. Markus envisioned a scenario where Leo had lit a cigarette in the truck and walked to the house, while Alex waited.

So Paul listened to those he considered very stupid people and was silent, and those people believed, as the only Micmac in the department, Paul was trying to thwart this investigation about a Micmac who had already confessed. It was a very slippery slope, they said, from enthusiasm to impeding progress. It was also, in the court of public opinion, something that would be looked askance at. Markus himself thought of it differently. That is, because of his race he was the enabler of their misdirection, and he knew it and could do nothing about it. He himself was the one red flag, and yet he himself had to keep pressing for their direction to change. Yet the more he pressed, the more he was the red flag, and the greater enabler of their misdirection did he become. If he stopped swimming against the current, took the easy road, he would be considered wise and brave, and Sergeant Bauer would applaud him and offer him the promotion he sought.

Markus Paul sat alone at lunch and most of the day, ate in the little restaurant by himself and went back to his apartment at night. He drank beer and stared out in hope at some spot in the trees as if some great magician of his people, the god Glooscap himself, who tamed the great bull moose by breaking his back, would make a path through the clouds and revisit him after four hundred years of his people being in the wilderness.

He even went along the road to small stores, to ask if anyone had come in to see about a lotto ticket. Though many, many did, no one remembered anything to do with Poppy Bourque. He would think this quest showed him to be a complete idiot. So he would try to reason other ways, and came back always to this: "Is it such an unusual thing, a lotto ticket—it must be—it has to be, but whose and why?"

He had no luck, however, so he thought long and hard about the truck in Chapman's yard, about the break-in at the Chapman property. There were two in the house, at different times. It was not hard to figure out. They were looking for something very small. Then, after a few beer, it always came back to this: Why did the nephew, long a major player in the fight for Indian rights, suddenly fudge his moral equivalency? Why did he backtrack on support of those who he had written about in the papers? What was the problem that he would not support this man now when the evidence was both flimsy and circumstantial?

How come?

This, in fact, should have been Alex's greatest fight.

Because he knows who did it, and Proud did not do it, Markus Paul thought. Which meant someone close to him or he himself did it?

"Glooscap will know," Markus Paul said. Thinking of the ducks in the air and birds in the great bed of the trees. "But Glooscap will not tell us mere mortals—for that we must figure it out ourselves."

That is, what Young Chapman suspected was true. Markus Paul was studying him and finding his love of justice to be a perverse and self-serving anomaly. He did not set out to find this; it is simply what he found, by process of elimination.

What made Markus ill and queasy about this as he drank his beer that late afternoon with the smell of fall in the woods? It was his pent-up desire to blame Alex, because Markus had liked old Jim Chapman, and was very fond of him. It was Jim Chapman who had helped him through university. And Alex did not know this.

So the last thing he was saying was that a white man couldn't feel the sting of injustice against the native. Surely he did not believe that it was only the native who understood the world? There was enough injustice in the world to go around. And most white men knew in some way the depths of betrayal they caused the First Nations people. In fact, what was strange, Old Jim had himself. And in some way Markus had had a relatively easy life compared to some whites, even Alex Chapman himself. No. It was something else: "REASON being."

So Markus bided his time and wondered about all of this energy, these small whirlwinds blowing back and forth just under the surface of things.

And Markus in a way (in a way he did not know himself until this moment) wanted to put a stop to Alex Chapman, and his assumption that he knew better than other white men, because he believed he could approve or disapprove of the value of people like his uncle and like Minnie. And now Markus realized it had all come to this moment on the lost highway. That he had long watched Alex do this, and he would try to put a stop to it here. He would do this because of the self-important picture Alex had taken beside Markus's sister, who was now dead and in the arms of Glooscap.

He shook slightly as he thought of it, toasted Glooscap, and said a prayer.

He just might quarantine Alex, who had damaged the reputation of his uncle for twenty years.

He just might show Alex that a man could and would appropriate everything in the world and anything from a life, except truth. Truth was something one could not, ever, appropriate.

He thought about the lotto ticket: What if the uncle, Jim Chapman, had the lotto ticket and Alex stole it!

Then he thought: It has to be wrong—he got everything in the will.

Still, he must decide to follow his gut instinct or not. It was follow the lotto ticket theory to the end of the line or not!

He sat smoking a cigarette and looking out at the darkness creeping over the bay and the foreboding look of cold coming in off the swells.

They are certain to do something else—something will force them, he thought.

So he decided to go once again to see Mr. Chapman.

THE DRIVEWAY WAS FLAT, WHITE WITH DUST AND COVERED in fine gravel, and the sun was still warm on his uniform. He sat on his haunches looking at the tires of Old Chapman's truck, and heard Alex coming up behind him in a kind of remote, hesitant way, peculiarly watching first from the trees, and then along the old creosote logs, and then up the path that 120 workers had taken over the fifty years of Chapman's company, coming and going, ebb and flow, like lost dusty planets circling some faint falling star called Chapman's Paving and Construction until that star imploded and drove them hither and yon into a botched universe.

Alex was about twenty yards away when Markus finally said, in his soft Micmac voice, "Do you know what I can't tell?"

"What?" Alex asked, startled that his presence was known and that it had been known, and that in some way because of his surreptitious movement a state of guilt might be registered by the man.

Alex stopped walking and then started once more. He had come over to get some books that he wanted to show his class. He had the list written down because he now forgot things so easily, his mind was often a vague whirr, as if some fan were inside and he couldn't stop it, like the fan you might hear in summer in another room and spend half the night awake in shadows. He certainly did not want Markus here, and he was wondering if he shouldn't make some kind of demand—this was, after all, private property, Old Jim had signs everywhere. But Markus simply said, "I can't tell if these are the tire marks."

"What tire marks?" Alex said, offhandedly.

"The tire marks at the old road, if they were—well, it just might be the reason."

"Reason—what reason?"

"The reason John Proud was at the house, to take and bring the truck back—that makes sense, doesn't it?"

"I am not sure," Alex said.

"Oh of course it does." Markus turned and smiled. "It would almost have to be him—if this is the truck—"

"Why—?"

"Well, it means he was here sooner, and it means that we know what he was looking for—and then why he came back—but of course you would have to notice if the truck was gone, wouldn't you?"

There was silence. Alex looked mystified, his blond eyelashes almost invisible when he blinked.

"The keys to the truck, that was small enough to riffle through jars and drawers—keys to the truck, that's what he might have been riffling through things for."

"Oh I see, yes," Alex said relieved. "That certainly explains everything—"

"Except why would he go upstairs to try to find the keys?"

"Well, they could have been up there," Alex said excitedly.

"Yes, they could have—"

Alex smiled at Markus, who didn't seem to know this, and walked himself to the door. Markus rose, came behind him, brushing off his knees. He suddenly remembered a line Alex had said once last year when he was speaking about his takeover at Chapman's Island. The line came to him now because he was thinking again of how Alex was fudging his moral responsibility, and he couldn't prove why. But Markus had thought this a wonderful line at first until he realized that what it actually did was enforce a quality upon both races that neither deserved, and therefore made both red man and white man less human. But he said it now as Alex started to open the shed door: "When the red man fights against the white man, I am on the side of the red man."

"Yes," Alex said quickly. He flinched slightly as he unlocked the door. They went into the cool small outer room of the house, where sunlight made a sudden dazzling entrance, and Alex did not turn around.

"Ah yes," Markus said after a moment, "I knew I was wrong."

"What do you mean?"

"Well, you said you never took the truck."

"I did not take it, no."

"Then the keys were hanging on the key holder—just as they would have been when your uncle went to the Restigouche—and here they are now—"

"But he could have taken them and put them back? Or I could have put them there after I got my uncle."

"Of course, well, yes—I know this, but you did not tell me that—that is, that you put them somewhere else? Then what was he riffling through the house for, what was he searching for—if the keys were there, and as you said, or hinted, they were there when you took them and went to get your uncle—but the bowls and jars and drawers were looked through—what, for a combination to a safe?"

"Perhaps," Alex said quickly.

"Do you have a safe?"

"No—but Proud wouldn't have known."

"No—" Markus paused, "but he wouldn't have searched to find the combination of something he didn't know you had or had not—and in many break-ins the people simply take the safe if it is small enough."

Alex was again silent. He looked perplexed, he blinked very quickly. His hair was caught in the sunlight through the kitchen window. Markus looked perplexed as well, looking at him closely. Then he shrugged and smiled and Alex gave a relieved: "I see— well, well, well."

Then he turned about, ran the tap water very quickly, and washed his face. But there was no hand towel, and he stood with his face covered in drops of water, smiling. Markus pretended not to notice this.

"So we are almost back to square one—unless you used the truck yourself, before the day you went to get your uncle, and placed the keys somewhere else—"

"No—" Alex said with some torment, for the time to say this

had come and gone. Now he could not say it without creating more suspicion.

"But we know that John Proud never used the truck either—"

"Why?"

"Well, to assume he did is to assume he came back and placed the keys on the key board exactly where they are, and then spent a lot of time riffling through papers—and though he was searching for things to rob, never took any item he could sell. He did not steal the 22.250 rifle in the upstairs hallway. Nor did he steal the truck!"

"No, he wouldn't have done that," Alex said, using both sleeves to wipe his face like a cat might use its paws.

"But you see, that's a problem."

"Why—I mean if you could just tell me why is everything all of a sudden a problem—that's the thing, everything is a problem now, just because John Proud is in a bind. I mean, I am not trying to say he is guilty, I know there are many who like to blame the First Nations, I am not one. You know how many articles I've written—and who had his picture taken with your sister. So there! But we have to deal with some kind of reality."

Markus paused for a moment. His hair was cut so that it was bunched at the top and shaved on the sides. It gave his cheeks and eyes a more pronounced and defining expression, which in some would seem sharp or aggressive but in Markus always made him appear jovial and dimpled, as if he was blushing. He stared at Alex a long, long moment—so Alex actually thought of running. Then he took a small pair of tweezers from his pocket and simply picked something off of Alex's sleeve.

"I wonder where that came from?" he asked, smiling.

"What is it?"

"I don't know," Markus said, holding a small worm up to the window on the tweezers' pincers. Then he said, "A maggot—on your sleeve!"

"A what?"

"A maggot."

Alex said nothing. In fact, he was on the verge of confessing.

But Markus put the maggot into the sink, and simply said this: "That's the thing, I am trying to deal with some kind of reality. Last year the Penniac man, who got off, left me shame-faced. Now I believe people want to blame an Indian for this, because of that. But it is not going to happen, not on my watch. For John Proud is innocent of everything except possibly trying to destroy himself."

"Me, me—wants to blame the Indian man—me—I'm Alex Chapman—that's who I am."

"No, listen, please don't get upset—I am not saying you."

"Me of all people," Alex continued, suddenly laughing at this absurdity.

Markus looked at him, stepped around him, ran the tap so the maggot would flush into the drain, and then said, "Well, we will figure it all out—come, I want to show you something."

Markus, taking the keys, turned and went out the back way, through the shed again. Alex turned out the kitchen light and fol-lowed him with his hands in his pockets, and every few feet he tried to yawn. But now this fan, this summer fan whirring in the back of his conscience, was forcing him to sweat, was forcing the valve in his heart to squeak, was forcing untold thoughts too. He saw the truck again, like he did when he was at the lighthouse watching it through the binoculars; it had its own animation, its own aura about it now, and this aura was in a way dark and sinister.

Markus turned to him and said, as if he were answering a dia-logue Alex had had with someone sometime before, "I do not know if there is a God."

"Pardon?"

"I do not know if there is a God—"

"I see."

"But I think God, if there is a God, directed me to this."

"Directed what to you where?" Alex asked now, squinting in the fading sunshine.

"I think I am right. And Sergeant Bauer is dead wrong. I think John Proud had nothing to do with this. You see, someone had this truck, and I think—I think Poppy Bourque was in it. I can't prove it—well, it would be circumstantial, as they say, but I will have a bit of evidence that I can match with something, I think. Then this case can be looked at in another way."

"How can that be if John Proud didn't take it?" Alex asked derisively.

Markus shrugged. "Well, it might mean—it might mean someone else had the truck—someone who knew where the keys were!"

There was a long and terrible pause, a thirty-second pause of incredible tension. But Markus did not seem tense; he simply watched Alex, with happy-go-lucky eyes. Then he said, "You don't mind if I show you—it might help the case if I could take a sample of something?"

"No," Alex said, "of course I don't mind!"

"I have permission to open this truck and take a sample—?"

"Of course!" Alex said. He was sweating and in a daze. He wondered what Bourque would say to this. But what if he said no—it would be worse.

Paul got on his knees again, and with his buck knife took a small sample of something at the edge of the door, placing it into an envelope. Then he unlocked and opened the door, and looked at the side of the door near the latch.

"It's small but I can detect it—can you see—it stretches from the tip of the door back to here."

"See what—I can't—what—I can't see blood—if you think I can see blood—I don't see any blood."

"No there is not a bit of blood as far as I can see," Markus said. "At least not right here."

"Then what, if no blood?" Alex said, squinting.

"Paint," Markus said. "Paint—this spot of green paint—here and here—from Poppy brushing against it while getting into the truck."

Alex's eyes closed for a long moment. He opened his eyes slowly and then shut them fast again. Then finally he opened them. He saw the truck keys Markus was handing him dangling in front of his face. Alex for a moment tried to think of blaming his uncle. But Markus stopped him with this: "We were a warring people—and our men were warriors of great skill."

"I know," Alex said seriously.

"We fought with the Beothuks, and the Inuit who came to our Northern Islands—warred with the Maliseet and Huron—killed and were killed—"

"I know that," Alex said.

"I do not expect the Maliseet or Inuit or Huron to apologize to me, nor I to them—"

Alex said nothing.

"What I mean to say, Alex Chapman, is I don't want forced apologies from people who are singled out to blame—besides, I liked your uncle, he was kind to my sister and me. But," he said, "you have the opportunity now to give the island to us."

Alex watched Markus leave, and walked out to the road to make sure he was gone. Then he went and sat in the middle of his worn and corroded property, with belts and motor housing stretched against the baleful sun. Here out of sight, he began to vomit and could not stop. The paint in the truck was certainly another terrible complication.

Alex was a man who was ill. He was like a man who, having an operation, believes he will be well, and yet a complication arises where they have to alter the prognosis. After an initial period of euphoria, thinking whatever embolism has been taken away, the symptoms come back. He is again operated on, and again feels he will be fine. But he has now entered the second stage, where the doctors are simply trying to correct some mistake made in the first stage, and since they do not correct it, the patient enters, because of the first and second stage, a third stage, where the illness is dire and life threatening. Still the patient hopes all will be well if the treatment in the third stage works.

This is where Alex Chapman now was, sick in body and soul, precariously knowing he was soon to be caught, and still trying to discover some way out. But the only way out for him now was to deal with Amy Patch—and yet even if he did, by now he was in such an advanced decline the operation might be worthless.

=

ON AUGUST 26 AMY LEFT FANNY'S AND WENT TO THE STORE to get bread and milk, using money from the jar in the kitchen, used only for Fanny, where every penny was accounted for. She clutched this money and walked along the ditch, spying the cat-tails now rising in the afternoon sun and the black daisies near the border of Annie Everette's house, a woman dead some forty years before. At the store she heard how John Proud should be hanged.

"It's not that he's an Indian, it's just that anyone to do that to an old man like Poppy Bourque—" Mrs. Hanson, in her large dress and her hair gray and pinned back, said while she rang in change and made adjustments to her hair every five seconds.

So as Amy left the store, holding her bread and milk for Fanny's breakfast, a greater responsibility followed her, here and there, as if a small human shape. She took time to cut some cattails and held them in her arm, and navigated the path up the slope and then back onto the Gum Road. And at all these moments, she saw the human shape beside her, perhaps as real as Bourque's and Alex's connection to themselves.

It was in its vague attachment every feeling of goodness wrestling with her hope that she not have to say anything. But over the last while, as her mother started to clear out the closets of the only house she had known, started to speak of a distant place, she knew she must complete the task God, if there was a God, had given her. No, she was not prone to thinking of herself as a mes-senger, she was prone as a teenaged girl to thinking of how some-day in the quiet of a field a boy would lay with her, and she daydreamed about this as other boys and girls her age did.

Yet the more she read the books assigned to her by Alex Chapman, the more she realized that for three thousand years man had the same hopes and desires and, moreover, the exact same responsibilities perhaps, and just perhaps given to them by the exact same God.

When she thought of Alex, and the lotto ticket, a strange tumbler was turned, and she could think clearly of the night she saw the truck. From that she could think of Poppy Bourque's movements, and from that she could think that Poppy had found out about this ticket and wanted to tell. Was Poppy with them, and had they killed him by then——? This was absolutely absurd and she cursed herself for thinking this.

Alex—that was the stumbling block. How could Alex be involved? It was impossible. And if it was impossible then she had no attendant shadow of responsibility, of duty far beyond her age.

However, she did not know why there was so much fear in her. Leo Bourque was absolutely right. If John Proud had not been arrested on suspicion of murder, Amy might never have felt an obligation to understand what she had seen. For this was what plagued her. And the more it plagued her, the more fear she had.

She thought she had seen a pair of sneakers sticking out just beyond the lights of the truck. But it may have been just two roots of the old pine tree that was there. She kept telling herself that her mind—a first rate mind it was, in its potential more powerful then Alex Chapman's, the one who had once wanted to destroy the potential of this mind (for he never thought of it as ever being a mind like his)—was mistaken.

But she knew in her heart this was on Alex's behalf, so she wouldn't send him to prison. In a way she was like every child who is taught to trust an adult who then proves to be untrustworthy. Some part of her was ashamed. She wanted to exonerate him. This is what her mind was trying to do. But by August 26, four days before her mom left, a week before her dad was to come home, she realized she just might have seen something—she might have seen the body of Poppy Bourque—and John Proud was innocent. She could not tell her mother this. That is, she wanted to prove that she was right before she did.

For there was one other thing. She knew it was problematic, and thought of it as a vague shadow across her reason. If she was wrong in any way about what she saw! If it was an innocent meeting between the two, her reporting she saw the body of Poppy Bourque would be thought of as terrible a miscarriage of justice as one could imagine on this river! If she was wrong (and she still thought she might be—because everyone assumed it was John Proud), then she would be marked as a young child who told fibs, who went to a seminar at the Catholic church about Saint Mark and the spirit of the law and then told lies about someone who did not believe and had fallen away from the church. (There was of course the history between her and Alex, which would make it look like a form of revenge—and after he had enrolled her in his modern egalitarian ethics course, it would look like a casting of stones against a kindly man.) It was also playing into Markus Paul's hands, and many were now saying he was a manipulator. That is, she would be taking sides with the man who wanted for his own gain to help his guilty cousin. This was the weight upon her, to keep silent. But what if Markus Paul was right?

Yet if she tattled and was wrong, she knew in her heart it would mark her family for years to come. She knew that she would be looked upon as a deceitful Irish Catholic girl trying to discredit a moderate secular man, who had always liked her and had tried to help her family. People would turn their backs on her. And then she would think of Rory and Robin! What would they say? What kind of a friendship would she have left with them?

All of this she had to think about, daily. She would not get the Beaverbrook scholarship that so many believed she was entitled to.

If she just kept quiet, would things not go away? She thought so, but as the days wore on she realized that she was frightened after dark. And every day, alone, she had to keep the old woman content. The dread would go away, and then come back. When it went away, she would be completely secure and sure that she was silly. When it came over her, she was surrounded by vague and insubstantial phantoms.

For a while, however, she thought they were just phantoms. So she started to take the old woman for walks again, along the lane during the afternoon, just after one o'clock, after the wind starting in from the bay moved the leaves on the tallest of birches, and they were separated from everyone else in the world by five hundred yards of twisting road and old-growth trees.

It was during the walk on August 28 that Amy suddenly had the overpowering feeling someone was watching her. At first she hoped it was Rory, who she hoped still liked her. Or Mrs. Hanson, who had come early to see them. Then she thought it was probably the buck deer in velvet who was gollywopping about for an apple.

"Stardust, you come out—now you come along out of there—come on now!"

But no one answered, and no buck deer named Stardust came forward. The silence made everything sinister. The trees waved, sometimes picking up scuds of dust upon the lane. She looked behind her, back down to the Jameson's old tote road being covered up in the shadows of afternoon, seeing big leaves being blown by wind across the empty friendless pathway, and then she put her hand up and covered her eyes to look. And when she did, shading her eyes to look, she saw something that made her heart fail. Stardust was indeed on the lane—but over three hundred yards away at the turn, looking back at her—or perhaps not at her at all!

So it was not Stardust, not at all!

On that day, when Fanny fell asleep, Amy placed the brake on the chair and went into the woods to see who it was. And then, after fifty or so yards she came to a gentle slope and a turn, where the path went down along the brook to Glidden's pool, and sunlight fell through the branches and glowed on some flat stones. At the bottom it was darker and more quiet. She saw a sparrow flit on a branch.

"Rory," she laughed.

No answer.

"Who are you?" she asked. But when she did the wind picked up and a few twigs rustled, and the branches moved. She thought she heard someone moving off, but she couldn't be certain.

"Who is there?" she pleaded. All about, the green leaves hampered what she could see, and left her alone. "Is that you, Mr. Chapman—Alex?" she asked.

"Go away!" she said, "You go away right now!"

Then she heard Fanny calling her.

"What are you doing?" Fanny said in her shriek garble. "What are you up to?"

The young girl turned, went back to the road, and took Fanny home. She locked the doors and drew the drapes tight, but this did not make her feel safe. In fact, it caused just the opposite sensation. She took a nail and hammered the bathroom window shut.

That evening the wind blew, and she could smell smoke from chimneys in the air. When she lay down on the cot near the kitchen, the wind made pitiful sounds, and it was so cold it was like autumn, and some of the bird nests had fallen from the trees.

"Tomorrow Mrs. Hanson comes. In two days Mommie goes— in five days Daddy is home—you wait and see if he lets anything ever happen to me!"

There was only one problem. For the very first time this summer she would be left alone with the old woman. Minnie only a stone's throw away would be gone, and Mrs. Hanson would on that one day be going down to pick her mommy and daddy up. For five or six hours in the evening, she and Fanny would be alone.

"I will make the best of it—" she decided, still thinking that she was mistaken, that she had to be—for things like this did not happen at all; at least not with men like Alex.

=

IT WAS NOW THE FIRST OF SEPTEMBER AND THE SHADOWS were colder, and the fishing boats in the bay distant, with the water dark. Markus visited the hospital and spoke to John Proud. He knew that men went insane on methamphetamine. But he wanted to believe that Proud, who'd had so much trouble in his

life, had not done so. He wanted to protect him, protect the reputation of his cousin, as shaky as that reputation at the moment
might be. His family had once been a great family, and Markus
knew it could be again. Markus knew that in time, someday, if
there was any justice, the First Nations would find their way
again. He knew they were as brave as any men and women alive.

"What did I do?" John asked him, his left arm with the intra-
venous tube inserted near his wrist, his head still bandaged, and a
small hose in his left ear.

"I don't think you've done anything," Markus whispered.
"Except try to steal a lamp."

"But others do? The chief came in, saying I did."

"Our chief," Markus asked in Micmac, "or mine?"

"Ours—so half the boys on the reserve think I did it. Besides,
I stole from most of them. So they all stand about the bed grinning. I told people I killed Poppy Bourque—I told them I cut him
up in pieces. Well I was bragging a bit and the story kind of got
away from me."

"Yes, you said that."

"Sometimes now I think I must have."

"Yes, many do—all the officers do. But I don't. First of all,
where was the blood—the bit of blood near the hunting camp
wasn't his. But Bauer said you are the prime suspect because you
insisted on being one."

"Well," John Proud said with some understanding of the plight
he had placed his cousin in, "that leaves you in a tight spot."

"Yes," Markus said, "it does—but of course I have been in tight
spots before."

"Well I can tell you this—I don't remember anything—"

"Do you remember confessing?"

"No—" Johnny smiled. "Except I do remember a story I
told—which as I say seemed pretty good at the time I told it."

Markus went back to his apartment. He showered and lay down on
the couch and listened to the sound of wind in the autumn leaves.

He was sure he had them—almost sure—and now it was all slipping away. Where would they go from here? If only there was a witness. But if there was a witness, perhaps he or she would be paid off—as horrible as that might be.

He fell asleep, into his deepest sleep in days. When he woke it was growing dark under the cold venetian blinds.

A lot of money, he thought, sitting up and going over his notebook with all the possibilities written in detail and then scratched away—except one possible thing, except one—which he had circled: "lotto."

To him it was terribly silly, and proved that he had lost his mind.

―

AS YET THE PRIEST, WALKING BACK AND FORTH IN HIS STUDY at the top of his house, listening to the first of the autumn rain rail against the roof, still leaned to the possibility of a mistake in all his and Markus Paul's assessments—arrived at independently of one another over the last two weeks. That is, the priest too had had a strange feeling when he watched Alex at the funeral. Something wasn't right. Now Paul wanted to see him, just to speak to him about his neighbor who he was investigating. Since Paul was a policeman, and Alex was a freethinking man, Father MacIlvoy thought it may be about marijuana or something—and did not want to give anyone up on that.

Still, something strange was happening. And strange, too, had been his life. So strange he sometimes wondered how he came to be Father—what had happened to him, the boy once drafted by Montreal?

"If you want God to laugh, tell him of your plans," he told himself once.

He had gone to fight a forest fire at Lean-to Creek. He thought of this as the turning point in all his dreams and ambitions, that one stream had plugged up and another had started with what he was sure would be clearer, more vibrant water.

He had been a tough, charismatic kid the likes of which a Leo Bourque would never go against. You looked at MacIlvoy's face from one particular angle and you knew he was as tough as nails. He took a job in the woods that summer, and by chance there was a fire. Three crews from the government garage he worked at went in—he went in as a pump man for one of the hoses, and set up at Lean-to Creek on a windy day in July, twenty years ago now. What was strange about it all was how quickly it happened. The wind turned the fire back into an area that hadn't initially burned, about four hundred yards from the brook where he was running the pump. They began trying to save the old Roach place, and cut the fire off from jumping the highway.

At five in the afternoon he heard a boy, who had been operating a hose, yelling. He heard an older man shout. He went to investigate, walked to the top of a hill through some black spruce, and could see a wall of fire that had leveled Roach's house and barn coming directly toward him. He could reach neither the boy nor the man. It was too late for them, so he turned to go back to the water but found he had already been overtaken. He was silly enough to climb a tree to try to get above the smoke. The fire burned under and about him for two more hours, and the trees beside him went up in flame. Below him the grasses withered and burned too, and he felt the sting of embers on his back, while the bottom of the tree he had climbed and his own feet were licked but did not burn. He placed his shirt over his face and thought he would die.

For the first time in his life he prayed, and in his prayers, heard by no one else in the world, said, "Keep me safe and I will give my life to you." That is, like so many, many millions and millions, in the end one's self was the only thing he could offer.

What was strange is he did not die.

So what could he do now but do what he promised? He didn't have to—so many people prayed, and then forgot the promises made immediately. And he was one of the toughest boys on the river. No one would give a thought to him not doing it. No one would even know. Besides, he had been drafted by Montreal.

Yet MacIlvoy did not join his team that fall. It was a long and painful winter, made more so by the number of requests he received from friends to go out with them to try to shake this imaginary debt. He did not speak of this debt, of course, but many knew something had happened to him there. Some internal metaphysics that had changed the registry of his clock. Some said he met the ghost of an old Micmac guide who led him out. Others said he became a coward and was now afraid.

"A gutless puke," as some said.

A great despondency overcame his house, and all that was in it. The girl he loved slowly drifted away, and began dating again. The snowbanks at the end of the lane sat in mysterious darkness, the street lights flickered on the ice. He stayed in his room, his broad sloping shoulders and quick powerful arms in quiet agony, and became in his very anatomy a question mark.

Vandermere, the center on his line in Junior, the man he looked up to, spoke loudest against him. His younger siblings spoke to him cautiously, trying their best to humor him, and then finally out of pain and frustration ignored him. It was true that that March his father brought a psychiatrist to the house, under the guise of friendship. But to no avail.

He entered Holy Cross a few years before Alex. For a long, long time the burden of having a perfectly healthy son, once as tough as nails, who had a great God-given talent he refused to use because he had climbed a tree, was almost worse than if the fire had taken him. After a time, he was forgotten. The world moved on. He took the job at this church—an out-of-the-way Catholic church along the battered highway almost no one in the world would know. It was (and he did not know this) the church Alex Chapman had dreamed of having.

Over the long years only heartbroken people, desperate and in need, were driven to seek his help. The ones who could not make it on the earth, yet as soon as they could they would disappear again, some to actually mock him for his help. Some he saw later, and they were embarrassed they had ever spoken to him when weak. And priests too were weak, and in weakness, with pale eyes and trembling hands, confessed things to him he had to keep in secret.

Many nights he wondered himself what he was doing. Lately, the little girl Amy had been coming to see him. It was after the course he had given on Saint Mark and not in time yet for the course on Saint John. When she spoke, she spoke so quietly that he couldn't catch what she said. But still and all it was her coming to him that kept his faith alive, if just barely. For his heart went out to her and her kind, loving face. People told him it was about a boy named Rory who Amy liked. That it was puppy love. So he spoke to her about love, and said that she should not worry, that her love would come, and she would be happy, and the man she fell in love with would treat her well. She nodded, looked timid, and left the church by the side door. In fact, by the end of the summer if she did drown herself in Glidden's pool, he wouldn't be surprised.

—

ON THE TWELFTH DAY AFTER THE DISAPPEARANCE, THE DAY after he visited Alex and took paint from the truck (he did this so he could get a warrant and do a Luminol test on the truck's interior), Markus Paul visited the priest. He had not at all forgotten about the maggot, and he wondered if someone hadn't had to move a body. This is what he was thinking of as he went to MacIlvoy.

They had known each other before, and MacIlvoy had coached him one year in peewee. Now Markus told him what he thought. There was a smell of autumn in the air, the wide white boards of the room they sat in were once used on a fisherman's shed.

"I think they have something to do with the disappearance of Poppy Bourque," Paul said. "I think it is over something—money, perhaps even a lotto ticket. I am not so sure." He asked the priest, opening his notebook with the eagle on the front, moving the picture of his sister to the back, if he could tell him anything unusual that was happening.

This was a strange, strange thing. All of his life, MacIlvoy had been torn about what he had done, whether he had sensed in the scalding wind on the day of the forest fire that his life was spared by some miracle. So he had followed this miracle to here—he had followed it away from the Montreal Forum and into this back-lane church. Here is where he came face to face with his soul. Here he saw disillusionment, crime, and hypocrisy within his own church and among his own priesthood. Over the tedious years, Alex had become more verbose against him and the little church. But then, why did this happen? There must be some mistake?

"Can you tell me anything—outside of a confession?" Paul asked.

But both knew that actions were very much like confessions.

Father MacIlvoy remembered one thing. He told Markus Paul what he had seen, had occasioned to witness, at the end of his drive, by the tall hemlock, early the previous Tuesday morning when he had come out after saying mass. It was a disturbance on Alex's property.

"What kind of disturbance?"

MacIlvoy recounted that he looked over and saw in the rather splendid morning fog a man chasing Alex from the garden, Alex running with a cucumber in his hand. Then Alex put his hands up over his head as if he were about to be hit, and MacIlvoy was prepared to rush over and enter the fray. The man chasing Alex stopped, and grabbed him by the arm, and started speaking to him. Alex calmed down somewhat.

"And who was this man?"

"The man was Leo Bourque."

"Did you hear what they were speaking about?"

"No—nothing—except one shout, and then they walked to the porch—and I had an appointment at the hospital."

"They have turned on each other," Markus said.

"If that is the case, can you pick them up?"

"No one believes they are responsible but me—"

MacIlvoy folded his arms and stared out the window.

"And we don't have the body."

"Ah—"

"And we have John Proud, who has already confessed to it—but he is so wild in the head he would confess to sainthood."

"Ah."

"So you see, I am in a bind."

"Yes," MacIlvoy said.

"Alex has done something he is trying to hide—and he did not know he would ever do it. So he is hiding it from himself. So, too, is Leo—but Leo is tougher and smarter, and has had a harder life—he is the one keeping them going."

"When," MacIlvoy stated, "will they come to their senses."

"I am not sure when! Nor am I sure if this is the end of it, or if we can prevent whatever will happen before they do. I am wondering if you could keep an eye on Alex for me—just for a few days."

"I could," MacIlvoy said, "but I am back and forth every day here, upriver and down."

They spoke about the milk route the priests were now on, the wee amount of priests there were left in the world to do what they believed was God's business on earth. Like a policeman sent somewhere at the last moment to stop the riot that had already ripped the town asunder, some of the very policemen sent entering happily and fiendishly on the side of discord.

"To find messes and fix a rioting of conscience," Father MacIlvoy now said. And what a dreary thing it was, to have come over to this life and given up the Montreal Forum on what his father had said was "a goddamn crazy whim!" His father had died alone, switched to the United Church, and refused MacIlvoy at the funeral. And still he was here. To hypothesize on your own about Saint Mark, or any other, to young and old, as if you had a direct line to the Vatican or some other special favor.

He had taken to asking himself this: I am now forty-one, so why am I here, and why can't I just go? Have I become like a skip man in a mine who has to be there every day to lift people up from the bowels of hell? And he thought, What will I see that will allow me to leave? And in the last week or so he had rested on this idea: he had seen Amy light a candle at the grotto one evening. He said to himself, If the candle goes out before I have to leave to go to the Church of our Lady of Perpetual Help, I will be released of my duty and will pack and leave. I will work in the oil patch and get some money—and, who knows, I might even marry. But he had said all of this off the cuff and did not respond to it as he went about putting out the candles with a candle snuffer after mass.

Immediately he began to ask himself why he had made this vow. So each morning he rose for mass, and each morning, the air cooler and sharper, he noticed the thin flame of the candle still burning.

"Surely it must go out before tomorrow," he said.

Yet the next day the wick still burned. He began to think then that God was certainly making fun of him. And now it was raining intermittently, and still the little candle burned. He had a heavy heart thinking he had made this pledge.

"Mother, let the wick burn, and let me go to the church in Millerton tomorrow and give old Cyril Corey communion."

Now he was pleading to remain in the arms of his stupid little church. How could a grown man be so naive? How, as Dylan Thomas once asked, could he not? He walked Markus Paul to the car and glanced again at the wick. The wick told him that nothing is really dependent on man. Certainly by now it should have burned its way out—and yet, like a spark, it glowed silently.

Father MacIlvoy let out a sigh, but said no more when Markus looked his way.

≈

THE RESERVE RAN EAST TO WEST ALONG THE MIRAMICHI bay to the south and the caribou barrens to the north. From the back of the reserve a man could see on clear summer days the houses of the French village beyond, along the road that led down to the Acadian coast, with a mirage of puddles and mists rising from the asphalt until noon hour.

Years ago they hunted caribou for the tourists that came here, American and German and Dutch, who all wanted the experience of killing something grand, and often grander than themselves. The Micmac were given tips by these men and women, and had their pictures taken in clothes and attitude not even looking like First Nations men anymore but poor cousins of the Enfield carrying hunters.

Markus Paul's great-grandfather shot the last caribou on these barrens, for an egotistical Dutch millionaire and his wife about the year 1911. That would have been John Proud's great-grandfather too.

Markus Paul had had a standoff at the reserve the night before, trying to talk a man—who was actually an uncle of his— into putting his shotgun down and coming outside. He was alone in the house and he was angered that his wife had gone to bingo and had not made him supper, and so he had not let her in when she had come home. Then when she went to get her son-in-law, to talk to him, he grabbed the shotgun.

Markus tried to talk him out of the house. This had been arrived at finally at twelve minutes after four. Markus Paul's attention, however, hadn't been completely focused on the standoff or the negotiation.

He was often sidetracked by the old hunting road that led through those barrens to the stand of hard trees against the soft, cloud-covered morning sky. The once principal and now forgotten hunting camp of his grandfather was halfway between the reserve and the highway, and he knew that John Proud, who was using this camp, would be in contact with many people along the road all summer long, and would have very likely spoken to Leo Bourque. So the standoff was important to Paul in this regard. (Besides, he knew his uncle didn't want to hurt anyone.) He decided, looking at the old hunting lane, that he would go to the camp himself.

So after the standoff, and after the dawn came, Markus Paul walked slowly up along the old path, through the trees, and into the camp, which seemed to be the epitome of a lost race. The rain had come and it was like those days moose hunting with his father, calling a long cow call in the dreary cold morning and hearing the bull coming from a mile away, cutting through the tamarack and birches, loud and still muted in the drizzle and the smell of pungent wood. No, the Micmac didn't have horses or know them like the Sioux, but they could trudge out and run a moose to ground, had hunted caribou the same way.

He could hear rain hitting the tin roof above his head, and running down the slope to the tiny east branch of Hackett Brook. It was all melancholy and soft and lonely. He was standing in John Proud's hunting camp, which had belonged to their grandfathers. They had taken many moose from here, at various times of the year when they needed. Too, too many moose were slaughtered now by some, in the kind of political retribution that fed the airways as being "native rights." His disposition was always to say that rights were not without obligation, and he was not liked for it among some of the men who some years took sixteen or seventeen moose out of the swampland off Hackett Brook.

Could he see the highway from here? No. But that did not mean it wasn't there. Now and again he could hear the drone of the cars approaching from the west or east, and then drifting away to the east or west. Through the small clearing, the old (ancient) hunting path of his peoples led now up to that road. The old barrens now trailing away with undergrowth, the blueberry fields that his people picked for cottagers.

Everything that Markus wanted to keep from the scene of Poppy's disappearance had been stuffed in three boxes at the back of the police station. There was only one set of footprints he was able to take. They were not prints of the men who had come to the truck, but of someone standing behind the truck, shuffling back and forth—perhaps waiting for the men in the house to come down the pathway. He had found out yesterday at six o'clock that these prints were not sneakers or boots, as he had expected, but sandals. Size 10, with the left sandal having a run-down heel.

Of course he knew immediately. Alex Chapman wore sandals. But so did others. And then there was the standoff and he couldn't go see Alex, who he was hoping to break. These prints had been lifted and photographed and fused onto plastic, an impression of an exact moment on the very night Old Poppy disappeared. Perhaps Alex, the consummate smoothie, did not know that his dancing a jig would be discovered in such a way. But of course he was no longer a smoothie.

There was something else impeding the case's progress. The paint he had sent off to Moncton had not been analyzed. He needed this analyzing done so he could confiscate the truck and do a Luminol test upon it. That is, he did not want to be wrong with the most significant piece of evidence in his life. If he was, it would be disastrous for him and the entire case and his reserve. If there was no blood, it would blow up in his face, and he would get no second chance. His cousin would simply be found guilty. The test on this paint would be done by tomorrow afternoon.

He was certain blood would be found in this truck, and it would be Poppy Bourque's. He had to bide his time a little, that is all. Tomorrow he was transferring Mr. Proud down to Richabucto jail, and therefore would travel later to Moncton to pick up the evidence about the paint. It all had to be verified, classified, and quarantined. He could have it all collected within the next day or two. Then he could bring the truck in for testing.

What Bauer wanted in assigning him this task was two things. He wanted to show people that Constable Markus Paul was a loyal enough policeman who would take his cousin down to Richabucto, that it was also compassionate for him to assign a native to transfer a native. And Bauer wanted to quell speculation that there was a bigger and more mysterious reason for the disappearance of Poppy Bourque, when they had this man who had confessed. Now the confession had been signed, and it made no sense to keep looking for someone else until you first proved the confession bogus. The only problem was, no one at all took the time to try and find out if the confession was indeed bogus. The other problem was Alex Chapman himself—was there any kind of vendetta Markus had against him, Bauer liked to wonder.

Of course Markus Paul knew all of these unsaid things, and kept quiet himself. He did not tell Bauer that tomorrow evening he would have the paint, and the sandals.

He took off his gun belt and lay it across a small table, and tried to find the picture of himself with the twenty-one-point moose that had been here for years. He couldn't. It could very well have been sold.

He thought about the standoff. It was actually comic. The man ordering spaghetti before he would come out, because he said this is what his wife was supposed to make him that night for supper.

"What did you say you wanted, Arnold?"

In the Days Before, when Glooscap ruled the heavens, the great moose hunts were done in both fall and winter. And Markus Paul's ancestor and John Proud's ancestor too, Osepitit, was chief of the Micmac tribe along this waterway—all the way into Chaleur, where the Iroquois had come down from the land now called Quebec. His ancestor was then the justice and the law, and the understanding of the law, of the spirit of the law, and there was little to dispute how great he was. So when the Iroquois made inroads into Micmac hunting and fishing land, south of Chaleur on those long ago days, Osepitit's people came to him. There was then no one to tell him what to do, and no one in the end to advise him. But he knew this: he knew the Micmac nation was not able to defend itself or defeat the more powerful tribe. Just as the Huron fought against his people along the Saint John, so the Iroquois fought here against them. Osepitit was an old man then, and had fought well fifteen years before, but he decided this: he would pit his life against the Iroquois chief, a younger, stronger man, to protect his people.

The bloodletting ended when Osepitit and the Iroquois chief fought to the death on the great rock out in Miramichi. They were paddled out by their warriors, and faced each other with one tomahawk in the center of the stone, with the bay all about them. The Iroquois grabbed the tomahawk first, and drove it into Osepitit's side. But it was his ancestor who snapped the back of the Iroquois chief, so the Iroquois left the land of the Miramichi to the Micmac. And this happened 150 years before the first white man arrived on their shores. The rock turned red in the late tide and had remained red ever since.

Markus Paul did not know that in many ways he was like that great man, in sympathy and appearance, nor would he ever think of being so.

Arnold, who would speak only to Markus in Micmac, came outside at about quarter past four, after eating some spaghetti. Many of the women and men who had gathered around to watch, yelling instructions first at Arnold and then at the police, started laughing uproariously because he had forgotten to take his bib off and still had some bread in his hand.

"What have we done?" Markus whispered aloud.

The rain fell over the tin roof, and along the streaked window, and felt of dreary autumn. This was once the great hunting camp of his family, but now had become a den of iniquity. Plastic bottles formed to blow pipes and pans, hydrochloric acid, and hundreds of empty containers of decongestion tablets that were opened and used with laundry detergent and old batteries for acid, all used for cooking methamphetamine. Here the seven men and women on the reserve who were hooked on crank came over the last three years, until late last month, when Markus finally put a stop to it. Now most of them were in rehab.

Rotted food and bones, stained and bloodied walls, soiled and ripped panties, condoms, and used tampons littered the sight. The people were lucky the camp had not blown up. And it had something unusual in the woods: small black eyes looking at you from the corners. Rats.

His people. My God, what had happened to them? As Markus looked about, he decided these ones had stepped off the cliff into hell. And he realized it was not only, or not just, the white man's fault.

Markus's own sister had been one. The one Alex so proudly said he knew. The one he had his picture taken with to appear in a paper, and make his name. She was dead now. Markus knew Proud had confessed because he felt so guilty about Markus's sister, who he had introduced to crank. In reality he was confessing to Markus about the death of Markus's sister, Peggy. It was one sure way to end his pain. Markus had seen this with alcoholics as well; all of a sudden they would confess to anything, to pay any price for what they had done to themselves, to their loved ones, and to their hope.

In thirteen months Peggy was dead. In her pocket she had something one of the native women had given her at the last to comfort her, a picture of Our Lady of Guadalupe, one of the ten pictures of Our Lady of the First People that Father Hut had given to the First Nations here long ago.

She had had two children, who Markus now supported. He put his gun back on, buckled the buckle, sniffed and stood, and went to the broken door.

The old path led away across the barrens, toward the houses, and Markus now followed it back, the rain slanting against his face. In the middle of a dense cluster of alders and small tangled spruce the path broke into three. One followed southeast to the upper end of little Arron Brook. One went to the northwest into the large country toward Tabusintac River. And one path turned directly north, and came out just below Poppy Bourque's house. This was the path John Proud had followed. It could well have been the path someone like Leo followed down to the hunting camp, on many occasions, to buy the pills he wanted for his back, or perhaps to sleep with Markus's sister, as many men did. (This is the one thing Markus had known.) And it may well have been Leo himself who sent John to Poppy's, saying there was money there, that he must have owed Proud. This would have been very easy—but now it might be something Leo regretted, with all the added attention.

There were tears in his eyes from being in the camp. He wiped them away.

The rain beat down on the sour little space about him, splashed against the terrible late flowers on the barren slope. Thunder came as if Glooscap were angry about all of this, all this treachery going on in all this brand new world. This new God, well, he tried, but he didn't do much for the hearts of men.

LEO BOURQUE SAW MARKUS COMING IN THE MIDDLE OF THE afternoon, his head down, as if inspecting the truculent mud. Leo was sitting at the table, eating a bowl of fish chowder, when Markus entered. He nodded and pointed with his spoon to a chair at the table, and Markus sat.

He nodded again and pointed to the pot of fish chowder, and Markus nodded and took some.

"Lobster in there," Bourque said, "and mussels and clams—pieces of sole, sister made it."

"Ah, it looks great," Markus said.

He took a bowl and sat at the table, and salted it, and ate. He had forgotten how hungry he was.

Leo opened a bottle of wine, and nodded. Markus took a small glass.

"Is the investigation over yet?"

"Pretty much," Markus admitted. "I'm taking John down to Richabucto tomorrow—so they will hold him on B&E and try to get more on him."

"Well it's a shame all around. Tomorrow?"

"Yes."

"And how long to lay charges about my uncle?"

"Oh I'm not sure—there is no body of the poor old lad. The thing is, with the methamphetamine and the B&E John could do almost as much time—"

"Well I'd like to get him for the murder too—I mean, since he did it and everything."

"Well we are working as fast as we can," Markus said. He kept eating, staring down at the bowl. "Did you ever see Alex Chapman and John together?"

"Who?"

Markus put the spoon in his mouth, chewed, picked up a piece of bread, and shrugged. "With John—I mean, as a native rights activist—Alex Chapman?"

"Never," Bourque said, with obvious disdain at the name. "Never—leave you Indians alone is what I say, then everyone could get along."

"Oh ya, you say that?"

"Sure I do."

Markus looked at him, put his spoon down and drank his small glass of wine. "Well there you go—"

Bourque did not answer this. Markus watched as Bourque lit a native-brand cigarette and offered him one.

"Sure," Markus said. He stared around the little shed, and across to Poppy Bourque's, and as if thinking of something his face lighted up, as it usually did, and he said: "So, Leo, what would you do if you won the lotto?"

Bourque said nothing. He simply stared.

Finally he said, "I don't know—who knows. I hear many who get it blow it."

"Is that what you would do—blow it?"

"I have no idea," Bourque said, with a tone of voice which indicated he did not like being condescended to, and he was tough enough even with Markus Paul not to have to be.

Paul acknowledged this with a smile. "Well I know you don't, and either do I—but someone you or I know very soon will have over $13 million."

"How—?"

"A ticket was sold here somewhere."

"Oh, well there you go," Bourque said.

They stared at each other uncomfortably, eye to eye.

"You know what I'd do?" Markus said.

"What?"

"You know how Cid Fouy had that old Corvette?"

Bourque shrugged.

Markus smiled again.

"I'd get myself a Porsche. Put him to shame. That is, if I ever got hands on that ticket!" He added: "Sure as hell!"

=

WHAT WAS COMING APART IN BOURQUE'S PLANS WAS THE actual physical aspect of the case. He knew this as Markus left—yes, it would all fall apart, trucks and tires and footprints in the sand. There was almost no way to alleviate this. He paced and grumbled and threw the almost full pot of chowder his sister had lovingly gave him over the floor. Then he had to mop it up, and felt all the stings of the world. He wondered about Alex, and what he might be doing. And was anything worth it anymore. That is, was tomorrow still the day? That is, though Bourque now realized it was all but over, he still looked blindly for a way out.

What was closing in on his partner was the mental fatigue and torture. They wouldn't see another few days without some desperate measure taking place. Neither of them knew what this measure would be. But both of them now lived constantly in each other's minds and skin.

The man known as Alex Chapman still paraded about, slowly of course, still elaborated on how he would find the cure for cancer once all of this was put behind him, still said he was doing it for his mother's memory, still wanted and insisted that people call him professor when he taught his course on ethics. Still thought that someday very soon, after he received his money, he would revive his career at another university—perhaps the wonderfully secular University of Toronto itself. That is, his whole life was as positive as a terribly right-thinking member of the New Democratic Party—except for the lotto ticket itself. Such is the prize that once had is soon taxing.

At noon tomorrow, Mrs. Hanson would leave the child alone with Fanny to go down and pick up Minnie and Samuel Patch coming in on the plane. Sam was actually named after Sam Johnson by his mother's doctor, Dr. Hennessey, who was reading Boswell at the time. But this Sam had grade 7. There would for the first time that summer be no attendant adults around. Only Amy and the old lady.

They had to entice Amy out of the house. The ruse actually was Minnie herself, and he, Alex, was supposed to be the ruser, for Amy knew him.

"Just tell her Minnie was in a car accident and is laying face down in a ditch somewhere, gurgling and kicking."

"That, however, may be a little offputting."

"Why?" Bourque had asked yesterday.

"She might expect a ruse if it is me."

"I daresay she won't."

"Well she might," Alex said peevishly. "And if she does, the game is over."

"I daresay she won't."

"What if she brings Old Fanny with her?"

"Then it's curtains for them both," Bourque said. "With all due respect to Fanny, she'd drown as quick as a kitten."

"But then will they say both of them committed suicide over the same boy?"

"Well no, but she might have tried to save little bitty Amy?"

Bourque had convinced Alex (and did it take so much convincing?) that if Amy lived, it thwarted his altruistic and humanitarian plans. This worked on a plain that took hours upon exhaustive hours of reasoning to reach. Then Alex teetered upon this elusive plain for a second, thinking all would be well, only to find himself one short hour later having to navigate the same murky and foul terrain to reach it all over again, with Bourque's help. That is why all of this repetition went on, day in and day out, with the same problems and same solutions discussed again and again. However, Bourque seemed already to have found a foothold on this plain and remained, teetering but balanced.

Bourque had found a military name for the campaign, to keep him in place: Emboldened Currents. They did not talk the last few days about "it" without this military name attached. For Bourque, this seemed so much better. The idea that this was an emboldened act was at least stabilizing. Made them seem mischievous if not quite heroic.

Alex drank some green tea and ate a peach. Again he would have to go over to his uncle's and get the books, for he had not gotten them the day Markus was there.

"But if he says the paint matches?" he asked Bourquey, the name Leo wanted to be called at times.

That is, what it came down to now had nothing to do with Amy.

"Even if she dies we are still in the crosshairs," Bourque did acknowledge.

"Then why must we do it?" Alex asked.

"It helps—for if she is not around there is still a good enough chance to charge Proud."

And so today—that is, the day before Amy was to be finally left alone on that lonely road—Alex proceeded in the dreary afternoon to find his books, for there was still a course on ethics he must teach. For what all this semantics did was show the lucid flexibility of his thought.

"Yes, I am a consummate thinker," he decided, as he crossed over the old lane where Amy had stood that night and made his way toward Chapman's house. However, he staggered now and again, and the pale cooling grasses sometimes trapped his sandals and made his toes pain, and he labored when he breathed, and if truth be told he had not taken his blood pressure pills, for he courted in some way oblivion now, and asked someone, in some way, for it.

The house was growing dark inside. The late shadows of afternoon crept over it, and when the rain stopped periodic bursts of sunlight came in certain windows and then faded as suddenly as they came. This happened when he was on the stairs walking to the third landing. A sudden ray of light pressed against the side of his face, bathing him in sudden warmth, and then just as spontaneously disappeared. For some reason he was shaken by this. It was simply because this used to happen to him on those long ago days after school, when he trudged up the wooden stairs to his apartment to see his mom, and for some strange reason this came back to him now.

It was also unnerving for him to be anywhere in the house. Too much of his belittled history was here, but this only reinforced his heartbreak that he was no longer as he had been—and the torment he had endured as an innocent boy and teenager was in many respects far more appealing to him then the nausea he felt at having become a denizen of hidden actions.

I will give my money to the church, the thought came suddenly. Why? He did not know. How insane for a man who believed in his own power and intellect.

So he approached his room knowing that the last time he had entered here he had been free, and now he was not.

The books were still there. His uncle for all his talk had not sold them, and not even moved them. There was his unfinished doctoral thesis (he was to finish it before tenure, but dropped it once he was pushed aside). His work, in part, was on the tragic imperialization of First Nations peoples, and the philosophical and moral duty one had to practice civil disobedience against this.

He trembled as he remembered Saint Francis's dialogue with Brother Leo: "In what way do we find true joy—"

"In being tormented and left outside, broken and cold—for only on the cross is the tree of joy found!"

He began to take the books out and lay them on his bed. He shrugged at every one he tossed, as if they no longer mattered to him. But he would have to teach them. Strangely, he could not find his Penguin edition of Aristotle's *Ethics*, the one with "Athena Mourning" on its cover. He looked through his bookshelf half a dozen times. He was puzzled, because like many men who love books he could go to any bookshelf he owned and find the book he sought. Yet he could not find it here. Perhaps it was the copy he had given to Amy? No, he had given her an extra copy.

He gathered the rest of the books and went to leave when he saw Aristotle on the bed stand by the window.

Strange?

He picked it up, carried it over to the rest of the books, and noticed a small piece of lined paper that must have come from a notebook. He wondered, for he didn't remember writing anything inside this edition, what it was.

What was written was simply this: Read page 124. Thanks a bunch, Markus.

Alex went downstairs with the book in his hand, the others littered on the bed because he did not take them. He shook like a timid child going to the principal's office. He could not stop shaking, and rubbing his mouth. He kept trying to rationalize why this was written, and whatever possessed Paul to ask him to do this. He hoped, or felt, that perhaps it was something benign and interesting. Something that showed that Markus truly respected him.

This then is what Alex Chapman read on page 124:

> A bad moral state, once formed, is not easily
> amended.
>
> Again, it is unreasonable to suppose that a man
> who acts unjustly or licentiously does not wish
> to be unjust or licentious; and if anyone, without
> being in ignorance, acts in a way that will make him
> unjust, he will be voluntarily unjust; but it does
> not follow that he can stop being unjust, and be
> just, if he wants to—no more than a sick man can
> become healthy, even though (it may be) his sick-
> ness is voluntary, being the result of incontinent

living and disobeying his doctors. There was a time
when it was open to him not to be ill; but when he
had once thrown away his chance, it was gone; just
as when one had once let go of a stone, it is too late
to get it back—but the agent was responsible for
throwing it, because the origin of the action was in
himself. So too it was at first open to the unjust and
licentious persons not to become such, and therefore
they are voluntarily what they are; but now that
they have become what they are, it is no longer
open to them not to be such.

He had let go of the stone and it was too late to get it back. If
only he had not let go of the stone, and become what he had
become, and now it was not in his power not to be such. This was
Aristotle, the man he was about to teach Amy and others. Many of
them were middle-aged, privileged women belonging to book
clubs. Some would dote on him and bring him cookies. He liked
the feeling of authority and being coddled at the same time. He
had wanted Amy to see this, too, so she would recognize him as
the same learned figure those poor ladies did. Their husbands
worked at the mines or in the mill; they would go to Christmas
parties where their husbands would dance half the night with the
secretaries. And there was at times much sadness in these women's
lives. At times, with all his mild manners, he liked to rebuke them
about their ignorant, self-satisfied husbands, and they would look
startled and guilty.

That is, in many ways he had really let go of the stone long,
long, long ago. The stone had fallen far away from him now. To get
it back he would have to become like Saint Francis said, broken
and alone, tormented and outcast. But would his own Brother Leo
ever acknowledge this?

He stood at six foot two. His thin body was becoming crooked,
and his back was bending down. He could still manage a hysterical
look whenever he was frightened or annoyed.

All I have done for everyone, he thought, all I have done—what will become of me now?

He crossed the darkening field and saw a buck deer, with its horns in velvet, standing in shadow down the way, near those trees that he associated with his aunt and his mother. Sunlight came on those velvet antlers and glowed, as if a halo. It was Amy's Stardust, which had crossed the road.

The deer turned and moved against the grain of the day, and like some elliptical shadow disappeared beyond the old woodlot. But Alex kept looking behind him for this deer, while coming into Chapman's lane. He turned his head to watch it again, seeing the antlers glowing as it made its jump, just where he and Leo had come to a stop on that horrible night.

Suddenly he tripped over a windfall, and found himself covered in mud.

"Damn," he said.

Yet what was even more startling was sitting right before him in the lane: a New Testament. He picked it up and looked at its soiled, wet pages, and the name on the inside cover: Amy.

He wanted to leave it there, where it was, but was compelled to bring it back to his cabin, to try to dry it out, to take care of it, for some reason, like a mother does a child. Not because it was the New Testament but because Amy was written on the inside cover.

He had intended to bring Plato and Cicero and Aristotle, and ended up with this.

After it was dried just enough, he closed his eyes for a long time, and decided that he would give this God a chance. That is, he would open the book and read one line. This line would in fact tell him if there was a God watching him or not. He knew this was a silly self-delusion. Yet—what James Joyce thought might not be what he any longer thought. Or could think. That is, the fact that he was implicated in murder had made him confront the very nature of himself and his relation with God, if there was one.

He realized when he opened his eyes he was sitting very much like he had when he was a child in his room. He opened the little faded book and read one line.

He stared at this line for ten minutes, wondering if it was real. That is, if the line was meant for him to read, at that moment, or simply a random bit of writing that had nothing whatsoever to do with him. That is, there was only one of two ways to look upon this. Either some greater force, mysterious and unseen as it was, had allowed him to read this line—the very line he was searching for (though he wouldn't quite admit to it)—or nothing he did meant anything outside this horrible little place. The one line was from the Gospel of John: "And you are unwilling to come to me that you may have Life!"

He suddenly thought that it was the first time Jesus had spoken to him in sixteen years. And what he said was—true.

Darkness was coming, night's sweet silence. He picked the knife out of the hiding place, the blood still on it from Poppy Bourque, and held it until the dark night fell.

So he thought suddenly not of Saint John but of magnificent five-foot-four John Keats: "Darkling I listen and at times have been half in love with easeful death." From a poem of genius almost no one read anymore.

—

AMY WENT TO TWO PEOPLE THAT DAY, TO SEEK HELP. BUT she did not find it. Her face in its troubled state was even more delightfully kind and human. It was the feature of its impish humanity, her unruly hair, her feet that seemed to dance when she walked, that Rory had loved as a boy.

Robin and Rory were now an item, and like all kids had moved off from the little world to the big world and had no time for people like Amy now. And Robin attended to a much more uniform philosophy of the world, where society dictated that her whims be taken seriously, and only her future, her ideas, her pleasures, and her hopes mattered, and her parents, and even her schooling, were there for the fulfilling of these as best they could.

Rory's father was an adjuster with Doan Insurance, and Rory looked upon his life as more positive because of it and the people his father dealt with, some of whom were influential men in the area. So he too had finally left his Gum Road sweetheart behind. He had stopped going to church, and shrugged with condescension that she still did. He had the stubble of a little beard he was trying to grow, his self-amused blue eyes staring out of a chubby, somewhat impertinent face. And Robin had her license now, so she and Rory were sitting in her mother's small car near the church lane, smoking and talking, when Amy walked up to them. When they realized she was there, they both looked at each other wisely and then began to giggle as Robin blew smoke into the silent late summer air in petulant superiority.

"What the heck are you doing?" Rory said like an older brother.

"What?" She smiled, her heart pounding at the disrespect he now was capable of showing for her, staring out the window as if she was the joke she herself didn't get.

"Yer damn pants, what have you got on them?" Robin asked.

"I put glitter snaps on them," Amy whispered. "I thought they'd look nice—so?"

"God," Robin said, "country bumpkin. Those went out of fashion ten years ago."

Amy smiled. Even more in her sorrow her face somehow looked wondrous.

"Well I've been waiting ten years to put them on," she said. "And I have mastered 'All Along the Watchtower.' That's over ten years old and that's not out of fashion! And there is no country bumpkin in that!"

She walked back down her lane by herself, and after a time, tears in her eyes, she began to run.

Who could she speak to now?

———

She made the call to Markus the next afternoon. The afternoon of September 2. The afternoon Mrs. Hanson went down to Moncton to pick up her mother and father.

Bauer took the call, but why should he tell Markus Paul, simply because a young girl said she had seen a truck off a back lane? The girl probably wanted attention. Bauer and Paul had just had an argument over charging Proud that had lasted three hours. Bauer had won an argument which he himself took to be irrefutable. So in this regard Amy was at least three hours too late.

MARKUS PAUL LOOKED INTO HIS BOOK OF NOTES WHILE sitting against the desk in the outer office of the small clapboard RCMP building, with the flag moving in the autumn heat.

It was now September 23.

The truck had been confiscated the day after he had taken John Proud to Richabucto. That is, on September 3.

It sat impounded in the yard, up on blocks, its tires off, its doors off, its seat taken out. The sky was deep, deep blue, the bay—not so far away that it couldn't be seen—was as blue, and wind chimes tinkled in the office like small angels were moving them.

Markus had found out, by miracle or accident or a little of both, that there was a lotto ticket sold by Burton when he stopped at the garage to buy some cigarettes for his charge, John Proud, on the day he drove him to jail in Richabucto, September 2.

Burton, when Paul asked the question about the now infamous lotto ticket, because he realized Burton sold them, said simply, "I sold it most likely." And looked very sternly at his friend.

"Oh, you did—well, to who—Poppy Bourque?"

"Not so likely," Burton sniffed. "No, not so likely—sold it to someone else."

"Who, Burton? I would appreciate it if you could tell me. Why didn't you tell us before, you must have known that I was interested—I asked a hundred people. It might solve everything."

"Yes, it might." Burton shrugged. "No one believed me in the first place," he said, sniffing a little sanctimoniously in the pulpy afternoon air. "So I sit here and say nothing—and you sent those other two in, and didn't come yerself, I figure you didn't care enough!"

"Well, try me," Markus said, "see if I will believe you," realizing the last thing to do was to become exasperated with a soul who had been belittled and beaten most of his life.

"Jimmy Chapman," Burton said, turning away and straightening some fall fliers on the counter, as if he was trying to hide the name behind his actions.

"Mr. Jim Chapman?" Markus asked.

"Why yes," Burton scolded, "Jimmy Chapman—I assume!"

Paul drove to Richabucto and then to Moncton, knowing that with this information, if it was true, the case would soon be solved. He did not tell his cousin yet. For his cousin had other serious problems, and he wanted to get him help.

"Alex found the ticket—the old man was fishing—Bourque got involved—why? Blackmail. So they went to Poppy—to get him to claim it?"

If that was the scenario, it was now very easy to see how things had gone wrong. Markus jotted this down, as he always did. "It was Poppy's honesty that killed him."

The one thing he never realized was the danger Amy Patch was in. That she was the one elusive witness to the two of them with the truck.

Now, on September 23, Markus was revisiting his notes. He came to a page that said, "Bodecia," and turned it to read what he had collected and written about her.

Amy was eighty-six pounds. She had spent the summer putting snaps on all her jeans and shirts and decorating her room, to make it more grown-up. She wore red sneakers with the tongues turned down, and she would try and make sure she stepped around every puddle so not to stain them. So her friends now said, when he asked why they had abandoned her, "Her life was random—"

It was more random because she was a girl on a lane and was leaving them to go away. They liked to talk that way—it confused the adults, without which confusion life itself would be no fun—and not move a muscle toward the future. It was strange that Markus, for all his driving the highway, never knew this little girl.

Still, Markus Paul had now pieced together what had happened that summer with her, from the moment she left grade 9 and took the bus back down the old highway to the night of September 2, when Mrs. Hanson drove down to pick up her parents in Moncton.

He knew the times she went for ice cream, or each time she went to the mall, telling her mother she was meeting friends. Most days were spent with either Fanny or her mother—or looking for Burton's hat, or his boat, which the kids hid on him. She would wade along the shore looking for it until she spied it, then find the oars and row it back up the Bartibog. Two or three days later it would have disappeared again.

Markus had made a note of this too, and those children now denied they hid Burton's boat on him or took his hat. This, in fact, was what put her in conflict with other kids, because many of them, bored and indolent, had taken to playing pranks on a man she was honor bound to help. So she would look for his hat and find it in the weeds, or look for his scow and find they had hauled it up on ground near the church—or that they had pulled the plug on his freezer full of ice cream. Amy went online and messaged her friends to leave Burton alone.

She had a handle: Ghosty. But she sometimes strayed and went, as they told Markus Paul, "Bodecia on us, which was the British warrior against the Romans!"

"She went Bodecia on you—is that right?"

"Yes sir."

"Why would she?"

"She was smart, and liked to say she lived in the woods, and had all the things collected on Bodecia."

"Is that right?"

"She was seriously smart—I mean space-station smart."

"Is that right?"

"Oh, that's right," one boy said, as if reprimanding Markus for his lack of understanding. "That's right!"

"Space station," another said, who had his head shaved except for two strands of green hair that hung down over his eyes.

They talked on, crowding about him at the small lace-curtained store, on the steps, as the traffic to and from Tracadie went randomly by. Messaging was a new language and a new way to write, and it took a few days for Markus to decipher it.

They told him she had started to go from random to spiritual. Took a course on Saint Mark. This came about because they, her friends, had abandoned her, though they did not admit this outright.

"Sometime in July."

"You lost touch with her?"

"Yes sir!"

Markus knew when she had written to Rory that summer. The messages were very ordinary until about August 9.

On August 9 things started to change.

"Bodecia has signed on, C U 2MORO 10, 2 put pollys in the pond?"

And Rory wrote back, saying, "K, c u at 10."

Markus discovered the child had waited that afternoon in the listless, boring heat. One thing she wanted to show was her sparkling jeans. So she signed on and wrote again: "Wh r U—

waiting near pathway? I won't go to pool alone—U know so, U come 2?"

He didn't answer. She messaged Robin: "U C him?"

Robin wrote back: "NO—U put wogs in pond?"

"Not so much yet—where is he?"

"Dunno—he's random, gotta go."

That day Amy left the house an hour later to go to Fanny's. The snaps she put on her jeans reflected the sunlight and water and her hair fell softly. She came to the path to Glidden's pool, which she didn't want to take alone. So she placed the frogs near the brook that led to the pond, and let them go there. For some reason she did not turn and go back to Fanny's, which she was supposed to do. She continued walking, thinking she would go check to see if Burton was being teased. But when she came to the very bottom of the lane she saw Rory's bicycle laying in the field of tall cow corn. She ran toward it, but stopped dead when she saw him and Robin tending to her bicycle. Fixing the chain, and Robin laughing. And so she knew. Later that week she heard Robin had her license.

So every day since then, she would go online to see Rory's last message, hoping for a new one. Rory, signing on as The Roaring Boy, had written: "K, c u at 10."

Yet time passed and the days got further and further away from his last message. As summer wore on she wrote: "Bodecia is on, U come 2 Me, Must C U—have something most important to say—secret I have to tell someone! K?"

She wrote August 12, 19, 20, 21, 23, 25 about this secret she could tell no one else. And then August 31: "Bodecia is on, Plez Roaring boy U come over, Redbreast is no longer my friend! You could stay with me at F G—just when Mrs. Hanson goes away to get dad and mom, on Sept 2nd. She is leaving at supper. I would be grateful for just that one day! I could make you Pizza? K??? Please??? I need to tell someone—I think I know something! You tell me if I do?? It is its own World."

Markus flipped a page with an energy that came from anger.

"The trouble with all of this is it was right before our noses," Sergeant Bauer said. "So, who knew?"

Markus knew Amy had phoned, but he said nothing now. Bauer had confiscated all of her messages.

Amy wrote Robin on August 31, saying, "Redbreast have U C'n R—I wn R to come to Fanny's with me—just that day when Mrs. Hanson goes to pick up mom and dad? That is the one and only time, and make U pizza?"

But Redbreast no longer answered.

Amy sent some emails to her father: "I am sure you are happy to be able to come home for a while, wait until you get my hug. My hug will last for an hour and two minutes. But I don't want to leave the Miramichi—do you think we have to?"

Markus read all of Amy's messages on a soft September afternoon when kids were now back to school. Little Bodecia, Markus wrote on one of the pages, was abandoned by most of us, most of it accidentally.

He paused. It was all there. That is, reading these things, as strange and as arbitrary as it seemed, everything was in place to make her drowning what Leo hoped it would be: a tragic suicide that all could live with after a certain length of time. Especially if they put a statue to her on Chapman's Island. Especially if Minnie came back to Alex, and Doreen to Leo.

The message to her dad was the last. September 1. The real trouble was, she knew something was wrong—a certain dread she felt.

By September 2 she knew exactly what it was. Why didn't she tell her mom?

This would all have to come out in the report now being handled in Moncton.

"Who would have ever known?" Bauer said now, insinuating Markus into his own lack of understanding.

"Random," Markus said, glancing at him, "totally random, my man." And he closed the notebook for good.

"Mrs. Hanson cooked them a chicken and a potato salad and a cheesecake," Bourque said at two that afternoon of September 2. "It's really nice of her—" Then he said this: "The thing about Minnie, which in effect is a balm to us, and allows a certain healthy healing to take place, is she is a good woman—not a dazzling woman like some of the trappers' wives I know, those insinuating little backstabbers who would wear a coyote and say it was a fox—but all in all a kindly woman, who as you know—what a body on her when she got her growth at about eighteen, do you remember? I am talking body, sweet, how do you say it, it melted when you hugged her, which I was lucky to do once at her wedding."

"Unfortunately I have never hugged her," Alex said. "I was too, too shy."

"Then you have missed a certain—charm." Bourque smiled. "For, you see, she gave in to a hug—a hug allowed her a certain predisposed submitting she had no control over."

"Shut up about her."

"Oh well. You should have been at the wedding. You should have been at my wedding."

"I missed it because of ecclesiastical duty."

"I know that," Bourque said, almost in timidity.

"Shut up about her or I will talk about your wife in the arms of you know who." And he looked up at Bourque with a calm and almost Jesuitical hatred.

"Anyway—Mrs. Hanson is already on her way—so we could go over now and do it—what do you think? This is when she is left alone up there—no one around at all—and Rory, that Rory—why he never visits her anymore!"

Alex shrugged.

They sat in the sullen cabin until almost quarter past four, not looking at each other perhaps like those about to witness an execution. For one whole hour or more they did not speak. Then

Bourque, who was wearing commando pants, went out for a little while. Then he came back.

The day had gone on. Bourque had come in to tell Alex that Amy was already there, at the house.

"But she is very smart," Bourque said. "She took the old woman for her walk when Mrs. Hanson was still there. You see, all summer on the lane she was only one call away from help. But today it is different." Here he broke out grinning in spite of himself. "I was so close beside her as she walked by me, I could have put the clothesline about her there and then." He was a little too energized, as if he wanted to instill a kind of excitement in the prospect.

"The clothesline—what clothesline?" Alex asked.

"Oh, don't you worry—I have a piece of clothesline if we have to tie her up." And Bourque reached into his pocket and brought out about three feet of line.

"But if we have to tie her up it will look like she didn't really commit suicide—for how in the world would she tie herself up?"

"It could be done—it is quite possible—and in fact it might show her ingenuity, coupled with her fierce determination to go through with it. If she ties her hands, she will have less ability to stop what she herself puts in process?"

"I will not go for tying her up. I don't want to scare her. I realize she has to go for whatever chance we have—still and all!"

"I am only saying that if there are certain other measures that have to be taken, just till we get her to the pond—but I couldn't put the clothesline around her because Mrs. Hanson was still there. She is looking at the puddle too."

"What do you mean, she is looking at the puddle?"

"Simply this: she is looking at the puddle, in the yard, for I have snuck back and forth and disturbed it. And though she has not seen me, she knows this—that is, that the puddle is disturbed. She is no one's fool, Minnie's little girl." He said this as a reprimand to Alex and in appreciation for people like him and Minnie. "And there is something sweet about her, she smells of wash and clean air—I like that about her!"

Alex was suddenly appalled at Bourque even suggesting Amy's body as appealing. But perhaps that is not what Bourque had meant. Perhaps he had only meant that her body was more sacred than he had thought.

"But I am trying to ask, what has that got to do with anything?" Alex said, trying to sound severe.

Bourque did not answer this. He stroked his mustache and nodded, deep in his own thoughts.

"Killing her will solve nothing," Alex said now. "If they impound the truck, which is what Markus is about, if they do so, we will be incarcerated no matter if we kill her or not. This is the fundamental flaw in our design and will work against us in the end."

"She is the key witness, and I believe that over the last two weeks she has figured it out. I am sure she saw Poppy and finally she knows she has, so we have no more time. As Elvis says, its now or never!"

Bourque did not know how right he was as far as the timeline went, and that over the last two weeks Amy had done just that, realized fully what she must have seen, and had been on the verge of telling her mother before her mother left to go out west. Was on the verge of telling her father in an email but realized once the email was sent how final it would all be.

Alex was silent. He, Alex, however, was no fool—he realized this. All of the crime so far had been committed by Bourque, really—the knifing and the tricking John Proud. He could go tonight and turn them both in, and perhaps, just perhaps be free of it all. But could he do this?

"Bourque is terribly right wing," he could say. "Not like me!"

Again Alex asked what it would benefit to harm Amy.

Bourque, drinking from a bottle of hermit wine, stared at him. "No man, no problem," he said.

This splashed on Alex like scalding water and he sat forward, suddenly, angrily. "Why did you say that?" he asked.

"Say what?"

"What you just said, why did you say it?"

"I dunno."

"Then don't say it again!"

"What did I say?"

"No man, no problem!"

"Seems like the thing to say."

"You stole it from Stalin!"

"I did no such thing."

"And that's not the first thing you stole—his mustache, his eyes—I've been watching you!"

"Are you nuts? Who is Stalin?"

=

MARKUS MISSED AMY'S CALL BY A HALF AN HOUR THAT DAY. In fact, his procrastinating made his departure for Richabucto late enough that he did not get back to the office and therefore was not told of the call until the following day. He reprimanded himself for this, but he was still sure they wouldn't have told him about this call, coming from the child. Because Bauer had had so many calls about the criminality of Johnny Proud.

The little girl had asked for Markus Paul, and only managed: "I know what is wrong with me. I saw a truck that night, about ten o'clock—"

The call came after one o'clock in the afternoon. She phoned from her house, because Fanny had no phone. When she hung up she realized that Mrs. Hanson had already gone, and she was alone on the sad old lane with the elderly woman.

=

MARKUS NOW WALKED TO THE TRUCK, WHICH HAD BEEN taken apart, piece by piece. It was the afternoon of September 23.

Blood under the seat belonged to Poppy. The smell of kerosene was prevalent, everywhere. Luminol showed passive blood drops on the carpet that had come from Bourque's cut hand. There was fiber from Alex, and most likely his DNA. There was nothing in the truck belonging even remotely to John Proud.

The tires, though scorched, matched what little marks they had, and the sandal prints matched Alex Chapman's. It was so easy, wasn't it, now that it was all over? A red-winged blackbird flew.

"Random." Markus smiled.

＝

THAT HAD BEEN BOURQUE'S IDEA, TO GET RID OF THE TRUCK by burning it, down in Chapman's lot, before dark. They could say, since the truck was old, that it was electrical, he maintained, a fire sparked by some short in the electrical harness under the dash. And he, Bourque, knew how to do it. He had done it for Cid Fouy before for insurance with the Corvette.

That would nullify the truck as a witness against them, he said.

He said, "It is our only chance, my big cheese."

"Well, when should we do it?"

"Now," Bourque said, looking out the window, "because it is starting to spit rain again—and that will stop the fire from spreading. We do it in the lower junkyard, behind all the rebar, so no one will see it from the highway."

"But couldn't they say that this is indication of some conniving guilt, as much as me going to buy new tires?"

"Oh sure, but then again the truck itself will be gone, the tires—we will burn them as well—"

"So we are in it this deep now—we burn the tires and we go kill Amy—is this what has become of my journey?"

"What journey?"

"The journey I started on the day my mother died, the journey that was set in stone, to defend my mother, as I must, from all who had harmed her. That is who I thought I was right up until last month!"

Bourque simply shrugged.

"So what happened to that fellow, the fellow I thought I knew?" Alex asked.

"What has to be must be," Bourque said kindly. And he added, not plaintively but philosophically, that when he was a child, crying out in the dooryard because his dad had hit his mom, little did he know that the knee of the man he was sitting on, Poppy Bourque, who made him toffee in a little bowl on winter days, he would later stab, and that would set off a chain of events that would make him prone to drowning children.

"But," he said, "it must be done now! Or give it all up. That is what we discussed throughout the late summer, when I could have been out fishing salmon. I was in that hole of a room with you, deciding what to do about her. I did not intend it and neither have you. But there is something else you must, must know."

"What?"

"Something that will burn your socks!"

"What—tell me, what!"

"He knows about it."

"Who knows about what?" Alex said, starting to tremble.

"Markus Paul has figured out it is about a lotto ticket."

"How in God's name could he ever figure that out?"

"It puzzles me as well," Bourque said, "but he came to my house and spoke of what he would buy if he won the lotto—and that he would buy a Porsche, just like I said I would. That scares me just a little bitty bit!"

Alex looked at him as if he had just suffered the deepest of betrayals.

"I knew it—I knew that would come back to haunt you!" he roared.

"Nothing will ever come back to haunt us if we stick together," Bourque said. "Keep your little chin up!"

But Alex now knew that was a lie, and that he must extricate himself if he had any chance to live.

=

THEY STARTED OUT IN THE PULPY AFTERNOON, THE WEEDS
gone yellow and the grasses trampled down, the trees themselves
all tinted by the cold and the bay water seemingly empty of summer life, and now again the rain spitting down on them, as they
moved solitarily across the trampled garden. What was even
worse, I suppose, is that both sighted Markus Paul's squad car at
Burton's. But they kept silent about this, even to each other.

They both of them smelled the wind, and smoke from chimney fires, and both realized the noble feelings associated with this
smell, the men who worked in the woods to keep their families
going, and all the thousands of winter storms fought, the children
protected, the mothers' sacrifice unto death.

Alex was quiet. They took the keys again and started the
truck, and drove it down the back hunting path to the old kiln
where Alex had tried at one time to forge out of his entrails his
essence as an artist and human being. He looked at it, as if wondering what had become of this wunderkind, this boy who had been
so amazed at life, so willing to debate it, and before that so willing,
so terribly willing, to love it.

"Gone," he whispered.

"What?" Bourque asked.

Alex lifted his hand, and said nothing more. He looked at
Bourque as the rain hit the windshield.

"She'll be having that chicken now, and all the things Minnie
made for them too," Bourque advised. "You see how nice Minnie
is—she was up so early making sure of everything before she left
for just a few days, making pies and chicken, and a blueberry
cheesecake—that's who nice Minnie Mouse is, and you, the big
cheese, didn't know it. You did not love her for who she was."

"Did so."

"Did not—you wanted to love her behind glass, so you missed
her completely, and will never get to fuck her."

"Well I'm not going to talk about it then."

"Well shut up about it then."

And both did.

This is tragedy, Alex thought, this is real tragedy, but then again the tragedy of whose life? Certainly not of little Amy's— but of Bourque's and mine? He didn't know. He would have to wash his hands of it.

Of course, what he pleaded about was this insistence that he now have to think of God and godly men, of the Virgin and of godliness. For this is what the last few weeks had opportuned. He knew now that one rarely thought of this, until they themselves were broken asunder by some calamity or crime, and then they must think of it too. Who doesn't pray until a maelstrom? This in fact was the absolute proof positive of God working in mysterious ways. Alex had thought of nothing in the last three weeks but of all that he had left behind when he set off to find the truth.

But what would happen if he was captured and said, "I have begun to think of Christ again, as being the one prophet in our lives. I scorned him too, too long!"

They would scorn him. No one would believe him, no matter how true it was. No one would think that this defrocked priest, as he liked to call himself, who had just murdered an old man short of his seventy-fifth birthday, and who then silenced a child by drowning her, was having any sort of self-debate about the nature of goodness.

"If only Christ had treated me with a little more respect," Bourque said suddenly, as if to foil what Alex was thinking, so ingrained to each other had their thinking now become. "Then I could have been different. It's probably a few weeks past the deadline now!"

After they drove the truck down, Bourque got out and made for the small dark kiln. And Alex saw him in a sad way, a small shadow against the forgotten machines of old Jim Chapman's life, wearing his woolen jacket and riffling through what in fact was the legacy of the old man, as their own life was coming to twilight, without the least qualm.

"For our lives are coming to a twilight one way or the other," Alex said, as his partner tried to strike the dash wires so they would go up.

After ten minutes of this he said, "The electrical fire will do nothing."

"There is some kerosene here by the kiln," Alex told him.

Bourque looked over, passively but with enough power in his passivity to cause a clammy sweat to break out on Alex's forehead. There was a moment when both smiled at each other nervously.

"You'd better get out, because I'm pouring the kerosene inside," Bourque said. "Unless you don't want to go up like little Joan of Arc."

The door was opened. The breeze off the bay blew up, sometimes still warm. This order to Alex seemed as though Bourque was issuing a direct challenge. And part of Alex wanted to accept it.

"Maybe I will," Alex said.

"Do, if you want," Bourque said.

"Maybe I will—for if there is an afterlife and I do go up in flames, it will I think be taken into account. The angels will sit about in the common room debating it and come to some sort of conclusion about me. Or if we are caught, which I think we very well might be, it will be nice to be remembered as the man who was burned to death rather than give up Amy Patch."

"It is very unhealthy and unwise to think that way," Leo said.

Leo began to pour kerosene on the floor and then up toward the seat. So Alex got out.

"But I am not saying I will," Alex said.

"I always liked the smell of kerosene. The way we used to do it out logging, right in the middle of winter, is to peel a tree right down the middle with our axes and pour kerosene on it, then stand around, light the whole thing ablaze, and keep warm. The problem here, Big Cheese, is that it burns slow but gets a great smudge going. Then the gas will go, so we will have to stand back."

"It will be seen and people will come over."

"No—a hundred things have been burned off in this yard and no one said a thing," Bourque answered, knowing the nature of the yard and its implication more than Chapman's nephew.

"I've never burned anything this big before," Alex said, a little amazed. Alex watched him, hands in pockets, rain spitting now, and the heavens lower and lower.

The day reminded Alex of a day long ago in Boston, where his mother had taken him looking for his father. He remembered they were in the Greyhound bus station. An old man was trying to comfort Rosa—and she seemed slightly insane. A rain fell down out of a gloomy sky. It was March, though the weather was warmer in Boston than it was in Saint John, and he smelled warm wetness in the soil, and wanted to stay there and play.

The old man, whoever he was, collected enough money for them to get the bus back. Alex remembered how grateful he was that his mother stopped shivering and crying, in that little part of his life long, long ago. He had never wanted to see a woman's tears after that. He could not stand to see them, yet he would now cause untold numbers to fall.

"We have to do something about those tires too," Bourquey said, "don't forget. Now there it blows."

Alex began to pour kerosene on the tires.

"Now we wait till night," Bourque said, "and do it before Sam gets home. You know Sam thought enough of me to get me a job out there. I shoulda took it—but look what I did, I got mixed up with you."

"Are you afraid of Sam?"

"There is not a man in his right mind wouldn't be—" Bourque smiled cautiously. "No combat man, no boxer, no kung fu man, no one would be safe if you injure a child, as far as Sam Patch is concerned. Don't let his size fool you—he could tear men twice his size up!"

They had to step back when the hood blew up and off, and fell near the kiln. Bourque gave a happy exclamation like one does at fireworks. It was almost as if they had done far too much and wouldn't be able to stop it from burning, and both were smelling of dirt and kerosene, both a little terrified of their excess.

"I didn't get to the fireworks this year, but look what we did," Bourque said.

The gas exploded and fumes caught and funneled up, and made black, thick smoke in the heavens that was seen well over a mile away. Some toads hopped and hobbled in the grass to get away, and both men turned in the direction of Groat's house.

They had decided that Amy's New Testament would be used for bait. This came after a long and separate argument.

"I can tell her I found it," Alex said, as if in a daze, "and wanted to give it back to her. That's better than telling her her mother is hurt."

But then they debated whether they could or could not speak—for if they did, Fanny would know they were there and know who they were, and if anything suspicious happened it would be they blamed.

This was a great concern, and they argued all the way through the woods.

"No, we cannot speak—we must be silent."

"Silent as thieves in the night."

Then an hour passed, then two, when no one saw either of them.

—

THE RAIN FELL AND DARKNESS CAME, AND IT WAS SILENT on the lane. For over an hour she wondered what to do, for she had realized by a process of elimination that if she just by the off chance happened to be right, then tonight was the night they would come to the house. Yet she waited and they did not come.

Finally Amy turned to the old woman and said, "Do you want to come upstairs?"

"Come upstairs—it's not yet seven o'clock—what do you mean? You have some boy coming here to visit, you have some boy coming here to see you? Show him your mustn't-touch-it?"

"No."

"Yes you do."

"No, I don't—"

She turned and went to the window and looked. She could see to the end of the lane and the trees waving. Now it seemed to her the most forlorn lane on earth, with its rocks and stubble that she had noticed all summer long. The very lack of it being sinister made it so. This was the road of her golden youth, her golden moment in the sun.

She was looking out every ten minutes, trying to tell herself the truck she had seen that night was not in any way "that" truck. And blaming herself for having taken that pathway, to cause herself unnecessary worry.

"Nothing is wrong," she said. "And he is a good man!"

But then, about ten minutes after saying this, came a little shock of terror. Suddenly and at once, though still not complete substantiation. After Fanny had her dessert, two shadows that had not been there ten minutes before were behind the elms. It was now after seven, so the shadows were lengthening even with the rain. She tried at first to dismiss them. She wanted to think they were the shadows of trees. But though she wanted them to be shadows of trees and nothing more, after she stared at them for five minutes she knew better. They were both there, thirty yards from the house. Her heart began to beat as fast as it had ever done.

They were just off the path. Amy had watched the lane too long not to know, had walked the road all her life, had fed the birds and herself hunted partridge. She looked at her wristwatch to see the time, to see how long before darkness came.

"I want to take you upstairs," Amy said.

"What about our game of cards—and—?"

"I said I'd play cards—I said I would, but we could play them upstairs," Amy answered. She did not once take her eyes off the lane as she spoke.

"Well it's not even seven o'clock."

"It's just after seven," Amy said, turning around a second.

She turned back, and saw only one shadow. She had missed someone. Someone had just gone by at the end of the driveway— she had just missed seeing who it was.

"You'd better not bring no boy here, I won't put up with it— you aren't supposed to. I'll tell yer mom."

"I'm not."

"I'm staying up until your mother comes home—right until she comes back, late at night—I am. I want to play cards, you said you would! Your mom said she'd bring me home a present and I want to stay up."

Amy walked past her quietly and made sure the door was locked. Then she turned and asked quite calmly, "Do you have a shotgun?"

"What's the problem, what are you doing?"

Amy walked by again and put the hook on the basement latch.

"I want a cup o' tea—go get it now—this is no fun, you said it would be fun. Mrs. Hanson should be here—I want Mrs. Hanson here right now."

Amy started to draw the curtains. "Didn't we have a picnic, just like I said, with chicken and cheesecake?"

"I hate cheesecake—too much cheese—and I'm going to tell," Fanny answered. "Ha—just you wait and see, I will tell—and everything!" Fanny was resorting to her only weapon: tattling.

"I will play cards in a minute," Amy said calmly. She thought she could see them both, almost clearly. It was Mr. Chapman who gave them both away. Up until that moment, she was hoping it was Rory and Robin come to tease. But her beau had not come.

Fifteen minutes passed, and she wondered the best way to keep them out of the house. The old lady had removed her phone three years ago, because she could never hear it, and so they were alone.

"I asked, do you have a shotgun?"

"Not since Hibbert," Fanny said. "Why?"

"Nothing. Don't cry and I will make you your tea," she said, to calm the old woman.

She went over and combed her hair.

However, her thin legs were trembling just slightly, and some of the snaps glistened randomly. Fanny could feel Amy's legs trembling and see her little jeans moving.

"You got a stump up yer arse—what is going on with your legs?"

"Just thinking of music," Amy said, "you know how I like it."

Though she had carried with her that book on Aristotle that Alex had told her to read, and had kept that as faith, there was no reason now not to believe he wanted to hurt her. Because she had seen something she had not known she had seen. From that moment, her life had been in danger. Now something she had never wanted to believe, she remembered. The tied sneakers of a man, lying there in the ditch. It was there in front of her as instantaneously as a flash from a welding torch. Suddenly she could never say she had not seen it.

She turned out the lights, and snuck upstairs to the window at the top of the landing. The birds began to sing their night song— and she remembered as a little girl going to bed in the spring, with the excitement of birds singing.

Ten minutes passed. All the shadows had lengthened in the dreary little house, with its gleaming living room floor, and the old cold kitchen, and all the tales of woods and forest, and walking bosses and laughter, gone now, but still present with the house so quiet and dark.

She came back downstairs so quietly Fanny didn't know.

"Do you have the drawer upstairs that you had when I was a girl and used to hide there, when Rory and I came over?" she whispered.

"What drawer, I don't know what drawer—you are making it all up. Why can't you make me tea?"

≈

Leo and Alex were standing just at the lane's edge, in the darkened autumnal trees, rivulets of muddy water running down the lane toward them, past pebbled ruts that had turned rust colored. They did not know they had already been spotted; they assumed the little girl would know nothing of their presence or their intention, though she had figured it out little by little and had procrastinated in self-doubt, which she promised herself if she lived she would never do again. The day was gone now, the clouds low and angry, and with each moment the puddles filled with red water. The pathways off the edge of the lane were overgrown, and rain pattered down against them, as the tops of the trees blew against each other, wildly as if cursing.

"We can't do this," Alex whispered. That is, he had to try to decide in his own mind what he could or could not do, separate from Bourque who was leading him. And for his own comfort, he pretended that this was simply another intellectual problem.

"Well then, go back and phone the police!" Leo said.

"I can't do that either."

"Stop shaking."

"You're shaking too."

Leo said Groat (as he called her) had no phone. Alex knew this, of course. He had been to her house, doing a survey on the plight of elderly women for the New Democratic Party last year.

But now Alex had returned to being quiet. He simply stared at Leo. There was, he decided, almost no way out. Going through with it was perhaps the only recourse.

Still, he said this, and it annoyed his partner: If he had doused himself with kerosene, he might have had a painful death but now be sitting in paradise. He shivered.

"Oh, you're back to paradise," Bourque sneered.

Bourque was right to sneer. There was simply no way out. The only possible chance they had was to go forward, Bourque cautioned.

No matter how they discussed it, this fact would not change. As soon as Old Poppy had said no, they had been frozen together in a dimension neither had predicted nor wanted. Like the two combatants in *Star Trek* placed in mortal combat for eternity.

"One right wing, one left wing." Alex laughed, remembering the joke about the hockey players in the seminary.

"It is not up to us anymore," Leo said, "it is part and parcel of the universe. What we must do is now written in the sky or in our souls—even if you don't believe it—for the course of events is predetermined, and was so when we first met at the tavern. Or we can say it is not, but then again, either way—either way in this horrible, dark world—and don't kid yourself, it is a dark world— you think it is a dark world? Go for a drive on our highway on an autumn night. Because, you see, when I went to see you in the tavern I had the note from Sammy in my pocket telling me to come out west and I could earn $160,000 a year. I must have been mad— but you see, like you and Minnie, I couldn't leave her—I couldn't leave Doreen—can't you see?"

Alex nodded a short, heavy nod that one does in the rain that makes the skin look somewhat elastic, as water had dripped down the back of his neck when he did. He was shivering and his legs ached. He had not taken his medicine, and that as much as anything could precipitate a heart attack. But now he returned to his overall lucidity.

"Except it was not when we met at the tavern. Every moment in our lives contributed to this moment now, and each syllable that we suffered through had something in its very measure for this, and the rain falling on us in this space. That is, if you believe that which you have just said, all else means that all pointed to this. From the first moment you disparaged me on the school bus—"

"I never did."

"You did so, you surely did—it is no time now to be less than honest. So then from that moment when you called me the big cheese, we have been locked in torment. And our relationship blossomed into only what it indicated it would, when you first threw my pens from the window or begged my money with a mischievous smile!"

"Well, did we create this dark old world, this Sodom and Gonorrhea kind of place? No, we were thrust into it, like little slaves, trying to eke out a living and everything like that there, don't you kid yourself. We are not the smartest puppies in the pen."

Alex nodded.

"So we are just doing only what we have to do— predetermined or not, it suits us. Build her her own rec center without any qualms."

Alex again nodded. It was once again Plato's rather esoteric principle of the noble lie.

Bourque spoke slowly into his ear.

Alex took the New Testament out and held it, its old faded cover turned back to expose the front page, with its quote from Joshua: "This book of the law shall not depart from your mouth." Alex glanced at her name at the top of the page, disappearing in the rainwater coming down from his eyes as if he was crying.

"She'd understand that you want to give it back," Bourque said nervously. "She'd understand it—"

What Bourque was conscious of at this moment was the road-blocks Young Chapman was trying to set up in their consciousness, and he was very angered by it. This was not the time for roadblocks or for turning back, now with the very road behind them washed out, and a cavernous gap between now and their former lives. Alex was saying that if they went back now, the cavern could still be traversed.

"Well, go one way or the other," Bourque said, challenging this philosophy.

But Alex couldn't budge. The rain poured over his jacket and flattened his curly hair, and he stood exactly where he was. The smell of smoke always made him think of Minnie. He now thought about the logic that had propelled him to this pathway at this exact time. It was logic, he decided, to do good with the money and the ticket. The ticket was actually a way to save his life. It was much more than just money—it was simply a way to refute all of those who hated him, to still win Minnie. Here is what he imagined, at its best, the death of little Amy could do for himself and his career:

"This is what you get," Minnie would say to Sam, "for trying to take the little child out west. She was trying to tell me how sad she was to go. So she went and threw herself into a puddle."

"She begged you not to go," Alex would say.

"When did you see her last!" Sam would command. (Perhaps he would be inebriated, Alex thought.)

"I brought her her New Testament and told her to keep her chin up," Alex would say.

"But you don't believe," Sam would appeal, astonished, looking at his wife who was now lost to him forever.

"No, I do not—especially not after the death of such a child as this; but I knew she believed, I knew and wanted her to have it back. I did not want to destroy the faith of a child as mine was destroyed harshly." (It was like a movie, with a somewhat British tone, or a puritanical one, yet he could see it being played out. The fact is, it could be played out no other way.)

"I am sorry, Mrs. Patch," Rory would say. "I tried to come up here and see her—for Mr. Chapman told me to." (Alex had not, but this was the best possible scenario he was imagining, and it could be accomplished, for in fact the noble lie allowed this.)

Sam would be devastated.

"That was kind of you," Minnie would say.

Oh, how beautiful the lie was, how close it was to altruism and truth, and how people of every stripe in every department, at every paper, and in every way clung to the lie as altruism, over and over again, for First Nations and women and people of color. And how millions had made money traversing the line between altruism and self-service—the idea and need to cover up a bad motive with a good one. This would in fact be just one more example.

"Think of all the little native children killed," Bourque said now. "The hundreds of years of misery and what we might do to help. So you see, what if she is tormented just a bit—it kind of makes up for the poor native children like John Proud! Especially if we help. You, in fact, could go down to Renous and counsel John Proud and everything would turn out!"

But here is what Alex said to Bourque: "How I wagged my finger, greatly annoyed and finding fault with all those who did not treat women just right. Now, unless I kill one, all will be exposed. And Markus Paul, the First Nations man, will expose it. Then John Proud will be free."

"Then we had better go and do it."

"But let's ask this," Alex said, holding him back. "What if, if, if there *is* a God?"

"Better off for it," Leo said.

"Why?"

"God forgives."

No lights came on, and the small tarpaper shingles, the yard littered with pulp and chips of wood, the small bleak windows, made it a reminder to Alex of his one-time plans to do some good in the world. Worse, they would be attacking two of the most vulnerable people on the river. Which in fact he had written an exposé about last year after his survey for the local New Democratic Party.

"This woman has one small fuse box, no phone, heats with wood, has arthritis, is vulnerable completely to some kind of menace or attack at night! Only a little neighbor girl comes over to give her comfort, and of course I do what I can!"

This would not look so good. This would not enhance his resumé.

"Well, I'm going to the door. You think I should?" Bourque asked. "We will wave the New Testament and smile. We have to get her just outside enough to grab her without the old bat knowing—okay?"

"Wait, it's not late enough yet," Alex said, with purpose holding him back.

"How late does it have to be?" Bourque replied, quite seriously.

"Please, please, a bit later than this."

≡

MARKUS PAUL TRIED TO REMEMBER HIS STEPS AND
movement that night of September 2, and then the next day. So
excited was he at having the paint established as being almost certainly the paint from Poppy Bourque's, he did not remember much
of that night.

But then he had to piece together Amy's steps. This is what he
discovered over the long hours the next day, and what he finally
told her parents as they sat at the table in the cramped little
house, Sam's homecoming jarred into the kind of freefall one has in
a dream, where to hit the ground is to die forever.

It was the late afternoon of September 3 before Markus
arrived at Patch's lane, dried with caked mud, some small maples
near the front steps and a small growth of windswept flowers
against the east window, which looked back toward Lean-to
Creek, and the divide of Arron Brook. He was visiting one of the
last family holdouts upon the lesser Gum Road, with its parallel
track along the river, and the long-forgotten Jameson tote road,
where many a boy and girl had popped or lost their cherries in the
past seventy years. As he walked, Markus looked at the Patches'
house and realized that in so many ways they had lived in the
same way his parents had, beguiled and stupefied by a world they
didn't quite belong to, resting assured and assuring one another
that they someday would, and never quite achieving that consis-
tency of knowledge the world imparted as wonder and wisdom
one day and scorned the next. So they, like his parents were and
always would be, in at least a certain way outcasts. The present
Sam brought home for Amy, with its yellow ribbons and pink
wrapping, sat in the center of the table, forgotten completely
from the moment Sam had set it down. A present that proved
their outcast status, a blouse and matching shorts already out of
date, which Sam wouldn't have guessed in a million years but
Amy realized in a nanosecond.

The new watch Sam wore—the only timepiece he had ever bought—seemed dazzling in its indictment against him, and Minnie, indicted too by the new diamond he had given her in the airport lounge, though neither were anything if not innocent of all. Yet the tragic scope of humanity now rested on their shoulders, and made Sam's watch, bought with exuberance at his new and carefree life where money could be earned, seem somewhat naive and then self-accusatorial. This did not go unnoticed by Markus Paul, as little ever did.

He had just been down at the truck, he said, and the house, he said, where they had found, he said, the ticket. And yes it was, he said, worthy of its estimate of $13.2 million, such was the ways of the world, he said. The truck actually burned only what was unnecessary to prove the case against the two, and made the evidence almost mythically stand out against them, as if some creature of God, or some fairy that Amy had boldly stated she had once been saved by, had herself boldly stood up and procured the evidence against the two, so startling the fire was, to enable them to see exactly what evidence was there. So he said. He smiled a little and put his hat on the table, and offered Sam a cigarette.

"Can you tell us, as best you are able, what happened to her last night?" Sam asked. And although Sam almost never feared, his body trembled.

Markus told them Amy knew she could not make a move until dark—that was wise, and very wise, so she didn't turn on the lights. She quietly sat watching the old woman nod off. She hardly breathed. She went about the house looking for the old shotgun she remembered being there. But it no longer was. A knife would be taken from her, she realized.

There were a hundred things she might or might not have done, but now they had been whittled down to one. She had to hide Fanny, and leave the house in the dark, and go, by one path or the other, through the rain, with one thought in mind, to get to a phone, and call 911 before they caught her. She realized with the giant clarity of a winged angel near her shoulder that if they caught her she would be killed. She knew, in fact, that they them-selves had become something other. That "it" that Leo Tolstoy spoke about was present in them, Markus said. Neither Sam nor Minnie had heard of Tolstoy. So he told them that now either one or both would not be able to stop—and if one did stop, it would propel the other to keep going, with more and more vigor until the task was done, blaming his partner of betrayal, and demanding all the money for himself.

"Do you see?" Markus asked, about the direction of his logic. Both nodded.

For they did not need Tolstoy to understand it. They had lived in its environs since they were born, been privy to all the grandeur and the indignity of man.

Amy was, after all, the only witness. But at least the dread of not being informed was gone, and she had decided, all eighty-six pounds of her, to fight.

JUST AFTER DARKNESS FELL AT ABOUT QUARTER PAST EIGHT she began to move Fanny to the stairs.

"But I don't want to go, you haven't made me my toast and tea." This was a ritual, the toast and tea, Fanny dunking her toast into the tea and telling stories about her countless beaux and her younger years, as the clock ticked quietly and comfortingly. It was the trivial ritual that had started in the summer but, then again, should not be overlooked. But initially Amy felt they had to forgo it.

But when she came near, and tried to get Fanny to take the walker, Fanny scratched her, saying she wanted to be alone. At first, like most arguments, it was contained and reasonable, but still and all Amy knew better what might happen if Fanny was privy to the knowledge Amy now seemed certain of—that on that little trip up the path, her mind swimming with the thoughts of some miraculous hope, she had come across men who had just murdered. And she herself at this moment had greatly figured out why, just as Markus had earlier in the day.

"No, you have to go now."

Amy's face was cut by one of Fanny's nails, so she grabbed the old woman's hands and pinned her back.

"I don't want to hurt you, but if I have to carry you, you are going upstairs and you will stay there."

"You are not my mother, missy—I will tell you that. Why, you couldn't hold a candle to my mother—"

"I am, however, your caretaker, and you are in my care!" Amy said, physically forcing the old lady, who was trying to hold on to the chair, to her feet. And all this time, too, Amy was trying not to indicate why she was being so unreasonable with the elderly woman.

"But I have to go to the toy-let, girl."

"Well then come along, but you will have to sit in the dark."

"I never heard anything so ridiculous, by a young girl. Why should I have to sit in the dark? Why do I have to sit in the dark?"

And she turned, and with Amy's help began to use the walker, with its shiny surface, seeming as if it had captured a wounded animal and was some strange kind of animated cage.

"Turn on the light, girl, so a woman can wipe her twat!"

"Just do what I say, please," Amy said calmly.

She now looked through the bathroom window. It led to a small back field of dark wet clover and some maples in two scraggly rows, near the alders where a small creek called Lean-to swept toward the indolent part of Arron Brook that would claim great ferocity near Glidden's pool. She could open it now. But, Markus told her parents, her best instinct was to protect the old lady. So she sat the old lady on the toilet and let her pee. Then she put the kettle on to make tea.

It was then that they started to come toward the door. But she knew they could not speak, for they would give themselves away to Fanny. One of them waved her little New Testament in the air.

—

"What did she decide?" Sam asked.

"She decided not to let them in the house—and therefore she gave herself away, because they knew now that she knew about them! She looked out the window at them, and they at her. So finally the three of them, staring for that terrible moment at one another, were certain of what had to happen!"

"Who?" Minnie asked, staring at her feet. "Who would try to trick a child?"

"They would," Markus said, without too much love for them at the moment.

So Markus continued, holding his notebook in the heat, his face suddenly sweating, and going over what he had discovered. Reading it off to them, he would stop at every half page and explain something, his hair cut close to his head except for the top, which made his cheeks look fat. The afternoon was very warm, and all of them were sweating. Though Sam had offered him a beer, as part of protocol he didn't take it. The doors were opened and the late summer flies buzzed uncertainly, as if not understanding why grand avenues were suddenly so available to them.

"Why," Minnie said, "would he do this to us?"

Markus did not answer this.

"I was always very fond of him," she said, and she could not stop her voice from giving away a kind of yearning.

Sam said nothing. His hands, so powerful they looked in a way deformed, were placed on his lap, his new watch gleaming in the late summer air. Her new and only diamond ever on the finger of her left hand. He said nothing. When she looked at him, his eyes stared straight ahead.

"He couldn't a been himself," Sam said. "Something must have happened to him." This to mitigate somewhat Minnie's statement.

"Yes," Markus said.

Sam himself was entertaining what all people wish to entertain, at certain moments, which is love for others. Love, even for Joseph Stalin, Adolf Hitler, or Saddam Hussein.

"Yes, I believe at that moment he was not himself, but he was wrestling greatly with himself. And soon he would come to some other determination," Markus said.

"What determination?"

"That he could not act, I suppose."

And so they paused just a little.

"Her bravery is what we want to honor," Markus said. "I am prepared to write to my commanding officer about it tomorrow, and see if she cannot receive some kind of citation."

But the night before in the house, no citation was thought of. They had descended the four of them, into hell. Fanny started to ask if there was someone there, and she began to shake. Her eyes became watery and dim, she looked about the warm old house trying to find comfort in it. But it did not seem comforting, or even her place anymore. The knitting basket she no longer knitted from, where she hid candies from the kids, as a joke. The plate with a picture of Pope John XXIII. She grasped at these items as signs of security, and looked at the frail little girl taking care of her.

"What is wrong, Amy—what is wrong?"

But then everything was silent. So Amy, her little legs trembling under jeans with those snaps she thought would impress her friends, went about as if making plans for a dinner party, regardless of the tornado at the door.

"Nothing—but I will stay here as long as you do as I say," Amy said. "You sit at the table and drink your tea."

And she poured the woman tea, and tried to think what to do. There was nothing except hot water to heave in their faces if they came in. Old Fanny was not so unbecoming or not so mean now. That is, her personality was imbued with some measure of infinity that Amy realized she would have to protect to the death.

Markus paused and spoke of how he had accidentally discovered the ticket was sold by Burton. Then he informed them that Burton, all summer, had been telling people that someone would hurt the children. So, Markus said, his colleagues went to Burton and asked him about this. They were afraid it was Burton himself who might, being a man-child, worry about hurting children. But Burton, no matter how many times they took his hat or hid his little scow, had no intention of hurting anyone.

"He simply felt over this long hot summer that someone else would, and he didn't know who. And in the end it came to these two."

"How strange can the world be?" Sam Patch asked, his whole body suddenly shivering, his new shirt still stiff at the collar and crinkly at the arms.

He said he remembered sending a note by email to Mr. Bourque's daughter, Bridgette, telling her to inform Leo of a job, where money would be well worth it. He did it as a gesture, to let Bourque, who was fired the same as he was, know he was thinking of him. Now he was sitting here, not a month later.

The idea, of course, could be construed as flowering from unrequited love on both their parts. It had happened to one and then the other over the years.

"What I am saying," Markus told them, his hat sitting on the table by Amy's present, and not mincing words even though Sam was there, "is that they both believed if they just did something grand, both would attain what they had lost, in some way, and that was love. They did not know they would ever be involved in anything besides the purloining of a ticket. And especially Mr. Bourque did not know—as he set his sights on Burton's to buy a Bic lighter that August day, he who was planning to go out and see you, Mr. Patch, and get a job—that he would be involved in the murder of someone he loved three nights later. But soon he felt Amy's death a matter of self-preservation—and not only that, a matter especially to young Mr. Chapman of saving face with the woman he loved, Amy's mother.

"The consequences would be dire, but allowable as long as it wasn't blamed on them. If it was blamed on them, Mr. Chapman's whole reason for living his life, the forty years he had lived, would be nothing. His believing that he could at long last have your woman for himself.

"They could, they believed, after time readjust their lives to this child's death. It was in fact—" he paused here, and then said, looking at his notebook, "a kind of seeking of great truth by the ultimate lie. For they were going to do good by her death, in a way, sanctify her afterwards."

"What do you mean?" Sam asked.

"Make her a saint," Minnie whispered. "Just as had happened to certain women throughout our history—like Joan of Arc."

The parents listened in a kind of vacuum. The idea of Minnie's and Alex's unrequited love was so painful to Sam that at moments he could think of nothing else, and then his eyes would focus once again, realizing that in a thousand ways it was all true. He looked at his watch, to see the time as if in a calculated hope of comfort. He did not want to blame, but he knew that his years and years of back-breaking, mind-numbing work, in heat and cold, in some ways meant nothing at all to her. She loved the man who read books that in the end he himself betrayed. He suddenly cringed a little, when she took his hand.

Minnie listened in despair about Alex, her feet in the new sneakers she had bought pressing together in a way she had done since childhood, making her look now, and perhaps for the first time, like a middle-aged woman.

In despair, she thought of that boy on the church lane so long ago, and his gentle, wounded smile.

—

AT ABOUT 8:30 THEY TRIED TO GET INTO THE HOUSE, BUT the door was locked. Neither knew where she was now. One went to the front door—but it was up off the ground and he couldn't reach it. The old timbers underneath looked as if the house wouldn't last another winter.

The other went to the bathroom window, but Amy had closed and locked it with a hammer and nail.

"Where is she?" one whispered to the other. "Where in the world did she go—can you see inside?"

Then, suddenly, an upstairs window opened and scalding water was thrown toward Bourque. He stepped back, and the window closed.

"Did you see?" he said.

"What?"

"Did you see! Imagine!"

"No—I saw nothing," Alex said.

"Boiling water!" Bourque said, looking up at the window in amazement.

The wind blew fresh rain again, against the forlorn shingles and tarpaper of Fanny Groat's little house, and then the rain stopped. And in the midst of it all, a magnificent rainbow appeared far over the bay just before dark.

Amy had thrown boiling water over the porch tiles toward Bourque and had slammed the window shut. She was now on the stairs with the old woman, pushing her forward. One step at a time, up the uneven stairs. She had decided that if she was killed, and Fanny witnessed it, they would kill her too. But if the old woman was hidden, she might have a chance. So Amy was actually pushing the old woman upstairs to hide her, and at the same time, in a kind of dark comic horror, telling her nothing was wrong. Old Fanny's feet hit the steps with a clunk, and the walker wobbled, and in trying to keep her equilibrium she said, "What about me muffin and me tea—what about that?"

"Tea, tea, tea, all you think of is tea!" Amy said. She stopped on the fourth stair and then the seventh. She rested, but did not let go her grip, though now and again the old lady tried to bite her.

"It won't work," she said. "You can bite me to the bone, and we still have to get upstairs."

But it was a great and fearful experience for the old lady. She did not know if Amy was now in some kind of adolescent meanness and was doing this against her. Besides, over the summer they had, as they do with old ladies and gentlemen, moved her downstairs. She had not been upstairs in months. She didn't remember it, and was in fact frightened to revisit it.

The rain had stopped, and though the trees sagged, everything was silent, except this pathetic clunk on the stairs, which was heard at the door.

The truck fire was out, yet both Alex and Bourque still smelled of kerosene. They could hear her whispering away to the old woman.

"That is," Markus said now, "she feared sooner or later they would break down the door. Because now they could not stop, and the terrible realization of all that had gone on that summer plagued her. The idea of Proud's innocence—and that she was the key to everything!"

"Please let me go, you little slut," Fanny was saying.

But Amy said nothing. She knew when and when not to answer. She finally had Fanny in the back room, and was holding her down on the bed, and was thinking what to do.

"You're trying to smother me for my money. Help! Police!" Fanny shouted.

As Amy sat upon the woman she counted the seconds in the dark, and thought she could smell smoke. For the world plays awful tricks upon you, and in the dark more than at any other time. The clouds were ragged just above the trees, sweeping away, so a cold moon was visible.

"What do you want—what do you want? I can't breathe, I have bumps on my tongue—I have bumps on my tongue and I can't breathe."

"Let me see your tongue?" Amy said. "Yes, well, your tongue is fine. Wait a moment, don't move—don't move! I'm going down right now for your muffin."

"You had better," Fanny said, straightening up. "And toast it!"

Amy stood and tiptoed downstairs, realizing how much glitter, even in the dark, her snaps, which she was so proud of once, gave off.

She blessed herself and stood by the kitchen table. She said the Hail Mary. She said, "Mary, save me tonight and help me."

"As long as they think I am here, I can get to my house," she decided. The way to do this was not through either door, but through a window and onto the porch.

And jump.

She had, she decided, little time left for important decisions.

=

"YOU ASK WHEN THE FIGHT BETWEEN THEM STARTED," Markus said (although neither had asked). "It may have started in infancy between two kind of men, stereotypes to each other but nonetheless seemingly virtuous to themselves. One who liked to believe he was a genius at university, but needed the university in order to be one, who did not seem to realize the special relationship between true genius and being jilted by almost everyone you held dear. The other a would-be businessman, seller of shrimp and oysters on the dock, a hopeful wannabe for Mr. Cid Fouy, and in the end his patsy. One intellectual and one physical, one trying to be physical and the other trying to mask as intellectual, both rounding each other's orbits until the end."

The fight started long before they reached the house, over exactly how to kill her—and if in any way they gave the lie away, then he, Alex realized, could not be magnificently innocent later. As he had in fact proclaimed himself during the Chapman's Island takeover. That is, he sided, as certain poets did, at the right time with those people who he'd never had to suffer as much as. It was in fact a fine feeling. And he now took it to the next logical step. He could suffer for Amy too, as long as she drowned.

For he had processed the information this way: one must continue to believe only what others did. That is, anything could be believed or not believed, approved or not approved. But the disapproval would come against him if it was considered murder. That is why with Bourque now becoming impatient, Alex realized how badly this might play out in the morning.

"Grab fagots," Bourque said now, "and we will smoke them out!" And he began by breaking off small limbs and placing them about the foundation of the old house.

"I said, grab fagots!" he roared, almost incoherently. His anger with Alex was increasing and becoming as hard as metal.

"Stop," Alex said, as Bourque went to light what he had piled up about the house with the Bic lighter he had bought three weeks earlier.

So he tried to explain to Bourque what he must. That is, if they did anything to the house, all the logic he had built in order to prosecute this little war would be moot, because it would be looked upon as a true crime, and not a suicide. Only a suicide helped them out of this spot they were in. It afforded the gravest claims against Sam Patch, if she killed herself, and the winning of Minnie. It allowed Bourque his money and the defeat of the Cid Fouy empire which he had helped create.

But Bourque was ready to kill her any way he had to. For, as he said, "It is time! And an accident is good too."

"Accident be damned, that's not what we decided, and we know we don't want to burn her!"

"Burn her, drown her, what's the difference!"

This is what Alex feared and what he argued with Bourque about. It had to be done in a way, nobly, for his secular opinions to hold water after the deed. In a way this thinking was absolutely understandable to a man in his position, not always given to passion or sentiment like some people, and quite remarkable and polemical in nature.

Not that it didn't have a spark of insanity. But it did have common sense.

"If I am to parade about as being the one who tried to teach her ethics, I can't be the one known to have killed her, which will happen as soon as the house goes up. And then," he said, grabbing

Bourque's arm once more, "what about poor Fanny? She walks with a walker now, she won't be able to get out."

"She can move along pretty good with that walker," Bourque said.

"Not fast enough—you know that?"

"So this will kick-start her, and she will move pretty good."

"But in all of this we make Amy afraid, and we promised not to do so. We really promised we never would!"

"We won't."

"We cannot do it without her fearing!"

This now is what the argument had degenerated into: a debate on what would make the child frightened.

"I cannot take time out from killing her to convince you that she won't be scared!" Bourque said.

So all the time Amy was wrestling with Fanny, all the time Fanny was complaining about bumps on her tongue, Alex was in a life-and-death struggle with his alter ego, Leo Bourque, and they were getting further and further away from each other. Because Alex was in the end, by his own impartial and somewhat brilliant logic, denying there was any way to kill her, if she was going to be afraid.

"We have to break the door down, and we have to get her now. You don't know what will happen—you don't know!" Bourque said, starting to panic. "They will kill us in jail—neither of us will see Christmas, you think they will welcome us in jail. We're dead as soon as we go to Renous or Dorchester, if it doesn't come off right! You talk about being frightened—you want frightened, know that you're going to get a shiv in jail!"

Both of them were sweating uncontrollably. Uncontrollably it clung to their backs and faces and chests, and uncontrollably Bourque was deciding that he must act alone if this man was not going to. They would have to separate at the moment when one needed the other most.

"I can't kill her if she is going to be afraid," Alex said, shivering now and indecisive, as he often was at moments when the opposite quality was required.

"She won't be—I promise."

"But she is now!" Alex yelled.

Alex looked at his shadow across the ground, stretching now because of the moon all the way to where Bourque had piled his huge pile of fagots, and shivered. He was just off the lane, and just where he once walked up to see Minnie, and just where he had turned down to Jameson's landing to meet her, and just where Harold Tucker had stopped him. He was in fact where he had been all of his life, and had not moved, and now could not. What is lamentable, he realized that almost every moment of his life had simply played out in his brain.

He turned and saw Bourque, then looked up at the sky. How turbulent it was, and how great in its turbulence. And he remembered one of Keats' lesser sonnets.

> I love to mark sad faces in fair weather
> And hear a merry laugh amid the thunder!

It was what he used to sing when he tramped through a storm alone, for he was our Alex Chapman, always alone.

But he did not know he had spoken those lines, until Bourque looked at him and said, "You will have all the money to do all of that."

"What Keats is saying is you don't need money to do all of that—he himself died broke, in fact gave his money away. He was at one time one of my great heroes—I must go back to him!"

"Where is he?"

Alex did not answer.

"Well, you can give your money away too," Bourque said. "I myself am not going to stop you. I still, however, am going to get my Porsche—drive it up to Cid Fouy's office just to see the look on his face."

They had moved out now, out into the lane, backing away from the house, because of the sudden feeling Alex had that this was useless and his life was over. He would not go to jail tonight. He decided he would die before he did.

Once that thought came it did not diminish, but in fact clari-
fied all other thoughts. He had been thinking this, in fact, most of
the day, from the moment Bourque had told him about the clothesline. There in that instant did he realize that nothing about this
protected him from the onslaught that would sooner or later come.
But there was also this—and it meant his end, if he said it. He
knew this now, as one of the great moments in his life. He knew
and thanked God he knew it!

"I cannot kill a child—and Bourque, you probably can't either."

He first told himself this while the truck was blazing in the
half-moribund yard, with the leftover rebar from the bridge sitting
like Picasso's wild stickmen on skinny horses. I cannot kill a child,
he had told himself, when he had reasoned that not to do so would
expose the very foundation of his theories on goodness and drench
him in contempt. So he had buoyed himself to do it and made his
way to Fanny's house, its very essence crying out for justice for an
old woman and a young girl who had saved up money to put snaps
on her jeans, so she would look like other kids who had ten times
the money. And he knew this. And was ashamed. Still he said it
had to be done, and they had gone to the door. And he had heard
the old lady peeing, and Amy wiping her and getting her up, and
again the horrible shame had come over him.

The shame had been growing, and he had tried to swallow it
until Bourque started to pile the bushes up.

Now he had backed this man out into the road where he had
played as a child, where he had hoped for kindness from others,
and much kindness he had never received. Where he had asked for
his mother's forgiveness, where he had prayed for Minnie's love,
where he had studied the stars with as wise an eye as anyone, and
for the priesthood with some humility, where he spoke about
terns and gulls and sandpipers to the sweet summer air, and sank
his feet into the muck, where his best dreams were never realized,
yet this road still was; he knew, now and forever, that he could not
do it. He could not. Yet, he had tried to do it once, and believed
in its wisdom.

As moonlight shone on the old drenched shed, he saw the faded words Minnie had written to him years and years ago: "Don't you know how I feel, look the writing is on the wall!"

"If I do this I am damned," Alex said.

"Shut up," Bourque said, accusingly, "You are talking just like Poppy! I won't take it—don't talk like Poppy or we won't get our money!"

Alex was silent, tottering on the ledge he had made for himself so long ago, the ledge he could climb to and hide on, the ledge that was crumbling.

"I can't," he said finally, "I can't."

There was a silence. Far away they heard a coydog yap; the moon was now out.

"I will die tonight and so will you," Alex said, for the first time realizing that the position he was in had allowed him this desire to "be half in love with easeful death."

"Do it and we will be free—you and Minnie will be one again!"

"I can't," he said, putting his hands in his pockets as if being stubborn. "Please, just let's go—who knows yet what good might happen!"

He tried to grab Bourque's arm, but Leo shrugged and stepped sideways. A chill came up from the ground, and the coydog became loud again.

Then Bourque turned away, and looked into the trees, as if turning his back on a former colleague forever. There were tears in his eyes. He was thinking of Doreen and how close he might have been to winning her approval just once more. He too knew that if this did not happen he would have to die, as going to jail was impossible for him.

When Bourque turned back, Alex had disappeared. He was absolutely furious at this betrayal, right at the moment. And just then, at that time, he saw a glittery form drop from the sky, land, and run, glittering under the moon. It was Amy, trying to make it back to her house, to phone the police. If he had not piled the fagots up just where he had, she would have broken her leg, but they in turn had broken her fall, like a springboard, and she ran, glittering as someone said, "all over her legs and arse up over the Lean-to hill!"

"How dare you?" Bourque whispered, and took off after her, hobbling because of his bad hip but knowing he had to hurry if he was to cut her off by Vince's rock.

If you run from someone, they almost always assume that you are guilty.

AMY HAD LEFT FANNY WHERE SHE WAS, JUMPED TO RUN around the shed, which allowed Leo to run diagonally toward her, passing by the far side of the house. But she was gone into the field, and only the sparkles on her pants kept her in view. He ran after her knowing what she knew—she would have to turn through the trees, toward the path, and get into her house to call 911.

Both understood this, and both were acting upon this insight. So just at the end of the diminutive crooked field, where an old deer trail was, and where laying deer had bent the yellow grasses, she turned into the woods, crashing the limbs before her in the dark. Then there was silence.

He walked off the cut and waited, in among some trees that had been scarred and brought leafless by blight. He heard Arron Brook moving down toward Glidden's pool. Certainly she could not cross Arron, she would drown, so since she was now between him and the furious heavy brook she would move north toward her house, which would bring her along the old apple orchard and the burned house of the unhappy Roaches, the family who had tried to destroy Chapman, and who had brought to life Charlie Roach, who had succeeded in establishing a son who seemed to have finally done the job. There were tiny foundation stones there in the moonlight, like some gothic picture, so wild and beautiful amid the curling fog. But she wouldn't be able to disappear so easily among them, as she was now in the deep undergrowth. So he waited for her to come out. Like one who knew how to hunt would wait on a deer.

The moonlight was eerie, and shadows had formed, and along the wall of stone turning into autumnal ashes—where there was once, if not laughter, at least a kitchen, and a pantry—was a ground fog that seemed to sweep over them. He looked up at the moon, close in its distant orbit about us. So he took to moving along the fringe of the derelict Roach property.

He picked up a stick and kept banging it against the trees in front of him, in part to find his way, and in part to scare his prey. He did not speak. She did not speak. At points, without knowing it, but which could be known by an owl watching, he was some fifteen feet from her, but she had tucked herself down under some plants and was almost lifeless. When he moved away, she took off her pants and sneakers and lay them across a branch. Then she slipped toward Arron Brook, and walked carefully along the bank.

He had lost her, he thought, as he walked back toward where he had come from. He stood silent once again, as if stand hunting for deer. Then he trashed ahead and behind him with the stick. He worked this way once again until he got to the remains of the small house, the stones crumbled with age and forgotten by men who would soon enough join them, and made his way toward the Roach orchard, the only thing they had managed in fifty-five years here.

Just then he turned. At the far end of this place, lingering in the stubble of alders and grasses where he had just come from, he saw something sparkle. He moved toward Arron Brook—that is, to his right—and missed running into her by ten seconds. He swept around on the fringe of the Roach property, toward what he assumed was behind where she was. As soon as he got fifteen feet from her, he rushed ahead, and slashed at her with the stick. To his incredulity he swished at nothing but a pair of jeans with glitter snaps, and a pair of sneakers with reflectors. The jeans flew a few feet and landed on a branch, and Bourque, still stultified, looked about for her, to see if she was under them.

He heard her crashing away to the north again, beyond Roaches' and the apple orchard.

He realized that she was on the far side of her house, and in fact he was closer to it. The moon was now high over the darkness of our land. Far away there was the sound of a truck on the highway, the pastures were wet and sullen, the water of Bartibog glistened in the night.

Her room was the same as she had left it that day. She had her CDs in a box near her small guitar, and her book of Aristotle's ethics—the same edition of the book Alex had sought a few days ago. Strangely, it was face up on the bed, turned to page 124. It was as she had left it. And Bourque waited under the porch, but she did not come.

He waited ten minutes, but she did not come. But she knew where he was. That is, on the very far side of the Patch ground, near the small fence and birdhouse, she was waiting to see if the house was safe. He realized after a while that this was perhaps the only place she could be; for to her right was the bog, and to her left was back where she came from.

He turned and went silently across the old Jameson tote road, and came up behind her.

He could see her pathetically shivering and looking toward the house. She had seen the skunk hobble off the porch as she got there, and realized someone had spooked it. So, knowing this, she had waited.

She was marblelike in the night air, her teeth chattering, wearing only her pink underwear and a T-shirt that said HILLBILLY HEAVEN!

"How are you?" he asked.

≡

SHE WAS BEING LED BY THE ARM, AS IF BY A VICE GRIP, straight through the dark woods, in her pink panties that were soaking wet, so she appeared completely naked from the waist down.

He did not speak, and she did not speak. Until they came to the path toward Glidden's pool she made no sound. Then she realized what he was going to do, and started to fight him, kicking and trying to bite.

"You come along now, missy—you just come along now," he said. "I want to tell you something."

He did not know what he was saying or why he was saying it, but she fought each foot of the way, both of her feet bleeding, her wrists swollen from him holding them. He wanted to cover her up but did not.

"If you come with me, if you do, nothing whatsoever, whatsoever will happen to you," he implored. "Scout's honor. Nothing."

THEY WERE SILENT AT THE SMALL TABLE IN THE LITTLE kitchen. Both Minnie and Sam had their heads down, and Markus had put his notebook away, and the flies still wobbled in the heat. The door was open to a smell of sweet air, being more clear and brisk than the stale summer heat, the air that was now coming down from the north to clean all things away. On better days, both Markus and Sam would have thought of moose hunting or partridge hunting soon to come, of the ducks and geese that would cross the marshes in the hundreds, of the nights to come when buck would move throughout the backyards scenting on doe. But neither of them thought this now.

"She fought then as best she could," Markus said quietly. "She still had only had a vague idea of why she was culpable in their eyes. She knew if he got her to the pool, she would have no chance."

They were very silent now, realizing as all folks do the immense stupidity of taking a child's life for granted. Realizing that the little thing couldn't swim. So she must have been doubly terrified.

Markus had the bad habit of speaking very officiously to white people, because it was best here to follow his training to the letter, and so he told them what he had to tell them in that impressive and direct tone of voice.

Bourque turned to pick her up and carry her down that long part of the path. He was on the grade going down, and had his hands about her, still trying to soothe her by saying nothing was wrong. The pool was eight feet deep and twenty-three feet wide. He could drown her very easily. Then he could get the ticket. Tomorrow he would stay in bed. He would see what happened with Alex. All of this must have been going through his mind.

When Alex came from behind the trees, Leo thought he had come to his senses, and was back with him to do what was right. But Alex did not speak. Looking at Amy, he believed that she was naked and Bourque was going to sexually harm her. This was not at all Bourque's intention. But Alex suddenly—in the only act of overt violence he ever committed—shoved the knife that had killed Poppy into his friend's side.

"Ooh," Bourque said, "Christ, son?" His face was puzzled and questioning, longing and hurt by deception all at the same incredible moment.

Amy found herself on the ground, dazed and bleeding, one of her legs caught up under her and her ankle sprained. Alex stood between them both, all three in this terrible small universe of themselves, while not three trees away two swallows that Amy had raised that summer had tucked themselves down, and the moon still lingered through the branches.

"Goddamn you," Bourque said, hauling away the knife. "Goddamn you, Alex, why did you do that?"

It was like a plea or penance, those words, like an entreaty to the betrayer he had believed in.

As Amy stood, Alex looked at her and said, "Run, sweetheart, run, and don't stop until you get to Father MacIlvoy."

"Christ, Alex," Bourque said, throwing the knife into the pool, where it twirled about like a propeller as it sank down.

Amy turned and fled, mud to her knees, and ran over both rocks and branches, cutting her feet.

Bourque realized his dream was floundering, and knew that the only possible way to have a dream left was to continue, and he managed to stanch the bleeding with his shirt.

＝

MARKUS NOW TOLD THEM IT WAS NOT JUST A CHILD ALEX could not kill; he really could not kill anyone. He looked at Bourque with sorrow, and a plea for forgiveness, as Amy ran. Bourque turned and went after her, pushing Alex down as if he were a rag doll, so Alex fell into the cold pool—fearfully cold, so he realized what Amy might have experienced at about that same moment if he had not intervened. Though he could not swim, he did manage to flounder forward and haul himself out. He had to go after them now, to protect her.

Down Bourque ran along the old fallow creekbed, toward the highway. He caught sight of her twice, her bare legs and almost naked behind, and then once more, as she moved across the highway. But as he came to the old respectable churchyard, Amy, who he had eyed running ahead, was not there.

The yard was bathed in gold and green, from the one floodlight and the sweeping moon.

Alex came up behind him, walking like a reluctant soldier who had lost his weapon and only did what he was told after all the other soldiers had complied.

Leo, now and again looking to see where Alex was, began to look for her in the graveyard, hobbling between the monuments and stones. The priest was gone to Millerton. No one was here. Now and again he leaned against these stones to rest and bled upon them, and upon the stone of the little boy who had died of leukemia all those years ago.

"Where is she?" he said.

Alex shrugged. He looked up at the sky. He felt weak, and his left arm pained. He felt suddenly that both he and Bourque would die soon. It was now almost essential that they do so. He uttered some kind of a prayer for them both.

"Go home," Alex said. "It is over."

Bourque turned then. "Where is the ticket?" he asked. "Let me see it—or I will knock your statue down!"

"The ticket—the ticket is Amy's," Alex said, and he moved down as if to protect the little grotto with the Virgin he had melted into life.

Bourque came up to it, and tried to grab at the Virgin herself. It was rather small, this virgin, and not very heavy. He put his hand out and tried to crumple it, but Alex for some reason prevented him.

"If you don't give me my ticket I will knock the head off the Virgin!"

"No, you can't—it's the best thing I have ever done and I won't let you destroy it. It's the only thing I have left to give away to the world!"

Strangely, just before them that little candle still burned. They grappled for a second, and though Bourque tried to knock it down, the statue remained, for he was growing weaker and had no determination, and some of his blood smeared the Virgin's face and seemed to run down her cheeks.

"Damn you, Alex," he said. "You have ruined my life from the moment you got on the bus!"

"You have ruined mine—but you will not ruin my statue," Alex answered. He waited, protecting this statue for some reason he had no real idea of.

Then Bourque, weakened and breathing raggedly, moved off, and walked back up the lane looking for Amy.

Alex left and went down the crooked steps to the shore. The night sky was brilliant and the shore light glittered. But he was worried, because when he turned, Bourque was following him.

"Go home," he said again, "it is over."

He could feel his heart, he clutched his chest. Soon he knew he would have a heart attack. He was going to go home, but Burton's little scow lay where the kids had hid it. So he put it into the water, to prevent Leo from following, but Bourque came behind and jumped into it too, demanding the money, for some reason saying it as a mantra and a prayer. There were no oars in the boat— they had been hidden elsewhere—and both were swept by the current toward the north cape of Chapman's Island.

AMY WAITED WHERE SHE WAS, UNTIL SHE SAW FATHER MacIlvoy's car drive into the yard at eleven o'clock. Then she squeezed out from behind the little statue of the Virgin and made her way toward him, telling him of such a fantastic tale. He got a blanket and covered her, and said he could at that time see them out in the rip on the north side of Chapman's Island, both of them locked against each other in silhouette, like mortal enemies in a death grip that would last forever, one type of mankind against the other, both somehow without recommendation to Christ.

He called to them twice but they paid no mind at all, so bellicose in their charges, one against the other.

He tried to get the oarlocks in his little dinghy, but by the time he got it to the water's edge the scow was gone, and all the water stilled.

When the police arrived, the scow had gone down a mile toward Hibbing's landing—it was adrift and turned over. No one in it at all.

The next morning, on what would have been Poppy Bourque's seventy-fifth birthday, his body was discovered by graveyard attendants. Markus Paul in fact told them where to look. It was not hard for him to comprehend.

The ground had softened by the rain, and the old man's poor body became visible, like an unearthed specimen from a former time, his sneaker laces still tied into bows.

≡

IT WAS NOW SEPTEMBER 23. THE DAY MARKUS FINISHED with his investigation, and the truck.

The ticket by will and testament of Jim Chapman was Amy's, for Alex had forgone his responsibilities to the estate. Both his and Bourque's body were found washed ashore on Chapman's Island.

The ticket was found too, by Markus, in the copy of Aristotle, where Alex had left it after he had read what Markus asked him to. Alex had signed Minnie's name to it. Markus had handed this ticket to Minnie and Sam on the afternoon of September 17.

On the day Markus filed his last report, and closed his book on the case, and was promoted to sergeant, Amy and her parents and Burton went down to Moncton, and with the requisite lawyer claimed the money. People who knew them said they tried to look and sound too fancy—and Amy was too dolled up for a little girl, and they had made her hair real frizzy so you wouldn't know her in the paper.

The Patches were the only three, along with Markus Paul, to attend both Bourque's and Chapman's funerals, after all the paper-work was done. Both Leo and Alex became names synonymous with betrayal on our river, names that measured immediate disgust with everyone, and it was strangely only these four who had compassion for the two, whose battered, forlorn bodies had been found three feet from one another on a lonely windswept shore, neither with a cent in their pockets.

≡

A YEAR HAS COME AND GONE SINCE THEN. JOHN PROUD IS out of jail and back on the reserve.

Life has returned to normal.

Did this windfall do the Patches any good? Who knows? They were able of course to get a bed for Fanny at the home, where Amy and Minnie visit her twice a week. The Gum Road houses are gone, and Sam, Minnie, and Amy live in the large Chapman house. But they don't and won't speak of the money much. Amy skipped a grade and is now in grade 12, thinking of her future. Sometimes Rory comes around to take her to a movie, and tells her with a somewhat obsequious smile that he is through with Robin. And she was asked to go to Prince Edward Island with Robin last Thanksgiving.

Sometimes, though, this money is a weight around all of them. Sam has taken over Chapman's enterprise, and they get a lot of requests from old friends who did not seem like friends when Sam lost his job.

Some say Sam and Minnie have not been to bed together since that awful time, and it is only the child, Amy, the beautiful child, that keeps them together.

It is true that there was a reunion between Burton and his mother.

Suddenly June, who says she is no longer any friend of the university, came to the garage one day, in a fall dress and hat, smiling and shaking her head at the scallywag, as she called him, the hat creating a shadow on one side of her face, and her eye shadow making her seem a bit predatory. It didn't take long for people to become frightened of her, though, and she is a force to be reckoned with. People say she dresses to the nines and has her own Lexus and a young man in Saint Leonard who she dotes on and convinced Sam to hire. She takes care of her son, makes sure he dresses in a suit, tries not to have him speak in public. And if Minnie and little Amy worry that Burton is spending too much, June is the first to say, "Leave him be—leave him be—please realize that he is, after all, a human being."

ACKNOWLEDGEMENTS

The author wishes to thank his editors Maya Mavjee and Martha Leonard, his agent Anne McDermid, his wife Peggy and sons John and Anton.